D0500491

Praise for Cindy Gerard's

TO THE EDGE

"Passion. Danger. Excitement . . . Cindy Gerard delivers top-notch sizzle."

—Cherry Adair,
USA Today bestselling author of *On Thin Ice*

"A tense, sexy story filled with danger . . . romantic suspense at its best."

—Kay Hooper, *New York Times* bestselling author

"Heart-thumping thrills, sleek sensuality, and unforgettable characters. I have one word for Nolan Garrett. Yum!"

—Vicki Lewis Thompson,
New York Times bestselling author
of *The Nerd Who Loved Me*

"An award-winning series author, Gerard expertly makes the transition to single-title fiction. Edgy and intense, this tale of romance, danger, and past regrets is a keeper. Readers will look forward to her next Bodyguards offering."

—*RT Bookclub* (4 stars)

"*To the Edge* is fantastic romantic suspense . . . The relationship between the two stars is a delight. The stalker is handled deftly . . . a fine opening gamut in the Garrett siblings' saga."

—*The Best Reviews*

"Great plotline with superior characters and a detailed backstory."

—Freshfiction.com

"The success of this book doesn't need any reviews— it's written in the pages! Not only is the mystery and tension from the stalker an edge-of-your-seat thriller, but Jillian and Nolan's relationship deserves accolades as well. Cindy Gerard's *To the Edge* proves she's not lifting the bar, she's already above it!"

—Readertoreader.com

"*To the Edge* was a riveting and exciting read. Fast-paced and action-packed, the story takes flight and doesn't land until the last page. This reader can't wait until the next book, *To the Limit*, featuring Nolan's sister, Eve, comes out!"

— Fallen Angels Reviews

"This is an absolutely wonderful book, filled with passion, sexual tension, excitement, danger, and most notably, a large dose of humor. The dialogue between these two extremely appealing characters sizzles and shifts as their sexual tension escalates and their relationship heats up . . . This novel marks Cindy Gerard's crossover into romantic suspense and I, for one, can't wait to read the next book in this three-book series . . . This is a phenomenal book . . . Don't miss it!"

—Romance Reader

ST. MARTIN'S PAPERBACKS TITLES
BY CINDY GERARD

To the Edge

To the Limit

TO THE LIMIT

BOOK TWO IN
THE BODYGUARDS SERIES

Cindy Gerard

St. Martin's

TO THE LIMIT

Copyright © 2005 by Cindy Gerard.
Excerpt from *To the Brink* copyright © 2005 by Cindy Gerard.

All rights reserved. No part of this book may be used or reproduced in any manner whatsoever without written permission except in the case of brief quotations embodied in critical articles or reviews. For information address St. Martin's Press, 175 Fifth Avenue, New York, NY 10010.

ISBN: 0-7394-5840-X

Printed in the United States of America

St. Martin's Paperbacks are published by St. Martin's Press, 175 Fifth Avenue, New York, NY 10010.

This book is dedicated to our fighting men and women who protect our freedom and our way of life while promoting peace and enduring all that is asked of them every day.

And to my kids, Kyle, Eileen, Kayla, and Blake. You are all things good and beautiful. I love you.

ACKNOWLEDGMENTS

What would writers be without readers? Simple. We wouldn't be. For your enthusiastic support and kind words, please accept my eternal gratitude.

Special thanks and unending appreciation go to Bobbie McLane and Donna Young of BASICALLY BOOKS. They are truly booksellers extraordinaire. Every author should have the support of two such savvy, well-read champions who know their stock, know their readers, and hand-sell books by the thousands. I wish I could clone you two about a million times!

Susan Connell—you're a real buddy. Thanks for helping me through my plot predicament!

Thanks also to Cynthia Lea Clark, Psy. D. forensic psychopathologist, and authors Linnea Sinclair (aka Megan Sybil Baker) and my buddy Kylie Brant for their invaluable technical assistance. To the KOD and the CNN loop, I'm a lurker most of the time, but I appreciate the invaluable tidbits I pick up from the many posts.

To the wonderful people at St. Martin's Press, particularly Monique Patterson, Jennifer Enderlin, and Matt Shear, I thank you for your faith and enthusiasm.

And as always, to my agent, Maria Carvainis, and her wonderful staff, thank you so very much for everything.

Note: I have, upon occasion, taken liberties with real estate to accommodate the story. Any mistakes are mine and mine alone.

Secret Service official motto:

"Worthy of trust and confidence"

I

DARK SHE COULD DO, EVE GARRETT thought as she sat by the curb, her Mazda's motor running. Rain was another story. She didn't do rain.

"Or wind," she grumbled as a strong gust rocked her little car and the downpour pelted the windshield like BBs.

Why couldn't she be curled up in her apartment, comfy and dry and reading a good "It was a dark and stormy night" mystery novel, instead of muttering to herself out here *in* one?

Because of Tiffany Clayborne, that's why.

Eve was a long way from her apartment. A long way from comfy. Instead, she was wiping steam off her driver's side window on a night that was also damp and muggy. And she wasn't even a little bit at ease about parking on this sleazy backstreet just off Blue Heron Boulevard in a seedy neighborhood that stank of garbage and rot while she waited for Tiffany to show.

She squinted into the rain. *Where is that girl?*

Despite the fact that Tiffany had stormed off in a huff the last time they'd talked, Eve cared about the little brat. God bless her. But she'd better have a damn good reason for dragging Eve out in this mess, or when she finally did show up, there might be serious hair pulling involved. Especially since Eve hadn't heard boo from her in three months.

And why the theatrics? Eve wondered uneasily, losing the

battle to clear a spot on her window. Eve had barely recognized Tiff's voice through the tears and the almost incoherent begging that Eve meet her here at one in the morning, no explanation provided.

"Just come, Eve. Please. Please hurry."

The last time Tiff had done something crazy she hadn't had an explanation, either. Starting with her eighteenth birthday six months ago, Tiffany had shown signs of turning into the quintessential spoiled little rich girl, monetarily gorged and emotionally starved for attention. In fact, if the newspapers were to be believed, she'd recently pulled any number of stunts to make sure she got that attention, really firing up the afterburners in the spoiled rich department—like anyone could really compete with Paris Hilton.

But Tiff still gave the local paparazzi plenty of fodder to sensationalize stories about her exploits. Eve figured it was a case of Tiffany's age proclaiming she was capable of making adult decisions but her brain not yet grasping the concept of maturity. Or coming to terms with the new reality that she was now an adult.

Come to terms, little girl. Soon.

The steam finally got the best of Eve. Giving up, she rolled down her window and killed the motor, thinking back to Tiffany's eighteenth birthday party—the one she'd thrown for herself at Club Asylum because her father never would have thought to celebrate the milestone event. Of course, had Jeremy Clayborne staged the party, Eve wouldn't have been within a hundred miles of the guest list. Tiffany was still speaking to her back then.

Anyway, you had your basic cake and balloons and candles. And then, in Tiffany's case, you had your instant access to a multibillion-dollar trust fund.

That kind of money would screw with anyone's head. Add a father like Jeremy Clayborne and, well . . . Clayborne was a whole other story and the main reason Eve put up with Tiffany's mercurial mood swings.

Rain blew in through the open car window and sprayed her in the face. "Come on, Tiff. It's getting wet out here."

Eve checked her watch and told herself that to an eighteen-year-old fifteen minutes did not constitute late. To a thirty-two-year-old who'd been on the job since seven this morning and had been anxiously awaiting the end of a roughly sixty-hour workweek, however, fifteen minutes constituted the beginnings of a very bad mood.

She flipped out her cell phone and punched in Tiffany's number. And got a no-service message.

"What the hell is going on?" Eve sputtered aloud, then sharpened her focus out the window when she saw a flash of movement by one of the buildings directly across the street. She leaned over in the seat so she could get a better look; through the rain, she saw movement again.

"Tiff? Is that you?"

Whoever it was stopped when Eve yelled, hesitated for a moment, then ducked between two buildings.

It didn't much matter that Eve had spent seven years as a Secret Service agent. Didn't much matter that she'd logged her share of stakeouts during that time. Neither did it matter that three years ago she'd teamed up with her brothers at E.D.E.N., a security firm that was regularly presented with its fair share of dicey situations. At least it didn't matter to her heart rate, because it ratcheted up several beats per minute.

Something was off here. Gut deep, she knew that something was way off. She just hadn't wanted it to be.

As the daughter of one of the most written about, speculated about, and richest men in the United States, Tiffany Clayborne was vulnerable. Prime predator bait. And the dark figure Eve had just seen duck between the buildings looked a lot more like predator than bait.

A healthy, intuitive wariness spiked an adrenaline rush and had her popping open her glove box and digging for her flashlight. She hesitated over the .38 S & W that she pretty much went nowhere without, then tucked it in her waistband at the small of her back. With a muttered oath, she stepped out into the rain.

Her white T and capri pants were completely drenched by the time she ran across the street and tucked in next to a dingy gray cinder-block building. She dragged her sodden hair out of her eyes and, reaching into her waistband, pulled out her gun.

The adjacent building was an ugly mustard brown brick. The walkway between the two was narrow and dark; the weeds growing in the dirt that had softened to muck were the primary landscape materials. Just like Tiffany was the primary reason Eve was soaked to the gills and, she suspected, about to put her life on the line.

She flicked off the safety on the S & W and, gripping the weapon in both hands, swung into the gap.

Water gushed from the roofs, bypassing debris-clogged eaves. Nothing. She could see nothing through the deluge.

And then she felt nothing. Nothing but pain.

An arm hooked around her neck and dragged her back against a body as hard and unyielding as the building she was suddenly slammed into.

She could barely breathe, wouldn't be on her feet if her attacker hadn't pinned her between him and the rough cinder-block wall. Somewhere at her feet was her gun. And somewhere in the dark she heard the wail of a faraway police siren. Too far away.

"You're dead," the man said, his hot, sour breath fanning her cheek as the rain poured down like a waterfall.

Oh God. "Wait—"

The forearm crushing her throat jerked viciously. Pain knifed through her windpipe. She gasped, fought for a breath that wasn't gorged with rain and pain, and willed herself not to pass out.

"You're dead," he repeated, his voice as void of emotion as the night was void of light. "You just don't know it yet."

Something hard jabbed into her ribs. Exquisite, mind-searing pain ripped through her system. She felt an involuntary scream boil up just as another jolt tore into her body and her muscles started to spasm. By the third jolt, her eyes had rolled back in her head.

And by the time he let her fall in a boneless lump to the muddy ground, the prospect of death was a welcome relief.

2

YOU'RE DEAD. YOU JUST DON'T KNOW IT YET.

"If you don't tell Nolan about this, I will."

Eve shook her head, then winced when pain shot through her skull like needles. She lowered her head back on the sofa pillow.

"No," she insisted while her sister-in-law hovered over her with a fresh ice pack. "Jillian, please. Not yet. Nolan will just tell Ethan and Dallas and then they'll all go big brother on me. Frankly, I've got all I can deal with right now without having them guard dogging me, too."

Jillian, a gorgeous redhead who'd made Eve's twin brother, Nolan, a blissfully happy man when she'd married him last year, gave Eve a concerned glare. "How did you even get home?"

Eve closed her eyes and pressed the ice to her temple. "Beats me."

Close to twelve hours had passed since the attack, and there were a lot of things Eve didn't know. Like what time she'd come to and dragged herself up out of the mud. Or how, when she could hardly walk, she'd managed to crawl behind the wheel and drive home under her own steam. And the bigger question: why hadn't her nameless, faceless attacker simply killed her if he wanted her dead?

"Look. I appreciate your concern, Jillie. I do."

"Right. And if I hadn't stopped over this morning on the

off chance you wanted to go out to lunch, you never would have told me about it."

"Yeah, well, if you weren't married to that knothead brother of mine, you'd have been the first person I would have called."

"You should have called a doctor. I'm not so sure I shouldn't take you to the ER right now."

"I'm fine. Or I will be. I just need a little time. Just give me the weekend to get it together before I tell the boys. Help me out here. You know how they are."

Eve could see by the sympathy in Jillian's green eyes that she knew exactly how they were. All of them former special ops, all of them overprotective. All of them tightly wrapped testosterone when someone they cared about was threatened.

And they cared about Eve.

"Promise you'll go to a doctor if you don't get to feeling better by tonight?" Jillian asked, clearly still filled with reservations.

"Cross my heart and hope to die. Sorry," she added when Jillian flinched. "Poor choice of words."

"And promise you'll tell them Monday morning," Jillian said, leveling another condition.

"Yes, Mom. I promise. Now go forth and shop or something. All I need is a little sleep."

"You'll call if—"

"Yes," Eve said, anticipating Jillian's request. "I'll call if anything comes up."

"And you'll stay put all weekend."

Eve nodded. And figured she'd go to hell for lying.

Later that night, Eve moved carefully through the loud, crowded dance floor at Club Asylum. She winced when someone bumped her and sent a sharp stab of pain slicing through her ribs where the bastard had given her direct hits with a stun gun. Had to have been a stun gun or she *would* be dead now. Of course, if bruised pride could kill, it would be all over but the eulogy.

She still couldn't believe she'd let him get the drop on her. Like a damn rookie. Like a wet-behind-the-ears newbie instead of a seasoned professional who had years of experience under her belt.

Not that her attacker had been a run-of-the-mill street thug. Neither had he been some cokehead jazzed on crack. The guy had been a pro. Big. Strong. Expert. He'd known exactly what he was doing. Known how to put the hurt on her without killing her. And it had been no random attack.

You're dead. You just don't know it yet.

His—what? Threat? Promise? Warning? Whatever. The words continued to rattle around the edge of her subconscious just as they had all day while she'd worked on getting a lead on Tiff. And since she could take care of herself— normally—and Tiffany couldn't, finding Tiff took top priority over the threat on her own life.

That's why Eve was here at Club Asylum instead of home, licking her wounds in solitary comfort as she'd promised Jillian she would do. Instead, she'd sucked it up. She'd covered the bruises on her face with makeup and dressed to blend with the party crowd in a black Lycra bodysuit and a black sequined waist-length jacket.

And here she was. It was pushing 1:00 a.m.—almost thirteen hours since Jillian had found Eve's bruised and battered self still in bed—and all she'd turned up for her efforts was more dead ends.

Dead. There was that word again. It annoyed the hell out of her. So did the fact that she wasn't yet up to full speed. Her head still felt as thick and murky as LA smog. Every step was still an exercise in pain as she worked the crowd at the current West Palm "in" spot and watering hole—and, more important, one of Tiffany's favorite haunts.

She'd made repeated and failed attempts to contact Tiffany on her cell phone today. She'd called a very short list of Tiff 's friends. The yacht club, country club, stables . . . anywhere she could think of, and had turned up nothing. She was running out of ideas and was pinning some hope on the crowd at Club Asylum providing some answers—or at least a lead.

The dance club and bar was billed as a retro knockoff of New York City's Studio 54, which had gained notoriety in the eighties for being the den of iniquity that it was. The music was loud; the smoke was thick and suspiciously sweet smelling. As with Studio 54, the name of the game at Club Asylum was to see and be seen—the more outrageous the antics and the outfits, the better. The bored and famous of Palm Beach high society, international celebrities, and even minor-level European royalty were known to frequent the place.

More to the point, all indications were that Tiffany had taken up with a band playing here and had recently dropped some huge coin. Since Eve had read in the papers that one of Tiffany's favorite stunts lately was to take off for a few days with the rock band of the month, it seemed a likely place to look.

"Haven't seen her," was the standard response as Eve worked the floor for information about Tiffany.

No one at the bar or in one of the many privacy cubbyholes or even on the dance floor had seen Tiffany for two, maybe three weeks. Or if they had, they weren't talking. One person did, however, remember the name of the band she'd been so taken with.

"Dead Grief?" Eve repeated above the head-banging beat of a glitter and glam band giving it their all from a platform suspended high above the packed dance floor.

"Yeah, they were sooo sick. That lead dude could really wail."

"They still around?"

"Nah. Played their last set a few weeks ago, then blew out of town."

A few weeks? If Tiffany had taken off with them, then where had she been when she'd called Eve last night?

If it had actually been Tiffany who had called.
More and more, Eve had been playing with the possibility that it hadn't been Tiffany. More and more, she wondered if whoever had attacked her knew enough about her to know that Tiffany was her Achilles' heel, and had taken advantage of that fact to lure her out and into the night. Where she would be vulnerable. Accessible.

You're dead. You just don't know it yet.
"One problem at a time," she muttered under her breath as the words came back with haunting regularity.

Regardless of whether it had been Tiff who had called or not, the offshoot of all this was that she was still missing. Or AWOL or something. And regardless that Tiffany hadn't been on speaking terms with her in three months, Eve needed to find her—if nothing else, to give her a little *"straighten your act up" talk* before she truly did end up in some trouble.

Eve moved among the dancers recapping what she had so far: that no one had seen Tiffany in two or three weeks and the name of a band she'd been "playing" with. Oh— and Eve knew that Tiff's cell phone was still out of service. Combined, it wasn't much, but warning bells were still clanging like crazy. Or maybe it was just the pounding in Eve's head that half a bottle of painkillers and close to a pound of M&M's hadn't been able to reduce to much better than a dull roar.

Time to regroup. OK. Dead Grief. The band's name was something to go on. A very minor something, as no one could come up with individual band members' names—Eve figured that had something to do with the weed that appeared to float around as freely as the drinks.

It left Eve only one option to get a lead on Tiffany. She needed to find out more about Dead Grief. Who they were, where they called home. Since she hadn't turned up anything in the bar crowd, the next best option was to get a look at the club's records—financial transactions, checks written, receipts that may have even been received from Tiffany.

Drawing as little attention as possible, Eve wandered off the dance floor toward the back of the club—and spotted a bouncer guarding the hall like the equivalent of Fort Knox was at the other end. Or possibly the boss's office.

She sized up the Steven Seagal wannabe, worked up a smile—no easy task given the shape she was in—and headed toward him.

Then she caught her first break. Turned out he wasn't a Steven. Fortunately for her, Leo, the not so lionhearted bouncer, also turned out to be a soft touch and an easy sell. Thank God. She was running out of steam when they finally struck a deal and she slipped quietly down the hall toward the first floor manager's office at the back of the building.

Sneak and peeks weren't her usual investigative methods of choice—not that she hadn't conducted a few when she was in the Secret Service—but desperate times and all that. She needed a lead on Tiffany yesterday.

Even though she had to do it on the QT, Eve always kept an eye out for her. Like she would a little sister. She'd tried to be there for her ever since Tiffany had been Eve's first Secret Service protective assignment three years ago.

They had a history. A complicated history. Tiffany—or rather her father—was also the reason Eve had been forced to resign from the Service.

Life is just too much fun, Eve thought as she quietly entered the office.

Her first impression was of stale cigarette smoke and one of those automatic air deodorizers that spritzed what was supposed to be a clean, fresh floral scent at programmed intervals. The smell brought to mind an unsettling combination of antiseptic, BO, and cheap perfume.

She shut the door behind her, flicked on her penlight, and shone it around the dark office. No sense turning on the overhead and inviting inquiring minds to want to know who was burning the midnight oil.

That's why she'd slipped Leo a hundred in exchange for a

few minutes' time in the absentee boss's office—so she wouldn't be bothered and ostensibly so she could look for signs that the lowlife was cheating on her. The cash had tempted the bouncer, but it was Eve's tears that had gotten results.

She felt a little guilty that the club's manager, Frank Leoni—innocent as a babe at least in the cheating on *her* department—was getting a bum rap. She didn't even know Leoni. Still, a little guilt hadn't stopped her from batting misty baby blues and tearfully thanking Leo for helping her.

She'd love to tap the computer but didn't think she had time, so when she spotted the file cabinet in the far corner of the office, she headed straight for it. It was a long shot, but with some luck she might find some financial transactions with Dead Grief's or Tiffany's name on them, since another one of her penchants of late was renting the place out by the night for private parties.

Naturally, the file cabinet was locked, so Eve had to sort of "unlock" it with the help of her pick kit, all the while trying not to think about the minimum sentence for a B and E.

She'd just finessed the top drawer open when she heard a sound that was out of place and out of time with the muffled rock beat bleeding into the small room through the office's thin walls and door.

She froze. Listened. And heard it again.

Damn it. She was too tired for this.

She flicked off her penlight and ducked into the shadows behind the desk, grimacing in pain as she crouched down to make herself as small as possible. Barely breathing, she reached for the .38 clipped on her belt and concealed beneath her jacket.

B and E with a deadly weapon. She was having some fun *now*.

It didn't take long for her pupils to adjust to the darkness. Or to figure out that whoever was joining her didn't have a key—which, sharp tack that she was, told her *they* didn't belong here, either.

God. She'd preempted a *real* break-in. Either that or the thug who had attacked her last night had followed her here—and that notion had her lips thinning and her trigger finger itching. Paybacks, as a rule, were hell. She may be packaged like a Twinkie, as her brother Nolan was fond of saying, but she had the disposition of a pit bull when someone pissed her off. And someone had.

She held her breath as an alley-facing window slid slowly open and humid tropical air leaked into the room. Shortly after, a black shoe attached to a leg also covered in black—she was sensing a theme here—was followed by the top half of a broad-shouldered man wearing a *black* turtleneck easing in through the jimmied window.

He was big and he was broad, but he was not her attacker. The guy with the stun gun had been Hulk Hogan material. This guy was big but lean. But he still didn't belong here.

On a disappointed breath, she stepped out of the shadows and trained the revolver level with the center of his chest.

"Freeze, dirtbag."

He stilled with one foot on the floor, then slowly twisted from the waist and turned toward her.

Eve flicked her penlight back on and watched as a slow grin spread across a rugged face that was half-hidden in shadow.

"Consider me frozen, cupcake, but for the record . . . am I still your *favorite* dirtbag?"

Her heart slogged to a stop.

She blinked, disbelieving, and glared at the rough and edgy features of the man grinning like he'd just won the lottery.

And then she thought about shooting him on general principles.

"What in the *hell* are you doing here, McClain?"

• • •

The moment he heard her voice Tyler "Mac" McClain knew
the woman wielding the gun was Eve Garrett.

Man, oh man, this is just too good.

And too weird. It had been a million years, a million life-
times, since he'd heard that silk and honey voice of hers, but
he'd never forgotten it. A million nights since he'd been a
cocky eighteen and pretty Eve of the beautiful breasts and
breathless sighs had taken him to heaven and back one moonlit night in Eddie Franco's cabana.

Yeah, the last time he'd heard Eve Garrett's voice—God,
had it really been fourteen years ago?—she'd been sighing
his name like he was a god.

Strike that. The *last* time he'd heard her voice, they'd had
a chance meeting at the beach a few weeks after they'd had
their close encounter of the hottest kind and he'd broken his
promise to call her. He'd just ridden into shore on a monster
wave. She'd been almost wearing a teeny-weeny neon yellow string bikini. One look. Instant hard-on. He could have
pole-vaulted off his surfboard to Havana.

"Dirtbag" had come up then, too. But unlike now, there
hadn't been any heavy artillery involved.

What was she doing here? With a gun no less? Somehow
he just couldn't see the daughter of a decorated Vietnam War
veteran and former West Palm police officer descending to a
life of crime. Mac knew he was here on the up-and-up—
unless someone decided to split hairs—but what was up with
pretty Eve?

He nodded toward the S & W. "Um . . . would you mind
pointing that thing in another direction?"

"Yeah," she said, drawing the one word out thoughtfully.
"I'd mind. You haven't answered my question. What are you
doing here?"

The edge in her voice was as sharp as a blade. Clearly,
she'd chosen to hang on to the pissed-off part of her memories

of that spring night instead of the incredible-sex part. But he'd save that discussion for another day.

"You'll understand if the same question has crossed *my* mind." He dragged his other leg through the window and faced her in a darkness cut by her wimpy flashlight and the muted glow of a security lamp slicing in from the alley. "But since you've got the firepower, I'll play nice. What I'm doing is working."

She processed that tidbit of information and from the look on her face discounted any *work* he might be doing as dirty. The word that came out of her mouth pretty much cinched it. And for a moment there—a moment that made him sweat—he thought she might actually shoot him.

"Easy," he said when she tensed as a result of his reaching into his hip pocket. "Just getting my wallet. Here. Check it out. Swear to God. I'm legit." He flashed a smile. "Unless you consider that a *bad* thing, and then I'm whatever you want me to be."

She didn't seem to find that funny. "Discovery Unlimited." She looked up from studying his ID. "You're a PI?"

"That's what it says on my license."

She pushed out a grunt that could have been disgust, disbelief, disinterest, or all three and tossed the wallet at his chest.

"Your turn," he said in his best *"plays well with others"* voice.

What he got for his effort was a hard glare. Big surprise.

OK. Time to get out the pickax and pry. "You a cop?"

The breath she expelled said she was weary of this entire scenario. "No. I'm not a cop."

He breathed a little easier. She wasn't the fuzz, which made things a whole lot easier for him, considering he was playing fast and loose with the law himself. Sometimes, it was just more fun that way.

"No way would I believe you're a criminal," he said, certain of that conclusion.

"Believe what you want."

What he believed was that he was tired of seeing the business end of that .38 directed at his chest.

"Yeah, um, Eve . . . about the gun?" He lifted a hand, then exhaled a relieved breath when she finally flicked on the safety and tucked the bad boy away. Not that Mac *really* thought she'd shoot him, but facing a royally ticked woman holding a grudge *and* a gun made for pretty limited breathing room. At least it did from his perspective.

"Thanks."

"So happy that you're happy." Stone-faced, she notched her chin toward the window. "Now gct out."

He tilted his head, considered her. "What? No, 'Hi, how are ya? How's the world been treating you after all these years?' " *And still no explanation?*

She heaved a weary sigh. "Hi. How are ya? How's the world been treating you? Gosh, I'd love to hear all about it, but at this very moment, I'm a little busy here." She turned back to the file cabinet and started rifling through the folders. "And I'm a little pressed for time."

"I can see that. Ready to tell me why?"

She glanced at him over her shoulder. He lifted a brow, gave a confidence-inspiring smile, and got another one of those stone-cold glares for his efforts.

"So I should take that as a no?"

"You're in my way, McClain. Now in case you missed it, that was your cue to belly crawl on back into whatever hole you slithered out of."

He scratched his head, took his sweet time following the lines of her slim legs and hips, the lush fullness of her breasts, all packed into a skin-tight black bodysuit. He'd never forgotten sweet Eve. She was sending some pretty clear signals that she hadn't forgotten, either. Or forgiven.

"After all these years? You don't really still hold a grudge, do you?"

From any other woman, the sound she made would have

been indelicate. From Eve, it was just plain sexy. "Don't flatter yourself."

Pissed. The lady was still pissed all right. Interesting. "OK. So you *do* hold a grudge. Shucks and golly. Didn't know it meant that much to you."

OK, that was a lie. She'd been a virgin. And so hot and sweet he'd damn near made the mistake of keeping his promise and calling her the next day. The fact that he'd even considered it had scared the shit out of him. He'd had an agenda back then that hadn't included a dewy-eyed, recently sullied virgin expecting things from him—like endless love and commitment. He'd had things to do. People to see. His life to fuck up.

Her shoulders were as stiff as a Kevlar vest as she very slowly turned away from the cabinet to face him again. Big surprise. She looked as annoyed as hell to see him still standing there.

"You could take advantage of me, you know," he suggested. "Tell me what you're looking for. Use me to help you out."

With one long look, she told him what a novel idea that would be. *Her* using *him*.

Right. So he'd told her he loved her that night. It wasn't the first time the line had worked on a woman. And it wasn't the last. He'd been a real shit, a first-class ass. And proud of it. Then. She didn't have a reason in the world to think he'd changed. If you asked his ex, she'd tell you he hadn't. But still, it *had* been a long time ago.

The sound of footsteps stopping outside the door had them both whipping their heads in that direction.

Heavy knuckles rapped twice. "The hundred bought you fifteen minutes, Mrs. Leoni. You've got five left; then I gotta have you outta there."

"Mrs. Leoni?" Mac whispered with an arch of his brow as whoever had delivered the message clomped away. "You

schmoozed your way in here playing the woman scorned?"
He grinned. "Cool."

And then a marginally disturbing thought occurred to
him. "Or *are* you a *Mrs.* Leoni?"

In answer, she turned back to the file cabinet, started on
the second drawer. Even in the semidarkness, he could see
how fine she looked. Fine bones. Fine blond hair. Fine, fine
breasts. But then she'd always had those. And now they just
might belong to Mr. Leoni.

Well, hell. Some guys had all the luck.

"So," he said, trying another tack, "what's a nice girl like
you doing in a place like this?"

Nothing.

He was getting nowhere . . . unless. He considered her
through narrowed eyes and decided to take a shot in the dark.
Hell. Why not? He didn't much believe in coincidence so it
was a stretch to believe that it was merely chance that he'd
run into pretty Eve in the exact same spot where he was
looking for his client.

"Your being here wouldn't have anything to do with
Tiffany Clayborne, would it?" he asked, just for the helluv it,
letting his cop's instincts lead the way.

She turned stiffly toward him, her eyes sharp. "What have
you got to do with Tiffany?"

Well, hell-o. She *was* here because of Tiffany. The question was, why?

"Well, darlin', I could tell you, but then I'd—"

He never finished his sentence. The office door edged
open a crack, then immediately slammed shut again.

The room fell into silence but for the sound of a heavy
object rolling across the floor. The distinct scent of kerosene
registered in the darkness along with the red-orange glow of
a lit fuse scuttling toward his feet, then rolling under the
desk.

"Holy fuck!" He flew across the room, snagged Eve's
arm, and jerked her with him toward the window at a run.

Grabbing her around the waist, he lifted her off her feet, shoved her through the open window, and bailed out right behind her.

"Go. Go. Go!" he yelled when he found her in the alley on all fours. He didn't wait for her to get up. He bodily lifted her again just as an explosion shattered the night around them into an inferno of fire and earsplitting sound and flying glass.

Eve's ears rang like a three-alarm fire. Her knees and elbows ached and burned from her crash to the ground. And thanks to McClain, her face was flattened into the filth of the pocked alley paving.

He weighed a ton; his hot breath fanned her face in labored pants as he lay above her, his arms wrapped protectively over her head. All around them, she could hear the sound of glass shattering against pavement, the muffled concussion of brick and stucco pelting the street.

Bomb. Someone had tossed a bomb into the office. And because of McClain, she was still alive to tell the tale.

Great. The last person on earth she wanted to be in debt to was him.

"Get. Off. Me," she grunted, and tried to squirm out from under him.

He moved with a muffled groan and pushed himself to his feet. "Who have *you* pissed off lately?"

She shoved the hair back from her face, took the hand he extended, and let him tug her to her feet. "You *really* want to talk about this now?"

"Good point. Let's get the hell out of here." Neither one of them wanted to hang around for the second act. Not to mention, they didn't want to be here when the police arrived.

With fire still rolling through the blown-out hole that had once been a window, she raced with him down the alley. In the background she could hear the serrated wail of sirens closing in fast.

"Are you nuts?" He snagged her arm when she headed back toward the blown-out wall.

"People could be hurt in there."

"That's what they pay paramedics for! Besides, that little piece of work was meant to be contained to a space the size of the office. And it was far enough away from the dance floor that even if—and that's a big IF—there was some residual damage, it couldn't have made it any farther than the hallway.

"Now, come on, cupcake. We don't have time to discuss logistics. Move it!"

She wanted to argue but didn't have the strength. She'd been beaten around one too many times in the last twenty-four hours; she was short on sleep and was running on adrenaline fumes.

Exercising wisdom instead of pride, she let him take control. He led her out of the alley, down two blocks, and into the cool, smoky darkness of a neighborhood bar. Once inside, she collapsed into a padded booth, leaned her head back, and closed her eyes. She didn't bother to open them when she heard a waitress approach. Didn't object when McClain ordered two whiskey shots.

"Eve." His voice was soft with concern.

She opened her eyes.

"Drink it."

He shoved a shot glass in front of her. She hadn't even heard the waitress return.

"Come on. Chug it down. You look a little shocky."

She pushed out a fatigued laugh—yet nothing felt funny. Surreal, yes. Insane, absolutely. But not funny.

She focused on the shot. With shaking hands, she brought it to her mouth and tossed it back.

Liquid fire. Instant tears. The whiskey burned all the way to her toes. And did its job. When the flames eased, a mellow warmth seeped through her blood and steadied her.

"Thanks," she said when she could speak.

Only then did he toss back his own shot. "You need another?"

She shook her head. "Coffee would be good, though."

Eve watched in silence as he eased out of the booth and walked over to the bar. Then she buried her head in her hands. And laughed. What else could she do?

It wasn't enough that she'd been attacked last night. It wasn't enough she'd almost been blown to bits tonight. She had to deal with Tyler McClain, too.

Who said Fate didn't have a sense of humor?

3

FOURTEEN YEARS. IT HAD BEEN FOURTEEN years since Eve had seen McClain.

Sure, it had been inevitable they'd meet up again someday, but in her wildest dreams she hadn't figured it would be in the dead of night, in the middle of a job, or that explosions would be involved.

She'd always sort of hoped it would have played out a little differently. Like with her behind the wheel of a Mack truck and him flattened on the pavement like a crushed beer can growing smaller and smaller in her rearview mirror.

She raised her head, raked her hair back from her face. OK. So it had been a long time ago. She'd been a kid. So had he. Neither one of them had known what love meant—and it sure as the world hadn't involved a quick tumble in a moonlit cabana.

But his great escape from her life that night had pretty much proven that Tyler McClain possessed what she'd since categorized as the triple-A factor. He was an arrogant alpha asshole—just like any other man she'd trusted like she'd once trusted McClain.

He returned to the booth with two heavy cream-colored mugs filled to the brim. One had a chip in the handle. She noticed he took that one for himself.

"In the stupid question department—are you all right?"

He studied her face with a grim scowl. His eyes were the same warm mocha brown she remembered as he considered her across the booth.

And she was not up for a stroll down memory lane even if just looking at his outrageously handsome face kindled memories of that first sweet crush.

Besides, it was a little late for him to be asking about her well-being. She'd needed to hear that from him fourteen years ago.

"I'm peachy." She wrapped her fingers around the coffee mug, disgusted to find that her hands were still a little shaky. "Now tell me what you have to do with Tiffany Clayborne."

"Sorry. That falls under *client confidentiality.* Just like Molotov cocktails fall under *somebody's royally ticked at you.* Ready to talk to me now about who's got it in for you?"

She would never be ready to talk to him. "That falls under *I have no clue.* Besides, what makes you think it wasn't meant for you?"

"I came in the back way, cupcake. If the boom boom had had my name on it, the joker who threw it would have followed me and tossed it through the window."

OK. So she couldn't argue with sound logic. But she wasn't about to discuss her life—or her death threat—with him.

"Tiffany Clayborne is a friend of mine," she finally said, skirting back to the issue of finding her. "I'm worried about her. Now what's your tie to her?"

"OK, disregarding the issue that you and Tiffany Clayborne don't strike me as the type to be 'chummy,' *why* are you worried? So worried that you're breaking into a private office?"

It all came back to one thing. She wanted an answer before she gave up any more information. "What do you have to do with Tiffany?"

He simply looked at her.

Stalemate. This was getting her nowhere.

"I've got to go." She eased toward the side of the booth.

"Wait," he said wearily, and reached across the booth to clamp her forearm in his hand. "Just wait a second."

She stared at his hand, far too aware of the strength and the heat and the roughness of his palm against her bare skin. "You know, I've had a bit of a rough night. If I were you, I wouldn't want to piss me off. Now get your hand off me."

He gave her one of those "are you for real?" looks, then lifted his hand in an exaggerated show of submission.

"You may have forgotten," he pointed out, and he didn't sound happy, "but I just got caught between a blonde and her bomber, all right? Further, I hauled your beautiful ass out of there or you'd be splattered from here to Miami by now. In *my* book that entitles me to more answers than you're entitled to questions.

"Now obviously, we both have some kind of a . . . let's say *vested* interest in the elusive Miss C. Maybe we can be of use to each other."

She didn't care if he'd walked over fire and chewed glass for her. Whatever he did now was too little too late. And she didn't trust him. "Fine. You go first."

He pushed out a grunt. "Not gonna give an inch on this, are you?"

"Now you're getting it."

He slumped back in the booth and shook his head. "OK. Fine. I've been hired to find her."

"That much I already figured. Hired by who?"

"Her old man."

Wrong, Eve thought, instinctively distrusting anything McClain said. Jeremy Clayborne was the stuff of legends and broad speculation. No one had seen him in years. Three years, to be exact. Word was the brilliant but eccentric businessman who'd made his fortune as, among other things, a firearms manufacturer had built the equivalent of a bunker in his twenty-story chrome and glass hexagon building in West

Palm Beach. Word also had it that unlike Elvis, Clayborne had not *left the building* during those past three years.

Three years almost to the day, in fact, that Tiffany, who had been under Eve's protection at the time, had nearly been abducted. Whatever Clayborne had been doing for the government at the time must have been big. So big that he'd insisted on and had been granted Secret Service protection for his daughter by none other than the president. Which was why Eve was on the scene in the first place.

"You're telling me you spoke with Jeremy Clayborne?" she asked with enough skepticism to make him shake his head again.

"No. I didn't speak to Clayborne. I spoke with Richard Edwards."

OK. This, she could possibly buy. Richard Edwards was the gatekeeper of Clayborne's private fortress within a fortress that was rumored to be stocked with everything he needed to survive away from the public eye into the next millennium, regardless that he wouldn't be around to see it. Edwards, reportedly, was paid big bucks to protect his boss's privacy. He did it well.

"When did you speak with Edwards?" she asked.

"Last week."

"Last week?"

"Yeah. Seems our girl hasn't shown her face in Palm Beach for a couple of weeks—maybe three."

Which was the same song Eve had been hearing all night at Club Asylum. Three weeks was a long time to be a no-show. And if Tiff really had been missing for three weeks, then Eve's speculation that it hadn't been Tiffany who had called last night was probably correct.

So what did that mean? Were Tiffany's disappearance and the attempt on Eve's life two separate issues, or were they wrapped up in each other in some way?

It made no sense at all that they would be. But then none of this made any sense.

Why she cared what McClain thought also fell into that category, but she asked anyway. "Do you think it's possible that she was kidnapped?"

"Whoa. Way off base. Edwards figures she's off on another lark, testing her boundaries, experimenting with her creativity or some such BS reserved for spoiled little rich girls who can't get their shit together."

She studied McClain's face. "You just told me what Edwards thinks. What do you think?"

He shrugged. "I think Edwards is right. He told me she seems to be dedicated, lately, to setting land speed records for blowing her trust fund. She's developed a yen for the West Palm Beach club scene, a habit of falling in with not-so-rising rock stars and taking them and their bands on pricey little side trips to Aspen or LA or wherever the spirit and her bank card move her. Usually she shows up again a few days later, her trust fund depleted by one to two hundred thou, and in total denial over the fact that she's been used. After resting and repenting for a few weeks, she starts the cycle all over again."

Man. Eve hadn't realized it had gotten that bad. Still, if that was Tiffany's MO of late it just generated more questions. "If Edwards knows what she's up to, then why did he hire you? If she runs true to form, he must figure that she'll show up eventually."

"He hired me because this time things are different. This time she's been out of contact for much longer than usual and her bank account has dropped by close to eight hundred thousand dollars."

A puff of air escaped along with Eve's disbelief. "Eight hundred thousand?"

"At least."

"So Edwards thinks what, then?"

"Same ole same ole. That whoever she's running with figures they latched on to the gravy train and they're riding it for all it's worth. They're using her for their fun while the neglected little rich girl is lookin' for love in all the wrong places, that sort of thing."

Sadly, it may come down to that. Tiffany was the product of an aloof, eccentric self-made billionaire and a socialite mother who had divorced Clayborne when Tiff was only six. The former Mrs. Money had then had the bad fortune to die, the victim of a car accident, barely a year after she'd gone wheels up and taken a healthy portion of the Clayborne fortune with her.

Tiff had moved home with Daddy Dearest. According to what Tiff had told her during those several months Eve had spent with her on protection detail and according to what she'd seen herself, Clayborne wasn't exactly father of the year material. Eve had seen the damage Clayborne's emotional and physical distance had done to Tiffany. She may have been there to provide Tiffany with protection, but more often than not, she'd played the role of surrogate parent. At the very least, big sister.

"Clayborne's no longer willing to let her get by with these little road trips," McClain continued. "He's pissed. Doesn't want her ruining her life hanging with trash rockers. Doesn't want her losing the portfolio he built for her. Per Edwards, Daddy's fed up with—how'd he say it?—'her reckless spending and flagrant disregard for decorum.' "

Eve conceded that McClain's explanation was plausible, but still . . . "Why isn't Clayborne using his own security staff to find her? Why, with the resources at hand to have his own people look for her, did he hire you?"

He lifted his coffee, swallowed. "I asked the same thing. The answer was, Tiffany can be very manipulative, especially where her father's employees are concerned. Apparently Edwards and Clayborne discussed several options and decided an outside firm would be better suited to finding her. And the sooner the better. The necessity for discretion was brought up several times. Clayborne doesn't want her latest stunt making the papers. The tabloids have been having too much of a field day with her exploits lately."

"And what if it's not an exploit? What if this isn't fun and games?"

His dark brows furrowed. "You're really worried that something's happened to her?"

"Yeah," she said, nodding slowly, thinking of last night's attack and the bombing tonight. She had nothing—nothing but the phone call that was sounding more and more like a fake—to give her reason to think that what was happening to her somehow involved Tiffany. "I think I'm really worried."

He leaned forward over the booth, his coffee mug cupped between his big hands. "Tell you what. If I were you, cupcake, I think I'd be more worried about things that go boom in the night."

If he only knew the half of it.

When she met his eyes, he was studying her face with concern. "Still not going to talk about it, are you?"

Not with him she wasn't. He wasn't a colleague. He wasn't a friend. What he was, was the first in a short line of men who had made promises, left her in a bind or let her down. And the fact that he'd come back on the scene in the middle of this, *"you're dead"* debacle was beyond strange.

In the meantime, she refused to be distracted by the brown eyes that had made her heart go pitty-pat at eighteen. Told herself it was their recent scrape at Club Asylum and her concern for Tiffany that was causing all the palpitations now. "If you find her before I do, ask her to give me a call, OK?"

"I can do that," he said, watching her with an interest that *wasn't* entirely professional curiosity but *was* entirely disconcerting.

She nodded her thanks. "I've got to go."

He rose when she did, steadied her with a hand on her arm when she wobbled. God. She needed a bottle of ibuprofen and her bed. Fresh air was the next best thing. She breathed it in, deep and slow, when they stepped outside.

She also needed to get away from this man whom she didn't like, didn't want to talk to anymore, and didn't want to thank for saving her hide tonight.

"I'll drive you home."

"No," she said quickly. "My car's not far from here."

"Then I'll walk you to your car. For all you know, it's blown to bits, too."

One thing she remembered about McClain from high school: he rarely took no for an answer. This wasn't a hill she chose to die on. "Fine. Whatever."

He smiled at her reluctant concession and shoved his hands deep into his trouser pockets. "Your gratitude just makes me warm all over," he said, falling in step beside her.

Gratitude. *Yeah,* she thought with a caustic frown. She had a lot to thank him for.

Eve groaned as she slipped a sleep shirt over her head, then eased into bed. Tyler McClain. She still couldn't believe it. *Of all the men in all the bars . . .*

"Urgggg."

This was not *Casablanca.* Still, someone might die a tragic death before this was over. It might be him if she let her anger get the best of her. If someone else had their way, it might be her.

It was too much to absorb. All of it. Tiffany's "disappearance," Eve's mugger, for lack of a better word. McClain. The bomb. And now, the note. The one she'd found on the front seat of her car after McClain had left her.

You're still dead. It's just a question of when and where. Tonight was just a little reminder. Boom!

She turned off the light. Tried to sleep. And thought about who wanted her dead. She thought about Tiffany. Mostly, she thought about McClain. And hated herself for it.

She needed sleep. But when sleep finally came it was with a distant but sharp replay of a night all those years ago when McClain had done what McClain did best.

. . . *She'd always been a good girl. Good student, good daughter, good sister. With a Sunday school teacher for a mother, an ex-Ranger, ex-cop for a father, and three big brothers riding herd on her every move, it was pretty much a given that "good" was the only option available. Until that night.*

Palm fronds rustled beneath an egg-shaped moon and spotlights shone up through the rippling water of Eddie Franco's swimming pool—and Tyler McClain offered her an irresistible chance to be bad.

"Come on, Eve." His breath feathered her cheek as he bent his head and nuzzled her neck. "Come with me. I'll make you feel so good."

Despite the tropical warmth of the May night, she shivered in anticipation of what would happen if she went with him. And she battled second thoughts.

Could she really do this?

But if not now, when? If not him, who?

She'd had a crush on Tyler McClain from the day he'd transferred to her high school last year. As of last weekend, graduation was behind them; this was the last senior party of the year, and he was asking her to . . . well. He was asking a lot. He was also offering a lot.

She glanced around at the crowd of partying seniors dancing by the pool, drinking beer out of Coke cans, and making out in dark corners and thought, I shouldn't.

But when Tyler ran his tongue along her neck and whispered, "Please," in that dark, dangerous voice that electrified every nerve in her body, then met her eyes like he would die if she said no, she found herself taking the hand he held out to her.

Her heart went crazy as he led her down the dark and narrow path toward a little cabana half-hidden from the pool by a squat pineapple palm and wildly flowering hibiscus trees. If anyone in her family knew who she was with and where they were headed—straight to hell, no detours, if the warnings were to be believed—it was a sure bet they wouldn't call her a good girl anymore.

They would call her reckless. Stupid. Damned for certain. But she held tight to Tyler's hand as he led her into the shadows. And she told herself she didn't care what they called her. She only cared about one thing: the way she felt when he kissed her.

Oh God. Could that boy kiss. And he'd always had a thing for her. Since the first time he'd seen her in government class he'd been wanting to ask her out. She couldn't believe it. He'd been too shy to tell her until tonight.

OK, right. Tyler McClain shy. Not in this lifetime. No, he wasn't shy, but he was trouble. The kind her overbearing brothers warned her about and usually managed to scare away. This particular brand of trouble had been on their short list of avoid-at-all-cost characters from the beginning.

Didn't matter. Not tonight. It was easy to believe Tyler tonight, easy to forget there wasn't a shy bone in his body. Easy to be charmed by the effort he'd made to make her believe him. It was easier still to give in to his boldness that made her heart race and her breath catch when he opened the cabana door, tugged her inside where it smelled dark and a little musty, then pinned her up against the door as it swung shut.

"You are so hot," he murmured, pressing himself against her and covering her mouth with his. It was thrilling. And a little frightening. All his intensity. All his hard, muscled strength. And he smelled so good. Like musk. Like male. Like temptation. And to an eighteen-year-old virgin—possibly the last eighteen-year-old virgin in her West Palm Beach graduating class—it was too much temptation to resist.

Because her brothers—especially her twin brother, Nolan—did such a damn fine job of scaring off any prospective boyfriend candidates, she was not only a virgin; she was a barely-been-kissed. Tyler hadn't been either for a very long time.

And the best news—he wasn't afraid of the Garrett boys. Tyler "Mac" McClain, of the bad-boy swagger and I-could-give-a-shit grin, had finally made his move. Even knowing what they could do to him, he hadn't tucked tail and run.

He'd led her into the dark instead.

Whispered that she was hot.

And kissed her.

"God, you're beautiful." He lifted his head to look into her eyes before he dived down to kiss her again. Open mouth. Wet. Hungry.

When his hand rose and covered her breast, she leaned into his touch, felt that frustrating and thrilling ache to know what sex was all about build low in her belly. She opened her mouth wide for another wildly carnal French kiss.

His eyes were smoky when they met hers again. His brown hair fell across his forehead and she was lost. She rose up on tiptoe, pressed her lips against his, felt the slight abrasion of his close-shaven skin brush her cheek, and let him lift her off her feet.

He laid her down on a cushioned bench that rimmed the octagonal walls of the small cabana. The Florida moon peeked through a vine-covered window, cast shadows on his beautiful face as he slid his fingers to the back of her neck and untied the string of her halter top.

Involuntary reflexes had her crossing her arms over her breasts, stopping him, embarrassing her. In the distance she heard a splash followed by laughter as someone fell into the pool, heard the heavy beat of metallic rock, and felt removed from everything that was real. Except that right here, right now, was as real as it got.

Wasn't this what she wanted? To experience life? Experience love? Her chance was looming above her, brown eyes questioning.

On a serrated breath, she lowered her hands. Watched his

face as he skimmed the backs of his knuckles across her col-
larbone, giving her time to get used to the idea of his touch.
Her entire body was trembling by the time he slid her top
down and finally uncovered her breasts. The night air felt
cool on her bare skin, but his gaze burned like a night fire.
And still, she shivered and her nipples tightened with aching
sensitivity.

"It's like opening up a present." He swallowed hard,
trailed a fingertip over her nipple, and watched her face in
the moonlight.

Everything inside her coiled tight . . . waiting. Wanting.

"Sweet Jesus, Eve. You are so flaming perfect."

With his hands braced on either side of her waist, biceps
flexing, he lowered his head, touched his mouth to the spot
where his finger had been. Wet heat. Unbelievable sensation
as he flicked the tip of his tongue over and around her nipple.

An arrow of fire sheared a path from her breasts to her
belly. And when he drew her into his mouth on a deep, ap-
preciative groan, any lingering trepidation gave way to a
flood of sensual pleasure.

It felt so good. What he was doing to her. What he was
saying to her. His mouth was everywhere. Licking . . . sip-
ping . . . sucking . . . tugging . . . drawing out all those deli-
cious yearnings to experience more and more as he pulled
back, dragged his shirt over his head, and tossed it on the
floor. Then he was kissing her again, his hard, bare chest
pressing against hers, rubbing against her breasts with an
electric friction that intensified the pulsing ache between her
legs and made her panties damp.

"Please."

She was barely aware that she was begging. Ultra-aware
that he'd unsnapped her shorts and was drawing them and
her panties down her legs. Then he was standing above her,
skimming his shorts down his lean hips, his erection huge
and jutting and glistening wet at the tip.

She lived with three brothers. It was inevitable that she'd

*caught glimpses of them naked, so she knew what the equip-
ment looked like. But she'd never seen them aroused.*

*Tyler's erection was beautiful. A little intimidating. And a
curiosity she couldn't resist. She reached out, touched him.
And he groaned.*

*"No. No, baby. It's OK," he whispered when she drew her
hand back, uncertain of his reaction. "Touch me. God.
Touch me all you want. Any way you want."*

*Still, she hesitated as she explored the sleek, pulsing silk
of him, the hard, steely thickness, the incredible way his skin
slid back and forth when she stroked him.*

*"Jesus," he hissed through clenched jaws, and closed his
eyes. "That feels so damn good. Too good." He drew her
hand away and bent over her.*

*Straddling her hips, he lowered his head to her breasts
again and nuzzled and licked and promised he'd make her
feel good, too.*

*She believed him. Every word. Believed him when he said
he loved her body. Loved the taste of her, the scent of her, the
sounds she made as he worked his way down until he was
kissing her navel, her hip point, then nestling his mouth between her thighs.*

*Oh God. He was going down on her. She'd read about it.
Heard some of her friends talk about it. Had considered it
with equal measures of disgust and excitement—until his
mouth touched her there and she almost went up in flames.*

*Stunned, saturated in sensation, she rose up on her el-
bows and watched his dark head as he dipped his tongue
into her cleft and with a long, slow stroke blew the top of her
head off.*

*She'd never felt anything like it. Never dreamed anything
could be so good. Her thighs went lax against the canvas
cushions; her arms collapsed as he used his fingers to
part her lips for better access and then sucked and stroked
her until she felt his hand cover her mouth to mute her
screams.*

"Sweet, baby," he whispered, crawling up her body to kiss her long and deep, filling her mouth with the taste of him and her own arousal.

She could barely catch her breath, was incapable of speech as he smoothed her hair back from her face and scattered kisses to her brow, all the while nudging his penis against her where she was still hypersensitive and swollen and so very, very wet.

"It's OK." He cradled her head in his hands, feathered his thumbs across her brow when she tensed at the insistent pressure. *"I need to be inside you. Let me in. Please I love you,"* He sounded desperate as he reached down and hooked her legs up and over his hips.

And yet he was careful as, ever so slowly, he pressed into her. Her eyes flew open when she felt him push deep and for just an instant a sharp stab of pain ripped through her.

"Christ." He groaned between gritted teeth. *"You really are a virgin."*

"Was," she managed with what little breath she could marshal. *"I was a virgin."*

And then he was moving inside her, thrusting his hips, driving with all his might. She felt as if she were going to rip apart at the pressure . . . until the stretching sensation eased and the most incredible pleasure replaced it. It felt like she was flying and falling, floating and drowning, all at once. And it was wonderful. The friction. The fullness of him. The amazing give-and-take.

She clung to him, moved with him, reaching, striving, pleading with him for something that was beyond her comprehension—until she reached it. She came on a stunning flood of release, a wash of raw, perfect pleasure that left her shattered and depleted and helplessly in love with sex and the boy who had just changed her world.

Moments later, he drove deep, one last time, and with a thick, guttural groan collapsed on top of her.

She wrapped her arms around him instinctively. Loving the

weight of him, the sweat, the thick pulse of his heart against her breast.

"I love you," she whispered.

"Love you, too, babe," he murmured drowsily, and pressed a kiss to her shoulder.

Much later, they dressed in between long, slow kisses and finally returned to the party. A little while after that, he drove her home. On the way, they stopped at a convenience store. She sat in the car while he went inside for sodas, then couldn't stop smiling when he brought her a bag of M&M's.

"How'd you know I like them?" It was the sweetest thing a boy had ever done for her.

He leaned across the seat and kissed her. "I know a lot about you. Come on over here."

She sat close beside him as they pulled to a stop in front of her house. In the shadows of the front seat their fingers entwined. She loved the feel of his long, strong fingers meshed with hers. She loved that she was deeply in love. For the first time in her life. Wow. She was in love. Had made love. Life was a wonder. Sweeter than sweet.

"You're incredible." He kissed her with such tenderness, tears welled up in her eyes.

"When will I see you again?"

"I'll call you tomorrow," he promised.

It was the one and only promise he ever broke. And he broke it right along with her heart.

She never heard from him again.

4

Eve woke up Sunday morning stiff and sore with residual aches and pains from Friday and Saturday nights' adventures. And with vivid memories of her dream. And that night. And the aftermath.

An old and familiar ache set up housekeeping in her chest.

"Get over it," she muttered as she dragged herself out of bed and into the shower.

She'd thought she *had* been over it. Thought that particular wound had been well and truly scarred over. And she didn't like herself much for giving in to self-pity just because she'd seen McClain again.

As the hot water poured over her aching bones, she cut herself some slack. Her anger wasn't just about the fact that he'd pulled a disappearing act all those years ago. It wasn't just about losing her virginity to him because she'd been stupid enough to believe him when he'd told her he loved her. It was about how he'd left her.

And what he'd left her with. An old sadness seeped through her.

He hadn't known. He couldn't have known that she was one of those unbelievable statistics—a virgin who got pregnant the very first time. In fact, McClain had been totally in the dark about her pregnancy, because a few weeks later he'd headed out for parts unknown on a road trip with friends before he would start college out of state in the fall. Except for that day on the beach, she'd never seen him again.

So yeah. He'd been oblivious to the fact that she'd gone through the scare alone, first worrying that she might be pregnant, then dealing with the stunning realization that she was.

She'd never felt so alone. Or so scared. She hadn't wanted to hurt her family, so she'd kept it to herself. Cried alone in her room, agonized over wanting the baby and not knowing how she would raise it by herself.

Then one morning she didn't have to wonder anymore.

She lost the baby. All alone in the bathroom.

She remembered the pain.

She remembered the blood.

She remembered the fear.

Most of all, she remembered the guilt. Maybe if she'd gone to see a doctor. Maybe if she'd confided in someone and hadn't been so emotionally stressed. Maybe if she hadn't been so stupid and young and scared.

Maybe . . .

Maybe she'd have a beautiful little girl now. Or a little boy. *Don't even go there.*

She lathered up her hair with shampoo. It was easier to resent McClain than think about the maybes. He'd stolen the option for her to even tell him about the baby. About what she'd gone through. She hated him for that. Resented him—no matter how unreasonable that resentment was—for not being there to help her through it, for not wanting to be there, for making her think he loved her and had wanted to be a part of her life. For leaving her.

And that resentment had festered for fourteen years.

Rinsing her hair, she tried to pull herself out of her funk. Yet when she stepped out of the shower she slipped in a little deeper. Because of McClain, she'd gone into every relationship with reservations and low expectations. So far, she hadn't had any reason to make her think all men weren't poured from the same mold.

"And thank you, McClain, for showing up and bringing all those old feelings to a head again." Feelings she'd evidently never completely worked through, because McClain had never been around to help her give them closure.

"And that's what you get for taking one year of psych in college," she sputtered. "Not merely self-pity, highly convoluted self-pity."

Fat lot of good it did her where McClain was concerned. Fat lot of good it would do her when she faced her brothers tomorrow morning. Of course, first she had to make it to the office.

She hadn't strapped on a shoulder holster since she'd been with the Secret Service. Yet today she didn't hesitate to wear one under her lightweight running jacket when she headed out the door for her morning jog.

She stayed out in the open. Took a different route than usual. And was constantly conscious of the possibility of an attack.

The wondering if and the waiting for were almost worse than the not knowing who or why.

And when she finally went to bed that night, she didn't know whether she should feel relief that the day had gone by without an incident or be more worried that he hadn't been waiting in the bushes to hit her with something really big.

"Just one fun possibility after another," she muttered, and with her gun at her bedside turned off the light.

The windowed door with bold black lettering identified the suite of offices in the Forum on Palm Beach Lakes Boulevard as E.D.E.N. Securities, Inc. The meshed glass window rattled in the frame as Eve—who just happened to be the second *E* in *E.D.E.N.*—dug into her purse for her keys early Monday morning.

The lights were on behind the door; she heard movement inside. On a deep breath she accepted that there was no hope of avoiding her brothers any longer. She'd wanted to beat them in and out this morning so they wouldn't see how rough she still looked on Monday morning after her Friday night run-in with the prince of darkness and her Saturday night bomb fest.

Oh yeah—and her "reunion" with McClain, who'd blasted her back to the past and spawned recurrent dreams slash nightmares that had shaken her up again, too. But McClain was the least of her worries. When she opened the door and the scent of White Shoulders assaulted her, she knew she was in for it.

"Eve! Holy cow. What *happened* to you?" Kim Creighton, their newly hired receptionist and White Shoulders devotee, asked in a voice that could have carried across the Atlantic.

"Shhh. Keep it down. I'm fine," Eve said in a whisper—but too late for damage control. She could already hear footsteps pounding down the hall.

"Jesus H. Christ." This blunt comment from her oldest brother, Ethan—the *first E* in *E.D.E.N.*—as he appeared in the reception area. "What in the hell—"

"It's not as bad as it looks," she assured him, brushing a fall of blond hair back from her eyes. As nonchalantly as possible, she reached up to rifle through her mail cubby, hoping it didn't show that the mere act of lifting her arm still sent a dull, lingering pain through her system.

If she ever caught up with the creep who had put the hurt on her, he was a dead man. At least, he was going to wish he were.

Dallas, brother number two and the *D* that held the *E*s in *E.D.E.N.* together, showed up about that time. He caught her wince of pain when she pivoted toward her office and ran smack into Nolan's broad chest.

"Jeez, you guys. What is this? Pounce on Eve day?"

"Conference room. Now." Nolan—her twin and the *N* in *E.D.E.N.*—took her gently by her arm and steered her in that direction. "Only the bruises excuse you for showing up without doughnuts," he added, in a droll and totally Nolan attempt to lighten things up a bit.

Dallas quickly squashed that idea. "What in the hell happened to you? Have you seen a doctor?"

"I don't need a doctor. I'm just a little bruised." She touched her fingertips gingerly to her temple and wished she'd done a better job with her makeup this morning. It wasn't the only bruise she'd brought out of her weekend encounters; she was covered in glorious color all over her body. But the biggest bruise was still to her ego.

"How many fingers?"

"Oh, for heaven's sake. Get away from me," she grumbled when Ethan parked himself in front of her.

"Nasty bump," Dallas observed with a grim look as he studied her temple.

"Any chance it knocked some sense into you?"

Nolan again. She smirked at him and shooed Ethan away when he suggested she might have a concussion.

"Look, at the risk of multiple redundancies, *I am fine,* you guys."

"And I've got a bridge in Brooklyn I'll let you have for a song. Now what happened?"

There was no avoiding it. Her brothers didn't just talk tough. They *were* tough. Ethan's uniform may consist of power ties and tailored suits these days, but her superserious eldest brother had separated from the army as a captain in the Special Forces a few years ago. He still ran his life with military precision. So, for that matter, did Dallas, who'd broken the male army tradition their father had started and opted for the marines and Force Recon instead.

Until six months ago, her twin brother, Nolan, had been career U.S. Army, an Airborne Ranger—a squad leader—but he'd ditched any strident military habits he'd picked up in his decorated career like a dirty shirt the minute he'd DXed out.

They may no longer have the might of the U.S. military behind them, but they remained forces to be reckoned with—individually and collectively.

"Call for you on line two, Ethan." Kimmie popped her head into the room. Short brunette curls surrounded her heart-shaped face.

"Tell them I'll call them back."

"It's Goodnight." Dark brown eyes swept the room. "And he wants to talk with all three of you. It's the third time he's called."

Ethan let out a heavy breath. "We've got to take this. Get your story straight while we're gone, little sis, because when we get back, I want information."

Saved by the bell. At least temporarily.

Eve watched them file out of the conference room, thankful for the chance to compose herself. And to worry about her oldest brother. Ethan remained true to form. All work, no sense of humor. Since his divorce five years ago, he never seemed to have any fun anymore. If given any encouragement at all, most of the single women in West Palm Beach— and some of the married ones—would provide him with all the fun he could handle. He maintained that as long as he had his work and his stock of cherry Life Savers, he was good to go.

She could relate—at least to the candy. Speaking of which, she dug around in her purse until she came up with a bag of M&M's. Life without M&M's was not worth living.

Like Nolan and Dallas, who in Eve's opinion was also way too picky when it came to the opposite sex, Ethan was tall, dark, and too gorgeous for his own good. To her eternal amazement, the person who greeted her in the mirror every morning appeared to have evolved from an entirely different gene pool. Unlike her brothers, Eve was petite and blond. In addition, she hadn't been blessed with the poster perfect looks the boys possessed. Oh, she'd do. And when she put her mind and makeup to it, she could turn her share of heads—but not the way *they* did by merely breathing.

She did share some similarities with her brothers, however. Like their blue eyes and the fact that to the last one they were all hopeless overachievers, and that they'd kill for one another if it ever came to that. So far, thankfully, it hadn't. Judging by the looks on each one of their faces when they'd left the conference room just now, however, they were tooling up for battle on her behalf, and they still had no idea what had happened to her.

In the meantime, they worked well together in spite of major differences when it came to personalities. Eve was the doer, Ethan the brooder, Dallas the negotiator. Nolan, well, Nolan was the heartbreaker and an insufferable—but cute, he reminded her regularly—pain in the ass. As of two months ago, though, Nolan was also off the market, happily and blissfully married to Jillian Kincaid, news anchor at KGLO TV in West Palm.

Eve still wasn't sure exactly what ghosts had haunted Nolan in those first few dark months after he'd left the Rangers and come home to West Palm. What she was sure of was that with Jillian's help he was slowly putting them to rest. Yeah, her as-tough-as-nails, stone-hearted brother had changed his tune when he'd met Jillian Kincaid.

Jillian was the daughter of publishing mogul Darin Kincaid and she'd been the target of a demented stalker—which was why Darin had hired E.D.E.N., Nolan specifically, to protect her in the first place.

Daddies went to great extremes, it seemed, to protect their daughters.

Speaking of daddies and daughters. Somehow, Eve had to find out what Jeremy Clayborne knew about Tiffany's whereabouts. No easy task. Clayborne had made it clear when he'd forced her resignation from the Secret Service that Eve was never to have contact with his daughter again. Tiff, being

Tiff, had found plenty of opportunities to buck Daddy's edict. And Eve, being Eve—a sucker for a sad little rich girl—could never find it in herself to send Tiffany away when she came around. Except for the last time.

The last time, even though she'd done it for Tiffany's own good, Eve had sent her away. Tiffany hadn't seen it that way. She'd seen it as rejection, and trying to explain that it was no such thing had been a tough trick when Tiffany had been peeling away from the curb in a snit.

Eve couldn't do anything about that now. And getting information from Clayborne was going to be tricky. But first, she had to deal with her brothers. Looked like now was the time, as they all came filing back into the conference room.

Nolan, in his proverbial black jeans and matching T-shirt, walked to the far side of the room, then slouched with his hip against the windowsill. Blue eyes grim, he tipped a bottle of root beer to his lips. Someday that crap was going to eat a hole in his stomach. But since it was better than the scotch he used to like a little too much, she didn't say a word.

Dallas, as always, button-down perfection in tan chinos and a white knit shirt, carried his laptop and a bottle of designer water as he sat down beside her at the table again.

"OK. Go," Ethan said, loosening his tie and popping a cherry Life Saver.

She didn't know if she could do this without coffee. As if reading her mind, Kim appeared at her side with a cup.

"Thank you, Lord. And thank you, Kimmie."

"We're waiting."

"OK, OK. Long story *long,*" she began drolly as her brothers glared at her with varying expressions of concern and impatience. "I got a call from Tiffany Clayborne Friday night."

"Should have known she'd be involved in this," Ethan grumbled. "Christ, Eve, when are you going to learn that girl is poison to you?"

"That girl," she said defensively, "is someone I care about. And that girl could be in trouble."

"So what happened?"

She told them. Everything. From Tiffany's three-week absence, to the frantic call that she'd thought was from Tiffany but had since decided had been a lure, to the thug with the stun gun, to her run-in with McClain, who'd been hired by Clayborne's camp to find Tiffany, to the blast in the manager's office at Club Asylum.

A silence loaded with testosterone vibrated through the conference room as the brothers absorbed and began to slowly, but quietly, fume.

"OK. What aren't you telling us?" It didn't surprise her that Nolan had picked up on her omission. Like most twins, they'd always had a special connection.

She pulled the note out of her bag. Gave it to Ethan.

You're still dead. It's just a question of when and where. Tonight was just a little reminder. Boom!

Her oldest brother read it and with clenched jaws passed it to his brothers. After reading it, Nolan summed up what all three men were thinking in one concise word: "Fuck."

Everything went downhill from there.

ATLANTIC CITY

The mirror above the bathroom sink in the penthouse of the Trump Taj Mahal ran the entire width of the room. Tiffany Clayborne stood naked in front of it. She tried to focus on her reflection through a thin curl of smoke. And wondered if what she saw was really her. She wasn't even sure she knew who she was anymore.

Thick black mascara circled her eyes and ran down her cheeks to blur the tiny tear she'd had permanently tattooed there. Red rimmed her lower lids. Her skin, she thought, in a fleeting moment of clarity, had sort of a pasty blue tint. Her lips were painted purplish black.

She looked, she decided finally, like one of those clown

dolls. A sad, broken clown doll with short spiked raspberry-colored hair and bruises on her breasts. She ran her pierced tongue around her lower lip, worrying the twin silver lip rings that had seemed like such a good idea at the time. They were infected now. They hurt.

But not as much as her heart.

Did clowns have breakable hearts? she wondered as she reached for the razor Lance had left in the sink along with stubble and soap scum. He was a sloppy pig. But he was a beautiful pig. And that voice . . . God, she loved to hear Lance Reno sing and wail on that guitar. Loved when he told her that he loved her. Even when he hurt her.

Fresh tears leaked down her cheeks. Amazingly hot. How could anything that hot come out of her when she felt so very, very cold inside? The tears burned her eyes. And made even more clown tears.

Everybody loved clowns. She stared at her garish reflection and took another hit off the joint she'd left burning in the soap dish. So why not her? Why didn't anyone really love her for her? And no one did. Especially not her father. Lance had explained it all.

The razor was wet and crusted with beard stubble and remnants of tiny popped bubbles farther down the handle. She held it up under the stark bathroom lighting. Studied it through drifting smoke as she touched the thin blade to her finger, drew it slowly across the pad. She flinched when it sliced her skin. Was amazed she felt pain as brilliant red blood oozed from the thin cut and dripped down her finger.

Like a tear.

How many tears does a person have? she wondered as she made an experimental swipe across the inside of her left wrist with the back of the razor. Was there like . . . a limit? Was everyone born with a specified number and when they used them all up, they couldn't cry anymore? It was that way with blood. Everyone had a certain amount—a quota—and when you lost it, you couldn't live anymore.

She took another deep, dizzying drag of some really prime Colombian weed. Set it on the lip of the sink with a shaking hand. And picked up the razor again.

How easy it would be to swipe it across her wrist. How horribly, horribly easy. No one to stop her. No one to care.

No one to care.

Why *would* anyone care about her? Even Eve had sent her away. She was bad, that's why. She knew that was why. She wasn't worth anyone's time. Not worth the trouble.

She felt so lonely. And so tired. Her head started to swim. Gripping the lip of the marble vanity for balance, she stumbled out of the bathroom and into the hotel suite's master bedroom.

She fell onto the bed, rolled to her back. Blinked drowsily up at the ceiling.

And wondered which limit she would deplete first.

Tears or blood.

So much alike.

No one seemed to be able to tell the difference in hers. No one cared which she ran out of first. No one cared that she was all alone. Especially not her father.

Lance had left her again. He'd be back. When he needed money, needed to score, wanted to get off, he'd be back. In an hour or two. Maybe more. He'd tell her he loved her. Stroke her like she was a lost kitten, lay out a line of blow, and coax her into snorting it. He'd even hold her head when she got sick.

Why couldn't he just love her straight? Why couldn't anybody just love *her*?

She wanted to go home. Even more, she wanted a home to go to. Someone to miss her when she was gone. Someone to give a damn that she was so unhappy. So desperately sad.

And lost.

She laughed, then cried. Lost soul. Lost person. She wasn't even sure she knew where she was. Wasn't sure anymore if she was safe. They'd been partying. Gambling at the tables. Lance had lost. Big-time. She'd told him to stop. He'd just smiled, that tight, icy smile that scared her. And then he'd grabbed her arm and dragged her back to this room, taken her clothes, ripped the phone out of the wall.

And left her.

Alone again. Alone always.

Her fingers went lax around the razor still clutched in her hand. She passed out to the feel of cool sheets against her naked skin and the tickle of hot tears leaking across her tattooed tear, then dripping into her ears.

5

Tuesday morning, Eve tugged open the ornate glass doors of the Clayborne building. As she walked across the Italian marble floor of the lobby toward the bank of elevators, she steeled herself for the meeting she'd requested with Edwards. Was surprised, frankly, that he'd agreed to see her.

As she'd anticipated, she was here against her brothers' wishes. They knew better than to issue a flat-out ultimatum, but yesterday they'd come close.

"You need twenty-four-seven protection until we get this guy nailed down," Nolan had insisted after the macho level had become manageable.

"That's ridiculous." She'd pinned all three brothers with a steely glare. "I can take care of myself. You know I can," she'd restated vehemently. "He got the drop on me the first time. It won't happen again. Besides, at Club Asylum he proved that it doesn't matter how many people are around; he's not afraid to make a statement, so one of you dogging me like a shadow isn't going to make one bit of difference.

"Come on," she'd wheedled. "It's pretty clear that he's just playing with me for now anyway. Whoever it is, he wants me to sweat. He wants me to be scared. What he doesn't want is to see me dead. At least not yet. Your time would be better spent trying to figure out who he is and why he's got it in for me."

"While you do what?" Ethan had asked with a sullen frown. "Hunker down somewhere until we find him?"

"Yeah. That's going to happen. I'm going to try to get a lead on Tiffany. Don't say it," she warned when she was met by looks of uniform disgust on those three handsome and belligerent faces.

"She's my friend," she reminded them.

Dallas grunted. "She's a pain in the ass."

"And you're our sister," Ethan added with meaning.

She couldn't help it. She teared up. "I love you, too, you big dummies, but don't ask me not to do this. Besides, the more I'm on the move, the more difficult a target I'll make."

In the end, grudging and grumbling, they'd relented—at least provisionally. They agreed to start looking. Dig up enemies she might have made during her Secret Service career. Check out the possibility of grudges over some of the work she'd done for E.D.E.N. And they'd let her take care of herself—until they felt she needed their intervention.

She'd taken the offer—and she'd cross any roadblocks they threw up when the time came.

Squaring her shoulders, she ran a hand over the lapel of her pale blue silk suit jacket, felt the comforting presence of her .38 beneath her breast, then tugged down the hemline of her matching short skirt and attempted to concentrate on the upcoming meeting with Clayborne's right-hand man, Richard Edwards. And get McClain out of her head—where he'd been in some way, shape, or form since Saturday night.

It bugged the heck out of her that she couldn't shake him—more specifically that seeing him again had shaken her.

She let out a gust of air through puffed cheeks and punched the up button on the elevator that would take her to Edwards's suite of offices on the nineteenth floor. It wasn't going to do a bit of good to bemoan the fact that the bullet she'd managed to dodge all these years had finally found its mark and blasted her and McClain together again.

When the elevator finally hit the ground floor, she stepped inside and punched 19 on the polished chrome panel. She'd thought she was over the disappointment of having to resign from the Secret Service, too. So much for what she'd thought. Seeing McClain had not only resurrected her anger and humiliation over what he'd done to her; it had also gotten all tangled up with her anger and frustration over whoever was running around with stun guns and bombs and in the man who had ultimately cost her her Secret Service career: Jeremy Clayborne.

A bigger person might have been able to forget about past transgressions. But, like her brothers always said, she was like an elephant. She didn't forget. Anything.

"And you don't forgive," Nolan had once accused her. "Just see where that's going to get you."

A lot he knew, she thought grumpily as the elevator passed the tenth floor. Just because her two semiserious relationships—one her senior year in college, the other her first year in the Service—had ended in near bloodlettings didn't mean she didn't forgive. She was passionate, that was all. Passionate and particular.

Specifically, she was very *particular* about the men in her life adhering to the same philosophies as she did. Like monogamy. Yeah. She'd been real particular about that. Just her good luck that the men she ended up getting involved with in her personal life always turned out to be triple-A's. Like McClain.

Life lesson: there are no good guys out there for her—either that, or she was destined to draw the bad boys who couldn't or wouldn't commit. Either way, she'd finally wised up. She wasn't going there again. Sure, she dated, but as soon as a guy started making noises that smacked of exclusivity, she was gone—saved her the pain of his letting her down later. Besides, long-term was a myth. And love—if there truly was such a thing—was overrated in the bliss department but deserved its reputation for pain. She'd concentrate on her career, thank you very much, and leave that rocky ground to those with a higher pain tolerance than hers.

When the elevator doors opened with a space age *whoosh,* she grounded herself back in the present, stepped out onto the intricately designed marble in the nineteenth floor's outer lobby—and walked directly into McClain.

"Whoa." He steadied her with the firm grip of his hands on her upper arms. "We've got to quit meeting like this."

He was all flashing brown eyes and five o'clock shadow—even at nine in the morning. He met her gaze with a cocksure grin as she tipped her head back to look up at him. She hated being short. Really, really hated it. Hated it more that she felt a slight stirring of an old memory when it registered that he still wore the same musky male scent she remembered from high school.

"But hey, at least you aren't holding a cannon on me this time," he added with a look that made her realize she'd been staring.

She took her anger at herself out on him. "That can be arranged. What are you doing here?"

He dropped his hands and the corners of his eyes crinkled; his tanned cheeks dimpled. "And here I was hoping a good night's sleep would cure that bad case of the crankies. Any more random bombings I need to know about?"

Eve smoothed a hand over her hair and headed for Edwards's office door, refusing to let McClain rile her. "Tell me you were just leaving."

"Sorry. Just got here. Now I'm serious. You had any more run-ins with the bad guys?"

"Only you," she said, and headed for the reception area.

"Wait. Wait just a sec."

She stopped, expelled an impatient breath. And went rigid when he reached out and hooked a strand of her hair with his pinkie. Their gazes locked and for the longest moment held. His eyes were mocha brown, warm, and just a little bit sleepy.

Bedroom eyes, she'd always thought. Sexy eyes that appeared to see more than they should.

With a gentle caress and a slow, intimate smile he drew the hair back and away from her face. Let his hand linger at the shell of her ear, let his fingers brush against her cheek as he finally pulled away. "There. All neat and tidy for the big showdown."

It took a moment, maybe two, for her to remember that she had no time for this man. Another to stall a shudder the heat of his touch had elicited.

She drew herself up to her whole five foot two—stretched to five-five in her open-toed bone pumps. "What makes you think this is going to be a showdown?"

He lifted a shoulder, a lazy, limber motion on a six-foot frame that was all lean muscle and corded sinew. "Did a little checking on you, *Agent* Garrett. You've got guts showing up in the lion's den, I'll give you that."

She felt her spine stiffen. So. He'd done some digging. Found out she'd been with the Secret Service. The lion's den reference also suggested that he must have discovered her history with Clayborne, which most likely meant that he knew she'd been assigned protection detail for Tiffany and that Clayborne had ultimately called for her dismissal from the Secret Service because of the abduction attempt. The information couldn't have been that hard to find. Eve could still see the headline: **FATALITIES IN ABDUCTION ATTEMPT FOILED BY SECRET SERVICE AGENT.**

She'd never forget that day. The would-be abductors had almost gotten to Tiffany. Would have if Eve hadn't killed them. Her first kills. Her only kills. Yeah. She'd gotten the bad guys. Too late, however, to save Clayborne's chauffeur and Jack Small, a good, solid agent. Both had died that bloody day.

"Hello?"

She blinked herself back—away from the hail of gunfire, Tiffany's screams, the bodies and the blood—and realized

McClain was watching her with both concern and compassion.

"What?" she snapped, not wanting either from him.

"It must have been tough," he said softly.

Yeah. It had been tough. She wasn't about to admit it to him.

"You OK?" he asked softly.

She drew in a bracing breath. "Right as rain."

"Yeah. I can see that."

When she didn't rise to the bait, he shook his head. "I'm surprised Edwards agreed to see you."

She mustered up a tight smile. "Life's just one big surprise."

She could see the moment when he decided things had gotten too heavy. The look in his eyes shifted from somber to smart-ass in one long blink. "Don't I know it. Came as a huge surprise when Edwards summoned me out of bed at," he checked his watch, a dollar-sized silver disk strapped on his well-defined left wrist with black leather, "eight thirty in the morning."

Eight thirty? He'd only been up for half an hour? No wonder he looked like he just crawled out from under a rock. Or a woman. He was wearing worn flip-flops, baggy, wrinkled tan cargo shorts, and an oversize tropical print shirt that looked like he'd dug it out of a clothes dryer—or a pile of dirty laundry. Her money was on the dirty laundry. As for his hair, it may be in style, but the look he was wearing was pure, real "bedhead," as opposed to the results of a session in front of a mirror with a bottle of hair gel.

And he was still one of the most devastatingly attractive men she'd ever seen. Damn him.

She averted her gaze to Edwards's office door. "If he needs you to run interference, he must consider me quite the threat."

"Or quite the nuisance," McClain suggested.

Yeah. There was that. She rapped on the door. And waited, feeling McClain's dark eyes watching her. Entertained. Amused.

He was still grinning when the door swung open. A tall, svelte brunette wearing a navy blue suit and a professionally distant air greeted them.

The woman's hair was styled in a sleek no-nonsense cut, and if there was any warm blood running through her veins, Eve got the impression there couldn't have been more than an ounce. A chill radiated from the brunette that made Eve shiver.

There was professional distance and then there was barely veiled contempt. Eve's money was on contempt.

The woman offered McClain a tight smile. "Good morning, Mr. McClain." Clear, cool gray eyes met Eve's with an icy stare. "And you must be Ms. Garrett."

"Eve." Eve extended her hand.

"Of course. I'm Jazelle Taylor, Mr. Edwards's executive assistant."

Jazelle's handshake, Eve noticed, was as reserved as her manner. And she'd been right about the blood. A dead fish was warmer.

To her credit, however, whatever opinion Jazelle, the EA, formed in a brief but assessing once-over, she didn't so much as let a hint of emotion flicker in her eyes. Of course, one had to assume she *had* any emotion.

"Please, come in," Jazelle said, stepping aside. "Mr. Edwards is expecting you."

With a phone to his ear, Edwards sat behind a black lacquered desk roughly the size of Miami. He lifted his hand, motioning Eve to sit in a plush black leather chair, then held up a finger indicating he'd be with her in one minute. McClain sat in her chair's twin beside her.

While Edwards finished up his call, Eve took in Jeremy Clayborne's inner sanctum. The office on the nineteenth floor was a study in chrome and glass elegance and priceless artwork. To the west, through floor-to-ceiling plate-glass windows, was the most amazing view of Lake Worth. To the east, the Atlantic, all raw power and white swells, crashed against the eroding Palm Beach sand.

And directly in front of her was a man who, by virtue of speaking as Jeremy Clayborne's mouthpiece, wielded more power than the heads of many small foreign countries. If she'd passed him on the street, however, she'd never have taken a second look—unless it was to shake her head over his comb-over.

It was a little hard to get past. Harder still to figure. Jeremy Clayborne's right-hand man—Jeremy, the new millennium's answer to Howard-trust-no onc-Hughes Clayborne—was most likely wearing a five-thousand-dollar Armani suit and five-hundred-dollar imported Italian loafers, but wouldn't spring for a decent hairpiece. Or plugs, for God's sake. This was West Palm Beach, Florida. Cosmetic enhancement capital of the world. Edwards had to be one of the highest-paid flunkies on earth, yet there he sat, a testament to wealth and power with a flipping bird's nest on his head.

"I apologize for that," Edwards said, disconnecting and rising to refill a cup of coffee from a small, sleek kitchen area toward the back of the office. In his wake, the scent of some spicy, pricey cologne mingled with the sterile air produced by a state-of-the-art air-conditioning system.

"It's all right. You're a busy man."

Edwards gave her a pointed look as he returned to his desk. Eve had to concede that with the exception of that ridiculous hair he wasn't a bad-looking man. He was about five-ten, a little on the stocky side, but in good shape. He had decent skin, pleasant features, and nice hazel eyes.

In all fairness, it was quite possible that if she worked for a wing nut like Clayborne—a man who had in the past three years morphed into an anal, distrustful, agoraphobic recluse—she supposed she might develop a few unusual peccadilloes of her own. Like a comb-over.

"Let's make this short and to the point, shall we?" Edwards said in a clipped, no-nonsense cadence. "I have no idea why you requested an audience, Ms. Garrett, but the very fact that you did raises all my antennae."

"I'm concerned about Tiffany," Eve put in before he could completely roll over her. "I was hoping—"

"Let's get something clear," Edwards interrupted coldly, part corporate gunslinger, part authority on everything in the world. "Tiffany is no concern of yours. Which brings me to the reason I granted this meeting. I want to make it clear to you, Ms. Garrett, that whatever feelings of attachment you have to Ms. Clayborne are misplaced and unappreciated. Mr. Clayborne could not have made that any more clear after the debacle in which you and you alone were responsible for placing Tiffany in harm's way."

"Mr. Edwards, I underst—"

"Ms. Garrett," he interrupted again with a hard look, "let me restate. You are here for one reason and one reason only. I wish to remind you in person that you are to stay away from Tiffany. You are not to contact her, not to call her, not to concern yourself with her in any way, shape, or form. If you do so, you will find a law enforcement officer at your door with a no-contact order."

Not to mention that Tiffany would pay a price, too. Eve had received a phone call from Edwards three months ago warning her that if she didn't keep out of Tiffany's life, the consequences were that Tiffany would be the one who would be punished.

Eve had thought then that the punishment would most likely be in the form of putting a lid on Tiffany's spending. Perhaps Clayborne would even disown her. For Tiffany's sake, Eve had backed away. The only problem was, Tiffany had seen it as yet one more person cutting her out of her life. She'd accused. She'd cried. And in the end, she'd told Eve she never wanted to see her again. Childish, yes. But she'd been hurting.

"Mr. McClain," Edwards said, and Eve realized she'd tuned out of the conversation, "your purpose here is to be apprised of Mr. Clayborne's vehement objection to any contact between Ms. Garrett and Tiffany. You are not, in any way, to confer, collaborate, or conspire with Ms. Garrett should you encounter her during your search for Tiffany. Additionally, should you choose to disregard Mr. Clayborne's wishes, your contract will be terminated immediately. Is that understood?"

She didn't have to look to know that McClain gave Edwards a sober nod.

"All right then," Edwards continued. "Then we're finished here. Good day to both of you. And Ms. Garrett—I truly anticipate that this will be the last we see or hear of you."

He depressed a button on his phone. "Jazelle. Please show Ms. Garrett and Mr. McClain out."

Jazelle appeared with the same cool, calm élan and held the door open for them.

Eve had little she could do but leave.

"Good day, Ms. Garrett," Jazelle said with a nod as Eve walked past her through the open door.

Eve could have sworn the woman was gloating.

Eve was hot. Sizzle hot, Mac realized as they walked together toward the bank of elevators. He couldn't help but wonder what she'd been thinking. Showing up here, asking for an audience.

A part of him admired the hell out of her for having the guts to confront the Clayborne machine after the way it had rolled over her three years ago. She was pretty cheeky about the explosion Saturday night, too—Mac didn't know whether to admire her or lecture her about watching her back. And though her safety wasn't his concern, along with digging up dirt on her background last night, he'd also found himself keeping an eye out for anything that raised warning flags— like who, from her past, might want her dead.

Secret Service. Hell. Sweet little Eve Garrett—single Eve Garrett, he was happy to find out—was also ex–Secret Service

agent Eve Garrett. Now she was a security specialist, a partner with her brothers—three tough, forceful men who had,
frankly, scared the hell out of him back in school.

When the elevator doors opened, he pushed the button
and they entered it together. Beside him, her face was flame
red, her nostrils flared, and if she crossed her arms any
tighter over her breasts, they were gonna pop right out from
under that sexy little white camisole thingy she was wearing
under a blue silk jacket the color of her eyes. Not that he'd
mind the prospect all that much.

It was a damn shame, though, that she was expending all
that energy on anger. He could think of a much more pleas-
urable way to let off steam. Actually, he could think of several. Some involved Jell-O. Not that he'd suggest it. He may
be horny, but he wasn't stupid.

Hadn't stopped him from spending a lot of time thinking
about her during the last couple of days, though—or from
finding out what he could about where she'd been and what
she'd been doing the past fourteen years. It hadn't taken
much digging to get the goods on Eve or her connection
with Tiffany. And as long as he'd been digging, he'd dug a
little deeper into Clayborne's closet.

Not that long ago—before he'd gone Howard Hughes the
hermit on everyone—Jeremy Clayborne had been tight with
the Oval Office. Real tight. He'd been working for the administration in some capacity, and the work sometimes took
him out of the country. When the shit had hit the fan with
Tiffany, Clayborne had been in Europe negotiating a contract for his own firearms company. Or so the story went.

If Mac had read between the lines correctly, however,
Clayborne hadn't been there on *private* business. He'd been
on *government* business—covert government business. Otherwise, why would a Secret Service agent be providing protection for Clayborne's daughter? The only way that happened
was for the president himself to request it. So, no, Mac
didn't buy the cover story for a second.

Anyway, whether Eve deserved it or not, Clayborne blamed her for subjecting his daughter—who by all accounts he'd given over to a nanny to raise anyway—to the danger and the trauma of the abduction attempt. Blamed Eve for the death of his chauffeur as well. Like she was supposed to know there were two men lying in wait for the limo when they arrived at Orlando for an equestrian competition.

Hell. Eve had done her job. Everything he'd read said she'd done it with bravery and skill. She'd protected the kid. Killed the bad guys even though they'd taken two of the good guys down in the process. But her heroism hadn't been good enough for Clayborne.

Clayborne had done some leaning. And his weight had toppled fences. Eve had been forced to resign from a career that, by all indications, had been the stuff that commendations were made of.

Mac looked at her across the elevator.

"I'm curious," he said as the cab hit the ground floor. "Other than pissing him off, what, exactly, did you hope to gain by meeting with Edwards?"

He'd probably have been wise to keep his mouth shut. But then, something told him she'd never accuse him of being the sharpest knife in the drawer.

The elevator doors opened and she walked out ahead of him. "The big question is: what are *you* going to do?"

He pressed a hand to his chest. "What am *I* going to do? What am I going to do about what?"

"About helping me find her."

"Cupcake," he said, stopping her with a hand on her arm and turning her to face him. "You heard the man. I'm out on my ass if I so much as smile at you."

Mac experienced the full measure of her accusatory glare. He exhaled wearily. "Look, if it were up to me, and you wanted to put in the time, hell, I'd say go for it. We'd work together. But it's not up to me. I've got to follow the rules according to Clayborne."

"Since when did you ever play by anybody's rules but your own?"

She had him there. "OK. Fine. Let's make them *my* rules. I need the job. I need the money. I'm not gonna blow this account because you've got a feeling that the girl's in trouble."

The money from this job—damn good money—was going to keep him afloat for several months. No way was he going to indulge a few lust-induced urgings to team up with her and blow it. This gig would more than pay off his divorce settlement. More important, it would ensure that Angie would have to stop making noises about terminating his visitation rights with Ali. He was damn tired of ducking the ax that his ex enjoyed the hell out of swinging on that count.

And maybe, just maybe, he could even eke out a down payment on that sweet little fishing boat he'd been dreaming about. Ali would love it. As long as she could bring her Barbies.

So yeah. Solvency sounded sweet. Frankly, though, so did the notion of going head-to-head with Eve Garrett. God, she was a looker. Maybe when this was over, he'd look her up. See if he could knock the hard edges off her grudge. Maybe get a little friendly again.

When she caught him staring at her breasts, she made one of those noises that only women could make. The kind that leveled volumes of accusation, denigrated his pedigree back a millennium or so, and put his IQ somewhere around a baker's dozen. Someday he had to find out how they did that. Today he really didn't care. In fact, he was feeling pretty damn fine.

"Why do you really care about Tiffany so much?" he asked, deciding to risk Eve's wrath. "Seems to me, she's been nothing but a thorn in your side since the beginning."

She tossed back that beautiful mane of silky blond hair. "It's something you wouldn't understand, since apparently it's all about the money to you."

He could be pissed but chose not to be. She didn't know

what motivated him. Let her think what she wanted. It was no skin off his nose.

"Well, hell yeah," he said with a cheery smile. "It's *always* all about the money. Keeps it simple."

Another sound of disgust. "There's nothing simple about it if Tiffany is in trouble."

"Look. Tiffany Clayborne is a party girl on a party run and she doesn't give a damn who she puts out in the process."

Eve shoved open the double glass and chrome doors and walked outside. The Florida sun was brilliant and hot. A stiff easterly wind shuttled in the scent of salt and brine from the Atlantic.

"I hope you're right. And I hope you find her. In the meantime, you won't mind if I conduct my own search."

The woman just wouldn't quit. "You're kidding, right?"

"Do I look like I'm kidding?"

What she looked like was a woman on a mission.

"With or without help from Edwards or Clayborne or *you*, I'm going to find her. As a matter of fact, I'll probably find her before you do."

He snorted. "Like that's going to happen."

"Like yeah. It is. Wonder how much money Edwards will pony up for you then."

One thing you could count on with women: the outside packaging varied, but inside they were pretty much all the same. This woman in particular hated being bested by men. His gender may have the physical equipment theirs lacked, but the woman standing beside him had her own equivalent set of balls. And he'd bet the farm that estrogen packed a helluva lot more punch in the mean department than testosterone any day. He ought to know. He still bore the scars from his divorce. And the deeper scars of losing Ali.

"If I didn't know better, I'd think you were trying to make this into a little competition."

She tucked her chin, looked him up and down. When she

met his eyes again she was smirking. "There's competition?"

He laughed. OK, so he looked like something a very in-discriminate cat wouldn't bother to drag in. "I remember you as being so much sweeter."

"You ought to see someone about that memory problem. See you around, McClain."

"Hey, Eve."

She stopped when he said her name. Turned slowly. Gave him a long-suffering look.

The wind caught her long hair and lifted it back and away from a face that was an intriguing mix of classic girl next door and wear-your-wrist-out porn star with her wide blue eyes and full, generous lips. The stout ocean breeze folded back her jacket lapels and molded that filmy little white top against her magnificent breasts—and some of his body parts started changing size and shape.

At this very moment, life was good. Life was sweet. He had a high-profile case, could almost see his ship coming in on the horizon and the prospect of a little competition from a hot woman to keep things interesting.

Pretty much in love with the moment and the fact that Eve Garrett was as much fun to needle as she was to look at, he dug into his pocket, pulled out a bag of M&M's, and tossed them to her. "Here you go, cupcake. These are for you."

She was too surprised to stop herself from snagging them out of the air.

"A little affirmation that my memory's just fine," he said when she looked from him to the bag of candy.

She smiled. Tight and brittle. Clearly remembering the last time—the *only* time—he'd bought her M&M's.

"If you think you're going to beat me to Tiffany," he said, unable to resist, "you underestimate me."

"No. I think I've pretty much got you pegged. You're a self-serving, self-absorbed rat-bastard."

He chuckled, as impressed with her mouth as he was with

her mind. OK, as impressed with her mouth as he was with her *body*.

"Yeah, well, you know what they say about self-serving, self-absorbed rat-bastards. We try harder."

"Try this," she said, and flipped him the bird as she turned and walked away.

6

KEY WEST

HE HADN'T ALWAYS BEEN A RAT-BASTARD, Mac thought candidly as he drove down Duval Street the next day, squinting against the late-afternoon sun, searching the row of shop fronts for the address he'd scrawled on his notepad this morning. At least he hadn't *consistently* been one, he amended as his stomach growled, reminding him that the Big Mac he'd downed for "brunch" around nine had been several miles and several hours back on U.S. 1 just south of Miami.

No, he hadn't always been a rat-bastard, just like he hadn't always been as lucky as he'd been last night when he'd connected with the big "D," Dave Johnson, in Atlantic City. Cops stuck tight with cops. Even ex-cops who had turned to private security or PI work to pay the bills.

"Got something for ya," Dave had said in his no-nonsense tone when he called Mac back early this morning.

Mac and Dave had been rookie uniforms together on the Chicago PD. They'd shared many a gut-searing morning cup of coffee at a little diner just off Calumet before heading out to their beat after roll call at division headquarters at Wentworth Station. For two years they'd patrolled the 213 together. Watched each other's backs. Saved each other's asses from the bad guys and even from the brass on a few occasions.

A lot of split shifts had gone by since then. A lot of

changes. Now Mac was back home in West Palm trying to make a go of his new business and Dave was head of hotel security at the Atlantic City Taj Mahal.

After he'd watched a royally ticked Eve Garrett stroll away from him yesterday morning outside the Clayborne building, Mac had first dug out his cell phone and punched in Angie's number, taking a chance that his ex was home. He'd gotten lucky and spent a good half an hour on the phone catching up with his daughter's latest Barbie adventures.

Then he'd gotten back to work searching for Tiffany Clayborne. Like her other escapades, this one appeared to be more a cry for attention than a calculated attempt to disappear. And after what he'd discovered, he was certain that the girl was running on her own steam and not against her will. Which was good. Eve may be worried about foul play, but Tiffany was just plain playing.

And she was playing hard. She'd been dropping a lot of coin up and down the East Coast—so said her credit card and ATM transactions. Roger Edwards had provided him with Tiffany's account information last week. The info had led him to Club Asylum Saturday night where she'd blown a bundle in the past month. Of course the small matter of an explosion had killed his shot at finding any useful information there. Now, however, thanks to the financial information, he had listings for several airlines, five-star hotels, and upscale shops as the benefactors of her latest spending spree.

Edwards had also provided Mac with Tiffany's photo, a list of her favorite haunts and acquaintances both in and out of the country, as well as her Social Security number.

Holed up in his office yesterday afternoon, Mac had gotten to work studying the info Edwards had fed him about Runaway Tiff.

The PI license and a U.S. map were the only framed items hanging on the wall of his ten-by-ten second bedroom that he loosely referred to as a den and currently doubled as his office. A laptop with wireless connection, a cell phone, a fax, and an answering machine and he was in business. God bless modern technology.

The U.S. map hanging on the wall was not for decoration— though God knew, the place could use a touch or two from a domestic diva. No, the map was a tool. Because Edwards had provided Tiff's ATM info and her Social Security number and DOB, Mac had been able to set up online banking and track her ATM use along the East Coast. Foolish girl, Tiff. She'd never bothered to set up a password on her account; consequently, he'd done it for her. No thanks necessary. The result was that he could monitor her account transactions real-time either by phone or by using his laptop.

It wasn't exactly kosher, but it was common practice in his profession, and since banks had some culpability for making access so easy, charges weren't usually filed unless theft became an issue. That wasn't gonna happen here—though Lord knew, the balance in her account was enough to have him thinking of opening up his own account in the Caymans and disappearing for the rest of his life in abject luxury.

Anyway, the last transaction had been recorded in Atlantic City, so he'd given Dave a call, figuring that if anyone had a finger on the pulse of the city, it would be Dave.

"That was fast," Mac had said, tucking his cell to his ear and reaching for a pen and paper when his phone rang, waking him around 7:00 a.m.

"Yeah, well, lots of freaks running around, but even a woman with berry red hair, a tear tattoo, twin lip rings, and accessorized by a rock band makes an impression. Especially when she's stoned out of her mind. People don't have too much trouble remembering a sight like that. Anyway, the whole tribe's been staying here at the Taj Mahal."

Mac and Dave had both made detective the same year. Had both been on career track to lieutenant. A high-cholesterol problem and a mild heart attack had permanently sidetracked Dave's public law enforcement career. Can't have a detective who might have the big one in the middle of a car chase or a drug bust. Just like you couldn't have a detective with a gimp leg making foot chases after law-breaking gangbangers who were pedaling on two good ones.

As he cruised down Duval, Mac rubbed his thigh, wished to hell he still had his badge instead of a banged-up knee and a line-of-duty disability pension that covered life's basics but not the luxuries like oh, say, pride. Or like frequent airfare to visit his daughter in San Diego. He'd followed Angie back to West Palm after the divorce so he could be close to Ali. So, of course, she'd relocated shortly after to San Diego with her new, not a cop, not a rat-bastard, husband.

That's what Discovery Unlimited was supposed to do. Provide the luxuries. He needed to make a decent living on his own. He wanted to see his kid more often. And yeah, the fishing boat was a ticket to a dream. So far, Discovery Unlimited had netted him enough to cover his investigator license, insurance, and office equipment. Oh yeah, and this piece-of-shit '98 tan Taurus that was good on gas and on blending into the background but was a gutless wonder on the straightaway.

"Your girl and the boy band she's playing with were here for several days but checked out night before last," Dave had said in that big booming voice that had put as much fear of death and dismemberment into a suspect as his size had. "Concierge overheard them talking about heading back south. Key West came up."

Thanks to big Dave, Mac hadn't had to resort to any additional, shall we say, back-door tactics as he had at Club Asylum. He'd upheld the law for over a decade. Still liked to stay within it—even if it was a little more fun to skirt the fringe of it on occasion like he had Saturday night. He did, however, plug into Tiff's account again, and sure enough, a new transaction popped up for an ATM withdrawal at a Key West bank.

So, here he was. Key West—or Key Weird, depending on

your perspective. Land of spectacular sunsets, Ernest Hemingway, 24-7-365 parties, and rainbow flags. And he was looking for a buddy of Dave's in the good-buddy network who might know someone who might know someone who might be able to give him a direct line on the Tiff.

See, that was one of the reasons Mac knew he hadn't always been a rat-bastard. The good guys were still his buddies. It was mostly women he had a tendency to piss off.

"Take my ex-wife. Please," he muttered under his breath as he drove slowly by a T-shirt shop that may or may not have had the number of the address he'd scribbled on his notepad. The purple paint was worn. He couldn't tell.

"And take Eve Garrett," he said, then did a double take and slammed on the brakes.

"What the hell?" He swore he'd just seen her walking down the street.

Tiny red tank top, tight white capri pants. Blond hair loose. Beautiful breasts bouncing.

He rolled down his window. Hot, humid tropical air smacked him square in the face.

Sonofabitch. It's her.

Mac couldn't believe it. Eve Garrett was here. In Key West.

He spotted her again—then lost her when she walked into the T-shirt shop whose address he'd been trying to make out. A car honked behind him. Next thing he knew, a buff blond beach boy drew alongside piloting a pedicab. He stopped by Mac's open driver's side window. Two middle-aged tourist-type women blinked and smiled from the pedicab's passenger seats.

"You lost?" the kid asked, tipping a pair of Oakleys—the kind Mac couldn't afford—down his bronze god nose and looking at Mac over the top of them.

"Not anymore."

He floored it, swore when he couldn't find a parking spot, and finally outmaneuvered an octogenarian in a tank-sized

Caddy for a spot three blocks away. The old guy was still shaking his fist and glaring at Mac from between the steering wheel and the dash as he sprinted back to the T-shirt shop.

"I'll be damned," he muttered. It *was* the address Dave had given him. And it *was* a T-shirt shop.

He walked in the open door of a long shotgun-narrow space—one of roughly 50 million such shops lining the Key West streets and designed to trap tourists and separate them from roughly 50 million of their dollars annually.

"Looking for something for a special woman?" A male salesclerk, possibly Syrian born, and heavily accented, flashed a broad smile.

Mac was looking *for* a special woman, but Eve was nowhere in sight. When he spotted a closed door with a **PRI-VATE** sign printed in bold red letters at the back of the store, though, he had a sneaking suspicion he knew exactly where she was. Not all PIs had to advertise their services. Not all wanted to. But you could bet anyone who needed an investigator's service knew someone who knew how to find one.

Stood to reason that Eve would know, too, but damn, she was good if she already had a line on the Tiff through the contact Dave had given Mac here in the Keys.

And now we were talking about pride. No way was he going to let her beat him to Tiffany.

The clerk held a hot pink T-shirt out for Mac's inspection. *Shuck me, suck me, eat me raw,* was stenciled in glittery gold letters across the front. The smiling crawfish clinging to the *w* in *raw* was white and very, very small.

"Your lady . . . she'll like this one."

Oh yeah. Any real lady would be proud as punch to wear that shirt.

Mac took a step around the clerk. "I'm looking for Bud Winchell."

The small man matched Mac's move with a wide sideways lurch. "Bud's busy right now. Would you like to wait?"

The clerk was five-six, maybe one-thirty if he'd been

soaked in rum punch. Mac particularly liked the worried look on the guy's face that told him he was a runner, not a fighter, because he intended to see Bud whether he was busy or not.

"Waiting's not my style," Mac said as he shouldered past racks of shirts and headed for the door in the back. "Neither, my friend, is that shirt."

Eve sat on the opposite side of Bud Winchell's battered gun-metal gray desk. Bud always made her think of a character drawn straight from a 1940s gumshoe detective novel—Key West style. So did his office, which was tucked discreetly away in the back of the "2-T's 4 $10" T-shirt shop.

The tiny office was a movie set complete with a slow-moving Panama fan sluggishly stirring the smoke-choked air and what appeared to be several years' worth of dust that had accumulated on every horizontal space. An old, faded ten-by-twelve framed photograph of a younger, slimmer version of Bud standing, Hemingway style, beside a trophy-sized marlin hung crookedly on the wall behind his desk. A coatrack in one corner sported a tan straw fedora, the black band stained from years of perspiration. A metal file cabinet occupied another corner. The top of the cabinet was cluttered with a slew of dog-eared papers, an overflowing in/out mail basket, and a sickly-looking good luck bamboo plant.

Evidently good luck did not extend to the plant.

Bud talked around a rattling cough and the unfiltered Camel jammed in the corner of his mouth.

"When are you going to stop smoking those awful things?" Eve asked as his barrel belly expanded beneath his white linen shirt, jiggling with the force of his cough.

"You sound just like your mother. Look like her, too, dar-lin'." His gravelly voice softened. "More and more every day. She's a beautiful woman and so are you."

Bud had been her father's mentor on the West Palm PD when Wes Garrett had returned from 'Nam, then graduated from the police academy. It was through Bud that Wes and Bud's sister, Susan, met and eventually married. And it was Eve's dad who had founded E.D.E.N. Securities, Inc., before turning it over to Ethan when he'd retired.

"When was the last time you called Mom?"

Bud lifted a hand, shook a disciplinary finger. "Last week, Miss Smarty-pants. If you kept in better touch with her yourself, you'd know that."

"No fair. I've been busy."

"And I rest on my laurels all day."

She grinned. Uncle Bud always made her smile, and frankly, she could use a smile or two today. Between worrying about Tiffany and watching her back for whoever wanted her dead, Eve hadn't done a lot of smiling lately. Oh yeah. And then there was McClain.

He made her think of mistakes and broken dreams—and lost babies.

She shook herself back to the moment and Uncle Bud, who had retired from the West Palm police force fifteen years ago and moved down to Key West. He'd set up a security slash investigation slash missing persons business shortly after. He hadn't intended to work more than a few hours a day, but as with most good PI enterprises, his work spread by word of mouth, and now he didn't get nearly as much time on his fishing boat as he'd like.

"Tell me, little girl—why are you and your smart mouth sitting in front of me today? And don't say you're on vacation. You've got that look in your eye."

"What look?"

"The one that says you're in a hurry, you have a need to know something, and you're betting your money on good ole Uncle Bud coming through."

"You're right," Eve said, feeling a little guilty because she didn't get down to see him more often. Key West was one of her most favorite spots on earth, and Bud was her favorite uncle. "I *am* hoping you can help me."

He rubbed the flat of his hand over his robust belly. "OK. Who do I gotta kill?"

Eve laughed. God, she loved him. He was as harmless as one of those old roosters wandering the Key West streets. All crow and no go.

"I'm looking for someone. Thought maybe you could put out a few feelers and see if you come up with anything."

He leaned back. Both he and the chair groaned.

"That hip bothering you again?"

He grunted and shifted his weight, wincing as he did. "Piece of advice for you, sweetie. Don't get old. Now who you looking for and why do you think they might be here?"

She gave him the background information on Tiffany Clayborne. "I managed to find out the name of the band she might be with." Didn't feel a twinge of guilt that she hadn't shared that information with Tyler McClain, either. Neither did she feel one bit comfortable with the idea that Tiffany was with them of her own free will. It was just a feeling. More than a hunch. Eve knew Tiff. Yeah, she'd grown a little wild, but she wasn't mean—and taking off like this, worrying everyone . . . well, it didn't feel right. Neither did the fact that Eve was still getting out-of-service messages whenever she dialed Tiff's cell phone.

"I called a few local booking agencies in West Palm and got lucky on the fifth hit. Seems the band was booked as a lounge act in Atlantic City, but when I called the casino they were a no-show. The manager was ticked, especially when one of his off-duty dealers spotted the lead singer at the tables at the Taj Mahal. The band had played this same casino before, and this dealer, a rock star wannabe, had struck up a friendship with them.

"Anyway, the manager was more than happy to bitch at length." He'd given her names and descriptions—at least of the leader of Dead Grief, Lance Reno, and the bass player, Abe Gorman. "I took another chance and called the Taj Mahal and sure enough, a Ms. Tiffany Clayborne had been

registered, but she'd checked out, purportedly headed for the
Keys."

"And you got them to spill all this from one or two phone
calls."

Eve grinned. "Yeah. I did." She'd learned the power of a
badge and credentials early on in her career at the Secret
Service. She'd learned the power of a bluff at the same time.
It still amazed her. Even over the phone and without any true
misrepresentation, it was exceedingly easy to convince people that (a) you were an important person, (b) they had little
choice but to divulge requested information, and (c) they
were providing a service of grave significance. It was human
nature to want to help. In many cases, that fostered a notion
of importance and inclusion—both elements many people
were sadly lacking in their lives.

"You know, you're the second person looking for information about that girl."

Eve snapped to attention. "Someone's already been
here?"

"A friend of mine from Atlantic City called. Said he was
sending a buddy down. An ex-cop turned PI."

Now he really had her interest. "Ex-cop?"

"Yeah." He shuffled around on his paper-strewn desk,
came up with a coffee-stained note. "McClain. Tyler Mc-
Clain. My friend used to work with him in Chicago."

Unbelievable. So, that's where McClain had gone when
he'd left West Palm. Chicago. And he'd been a cop. This was
also news. Of course, anything about McClain would be news
to her. Sure, she'd known he'd gone to college—after all, she
ran with the same circle of friends for a while and his name
had come up occasionally. But she'd lost track of him after
that. Frankly, she hadn't wanted to know where he'd been or
what he'd been doing all these years. She'd known only that
he wasn't in West Palm, and once he'd left without a long look
back, wherever he'd gone couldn't have been far enough.

Unfortunately, now she knew he was back. It was already bordering on too much information.

So, the quintessential bad-to-the-bone bad boy had been a cop. Go figure. Now he was just a jerk. And he was zeroing in on Tiff. At least he was good at what he did. Eve, however, was better.

"You know this McClain guy?" Bud asked.

"Yeah. I guess you could say I do."

"And?"

"And I don't want him to find her just yet," she said, making that decision on the spot. If Tiff was on a fun and games road trip and McClain found her first, he'd take her back to her father. Eve wasn't so sure that was the best place for Tiffany right now. She'd like a chance to talk with her and make things right between them.

If, on the other hand, Tiff was in some kind of trouble . . . well, that was another bridge she'd cross when she came to it. If need be, she'd fill McClain in then and use him to help her if she needed help.

Bud pushed out a grunt. "So, you want I should keep this McClain guy in the dark?"

"Yeah."

"You got it. In the meantime, it's not like there are a helluva lot of places to hide down here. I'll make some calls. See if anyone's spotted your girl."

"Thanks, Uncle Bud. I think I'll hoof it around town. Hit as many bars as I can. If I shake the trees hard enough, she might fall out."

"I've got your cell number. Something turns up, I'll call."

Eve stood and walked around behind the desk. She bent down and kissed his cheek, smelling Old Spice and smoke when she hugged him hard. "Quit smoking," she whispered, and kissed him again. "And get that hip checked."

"Go away."

"If McClain shows up—"

She stopped midsentence when the door swung open. And there he stood. Tyler McClain in all his laid-back glory.

She couldn't hide her surprise—or her disgust at seeing him in basically the same stellar form he'd been in yesterday for their meeting with Roger Edwards. The only thing he'd changed was the color palette. Instead of orange, black, and green, his tropical print shirt was blue, gold, and tan. His shorts were olive.

Somebody call the fashion police.

Uncle Bud squinted up at McClain through the cigarette smoke curling toward the ceiling. "This your man?" Bud's gaze drifted from Eve to McClain.

"Yeah," she said grimly. "It's him."

With barely a glance at Eve, McClain extended his hand and a good-ole-boy smile. "Tyler McClain."

When Uncle Bud just stared, McClain withdrew his hand, but the wattage of his smile never dimmed. "Dave sent me."

"Good man, Dave," Bud said with a slow nod before averting his gaze back to Eve. "You want I should call the boys to work him over?"

God love Uncle Bud. It was all she could do to keep from laughing at the shock that literally bled McClain's face of color along with his cockiness. There were no boys. And her uncle wouldn't harm a flea. A rat-bastard, maybe, if she asked him to. Admittedly, it was tempting.

"Nah," she said when she'd figured McClain had sweated enough. "He's harmless."

She squeezed past McClain, then paused to look back over her shoulder when she reached the door. She gave Uncle Bud a pointed look. "See you around."

"Sure thing, sweetie."

"Sweetie?" she heard McClain ask, his voice a little squeaky and not nearly as cocksure as when he'd barged in on them.

She grinned and walked out of the office.

. . .

"Sweetie?" Mac repeated as his head swiveled from the trop-
ics version of a Colonel Sanders look-alike to the woman
walking away.

"My niece."

Mac's head snapped back to Bud Winchell. *"Niece?"*

The old boy folded his hands together over his rotund
middle and gave him a look.

Mac shook his head. Pushed out a disbelieving laugh.
"Well, that works out well, doesn't it?"

"Yeah," Winchell said with a droll look. "I'd say it does."

Didn't it just beat all? Didn't it just beat fuckin' all?

He'd pinned a chunk of hope on Bud Winchell being
his best source on locating Tiff Clayborne well ahead of
Ms. Blond, Blue-eyed, and Beautiful. He'd just as well have
pinned it to thin air. She'd made this into a fricking contest—
and *Uncle* Bud was sure to want to stack the deck in her
favor.

Still, Mac gave it the old college try. "So I guess it would
be a pretty good bet that I'd be wasting my time asking for
professional courtesy."

Bud's mouth folded into a scowl. "Dave said you were a
sharp one."

Mac couldn't help it. He laughed again, and this time, he
actually found it funny. Hell, it *was* funny, even from his
perspective.

The next words out of Winchell's mouth had Mac sober-
ing like a judge in night court.

"If I hear from Evie that you did anything to hurt her,"
Winchell said, with that slow-paced tropical cadence that
spoke of years of laid-back comfort overlying a foundation
of steel, "you're fish bait. You understand me, boy?"

Oh yeah. He understood. He understood that this was
Winchell's turf, not his. He understood that while the man
hadn't been serious about "calling the boys to work him

over," he probably did know some "boys." And he could make it real hard on a man who crossed him.

Mac nodded like a good soldier.

"Swell. You have a nice day now," the detective added, and, leaning forward in his creaking chair, gave a dismissive nod toward the door.

Since a nice day was pretty much off the radar screen, Mac decided that what he needed was a nice drink. And he was going to have one, just as soon as he caught up with "the godfather's" niece and figured out a way to convince her to play well with others—specifically with him.

It could work. Stranger things had happened. Some bubba from Arkansas was always being abducted from a 7-Eleven by aliens. Men read *Hustler* for the articles.

So hell, yeah, Mac could bring one short, sexy blue-eyed blond woman around to his way of thinking. And if he could get someone to believe that, he had a spacious high-rise in a quiet, peaceful neighborhood on the Gaza Strip he'd enjoy the hell out of selling them.

7

THE SUN WAS STILL BURNING AS HOT AS A jalapeño when Mac stepped outside the shop—without a new T-shirt, much to the dismay of the salesclerk. Mac looked up and down the street. Eve couldn't have gotten too far. Hell, the entire key was only two miles by four miles. How far *could* she go?

He hooked a left and started walking down Duval. It shouldn't be too hard to spot her.

Or it wouldn't have been, he amended a couple of hours later, if he hadn't had the good luck to arrive at Key West smack in the middle of spring break. The city was overrun, it seemed, with gorgeous blond coeds. And brunettes and redheads. Tall ones. Short ones. Drunk ones. Lots of drunk ones. And lots of drunk young men hoping to get lucky.

Oh, to be young again. He remembered that age when life was all about partying, drinking, and scoring to a war cry of *"get drunk, get laid."* Eventually, reality had grabbed him by the ass and gotten his attention. That kind of life cost money. Required a job. A "normal" life. And things got a whole lot more serious than this laughing, dancing throng of coeds, sashaying through the streets in their bikini tops and shorts, pouring out of the restaurants and bars, making out in broad daylight and dark corners.

It was close to one of those dark corners where he finally found Eve several hours later.

. . .

Sloppy Joe's was a favorite hangout for any kind of crowd, but the party-hardy contingent had turned out in droves today. They hung out of the doors and open-air windows. They littered the sidewalk, drinks and beer bottles in hand, while music flowed into the late afternoon like sunlight and had them dancing in the streets as well as inside the bar. Suntan lotion was the scent of the day.

Barry Cuda and the Sofa Kings were the featured bands according to the board posting both the daily specials and the talent. Sloppy Joe's was clearly the best party in the Conch Republic, and the standing-room-only crowd inside, moving to the music, swaying to the beat, and drowning in their beer, weren't giving a thought to the brain cells they were killing and would sorely miss when they returned to class in a mere few days.

Mac shouldered his way inside through the glut of bodies. He was tired, he was thirsty, and despite the fact that everyone he'd quizzed had seen a pretty blue-eyed blonde at some time during the day, he still hadn't spotted Eve. Neither had he seen any sign of Tiff. When he'd fished her picture out of his pocket and flashed it here and there, he'd come up with a lot of, "Man, I'd remember that weird chick if I'd seen her."

Of course, since those same expert witnesses had slopped beer on the snapshot and had to occasionally rely on a wall to keep vertical, he hadn't taken a lot of stock in what they'd said.

Somehow, he managed to squeeze his way up to the bar.

"Beer," he yelled above a noise level that would have tripped the meter at a Bulls game over the top of the scale.

"Thanks." After sliding a five across the bar, he turned and leaned his elbows back against it, watching the crowd with a mixture of envy and fascination. That used to be him, and not more than ten years ago. Now he felt like an old man as he wondered where they came up with the stamina to not only pull it off but also live to tell the tale.

Clyde College at the end of the bar was slamming tequila shooters to the roaring approval of his pals. Coed Cathy was crying in her beer while her girlfriends tried to sober her up. And—*hello*—in the corner, Larry Linebacker was putting the moves on a petite blue-eyed blond in a tiny red tank top and white pants.

Jackpot.

And what a haul it was. It was the first time since he'd looked down the business end of her .38 that Mac had had an actual opportunity to observe pretty Eve without her barking orders or leveling insults. She was completely unaware of his presence. And he was a tad too aware of hers.

She still took his breath away. Didn't look much older than the eighteen-year-old girl he'd talked into going all the way fourteen years ago. A sharp arrow of pure unadulterated lust shot straight to his gut and curled tight at a vivid memory of how she'd looked that night, all pretty and pink and naked.

Not now, numb nuts. This was not the time for a little X-rated stroll down memory lane. The present was pretty damn pleasant anyway.

He tipped back his beer, never taking his gaze off her. God, she looked good. She wore her hair a little different now than she had back then. Longer. Fuller. A thick, sexy mass, streaked white and gold and subtle colors in between, that hit her bare shoulders and fell midway down her back.

He wasn't usually such a detail man, but this woman's details were just too lush to overlook. Full, pouty lips. Wide summer blue eyes. And that body. Jesus. No wonder Larry Linebacker was primed to light up her life. She was like a banquet of desserts. A small, delectable treat. What man in his right mind wouldn't want to nibble on her good parts before eating her whole?

A man who knew that the sugar-and-frosting-wrapped package was only window dressing, that's who. Eve Garrett was no simple cupcake, even though he took endless delight in calling her one. And she sure as hell wasn't a twinkie. She had a shrewd mind, a rapier tongue, and a degree in criminology. Tiff's flight path wasn't the only thing he'd studied last night. He'd taken a little time to check out E.D.E.N. Securities, Inc., on the Web.

The Garrett boys had been tough in high school—protective as hell and mean as caged tigers where their sister was concerned. Their military background and the credentials listed on the firm's Web site confirmed nothing had changed in that venue. Their little sister was no slouch, either.

No. This was no crumbling cupcake Mac was up against. This was a highly trained, experienced, and, given the fact that she'd beaten him to Key West, excellent investigator.

But right now it appeared she might be in a little trouble. The big bruiser was all over her, and when she finally spotted Mac watching her from the bar, damn if the first thing that registered in those baby blues wasn't relief.

Well, well. Wasn't that interesting?

Tough as nails, my-bad-ass-is-meaner-than-your-bad-ass Eve Garrett actually looked like she might have found herself in a position where she could use some help. Specifically, *his* help.

Hell, he could get into this. Thoroughly enjoying himself, Mac leaned a little farther back into the bar, grinned, and lifted his beer in greeting.

Her eyes glazed over. Anger? Warning? A little of both maybe, as her besotted and very drunken admirer braced a hand on the wall above her head and, leaning in close, slobbered something romantic in her ear.

Mac grinned a little wider, wondering if she'd actually swallow her pride and ask him to help her out. Clearly, she had a very amorous suitor who was emboldened by beer and dedicated to winning her over with his debatable charms.

She shot Mac another look. Hitched her chin. The significance of the gesture was as clear as any shout-out. *Get over
here and help me.*

Better and better.

Still, he played dumb—not much of a stretch if he read
the look on her face right.

Finally, he decided to take a little pity on her. OK, maybe
pity was the wrong word. He decided to play hero and wind
up in her IOU department. He knew exactly what payment
he'd take on that debt. Information. Whatever she'd turned
up on Tiff Clayborne so far today would do nicely—and if
any other talk of reward came up, hey, he was game.

He lifted his beer for a final deep swallow, then pushed
away from the bar and sauntered over, magnanimous as hell,
to help her out.

"Hey, babe." He edged a shoulder under the musclehead's
armpit and hooked his arm around Eve's neck. "Thought I'd
lost you."

He dropped his arm around her waist, hugged her hard—
partly because she stiffened the minute he touched her and
he knew it would piss her off and partly because he'd been
itching to get his hands on her since she'd caught him sneaking into Club Asylum.

Her bare shoulders felt warm beneath his arm. She smelled
like summer and subtly of sex—or maybe that was him.

"Who the fuckareyou?" Larry demanded, beyond drunk
and clearly perturbed that someone was cutting in on his
action.

"Tyler McClain," Mac said amiably, and extended a hand.
"My friends call me Mac. Hey, thanks for taking care of my
girl here."

College boy scowled, weaved on his feet, and batted Mac's
hand away. "*Your* girl? Wha the fuck you talkin' about?"

Beside him, Eve forced a smile. "I've been trying to tell
you I was waiting for someone."

"Fuck that," Larry slurred, cutting a bleary glance Mac's

way. "Me and the blonde here, we got a fuckin' thing goin'. So get fuckin' lost, ole man."

Clearly, they were not dealing with a language arts major.

"Happy to oblige," Mac said. "Come on, sweetie. Time for us old codgers to hit the hay."

"Not her, you fuckhead," Larry growled through a belch, and wrapped his beefy fingers around Eve's arm. "She fuckin' stays with me."

Mac saw her wince when the drunken Lothario grabbed her arm. Something he rarely let loose unraveled inside him. Rage. He'd taken the "ole man" crack in stride. But he wouldn't see her hurt.

"You've got about a nanosecond to get your hands off her, pal."

The kid, who was ten or twelve years younger and outweighed Mac by a hundred pounds, laughed. "Or what? You gonna fuckin' talk me to death?"

"Actually, I was thinking something more along this line."

The kid was on his knees, doubled over and moaning in pain, before he knew what hit him.

"How'd that *fuckin'* feel?" Mac asked cheerily as a shout of, "Fight!" rose like a battle cry through the bar.

"Great," Eve sputtered. "Just what I was trying to avoid. A scene."

Mac couldn't believe it. "You're welcome as hell," he ground out. "You want to avoid a scene, cupcake, you might try covering up some of the goods."

"You fuckin' sumbitch!" Larry roared, and, apparently numbed by alcohol and back in *fuckin'* business, grabbed Mac around the knees.

Only pride and clenched teeth kept him from screaming like a girl when his bad knee buckled. Pain shot through his leg like a bullet. He hit the floor face-first, tasted blood and excruciating pain as Larry fell on top of him.

. . .

Eve left McClain on a park bench in Mallory Square and went in search of ice and chocolate. By the time she returned, a crowd had started to gather in the warm tropical dusk in anticipation of the nightly occurrence of a spectacular Key West sunset.

He didn't see her return. His eyes were closed, his arms stretched out on either side of him on the back of the bench. His head hung back.

And he didn't look one damn bit appealing, she told herself grumpily as she cataloged the clean, sharp lines of his profile, the presence he made filling up that bench. What he looked was pathetic. Exhausted. And in pain.

Despite the fact that she was royally torqued at him, Eve couldn't help but feel a kernel of sympathy. OK, maybe more than a kernel, and that made her angrier still. He didn't deserve her sympathy, and she was a sap if she let down her guard around him.

She walked up to the bench and sat down. He stirred, winced, and slowly sat up a little straighter. When he looked up at her through his swollen eye, she shook her head and handed him the plastic cup full of ice she'd bought from a street vendor.

"For your eye."

He pressed it against his left knee and said exactly nothing.

She scooped her hair up off her neck and let a hint of a breeze, scented of sea and the dozens of food stands, dry the perspiration at her nape. It had been almost an hour since they'd managed to crawl out from under a full-blown riot of a bar fight, hail a pedicab, and ride away toward the sunset, the whine of police sirens rending the air behind them.

She was hot. She was tired—not to mention hungry—and she wasn't particularly pleased to find herself playing nursemaid to a man she didn't even like, let alone want to feel responsible for.

She ripped open the bag of M&M's, popped a couple, and offered the bag to McClain. When he shook his head, she thought, *Fine, more for me.*

"You need to have a doctor look at that leg."

"While your concern is touching, don't worry about it. I'm fine."

"Yeah. I can see that. You're just like my brothers. Tough guys one and all. God forbid you knuckle under to a show of human *frailty,* like emotion, or pain."

Disgusted, she looked away. Munched on chocolate and watched the unorganized circus of events that began to unfold every afternoon in anticipation of sunset, when the tourists started to find their way to the square. A fire-eating unicyclist had drawn quite the crowd. A comic was happily insulting hapless bystanders to the amusement of those fortunate enough not to be singled out as targets. Little dogs that looked like pound rejects jumped through hoops and rode big dogs' backs near the seawall. A one-man band—the guy looked amazingly like Jimmy Buffett—played and posed for photographs for dollar bills. And a good time was had by all.

Well, maybe not all.

She glanced back to the man sitting stoically by her side. God, he was a mess. His lip was bleeding. He was probably going to end up with a heck of a shiner around his left eye. He'd also done a darn fine imitation of a man with a really bad leg when she'd dragged him out of the bar. But he was tough. He hadn't uttered one word of complaint. He was hurting, and hurting bad, but he wasn't about to admit it.

It was his own fault, she thought in disgust. Then, because she felt herself softening toward him again, she did what she did best whenever she was around him. She bitched.

"You followed me, didn't you? Can't say that I appreciate it."

He lifted his head, gave her a bland look. "Imagine your

surprise, then, when I tell you that I could give a damn about what you appreciate. And I didn't follow you. I followed a lead. And you're welcome, by the way."

"Just what am I supposed to thank you for? Drawing everyone's attention to us?" She snorted. "Yeah, that'll help me find Tiff."

"You could start with thanking me for saving your ass from that beer-swilling Romeo. And don't say you didn't ask for my help—or that you didn't look *appreciative* when you saw me."

"What I was hoping for was a little professional courtesy, a low-key extraction, not a street brawl."

"Which is exactly what I was trying to accomplish until the sonofabitch hurt you."

Eve blinked, taken off guard by what he'd said. Unconsciously she rubbed her arm where bruises were already forming. The football player *had* hurt her. But everything had happened so fast that it hadn't registered until now that the drunk's rough handling had been the catalyst that had set the match to McClain's fuse.

"Oh," she said, feeling contrite suddenly but grappling for a reason not to be. She didn't want to feel grateful. Or beholden.

When she looked at him again, she realized he was still staring.

"That hadn't occurred to you, had it? That I was actually trying to help, not muck things up?"

She looked away and thought about what to say to that. Finally, she just stated the truth. "Honestly, no. It hadn't occurred to me."

He grunted, oozing disgust. "And you want to know why?"

"Because I could have handled him the same way myself if that's what I'd wanted to do?"

"Because you're looking for reasons to be pissed at me."

OK. This was true. She did look for reasons. Not that she had to look too far.

"I'll tell you something else," he said, shifting the ice from his knee to his eye. "You're a tight-ass. You need to loosen up. And you need to let things go. So I screwed up. It was a long time ago. Years. Believe me, I've screwed up a helluva lot more since."

Scowling over the tight-ass remark—not just that he'd said it but because he'd hit a little too close to the mark—she searched his face. It really was an interesting face, she admitted grudgingly—bloodied lip, bruised eye, put-upon glare, and all. She'd seen the promise of a handsome man in the boy's face at eighteen. Even then, his dark eyes had invited; his full lips had enticed.

He wasn't that boy any longer. Despite his smart-ass facade he was harder now. His eyes were a darker life-worn brown. And there was little of that teenage boy in the mature man's face that was all interesting angles and sculpted planes. All devastating, dangerous, and lived-in good looks—even bloodied and bruised.

She dragged her gaze away. Quelled the unexpected eddy of sexual awareness and thought about what he'd just admitted.

I screwed up.

He didn't know the half of it.

Knee-jerk responses to a dozen shifting emotions had her twisting the screws. What he'd just said was long overdue. "Did I actually hear an apology in there somewhere?"

He sniffed, fished a chip of ice out of the cup, and, looking surly, touched it gingerly to his lip. "I don't know. Maybe."

God. He just kept surprising her. Against all odds she smiled at his grumpy concession. Not just because of his reluctant admission, but because of the irritation in his tone when he made it. Or maybe she was just tired and her guard was down. It had been a long day. Despite a call earlier from Uncle Bud telling her the bartender had spotted Tiff at Sloppy Joe's last night, she'd run up against another dead end. Just like she'd run up against dead ends all day.

She was also tired of bickering with McClain. And maybe, just maybe, she was growing weary of holding a grudge.

"Well," she said finally, "maybe I accept your apology— if you made one."

He grunted. "Did hell just freeze over?"

She stared toward the crowd sardined together on the wharf and facing the bay. "And I'm sorry you got hurt."

"Because of you," he reminded her, one corner of his mouth tipping up with a hint of amusement and expectancy. A wince of pain quickly followed when the action tugged on his split lip.

She smiled, too. Didn't even try to fight it. "Don't blame me."

"I don't think Joe College liked my shirt."

"*I* don't like your shirt, but it doesn't provoke me to violence. It has crossed my mind to rip it off, though."

"Now you're talking," he said with a smart-ass smirk.

"You wish."

For a long moment she just sat there, getting used to this surprising turn of events. They were actually bantering with each other—no heat, no anger. Evidently, it took a while for him to get used to it, too, because he was also quiet.

"I was an ass," he said after a long moment. "Back then— you know. I should have called."

When she met his eyes, he looked away. But not before she saw the guilt in them.

"Anyway. I'm sorry. You didn't deserve to be treated that way."

She was stunned. First peace. Then an outright apology. He was giving her reason to let it go. But there were things he didn't know. And there were things she could never let go of.

Still, she almost told him then. About the baby. Almost blurted it out. But in the end, she didn't. She couldn't. It was a secret she'd kept to herself for too long. She didn't want to trust him with it yet. She didn't want to trust him at all.

For now, he was going to have to settle for a truce. While she thought it over. In the meantime, the chocolate wasn't doing the trick.

"Are you hungry?" she asked rather than commit.

"God, yes."

With little argument, he agreed to let her go pick up something for them to eat if she let him pay for it. She opted for the shortest line and came back to the bench with foot-longs and lemonade.

"Hope you like them loaded."

When he dug in with a mumbled, "Thanks," she laughed.

"I'll take that as a yes." She started in on her own.

While they couldn't see the line of the horizon beyond the bodies packing the wharf, they ate in an almost comfortable silence, watching the twilight sky transition from orange, to red, to muted lavenders and pearly pinks, listening as the crowd applauded and cheered, paying homage to the striking beauty of the setting sun.

"Where's your car?" she asked as salsa music played in the background and the crowd slowly dispersed to the outdoor gardens and clubs and any number of eateries leading to and lining the square.

"A helluva long way from here."

So was hers. "Want to split the fare on another pedicab if we can nab one?"

He wiped his mouth with a napkin, taking care around his split lower lip. "I think that would fall into the category of working with the enemy. Edwards might find out."

She knew that Mac was kidding as she balled up her napkin and gathered up the rest of their trash. "I won't tell if you won't."

"Fair enough. But just so you know, I still plan on finding her first."

"We all need fantasies to cling to."

He just smiled.

They sat in silence for a while longer before she decided

to take a chance on confiding something that had been eating at her. "Do you still think Tiffany is just running wild?"

"Nothing tells me otherwise."

"Clayborne is such an ass," she said after a long while.

"This is news?"

"What kind of a father wouldn't be out looking for his own daughter? I mean, if Clayborne cared, wouldn't he want a hand in finding her? I can't help but think of this from a parent's perspective. If . . . if Tiff were my child, I wouldn't be able to stand sitting back while someone else did the work. Don't you agree? What if *you* were a father—"

The look on his face stopped her cold. He turned his head away, but not before she saw a bleakness in his eyes that made her heart race.

And she knew.

"My God. You have a child, don't you?"

He looked past her toward the darkening sky. "Careful. You might find out more about me than you want to know."

Yeah. She just might. She'd decided to opt for wisdom instead of curiosity and not press the issue when he took the matter out of her hands.

"It will come as no surprise that there's another woman in the world other than you who thinks I'm a rat-bastard. She's in San Diego now. Happily remarried." He stared at the hands he'd clasped between his knees. "To a man who tells my daughter she doesn't have to call him Daddy, but he'd sure like it if she did."

8

OK, Eve thought, wishing she could close her heart as easily as she closed her eyes. This was too much information. She hadn't wanted to know this. She hadn't wanted to know that McClain wasn't just a smart-ass ex-cop PI who'd taken her virginity and her innocence and left her pregnant when he was pretty much a kid himself. She hadn't wanted to know that he'd lived through a divorce and suffered the loss of a child.

There might have been another child, a sad voice reminded her. *Another child for him to miss.* And because she heard pain in his voice for the child he loved and missed, she found herself resisting the urge to touch him when she needed to be irritated with him.

"Ali," he continued, still not looking at her. "Her name is Ali. She starts school this fall."

And clearly, Tyler McClain, absentee father, was mourning the fact that he wasn't going to be there for his little girl's first day of school. Or for many other firsts.

Crap.

Crap, crap, crap.

He'd done it. He'd gotten to her. Was becoming far too human, with human wants and needs and loss and pain. Like she'd known loss and pain.

"That's got to be hard," she heard herself saying, unable to hide the empathy in her voice.

He, of course, possessor of the macho gene, heard pity. So naturally, he bristled right up to make sure she understood he didn't need anybody's sympathy.

"That's why I took this job. For the money. Like I said. It's all about the money. Divorce settlements are a bitch. So is frequent airfare to California."

She was going to hate herself tomorrow. "What happened?"

He cocked his head, looked at her for a long moment that relayed how surprised he was that she'd opened herself up enough to ask such a personal question. "To my marriage?"

Yeah, well, color *her* surprised, too. And stupid, because she nodded.

"The decree called it irreconcilable differences."

Deeper and deeper. "And what did you call it?"

He pushed out a weary grunt. "I called it quits."

All around them people talked and laughed and walked across the square without care.

"She got bored being the wife of a cop," he added after a while. "And we had different interpretations of the word *fidelity*."

That Eve really didn't need to hear. She'd been on the wrong end of the cheating game herself. Knew how it felt. How deeply it cut.

"But enough about me," he said with an abrupt attempt at levity that didn't quite succeed. "You never got married?"

She shook her head.

"Come close?"

"Not even close." It was a lie, but he didn't need to know that she, too, had discovered a cheating partner she'd trusted and thought she might actually want to build a life with.

"Spoiled you for any other man, did I?"

She was too tired to rise to the bait. And he *was* baiting her. Cease-fire or not, it seemed to be a mandatory part of their relationship.

Whoa. They did not have a relationship. What they had

was ancient history and current competition. And that's where it started and ended.

"About that pedicab."

His eyes were full of questions as they held hers, but thankfully he let it go. "Yeah," he said at length, and rolled his head on his neck. "About that. And about Clayborne's methods—I think you're chasing smoke."

"Maybe," she said, but she wasn't sure she agreed. Something felt wrong here. She'd figure it out eventually. In the meantime, she had to figure out something else.

Like why she was having such a hard time disliking this man. And why he'd struck a nerve with his crack about spoiling her for any other man. It should have been outrageous, but what it was, was unsettling.

She walked slowly to accommodate his limp. They'd just gotten a pedicab driver's attention and were about to board when a beat-up older-model blue van came careening around the corner on two wheels.

"Look out!" Mac yelled, and, grabbing her, dived toward the curb.

Taking her down with him, he twisted at the last moment and took the brunt of the fall. She landed on top of him to the sound of squealing tires and a string of swear words from the pedicab driver who'd barely managed to jump the curb with his bicycle to avoid being hit.

The pedicab driver shook his fist and took off in hot pursuit of the van that never stopped, never even slowed down, to see if anyone was hurt. Like he could possibly catch it. The vehicle had already disappeared in traffic.

"You OK?" Mac asked as she braced herself on top of him.

She took stock, nodded. "Yeah. I think so. How about you?"

"Great. Nothing like a little hit-and-run to get the old juices flowing. Asshole must have been stoned or something."

"Or something," she speculated, a familiar sense of unease sending a shiver down her spine. It had been several days since she'd been attacked. And that little hit-and-run scenario was just a little too coincidental.

But she kept her suspicions to herself as Mac set her aside, rose painfully to his feet, and held out a hand to help her up.

His heart had settled down and the throbbing pain in his leg had downgraded from bullet-biting intensity to stalling the urge to whimper by the time they managed to hail another pedicab.

They reached Mac's car first. He eased carefully out, limped to the driver's side, and scooped a fistful of parking tickets out from under the windshield wipers.

"Nice to know that Key West's finest are Johnny-on-the-spot," he muttered, and tossed the tickets into the backseat. "Too bad they couldn't have been on the square when we were scrambling for our lives."

"You really ought to see a doctor about that leg," Eve said, ignoring his grumbling. "And get some antiseptic on your lip and eye."

Interesting, Mac thought, casting a glance back at Eve where she sat in the pedicab, the driver patiently waiting. That was twice she'd mentioned a doctor. And she'd gotten him ice. If Mac didn't know better, he'd think she might actually be worried about him. "I'm fine. You driving back to West Palm tonight?"

"Have I found Tiff?"

"Right. Stupid question."

"What about you?"

He looked down the street. If possible, it was busier than it had been during the day. *Nightlife was the right life in Key West.* "I'm not going anywhere."

"Well," she said, looking uncomfortable with all this civil chitchat. "Guess I'll be heading out."

He dug into his hip pocket, fished out his wallet, and shoved some bills into the driver's hand. "Take her wherever she needs to go."

Then Mac turned to Eve, intending to tell her good-bye, and got lost for several long moments just looking.

Her cheeks were pink from the Key West sun. So were her shoulders and the tops of her breasts above the low neckline of her little red top. Her hair had been combed by the wind; delicate violet smudges colored the skin beneath blue eyes, showing hints of fatigue. She had a dab of mustard and dirt from their scrape with the crazy driver on the thigh of her white pants, and the toes that peeked out of her sandals and sported siren red polish were powdered with Key West street dust.

She looked messy and amazing. And the best part of it all—she didn't care. Didn't bother her at all that she wasn't fashion-plate put together, that her lipstick had worn off hours ago and her makeup couldn't conceal her fatigue.

He thought she looked damn near perfect. Real. Genuine. Tough. And juxtaposed against it all was a stunning vulnerability she'd never, in a million years, admit to.

She'd been vulnerable that night in the cabana. He should have felt more guilt over running out on her. He hadn't then, but he did now. Now that it was too late. Story of his life.

He dug back into his wallet, finally came up with a business card. "My cell number," he said, handing it to her.

She stared from him to the card.

"In case you missed it, that was your cue to give me *your* number."

She smiled and tucked the card in her purse.

Well, it had been worth a try. "Call if you need anything."

"Like someone to instigate another bar brawl?"

He grinned. "Yeah. If you need someone for that. Or if, you know, you find yourself in trouble."

She looked away from him and down the street. "You have a room booked somewhere?"

He shook his head. "Gonna have to fire my travel agent for that misstep."

She expelled a heavy sigh. They both knew he didn't

have a prayer of getting a room with the college crowd in town. What he hadn't expected was that she actually looked a little worried about him. Again.

"Hey—I'll be fine. Won't be the first time I slept in my car."

"Or in your clothes," she added with a dry look.

"I like to travel light."

She looked like she was about to say something else, then thought better of it, so he picked up the thread. "What about you? You have someplace to stay?"

"Uncle Bud's."

Oh yeah. Good ole Uncle Bud.

"Well," she said, a clear precursor to *adios*.

"As long as we're in competition over this, how about a little side bet?" he asked abruptly. Partly because he didn't want her to leave just yet. Partly because he couldn't pass up one last chance to rile her. Just a little.

"Side bet?"

"Yeah. Just to make things more interesting."

"This ought to be good."

"Oh, it is. If you find Tiff first, I have to take you to bed."

She snorted. "Yeah, *that's* going to happen."

"No. No. It gets better. If *I* find Tiff first, then *you* have to take *me* to bed." He grinned when she rolled her eyes. "What do you think? Win-win all the way around, right?"

"Good night, McClain," she said, and asked the driver to start pedaling.

"G'night, cupcake."

Weight slung on his good leg, Mac stood and watched them pull away. He watched for a long time, until the motor traffic and the foot traffic swallowed them up. She hadn't turned around to see if he was watching. But then, he hadn't expected her to.

"And what exactly do you expect of the lady?" he asked himself aloud.

Big surprise. Another question he had no answer for. He

didn't know what he expected. He really didn't know. But he couldn't quite block the images he'd offered up in the form of a side bet. And he couldn't help but think about that night all those years ago.

A man didn't forget a night like that. Just like he didn't forget a woman like Eve—even if she hadn't exactly been a woman at the time. She'd been a good girl with a yen to go bad—at least that's what he'd told himself at the time—and he'd gladly provided the ticket for her walk on the wild side. For a long time afterward, he hadn't felt nearly enough guilt over what they'd done. She had, though. Just like she'd expected more from him than he'd been able or willing to give.

His guilt had come later. Much later, when he'd become a father and he thought of some superstud asshole hurting his little girl the way he'd hurt Wes Garrett's little girl.

He wiped a hand over his face as a horse-drawn carriage rolled by, shod hooves clicking on the pavement. Hell. He'd only been eighteen himself. If he'd stuck around, then he'd have done something really stupid, because what pretty Eve had made him feel was heat—so much heat he'd dropped her like a hot poker and run as far and as fast as he could go in the opposite direction. No way was he going to get himself tied up in knots over that elegant little blonde with the kiss-me mouth and promise-me-forever eyes.

Georgia Tech had been far enough. And later, Chicago had been even better. The Chicago PD had been job enough to make him forget all about Eve and get stupid enough to decide it was finally time to settle down and marry the absolute wrong woman. He'd tried to make it work for six long, wasted years. Wasted, except for Ali. Ali was the best thing that had ever happened to him.

When the marriage was over, at least he'd still had his job. And then he didn't even have that anymore. Now fate, it seemed, had brought him back in contact with Eve Garrett.

Helluva deal. Helluva rush when he'd seen her standing there that night at Club Asylum, sleek as a cat, dressed all in black, all centerfold curves and .38 caliber of firepower aimed dead center at his heart. And damn if he didn't find himself wondering if picking up where they'd left off wouldn't be such a bad idea after all.

He was no romantic. In fact, he was cynical at best when it came to the opposite sex—and with good reason. Angie had damn near gelded him, and when she'd gotten done with him, her lawyer had taken a turn at working him over, too. But there was something about this woman that got to him. Had always gotten to him. God's honest truth, Eve Garrett still scared the living shit out of him. He felt too many things when he was around her. Alive for one. Wired for another. And just a little too open. Hell. He'd told her about his divorce today. About his kid. What was that about?

Just because she made him hot? And heat was all he was willing to cop to. Any other possibilities sent him into a cold sweat.

He let out a long breath, braced himself for the pain, and maneuvered his bad leg into the car. If he ran into Larry Linebacker or the sonofabitch in the blue van again, he was up for a little payback. Leaning across the seat, he opened the glove compartment and rummaged around until he found his bottle of ibuprofen. His prescription pain medication was in there, too, but he didn't want it. He had work to do tonight and that stuff always made his head murky.

Because he had nothing to drink, he downed three ibuprofen dry, then shoved a stick of gum in his mouth to generate a little saliva. He found a little packet with a wet wipe in it and dabbed it on his lip. It stung like hell, so he counted it as antiseptic and, because it was wet and cool, held it against his eye for a second or two.

"Good to go," he muttered, tossed the wipe in the ashtray, and pulled away from the curb.

It was back to business. Tiffany was out there somewhere. Because of his bum leg he didn't particularly want to walk, but he could cruise around on the off chance that he'd spot her. He'd cracked more than one case on a lucky break. Nothing said it couldn't happen on this case—and it might take staying up all night to do it.

And nothing said he had to think about Eve Garrett. Nothing said he had to think about how he'd like to sink into all that silky softness and experience something just short of what he knew would be a near-religious experience.

Eve let herself into Uncle Bud's little bungalow with the key he'd given her years ago.

"Uncle Bud? You home?"

Silence. Possibly it was poker night. Possibly he was at Juanita's, his longtime companion.

Whatever, Eve closed the door behind her, leaned back against it, and let out a deep breath—glad to have a moment to herself. A moment when she was not behind the wheel of a car, in the seat of a pedicab, or searching for Tiffany Clayborne.

A moment to get a little distance from the unsettling concern she felt for Tyler McClain.

She pushed away from the door, walked over, and turned on the brass and stained-glass lamp that sat on top of a rattan foyer table.

How about a little side bet?

McClain was a jerk.

After turning on a ceiling fan to move some of the stuffy air, she plopped down on the sofa. Stared at the far wall.

A jerk of an ex-cop with a bad marriage behind him and a little girl clear across the country. He missed his daughter so much that the pain on his face when he spoke of her outdistanced the pain in his leg. Oh yeah. And he'd played hero twice tonight.

She shook her head, called herself ten kinds of sap, and dug her cell phone out of her purse. She debated for all of a deep breath before she punched in the phone number on the business card McClain had given her.

He answered on the second ring. "McClain."

"Um . . . look," she said, suddenly wishing she'd worked through the blond moment that had prompted her to call him. "I was just thinking . . . I could maybe make some calls for you, see if I could turn up a room."

The momentary silence on the other end of the line told her he was as shocked as she was that she'd called.

"Am I growing on you, cupcake?"

She closed her eyes, rubbed at her temples. "Yeah, like a wart. Listen, forget I offered."

"Not a chance. Random acts of kindness don't roll my way all that often."

"Can't imagine—what with your stellar personality and all."

"Yeah. It's a real shocker, isn't it?"

She grinned—caught herself and sobered up. She was not going to let him suck her into liking him. "Look, I just feel a little responsible for you getting hurt is all. It seemed like the right thing to do. Now do you want me to find you a room or not?"

"Appreciate the offer, but I'm fine."

"Which is why you can hardly walk."

"OK, let me ease your troubled mind on that count. The knee was bad long before Mr. Football clipped me or the phantom tried to run us over. It's just riled up a bit. It'll be fine in a day or so. But, if you want to massage it—or any other little thing that needs attention—hey, I'm all over that idea."

"Good-bye, McClain."

"So that would be a no?"

She hung up on him. Laid her head back against the old dusty-smelling sofa and swore under her breath when she realized she was grinning again.

Mac stared at his cell and smiled.

He *was* growing on her. Even better, he now had her cell phone number.

He pulled up his call log and there it was. After transferring the number to his phone book, he punched it in.

"What do you want?" she asked with the weariness of the aged.

"Just wanted to thank you—right this time—for offering to find me a room. It was sweet."

"If that's what you want to believe," she said, sounding grouchy.

"Yeah. That's what I want to believe. Thanks. Get some rest."

"And you'll give me a call if you get a lead on Tiff, right?"

He laughed and this time he disconnected first.

Two hours later, he was wishing he'd taken her up on her offer of finding a room. The notion of sinking into a queen-size bed in an air-conditioned room—right after he'd had a long, cool shower and soaked his throbbing knee in an ice bath—held more and more merit as the night wore on.

He pulled into a parking space on Whitehead, windows down, eyes open for any sign of the Tiff. The heat of the Key West night was beyond muggy. What breeze had stirred the air had gone down with the sun and now, around midnight, music, laughter, and the mingled aromas from the open-air restaurants permeated the air as thick as the humidity.

He was beat. He was miserable and he'd cruised every front street, backstreet, and alley in between hoping to catch a glimpse of Tiffany Clayborne.

Like a good little PI, he'd checked his answering machine an hour ago. There'd been a message from Agnes Boudreau. Agnes paid well and on time. Agnes was also a whack job, and no matter how many times he'd tried to convince her that her husband of forty-five years really did play poker with the guys one Thursday night a month, she insisted the "old goat" was cheating on her.

Mac had another message from a company wanting a number of background checks on potential employees. He'd make sure he called them back in the morning, as it sounded like a nice, steady stream of income.

Roger Edwards had also checked in wanting a progress report. Mac called back and left a message that summed it up in four words. "Still working on it."

His gaze scanned the busy streets.

If I were a spoiled, bored little rich girl, where would I be?

Like it or not, he wasn't going to find out languishing in this heap of a car.

He downed three more ibuprofen and sucked it up. Then he hit the pavement and limped into every bar he could find, flashed the Tiff's picture, and posed the two-hundred-K question: "Have you seen her?"

It was a long fricking night.

9

A MUGGY KEY WEST BREEZE BLEW IN through the open hotel window. Tiffany sat on the bed, chewing on her nails as she eavesdropped on a conversation between Lance and his bass player taking place in the living area just outside the bedroom door. Abe Gorman's voice was like Abe. Harsh and hard. As mean as the licks he plucked from his bass guitar.

Lance's voice was soft, lilting. When he sang, the sound of it was mesmerizing. Hypnotic. She could listen to him sing for hours. Only he hadn't done any singing since Club Asylum. Instead, he'd canceled dates—like the ones in Atlantic City. All he seemed to care about now was partying. Partying so hard, sometimes it scared her. Sometimes *he* scared her. So much that like now, when she was almost sober, she thought about going home.

Only at home there was no one who cared where she was or what she did, unless she did something to embarrass them.

She fought back tears of anger and pain and humiliation and wondered if she'd merely exchanged one form of degradation for another.

"You heard this guy ask about her?" she heard Lance ask Abe.

"I just said so, didn't I?" Abe sounded mad. "And he was

flashing her picture around in the bar. This is all going to crash on us. I can feel it."

"Chill, man."

"Fuck chill. I've been listening to you. I've been letting you play mastermind, Reno, following your orders like a goddamn flunky. So help me, if you blow this—"

"Shut up. Just shut the fuck up," Lance growled. "I know what I'm doing."

"You'd by God better."

"Or what? You going to split? Fine. Go. Makes more for me."

"Just make sure you don't screw this up. I don't know why you haven't taken care of h—"

"Shut up, goddammit! I'll do what needs to be done in my own good time."

Tiffany had heard them fight before. It always gave her a sick feeling in the pit of her stomach. She couldn't see Abe, but she knew exactly what he looked like. His face would be blotchy red. Even his shaved head would flood with color. The heavy Celtic cross he wore in his left ear would be flipping around like a kite tail caught in gale winds.

Straight, she despised Abe and the gross tattoos he wore all over his body. Stoned, she managed to ignore him. She didn't like what Lance often threatened to let Abe do to her. Sometimes she actually believed Lance would let Abe use her that way if she displeased him.

So she did everything she could to keep Lance happy. She gave him money. She did his drugs. Anything to keep him loving her. Sometimes she wondered why. But then he'd get her stoned again and she knew why. She needed him to love her. He told her so. He loved her like no one ever had.

"Tiffany. Hey, Tiffany, you awake, baby?"

She jumped when she realized Lance was calling her. Was afraid he'd caught her listening, which was something she shouldn't do. Lately, she felt like that around Lance. Like she was always on the edge of pissing him off. She didn't want to mess things up between them. She didn't want to blow it—like she had when he'd hit her last night. It hadn't been the first time, but it always came as a surprise.

On a deep breath, she walked to the door, opened it slowly, hoping he'd notice the trouble she'd taken cleaning up. She'd dressed up for him, taken pains with her makeup. She hadn't slept after they'd come back to the hotel around three, and whatever it was he'd given her had pretty much worn off, so she wasn't so messed up.

She checked the clock. It was almost 5:00 a.m. Only two hours later. Yeah. She was almost straight. Lance said she disgusted him when she was stoned and yet he was always giving her stuff to make her high.

"Hi," she said, walking to his side.

Lance looked her up and down, his beautiful curtain of waist-length black hair hanging loose and flowing over his bare shoulders. He wore only a pair of cargo shorts. His feet were bare. God, he was gorgeous. Even his toes were sexy. He wasn't much taller than she was—maybe five-eight, five-nine—but he was bigger than life with his poet's mouth and artist's hands. His skin was a soft caramel color, like he spent hours in the sun.

His eyes were as black as his hair. Exotic. Mysterious. And when his full lips curved up into a smile, she felt like crying because she loved him so much.

"Sweet," he said, reaching for her. "You look real sweet, babe. Did you get all styled up for me?"

She nodded and snuggled up under the arm he wrapped around her shoulders. He smelled like expensive cologne, the cologne she'd bought him. And he felt so solid and warm. So loving as he nuzzled her neck, then kissed her long and deep.

The first time she'd seen him she'd fallen in love. Three weeks ago? Four? She didn't remember. All she cared about was the way he looked at her. The way he made her feel loved for the first time in her life.

"Abe says some dude was looking all over town for you. You got another guy on the side? Do I need to be jealous?"

She looked up at him through heavily made up eyes, tried to get a read on his temper. When he was loving, she felt wrapped up by him. Protected. Secure. But his moods sometimes shifted like shadows. Sometimes he'd fly mad at the slightest provocation. Like he had last night at the Hog's Breath. He didn't look mad now. He just looked curious.

"You know there's no one else for me but you. That bartender guy—Jimmy? Hey, I just thought, you know, that you'd like to party with him. That's the only reason I asked him to come back here. Because of you."

Lance stroked her hair. "That's what I needed to hear, babe. Tell her what this guy looked like, Abe."

Abe pinned her with a mean glare. "Six-foot or so. Brown hair. Put together. Maybe thirty-something. Walked with a limp. Smelled like a cop to me. Had that look about him."

"He sound like anyone you know?" Lance asked, still stroking her cheek, though his eyes hardened as he searched hers.

She shook her head. "No. I mean . . . I don't know. That's not much to go on."

"Could be someone your daddy hired to find you, you think?"

The mention of her father made her stiffen. "My dad could care less about where I am."

Lance hugged her. "But he cares about your money, doesn't he? Enough that he might send someone looking for you?"

She shrugged. "I suppose. I don't know." But she did know. Money was the only thing her father cared about. He sure didn't care about her.

Abe exchanged a look with Lance. In the corner of the room, Billie . . . Billie *something* slouched in a chair, sound asleep. His guitar lay across his lap; a piece of sheet music lay on the floor at his feet. She couldn't remember his last name. He never said much. And he never partied with them. Mostly he just played his guitar and wrote his precious music. And except for the occasional glance that both accused and judged and sometimes made her feel shame, he left her alone.

"Think it's time to move on." Lance walked away from her toward the bedroom of the hotel suite.

"But we just got here yesterday," she said, and immediately regretted it when it came out like a whine. "I mean I . . . I thought we were going to go out and party again today."

"Plans change, darlin'." Lance smiled, but without affection. "You don't want to take a chance on Daddy putting an end to our road trip, do you?"

Yes. No. Maybe. She didn't know anymore.

"You know he'd make me leave if we went back to Palm Beach. I love you, babe, but I'd have to go. Your old man's machine—hell, it would roll right over me."

He was right. And her father's stooge, Richard Edwards, the bastard, would make sure something happened to convince Lance to go. Including paying him off.

And yet she was pretty scared. She'd never been a cabbage head. She'd been particular about drugs. Had never done the hard stuff. Lance made her try all kinds of shit.

"Maybe I just need to take a little break," she said carefully. "I could catch up with you later, you know?"

"Now you're talking stupid." Lance's eyes were hard as he drew her into his arms. "I need you with me, babe. Always."

His embrace tightened until he was hurting her.

"And I say when and if you go anywhere, got it?"

She nodded, close to tears of pain when he finally loosened his hold.

"How about this? You pick the place."

She blinked up at him, a little afraid. Until he kissed her. It was so tender. So, so loving.

"Now get packed." He reached for the shirt he'd tossed over the back of a chair. "I need to get some bread. You have your mind made up where we're going by the time I get back."

He dug her ATM card out of his pocket and headed for the door. "Be back in thirty. Abe—book a charter."

Tiffany fought tears. And told herself not to let ideas bring her down. Stupid ideas. Like . . . like maybe Lance only loved her as long as the money flowed. Like he was manipulating her with drugs and slow, deep kisses and the amazing way he made love to her.

"Go ahead," he said, softly now. "Pack your things. Or would you rather spend a little time with Abe?"

A wave of shame washed through her, making her nauseous. Love had a price. Sometimes it was terrible. Frightening. And sometimes it made her wish she were strong enough to leave him.

But the thought of leaving him was so frightening it hurt. She couldn't leave him. Life without love was worse. She knew.

She caught Abe smirking as she turned back to the bedroom. With shaking hands, she shut and locked the door behind her.

Then she dug her stash of weed out of the hiding place in her makeup case. Only after she'd lit up, dragged deep, did she feel a little steadier. Only after she'd finished it did she feel good again. And after she smoked a wet stick—Lance had told her it was marijuana, PCP, and formaldehyde—she was high as a kite.

Sometimes that's what it took to remember that Lance loved her. Sometimes it was all it took to shake the fear. His love was all that counted. It didn't matter that he spent her money. Nothing that he did to her mattered. As long as he didn't leave her.

10

It happened the same way with police work. You worked a case like a hound dog and sometimes it came down to luck. That is, if you consider playing every angle and turning every stone as getting lucky. No matter, after a night of searching, Mac was cruising by the Ocean Key Resort Hotel around six the next morning and spotted Tiffany Clayborne stepping into a stretch limo.

He jerked his head back around in time to see a slim dark-skinned man with a long black ponytail duck into the limo behind her. Pulling over to the curb, Mac turned on his emergency blinkers and grabbed the city map he'd laid out in the passenger seat so he'd look like one of the many lost tourists trying to find their way back to Old Town.

After adjusting all three rearview mirrors, he got a line on the limo as it pulled out from the hotel's portico and eased into traffic. Since the stretch was big and black and roughly as inconspicuous as an aircraft carrier, he let it get a couple of city blocks ahead of him before he pulled out into the stream of traffic.

He maneuvered along a safe distance behind the limo, following when it turned south on U.S. 1. After crossing over Stock Island Bridge, the limo hooked a left onto South Roosevelt Boulevard. That's when Mac spotted the Key West International Airport sign.

Hell. Fate giveth; fate taketh away. He'd actually discovered the chicken and it looked like she was about to fly the coop. He'd hoped that when he found Tiffany, she'd be settled in—at least for a couple of days. The plan had been to give Edwards a call, lead him to the prodigal daughter, and collect his fat paycheck. As neat and tidy as a laundered shirt. Unless he figured out a way to delay Tiffany getting on a plane, however, there wasn't going to be anything neat and tidy about it.

Speaking of neat and tidy. He caught a look at himself in the rearview mirror, then leaned over and dug his electric razor out of the glove box. If Tiffany was, in fact, leaving, he thought as the razor buzzed across his face, he might be able to get a lead on where she was headed. But not if he looked like he'd just crawled out of a drainage ditch.

Just his luck, the security guard on duty was diligent as hell when he pulled into the terminal drive, two cars behind the limo. At least he'd had the foresight not to pack his Beretta. Not only would he not be waved on to a parking spot; he'd probably be spread-eagled against his Taurus by now.

He hadn't been back in Florida long enough to make any key contacts—especially down as far south as mile marker number 1—so he was on his own coming up with a ploy that might detain Tiffany long enough to get Edwards down here.

And all of this on a bum wheel, a couple of hours' sleep in the backseat of the Taurus, and clothes that looked exactly what they were—past their prime. Not much he could do about that, but he finger combed his hair and popped a Tic Tac. Another hit of ibuprofen an hour ago had taken the edge off, but his knee was a far cry from ready to go.

Tough. He snagged his cell phone, covered his banged-up eye with his dark glasses, and shouldered the car door open. And damn near dropped to his knees.

"Jesus H. Christ."

Mac didn't know which ticked him off more. The pain that shot through his left leg and arrowed all the way to his gut or the fact that it slowed him down. He gritted it out and made it into the tiny terminal that handled mostly charter flights. Fortunately for him, terrorism and security didn't appear to be high on the priority list this far south of D.C.

The terminal was open-air, as laid-back as a day on the beach, and consisted of a circular concourse with open walls of windows that afforded a bird's eye view of the concourse that could be accessed by three open gates. He arrived at the far gate just in time to see Tiffany, and what he could only assume was her boy band, walk across the tarmac to a charter jet.

Disgusted, he hobbled toward the window. Careful not to draw any attention to himself—it was always possible that someone with a badge and a gun might get jumpy—he whipped out his cell phone and snapped a few pictures. Then he watched as the pretty boy with the ponytail motioned for Tiffany to board. Leader of the band, calling all the shots, Mac decided as Tiffany obediently climbed the ramp and ducked inside. The guy milled around on the tarmac, overseeing the loading of a couple of guitar cases. In addition to the dude with the black hair, there was a big ruddy-faced bald guy covered in tattoos and a slighter, skinny urban cowboy type who carried his guitar case onto the plane with him.

Mac didn't have names, but at least he had faces now. And possibly a jump on their next destination if he played his hand right.

The jet was already preparing to taxi toward the runway when he approached the desk at the charter gate and put on his frazzled face.

"Oh hell," he muttered, and ran a frantic hand through his hair. "I missed 'em, didn't I?"

The woman behind the service desk looked up as the whine of jet engines winding up and the scent of jet fuel floated in through the open airport terminal. "You have a problem, young man?"

She appeared to be in her early sixties, tight gray curls, crisp white blouse, carefully painted-on eyebrows that were

arched ever so slightly as she looked him over, trying to decide if he was a mere annoyance or, in this day and age, a
terrorist threat.

"Lady, you don't know the half of it." He limped over to
the desk, propped his forearms on the counter, and made a
big show of catching his breath.

"Is there something I can help you with?" She smelled
like the perfume his mother used to wear. Chanel? Estée
Lauder? One of those French broads.

"No," he said, shaking his head. "I am so screwed. That
was Tiffany Clayborne, right?"

Mae, according to the shiny gold nameplate on her blouse,
tilted her head to the side, studied him but said nothing.

"It's OK. I know you have your confidentiality rules. You
don't have to say anything. Besides, I know it was her. Just
like I know I'm out of a job. God. What a frickin' morning."

"Why would you be out of a job?"

He pushed out a laugh. "Because my boss at Ocean Key
is gonna boot me out the door the minute he finds out I didn't
catch Ms. Clayborne and make sure she paid her tab."

He turned around, slumped with his back against the
counter, and let out a deflated breath. "He's gonna see it as
my fault she left without giving us her credit card imprint."

Silence.

"Leave it to management. You know? The suits with the
high-ticket jobs? Anyway, one of them opened up the penthouse suite to her and her friends simply because she's the
daughter of some Palm Beach billionaire and told her they'd
worry about payment later."

He flayed a hand in the air, disgusted. "Only Ms. Clayborne, she didn't seem to worry about payment at all—then
or later—and since I was the desk clerk on duty when she
hightailed her high-class butt out the door half an hour ago,
that same high-ticket suit decided to sacrifice my ass to save
his. He sent me after her and told me not to come back unless
I had cash or her signature on this bill," he patted his hip

pocket as if a bill were actually in it, "or a line on where to find her to send it."

Behind him, there was still nothing but silence. He took it as a good sign that Mae wasn't telling him to peddle his tale of woe to someone who gave a damn.

"Oh well." He pushed away from the desk, the picture of absolute dejection. "Sorry I bothered you."

"What did you do to your leg?" she asked when he'd limped a few steps away.

He stopped. Gave a weary laugh. "I think I sprained it when I ran out of the hotel after her. Banged it hard against the side of my car anyway. Well, it *was* my car. No job, no payment."

Mae made a pinched face. "Don't you think you're laying it on a little thick?"

He grinned, sheepish and contrite and just a little flirty. "Yeah. But I'm desperate. Is there a prayer that it's working?"

God love her, she grinned. Then she sobered, studied him, and scowled. "The charter flight is headed for La Guardia," she said, leaning forward so no one else would overhear her.

Fuckin' A!

He'd started to think he was going to have to wait until he could tag an ATM withdrawal from Tiffany's account to get a line on her location, and by that time the whole happy tribe might be a couple of days ahead of him.

"You're a doll, Mae."

"I didn't do a thing."

"Right. Didn't say a thing, either. Nothing that anyone will hear from me. Thanks again. Thanks a million. I don't suppose you heard where, in New York, they were staying?"

"Now you're pressing your luck."

He nodded and took off. His leg didn't feel nearly as bad as he limped out the door. At least he had a destination city. And as he hit U.S. 1 headed north and beat a fast track back to West Palm, he didn't give much of a thought to sharing the information with Eve Garrett that Tiffany was on her

way to NYC. Well, not much of a thought, except that after
this was over he was definitely going to give Eve a call.

If nothing else, just to hear her rail at him. There wasn't
too much the woman did that didn't make him hot, and being on the receiving end of one of her tirades—well, let's
just say that even thinking about it made him rise to the occasion.

"OK. Extract your head from your ass, McClain," he muttered. It was time to get serious. There wasn't one damn thing
he could think of that justified even thinking about Eve that
way. He'd screwed with her life once. If he were any kind of
man, he wouldn't screw with it again.

Besides, she considered him the equivalent of roadkill.
And yet she'd called last night, offered to find him a room.

Because she felt guilty. It had nothing to do with him.
More to do with the kind of woman she was.

He pulled into a fast-food place to get a cup of coffee to
keep him awake. On the road again, he made a call to Roger
Edwards. New York was a big place. Edwards had a couple of
ideas on some of Tiffany's favorite haunts, which was good.
Without them, it was going to be like sifting through sand in
a sandbox.

Unlike Little Miss E.D.E.N., Inc., at least Mac knew
which sandbox to look in. If push came to shove, he wasn't
above playing with the definition of *lawful* again if it would
help him get the information he needed. Once Tiffany and the
boy band settled in, he'd access her account again and close
the deal.

And unlike Eve, and over and above what he'd said, it
wasn't all about the money. It was about what the money
could do. It was about seeing his daughter. And Ali was the
most important thing in his life.

Eve was in the shower when her cell rang at seven the next
morning. It was Uncle Bud.

"And where were you all night, young man?" she asked in

her best mother of the house voice as she grappled with the shower curtain.

"I quit answering to women a long time ago—and I've never answered to little girls. You find everything you need?"

"I'm good. Thanks for the five-star digs. What's up?"

"Your girl was at the Hog's Breath last night. Partying pretty heavy according to Jimmy."

"Jimmy?" She wrestled with her phone and a towel and blinked shampoo out of her eyes.

"The bartender. Happens that Jimmy sometimes does some legwork for me. He'd heard I'd been putting out some feelers, so he called. *Just* called, because he just heard I was needing info. Anyway, your girl took a shine to Jimmy and invited him to come back to her suite at the Ocean Key to party a little more. A boyfriend type put the kibosh to that idea with some sharp words and roughed her up a little."

"He hit her?" The uneasiness Eve felt over that news outdistanced her excitement at getting her first solid lead on Tiffany.

"Yeah. He hit her."

Since she'd first heard Lance Reno's name in her conversation with the casino boss at Atlantic City, Eve had figured that the lead singer in Dead Grief was the boyfriend. She asked anyway. "I don't suppose he caught Prince Charming's name."

"Nah, but I got a description. Got a pen?"

She was losing the battle with the shampoo. "Got a memory. Shoot."

"Latino maybe. Black straight hair in a pony all the way to his ass. Under six-foot—late twenties, early thirties."

It was Reno all right. Eve felt her uneasiness over Tiffany's situation grow, then spike up another notch when Uncle Bud continued.

"There was another guy with them. Big. Silver cross in his ear. Shaved head. Lots of tattoos. Full of attitude. Mean."

That had to be Gorman. "OK—so," she groped for

a washcloth, wiped her stinging eyes. "Any chance you've got connections at Ocean Key?"

He grunted. "Honey, there's not a place on U.S. 1 I don't have a connection. Try the bell station. Ask for Randolph. If you're lucky, he's working today. If not, call me back."

"You're a peach."

"Yeah, yeah. Sweet as syrup. Call your mother."

"Quit smoking."

She'd ducked back into the shower and rinsed the shampoo out of her hair and eyes. Then she got herself together and headed out—to find a note on the windshield of her car.

She didn't bother to look around her. She knew that whoever left it was long gone.

You're dead, of course. Or perhaps someone you love will die. Who will go first? I wonder. Watch out for traffic.

In the heat of an eighty-degree morning, a chill spread through her entire body. In its wake rolled white-hot anger.

Damn him! It was one thing to threaten her. It was another to threaten the life of someone she cared about. And do it in such a cowardly way.

"Dammit!" she swore loud enough that a neighbor poked her head out her front door.

"You OK?"

Eve swung around, saw the concern on the face of an elderly woman wrapped in a cotton housecoat.

"Did you see anyone around here? Last night? This morning?"

The woman shook her head and, evidently deciding Eve was all right, ducked back inside.

. . . someone you love.

Oh God. She fumbled for her cell phone and dialed Uncle Bud from her call log.

"Thank God." She breathed a sigh of relief when he answered.

"What's up, little girl?"

She leaned against her car, rubbed her temples, and told him.

An hour later Eve pulled up to the Ocean Key Resort Hotel. Uncle Bud now knew to watch his back. She'd also called Ethan and filled him in on the latest—including the incident with the van that had almost hit her. So much for chalking it off as a drunk driver.

"You'll stay exactly where you are," she insisted when Nolan, on speakerphone, informed her he was coming to the Keys.

Fifteen minutes' worth of arguing later and she'd calmed the waters by threatening to stop updating her brothers if they reacted with macho mania every time she did.

"Trust me to take care of myself," she'd pleaded, and finally gotten them settled down.

Distancing herself from thoughts of her unknown attacker, she marched into the lobby of the upscale Ocean Key Resort Hotel. There wasn't anyone at the bell station when she walked in, so she turned her attention to the registration desk.

"Ring Tiffany Clayborne's room for me, would you please?" she asked a perky blond clerk who looked like she might be a surfer in another life. She was all white teeth and toasted tan.

"I'm sorry, but Ms. Clayborne checked out this morning."

All the authority, finesse, and pleading in the world couldn't pry Tiffany's destination out of the clerk. Who'd have figured Ms. Surf and Turf would have a head on her shoulders?

Eve headed back to the bell station. It was still empty, but a tall sixtyish-looking man in a bell uniform exited an elevator right then rolling a full luggage cart.

Eve followed him out the door. "Randolph?"

He was indeed Randolph. All six long, rangy feet of him.

But for the gray beard and his height, he was another Jimmy Buffett look-alike. Must be something about the sun and tequila this far south that produced so many clones.

Randolph's beard was neatly trimmed, his graying hair just long enough to pull into a little tail at his nape. His uniform was dark green; his hands were huge. He had a tendency to answer almost every question with a question—like he needed confirmation of what he was saying. Eve didn't doubt what he said one bit—especially when he smiled at the mention of Uncle Bud and told her everything she wanted to know for the grand sum of twenty bucks.

"Called the limo service for them myself. Settled the four of them into the stretch, you know? Told the driver to take them to the airport. They left at, oh, let me think, six this morning?"

Three hours ago. "Did you happen to catch where they were going?"

"You know the slim guy? The one with the long hair? Him and the big dude, they were talking about all the clubs they were going to hit when they landed in the Big Apple."

So Tiffany was headed for New York. Eve could have kissed Randolph. Instead she asked another question.

"Gut instinct, Randolph—did you notice anything wrong with the picture?"

"Wrong?"

"Was everybody on board with where they were going? Any bickering? Or were they just one big happy family?"

"Didn't see any smiles, if that's what you mean. Rich kids. Go figure. Mostly they just seemed stoned."

"All of them?"

He let out a breath. Thought. "Maybe not. Maybe just the girl. The staff talks, you know? Carmen—one of the day maids? She was saying one day when she cleaned the room that the men, they were mostly gone. The girl? Not so much. She was too out of it most of the time, passed out in bed." He shook his head. "Lost cause, that one."

"Anything else?"

He firmed his lips, sniffed. "Boy with the hair? Seemed like he just led her around like a rag doll."

"Led her around? Like he was helping her?"

A deep furrow formed between Randolph's bushy brows. "No. More like he was, you know, pushin' her around? Got no time for those types who think they've got to handle women." He shook his head. "But then, she was so out of it, maybe it just seemed that way?"

"Did she look like she was in trouble?"

"That girl was way past trouble. That girl was wasted."

"Happy wasted? Sad wasted?"

"Lost wasted," he finally said with a sad shake of his head and no question at all in his tone. "Those guys she was hanging with? My bet is they could lead her a whole lot deeper into the wasteland."

Lost wasted.

And heading deeper.

All the way back north on Highway 1, she couldn't shake the chill that had run down her spine when she thought about Randolph's words.

If she could have saved time, she'd have flown directly to New York City from Key West. A quick call to the Key West airport from Ocean Key, however, confirmed that there were no direct commercial flights to New York. Several phone calls later and it was obvious she could make just as good time driving back to West Palm and catching a flight there.

OK. That was fine. She needed some think time anyway. Wouldn't hurt to grab a change of clothes. Yet all the way home, her sense of urgency over Tiffany Clayborne kept hitching up by degrees.

. . . Someone she loved . . .

Someone she loved could die.

It was beginning to seem less and less like a stretch: what if that someone was Tiffany?

11

NEW YORK CITY

Eve had broken a few speed limits on the drive back to West Palm. Her apartment had felt cool and dark when she'd let herself in. She'd checked her voice mail, reconfirmed her flight time, then thrown some things into a suitcase.

She'd made a quick call to Uncle Bud on the drive to the airport to let him know she'd arrived safely back in West Palm and to caution him again to watch his back, just in case. She waited until her flight was called, however, to call Ethan.

"I'm about to catch a flight to New York. . . . Because that's where Tiffany's headed. . . . Yes. I know. She's a mover. Look, I've just got a few minutes, but I wanted to check in and I need you to check out some things for me. Got a pen? . . .

"OK," she'd added when he'd said, "Shoot." "Lance Reno, Abe Gorman. Those are two of the guys Tiffany is running with. I don't have anything on the third. And find out what you can for me on Roger Edwards, too, would you? . . . Yeah. Clayborne's man." She'd been thinking about Edwards quite a bit. Something about him didn't feel right.

"I don't know," she admitted when Ethan asked what she was thinking. "Something just feels funny about this whole thing and I want to double cover my bases. If you turn up anything interesting, give me a call. Oh, and while you're at it, might as well run a check on his executive assistant, too. Jazelle Taylor. . . . Yes. I know. I'm thorough. I am *not* anal. And Ethan—so you know, I'm beginning to wonder if this thing with Tiffany might be linked to whoever's after me. . . .

"Nothing solid, no. Just a feeling. Look, I've got to go. Check in on Uncle Bud now and then, OK? And you'd better call Mom and tell her to get on him about his hip. It's giving him trouble again. And you guys be careful, too. Make sure the folks . . . well, just watch out for them, OK?"

She couldn't do anything else about her situation, so she'd used the flight time to make a plan of action to find Tiffany. She needed to make something happen fast, and other than a destination, she had little to go on. If she remembered right, there were, however, two distinct possibilities for leads in New York. Margaret Reed and Katrina Hofsteader.

Margaret Reed had been Tiffany's nanny. After her mother died, Margaret had been the closest thing Tiffany had had to a parental influence. During her childhood, if Clayborne hadn't been jet-setting around the world on business or pleasure, he'd been holed up in his crystal castle. Margaret was currently employed as a nanny by a prominent cable TV talk show host. If anyone understood Tiffany, Eve was betting it was Margaret. Eve remembered Margaret as being a warm, friendly person and was glad that Tiffany had had the woman in her life.

Katrina Hofsteader, a twenty-something daughter of a Frankfurt industrialist, also looked like a good bet. Katrina was a close friend of Tiffany's although Eve had never met her. Tiffany and Katrina had participated in competitive equestrian events in Europe together for several years. Eve knew through Tiff that Katrina kept a co-op apartment in SoHo and spent time there when she wasn't staying in the family's Aspen condo or Tuscan villa. God forbid she'd have to land at home in Frankfurt long enough to account to anyone.

Eve was checked into the West Park Hotel on West 58th

and on the phone in her hotel room at four o'clock that afternoon. Fortunately, both Margaret and Katrina were listed in the phone book. Eve dragged a hand through her hair as she waited for Margaret Reed to pick up. She got an answering machine instead.

"I'm sorry, but I'm unable to take your call. Please leave a message."

She left a message, then tried Katrina Hofsteader. It was a long shot that she'd find Katrina in the city, but Eve gave it a try anyway—and got lucky.

Hofsteader's housekeeper answered on the second ring. "I'm sorry, Ms. Hofsteader is out."

"Can you tell me when you expect her back?"

"I couldn't say, ma'am. Possibly later this afternoon. May I take a message?"

Eve left her cell number, as she had with Margaret Reed's voice mail, asked that the housekeeper relay to Ms. Hofsteader that she was calling about Tiffany Clayborne and to impart the urgency of returning her call as soon as possible.

Now all she could do was wait. She checked her watch, gave a passing thought to McClain, his black eye and bum leg, and grabbed her jacket. McClain accounted for too many passing thoughts, she decided in disgust as she headed out of her room.

She didn't get it. Other than the fact that he was an aggravation—which upgraded his status from triple-A to quad- —there was no reason to waste gray matter thinking about the man. And his disarming smiles. And wiseass remarks. And that sleepy, sexy question he'd posed last night in the heat of a Key West night.

Am I growing on you, cupcake?

In his X-rated dreams.

Tyler McClain proved the axiom: Growing old is mandatory. Growing up is optional. He hadn't grown emotionally. He was still just a big little kid.

"So, that makes him what?" she muttered to herself when

the elevator doors opened and deposited her on the lobby floor. "A jumbo shrimp?"

Amused with her little joke but peeved with herself for getting sidetracked, she double-checked the address she'd pulled from the phone book with the concierge, then headed out of the hotel toward the subway stop.

Things had changed since she'd last been to the city. No more tokens. Only MTA cards. She bought a rechargeable yellow card and caught the F train to Brooklyn. She still had friends in the Secret Service in the field office. Friends she could count on and who were nothing like Tyler McClain, on whom she could *not* count. At 4:40 she was sitting across the desk from one in her old boss's office at 335 Adams in the Carroll Gardens neighborhood of Brooklyn.

"I'm fifty-five fricking years old and you're asking me where the 'in' spots are? You're asking me about—what the hell was it?"

"Raves. Clubs where the rich and famous go to party. Where they play punk, glam . . . maybe some new wave or Gothic. And metal. It's music, Bob," she added with a laugh when he looked at her like she was speaking Martian. "God, I've missed you."

Bob Gleason had been supervisor, mentor, and friend when she'd spent her six years as a Secret Service field officer in the city. He was overworked and overweight, with the drooping bags under his eyes and the bulldog jowls the most obvious tells, but the gaze from his silver-gray eyes was still as sharp as a stiletto. And he still smelled like mint and comfort. Just like she remembered.

Eve had just transferred out of New York City to D.C. and protection duty for Vice President Hargrave's daughter when the world changed on 9-11. As usual, Bob had been at work on the ninth floor of Number 7 World Trade Center, where the field office had been located until that horrendous day. He'd saved lives. He'd made a difference.

Eve missed making a difference, too. Sometimes she wondered if that was why she was so certain Tiffany was in trouble. Maybe she needed to make a difference for Tiffany more than Tiffany needed to be found. Maybe she needed to know she wouldn't screw this up the way her career had been screwed up and she'd been screwed over.

In the meantime, she really did miss Bob. The framed photograph of the Twin Towers on the wall behind his desk spoke of his respect and sorrow for another time when their office was in another place. When they'd lived in another world where terrorism happened everywhere but here.

Bob leaned back in his chair, shoved his bifocals up on his nose, and laced his fingers across his middle where his white shirt tugged at the buttons. "So, how you doin', kiddo? Things goin' OK?"

She hadn't given him a chance to ask that question yet, but she'd known it was coming. "Things are great."

"You're good with the security business, then?"

"Sure. Never a dull moment."

He considered her, then shook his head. "You should still be with the Service. You were one of the best. Those bastards sold you out."

She agreed. What had happened to her—losing her job—wasn't right. But it was the way things worked in the bureaucratic food chain. Big fish ate the little ones. One chomp. It was all she wrote.

"Yeah, well. You want to argue with the president of the United States?"

"'Worthy of trust and confidence,'" Bob muttered the Secret Service motto. "You were worthy of both."

"It's old news, Bob. I've put it behind me." At least she'd tried. "And I do like what I'm doing now. It's a plus being back home. A plus working with my brothers, although, I've got to tell you, there was a time I would have choked on those words before admitting it."

"Well," he said, seeing that she didn't want to rehash ancient history, "I'm glad. And you look great. Florida must agree with you."

"Being home agrees with me."

"Which begs the question, if home is so great, why are you here looking for nightspots? And don't tell me you're on vacation."

"Actually—don't get bent out of shape now—I'm looking for Tiffany Clayborne."

He blinked. Then swore. "Are you nuts?"

"Probably."

Very briefly, she filled Bob in on her search for Tiffany and her fear that she might be in trouble.

"And then there's this other little thing."

He searched her face. "How little?"

"OK. Maybe it's big."

She told him about the attacks and the notes.

"Fuck."

"My brothers pretty much sum it up that way, too," she said, and in spite of the gravity of the situation found herself smiling.

And in the end, that's why she was here. She hadn't really expected Bob to be of any help with the club scene information, but she couldn't resist the chance to talk to him. He always made her smile.

"Someone you bumped noses with in the Service?" he speculated with a frown.

She shrugged. "Don't know. My brothers are doing some digging."

"Have 'em call me. I'll do some checking tomorrow."

"Enough of this. Tell me what's happening with you," she insisted, and for a few minutes more he did. They kibitzed about his wife, and Eve made the right noises over photos of his beautiful grandkids before she decided it was time to let him go home to his family.

Her cell rang just as she stood up to leave. When she dug

the phone out of her purse and checked the digital readout her heart gave an excited little lurch. And because it did, she considered not answering.

Disgusted, she punched talk, lifted the cell to her ear, and gave it her best bothered voice. "What do you want, McClain?"

"We need to talk."

"And obviously I need to change my cell number."

"Here I thought we were getting to be good buddies."

"What do you want?" she repeated.

"If you haven't left Florida yet, catch the nearest flight to New York. Call me with your flight number and I'll meet you at the airport."

Her oversize purse landed on Bob's desk with a thump. "You're in New York?"

"Look, we don't really have time to play Twenty Questions. The thing is, I think you're right."

She was still processing the news that McClain wasn't limping around Key West following a very cold trail when he spoke again.

"I'm beginning to think Tiffany might be in some trouble."

He had her complete attention now. "And?"

"And we need to talk," he restated with staged patience. "Now would you quit wasting time and just get on a damn plane?"

She debated for the length of a wary breath. "Hold on a sec." She turned to Bob. "Is Time Squared still open?" she asked, referring to a bar where a bunch of them used to sometimes congregate after work. They'd catch the subway, tip a few, then scatter to the various parts of the city and their own private spaces.

Bob nodded.

"Where, specifically, are you?" she asked McClain.

When he told her, she gave Bob his location. "What do you think? Take him an hour or so to get there?"

"If he can snag a cab."

She turned back to the phone. "Got a pen?"

"Shoot."

She rattled off Time Squared's address. "Got it?"

"Yeah, but—"

"I'll be waiting."

"Waiting?" Silence. "Well, shit. You're already in New York." It wasn't a question. More of a "why didn't I already know that" statement.

"Now who's underestimating who?"

His chuckle held more resignation than humor. "Guess neither one of us will make that mistake again. See you in an hour."

She disconnected, then caught Bob's concerned look and grinned. "Life's just one surprise after another, isn't it?"

She filled him in on McClain—leaving out the parts that were giving her trouble, which made it a very brief briefing— as she gathered her things to go.

"Come on," Bob said. "I'm ready to blow this pop stand. I'll ride partway with you."

She'd been thinking of hailing a cab but decided that catching the subway with Bob would be like old times. By the time she'd trudged down the subway stop steps, bought her card, and pushed through the turnstile, she was having second thoughts about the car.

"How could I have forgotten rush hour?"

Beside her Bob just grinned, the rumble of the trains and the screech of brakes in the cavernous tunnel making it almost impossible to talk. So did the glut of bodies. The subway station was packed. It was body to body as she stood beside Bob on the platform, a little too close to the edge for comfort.

She'd just decided to step back when someone shoved her from behind. Hard.

She might have screamed as she felt herself falling. But all she could hear was the roar of the train speeding by like a bullet. All she could see was harsh light glinting like splinters off polished steel. The glare of glass spun by in a blur. She couldn't catch her balance. Couldn't break her fall. Was sure of only one thing: she was going down on the tracks.

They'd find her body splattered from here to Upper Manhattan.

And she hadn't wanted to die like this.

12

"DEEP BREATH. YOU'RE OK. YOU'RE OK."

Eve blinked up and into Bob Gleason's tired eyes. Eyes that were wide and worried.

"Jesus," she said, and let out a breath that felt fractured and too full for her chest.

"Yeah." Bob gave her a hand and helped her stand on rubber legs. "I'd say he had a hand in helping me get to you."

The crowd had parted, Eve noticed; the faces of several onlookers were studies in curiosity and concern. She brushed herself off and made a quick body check. All digits present and accounted for.

"Someone pushed me," she said, finally meeting Bob's eyes.

"I know. I saw. It was either go after him or go after you. I made a grab and got lucky."

She couldn't help it. She threw her arms around him. Hugged him hard, which of course had him flushing about three shades of red and setting her back.

"Lucky for me you've got good hands," she said, very much aware of the unsteadiness in her voice and the rapid-fire beat of her heart, which was still reacting to the close call. "Did you get a look at him?"

"Just his back as he cut out of here. Arms were bare. He

was Caucasian. Big. Broad. Wore a stocking cap, so I couldn't see his hair. Sound like anyone you know?"

"I've never seen him—but I know he was big and muscular."

"Come on." Bob gripped her elbow when their train pulled in. "He's long gone. Let's get out of here."

Still a little unsteady, Eve let him steer her into the car. Again they got lucky, and found a pair of seats. She stared, without really seeing the advertisements posted above the windows on the train.

"Tomorrow, I'm pulling your case files," Bob said, his frown deep and troubled.

She nodded, shifting her purse from under her shoulder to her lap, feeling very weary suddenly. And something else. Vulnerable. She hated both feelings.

"My money's on finding some answers in them."

"It's possible, sure. You might want to start with the Clayborne case."

He lifted a brow, then nodded. "You sure you're OK?" He placed an arm around her shoulders. He felt solid and protective next to her. Yet his face was lined with worry.

"Good as gold," she assured him—as much for her sake as for his.

"I'm going with you to this meet," he said.

She shook her head. "Not necessary. He made his statement for the day. And McClain's solid. I'm safe with him," she assured Bob, surprising herself when she realized she believed what she'd just said.

When they reached Bob's stop, she hugged him again before he stepped out of the car. "You always were my guardian angel."

He squeezed her arm. "Watch yourself, kiddo, OK?"

She nodded and waved good-bye, a persistent sense of unease gnawing away as the subway train picked up speed again on the way to Time Squared.

It was close to six when she climbed out of the subway stop, walked the few blocks to the bar, and stepped into the dark, cool confines of Time Squared. A quick sweep of the place told her McClain hadn't made it yet.

She'd just sat down at a dark corner table with her back to the wall when he walked into the bar. At the sight of him her heart kicked her a good one dead center in her better judgment. Just that fast, she forgot all about her close call and experienced a momentary urge to duck out the back door.

Lord, he was a presence. His gaze swept the bar with the practiced eye of a cop. For the first time, she could actually see him in that venue. Even though he didn't spot her at first, she could definitely see him. Alpha male on the hunt, all dark dangerous looks fueled by pure testosterone.

Well, hell. This wasn't good. This wasn't good at all. Sure, she'd had moments of awareness around him, but it had always been marginally easy to sweep them under a rug of dislike and disgust. And yeah, she'd felt a tug of empathy when he'd talked about his little girl, all the while holding ice on his swollen eye and limping without complaint to his car. It had been an understandable, even acceptable reaction. She'd gotten over it. After all, he was still a rat. She didn't want him anywhere near her life again. She'd been royally ticked over him showing up in West Palm. He'd made it pretty darned easy to stay that way and to ignore certain knee-jerk reactions—like gut-deep attraction.

Until now. Maybe it was the stress. Maybe it was the uncertainty. But now . . . now she just plain couldn't ignore them. The breadth of his shoulders was no longer minimized beneath a loose, painfully ugly tropical shirt. The underlying tension of a warrior and the rugged appeal of his lived-in face—black eye, split lip, and all—were no longer overshadowed by his cabana boy air.

That man—the Peter Pan "party dude" beach bum in worn flip-flops—must have taken a slow boat to Tahiti. In his place was a devastating combination of urban cosmopolitan and retro *Miami Vice*. A dove gray mock turtleneck hugged his broad chest and flat abdomen beneath a lightweight navy hip-length jacket. Pleated black pants emphasized a narrow waist, lean hips, and the length of long, muscled legs.

As she watched him, sexual tension coiled low in her belly and radiated to all points above and below. Without the loud shirts screeching at her, she could hear the call of the wild. Felt a little like howling herself.

Just what she needed. More trouble.

"What'll you have?" a forty-something waitress with bleached blond hair and hot pink nails asked as she placed a cocktail napkin on the table.

"Hemlock, please."

Eve got a long, bored blink and ordered a club soda.

Eve thought he'd underestimated her? What Mac thought, as he shouldered out of a cab and spotted a sign above a recessed door that ID'd the place as the Time Squared Bar, was that Eve Garrett was freakin' brilliant. He should have known she'd be ahead of him. And he should have known to trust a woman's instincts and heed her concern about Tiffany.

He'd just come from Margaret Reed's West Side apartment. After his conversation with Tiffany's old nanny, he was damn concerned himself.

The longer they'd talked, the more certain he'd become. And the more resigned he'd become to paying attention to the sinking sensation in his gut. It was the same kind of sensation he felt every time he thought of Ali. It felt like guilt, tugged like responsibility, and gnawed like a conviction to do the right thing. In this case, doing the right thing could cost him a whole lot of money. If Edwards got wind that he was considering teaming up with Eve, it could cost him this contract.

With luck, it wouldn't come to that. He wouldn't let it. He needed that money—and he was going to get it. Angie's constant threat to terminate visitation rights if he didn't keep up with child support was like a five-hundred-pound gorilla sitting on his chest. He wanted it off. He wanted breathing room, and the money from this job was going to buy it.

He opened the door and stepped inside. Time Squared had all the essentials to make it a perfect place to unwind after a day of warfare in the trenches—whether the battle was fought in the boardroom, on the sales floor, or deep in the subway humming nonstop beneath the city. It was small, it was dark, and it smelled like spilled beer, salted peanuts, and the ghosts of cigarette smoke that still lingered in the wake of the city's public-smoking ban.

As his eyes adjusted to the light, he noted a dozen or so suits clustered at a round table gulping martinis; some blue collars tipping tap beer at the bar. The pool table in the far corner was idle; the TV above the selection of call liquor was turned to a Yankee game. The beautiful blonde with the "this better be good" scowl and frosty blue eyes was alone at the corner table.

"Eve," he said cordially as he walked over to her.

"McClain."

Oh, so formal, he thought, suppressing a grin as he pulled out a chair, sat, then signaled the bartender for a beer. Then Mac did what he'd been wanting to do since he'd left her a little less than twenty-four hours ago. He looked his fill.

She had to be as drained as he was. They'd both been on the move for days. And yeah, she looked tired. Tired and incredibly beautiful. She'd been hot and spicy in her little red tank top and white capri pants under the Key West sun. She was cool and sexy as hell in a tailored black pantsuit beneath the bar's diluted light. And like damn near every time he saw her, his mouth dried up and key muscle groups did a lot of involuntary clenching and flexing and ruined the clean line of his trousers.

He made a subtle adjustment to his fly under the table. "I just came from a long visit with Margaret Reed."

Her eyes narrowed.

Yeah. He'd known she'd probably be hot over that. "She won't be returning your call, by the way, because she thinks we're working together.

"OK, simmer. Just simmer," he suggested when she looked like she was about to fly across the table at him and blacken his other eye. It wouldn't be the first time he'd have a matched set, but he'd just as soon pass on another one.

God, she was something. If the situation weren't so serious, he'd have some fun and needle her for a while. Just to watch her get all fired up. The lady was a sight riled. And aroused. He wondered if she still made those little throaty purring sounds when she came.

"Let's just get the cards out on the table, OK? This is not a scam. Not a test. I'm here to share information. Because," he interrupted when she opened her mouth to voice a distrustful "why?," "what Margaret Reed told me has brought me over to your way of thinking."

She leveled him a cynical look. Judge Judy about to pronounce sentence on the biggest rat in the pack.

"Among other things, I learned that Tiffany Clayborne used to sleep with a pink stuffed kitten. She named it Fuzzy. Fuzzy was her best friend. Her family. When she was tired and feeling insecure, she'd cry for Fuzzy if she'd misplaced it. She couldn't sleep without it. Had to supervise directly when Margaret tossed Fuzzy into the washer every week. Tiffany actually sat in the laundry room until the thing was fluffed and dry. Until she turned eighteen, next to Margaret, Fuzzy was the only thing that never left her.

"At twelve," he continued, seeing that he had Eve's reluctant attention, "she still slept with a night-light. She saw her father on Clayborne's schedule. Once a week. On Monday morning for an hour. When she turned fourteen, Clayborne cut it back to half an hour. Guess the bastard figured he was spoiling her.

"When she went out and had her tongue pierced for her

sixteenth birthday, desperate to do something to get his attention, Clayborne cut off even the Monday morning appointments until she had the thing removed."

All the time he talked, Mac watched Eve's face—not exactly tough duty. A poker player she was not. Empathy, sorrow, anger, it all flashed in those wide, expressive eyes before she tucked her emotions away again and repositioned her mask of distrust.

She toyed with her glass. Rocked it on a damp napkin. "So you had a nice chat with the nanny. Now tell me something I didn't already know about Tiffany."

"It was more than a chat. It was an education. Margaret agrees that Tiffany could act out when the spirit moved her. God knows she had good reason—especially after Clayborne went hermit a few years ago. Even before that, though, Clayborne was a cold piece of work. But Margaret insists that Tiffany is a good girl. She may have experimented with pot, but overall, she was afraid of drugs. And she's big into horses."

"I know. Equestrian events. Jumpers," Eve said with a nod.

"Which required random drug testing for her to compete," he supplied, noting that Eve had let her guard down enough to add to the conversation before she could stop herself.

"She always passed. And she's a good athlete. But again, you're telling me all of this like it's something I don't already know. You forgot, I spent several months with her. So unless this story is going somewhere—"

"It is. Just bear with me. According to Margaret," he continued, "it wasn't until after Clayborne went off the deep end that Tiffany started getting a little out of control. But still, Margaret insists Tiffany wasn't into drugs. She'd go out and drink too much, party a little too often, but she limited her illegals to marijuana if she did anything at all."

"Yet according to someone I interviewed in Key West, she was pretty much stoned the entire time she was at Ocean Key."

He nodded. "My guy at Atlantic City says the same thing. She was wasted most of the time she was there, too."

"It's the band," Eve said, too caught up in concern and conviction to realize they were no longer arguing. "More specifically, the boyfriend."

"Reno. Right."

Again, a look of surprise. That'd teach her to underestimate him.

"I caught up with them at the Key West airport. Shot some film. Had a friend of mine on the force run his picture through VICAP and got a hit. Lance Reno is a wannabe rocker with a bad drug habit and a penchant for high living. He's got a short rap sheet—minor stuff mostly. But he's not likely to be someone Clayborne would want to see Tiffany bring home to dinner. His buddy with the tattoos—"

"Abe Gorman," she supplied.

"Yeah," he said, impressed again. "Gorman's small-time, too, but likes to mix a little petty larceny and assault and battery in with his illegal activity."

"What about the third guy?"

"I was hoping you had something on him. I didn't get any pictures. He was already on board when I started shooting so he's still a mystery man."

"OK, McClain," she asked after she'd absorbed the information to date, "so what are you thinking?"

"I'm thinking that what on the surface appears to be a lark for Tiffany Clayborne has taken on some darker elements. I'm thinking that little Tiffany has fallen in with some bad dudes who love their first-class ticket to ride the gravy train."

She pinched her lips, slowly nodded. "They're manipulating her to the point she no longer knows what she's doing."

"Yeah. Tiffany is definitely looking for love in all the wrong places."

Worry pinched Eve's brows even though she fired one of her zingers. "Could you throw in a few more clichés, do you think?"

He smiled. "If I put my mind to it. The fact that Tiffany is deep into the hard stuff," he continued without missing a beat, "is totally at odds with the nanny's take on her. Margaret is adamant that *her* Tiffany would never willingly sink that low. She's worried about her. Even more, she's afraid for her. Her old man should care about her half as much," he added, remembering the tears that had filled the older woman's eyes when she'd begged him to find Tiffany and get her help.

He drained his beer, then met Eve's gaze. At least curiosity now seemed to outweigh her suspicion.

"So, even though I told you from the beginning that I was worried about her, it took a talk with Margaret to make you come around."

"It helped," he agreed, rocking back on his chair, "but it was something else that brought me over."

Her gaze sharpened.

"Tiffany's horses," he supplied.

"What about them?"

"Margaret said Tiffany loves them like children. Felt about them the way her father should feel about her. Per Margaret, during all the time she spent with Tiffany a day didn't go by that she didn't go to see them or call the stables to check on them. Not a day," he restated for emphasis, "regardless of where she was."

"I know," Eve said. "I remember."

The look on her face told him that she already suspected what he was about to say.

"Margaret still had the phone number in her address book, so I called the stables from her apartment. They haven't heard from Tiffany in three weeks."

She drew in a deep breath. Let it out like she was very tired.

"And that's when it changed for me. Now I'm certain we're looking at a victim, not a runaway."

Even though she'd been pursuing the foul-play angle,

Mac suspected that Eve had been holding out hope that Tiffany would just wander home on her own steam. His news had just shot a horse-sized hole in that hope.

"So. What now?"

"Now I figure two heads are better than one."

She didn't look like she was sure she liked that idea. Interesting. Once she'd asked for his help. Now that he was offering it, she seemed hesitant.

"What about Edwards? What about your pay?"

"You let me worry about that. Tiffany's the priority and we can find her faster together than we can apart. And fast may be all she's got going for her right now."

The waitress wandered over about that time, asked if they wanted another round. Without looking up, they both shook their heads.

And still, Eve hadn't indicated she wanted to team up.

"So . . . are we in this together from here on out or what?"

She hesitated and he could see by her closed-off body language that she was actually considering telling him no.

"OK, what, exactly, is the problem?"

She finally met his eyes. "That's just it. I don't want there to be any problems."

"Like?"

She stared at her empty glass. "Like I don't want you getting the idea that if I decide to work with you it means that I'm up for anything else."

Ah. There it was. He knew where this was heading. "Anything else? Like sex, you mean."

"Yeah. Like sex. Or sweet talk leading up to it or—" She lifted a hand, searching.

"Seduction?" he suggested, feeling ornery, and damned if her cheeks didn't turn red.

"I was going to say like side bets."

Like the one he'd suggested in Key West.

Interesting that she felt she had to level terms. It made

him wonder if she wasn't thinking about sweet talk and sex and side bets just a little too much to make her comfortable.

Just thinking about her thinking about "it" turned him on like a strobe light.

"So. Just business."

She nodded but wouldn't look at him. "Just business."

Behind him, a roar rose from the bar area—apparently in response to something that had happened during the baseball game. He barely heard it. Instead, he took in those blue eyes that had grown flinty and tough; the lush mouth that protested just a little much to ring true; the set of her slender shoulders that said she was tooled for battle on this front. Eve, warrior princess, ready to defend womankind.

And he thought, *Fuck it.*

If he was going to get shut down before he ever got out of the blocks, he at least wanted a taste of what she wasn't willing to share.

Since the first time he'd seen her at Club Asylum with her gun drawn, her expression murderous, and her schoolteacher mouth spewing four-letter words, he'd pretty much been in a perpetual state of rut.

He wanted this woman. Spitting fire and claws bared, restless beneath him and begging, submissive and on her knees in front of him, he didn't care how it went down, but he *was* going to have her—today, tomorrow, when this was over—and it was past time he laid it out on the table. Damn the scars. And damn her conditions.

"Fine. Just business," he said, "as soon as I get this out of my system."

And then he reached for her.

While she was still mired in surprise, he wrapped his fingers around the warm skin at her nape. The silk of her hair caught in his hand as he drew her toward him and slammed his mouth over hers.

And sank into pure unadulterated lust.

He wasn't a kid anymore. Neither was she. And he hadn't

felt this much life in his cynical old bones since—hell, since he'd taken her into his mouth all those years ago.

He caught her so completely off guard she didn't have a chance to wedge her hands between them and shove him away. That didn't mean she didn't put up a fight.

She opened her mouth to rail at him. That worked out just fine. He slid his tongue past the seam of her open lips and tasted his fill. When she didn't bite him, he took it as a good sign. And when her hands rose to his shoulders and gripped as if to push him away before the rigid tension in her body let go with a soft moan, he embraced it as invitation.

He kicked back his chair and drew her with him to her feet, wrapping her flush against him. He needed to feel the lush heat of her breasts crushed against his chest. Needed to wedge his thigh between hers and press against her pubic bone and just wallow in the promise of her.

Jesus. She was as amazing as he remembered. And as wild. Her mouth as hot and wet and hungry. And as greedy as that other part of her he'd never forgotten. He lifted his head, changed the angle of the kiss, and took things to a whole other level.

When she made a little shivery sound in her throat, he gentled his hold, gave her hands room to roam—and immediately realized his mistake.

Her hot little fist wrapped around his balls and twisted.

"You just couldn't quit while you were ahead, could you?" she hissed against his mouth as he sucked in a breath and thought about begging.

All he could manage was a tortured, "Murppffhh," as he met her hard glare from less than an inch away.

The lady played hardball. And he was pretty damn certain he wasn't going to be able to let anyone play with *his* balls any time soon.

It was all he could do to keep on his feet. He could barely breathe. His ears started ringing—or was it a phone?

It rang again and mercifully, she let him go.

"Eve Garrett," he heard her say through a groundswell of relief and a surge of blood shooting back to his head.

"Ms. Hofsteader. Yes. Yes. Thank you so much for returning my call.

"What? . . . Yes. I'm worried about her, too. . . . Absolutely, I can do that. Where? . . . OK. Got it. I'm about a half hour from there. I'll see you soon."

Mac was still sucking air, his hands braced on the table, when her gaze met his, cool as frost, hard as ice.

"Don't play games with me, McClain. You'll lose. You want to do this? Then you do it my way. And that means that's the last time your tongue comes anywhere near my mouth. Understood?"

Since he wasn't sure he could speak yet, he took the low road and didn't even try.

"And so you know, if I didn't think Tiffany's life might be on the line here, I'd drop you like a bad habit. But the fact is, you're right. We can find her faster working together."

"*Working*, McClain," she restated with emphasis. "Our association ends there."

He nodded, but as cognizant thought slowly returned along with blood flow, he recognized the truth. She was lying through her teeth. *No way in hell did their association end at work.* She hadn't damn near neutered him because she wanted him to stay away from her. She'd put the screws to him because she *wanted* him. Period. And she didn't know how else to defend against that want.

She'd been totally on board with that kiss. And despite the knifelike pain shooting through his equipment at the moment, one of these days he was going to spread her like butter, because the woman was toast.

"What?" She glared at him. "The king of the comebacks has nothing to say?"

"Ice," he managed in a strained voice. "I could probably use some ice."

13

JESUS, JOSEPH, AND MARY, EVE THOUGHT as she hailed a cab, then waited for McClain to limp carefully off the curb behind her. She scooted over to the far side of the backseat to make room for him, then scrabbled around in her purse, searching frantically for a bag of M&M's.

Swearing under her breath when she turned up empty, she dragged a hand through her hair. What had gotten into her? She'd let McClain kiss her. So what if she was still shaken from her scare at the subway? So what if McClain had also taken her by surprise? She could have had him on his knees and singing soprano long before she'd come to her senses and put an end to it.

Just because he'd grown into his shoulders and had the kind of rugged, lived-in face that prompted all kinds of questions about what experiences in his past had shaded his present, didn't mean he'd matured where it counted. He was still testosterone on a half shell, a hormone on the make. And she needed to stop getting all fluttery inside and out thinking about him.

Fluttery.

That soaked it. She had a job to do that did not include fantasizing about what it could have been like between them if he hadn't been such a first-class jerk years ago. What it could *be* like if he wasn't *still* such a jerk.

"Where to?" the cabbie asked over his shoulder when McClain had shut the door behind him.

Eve gave the cabdriver Katrina Hofsteader's SoHo address, then stared out the window at the traffic and the lights of the city and settled herself.

OK. She'd been curious about what it would be like to kiss McClain, she conceded, cutting herself a little slack. It'd been a long time since she'd experienced any man–woman chemistry. So long that she'd forgotten what it felt like when that chemistry was good.

Really, *really* good.

Beside her, McClain was slumped down low, his head lolling against the seat back.

"How's the knee?" she asked grudgingly.

He pushed out a pained laugh. "Not at the top of the agony chart at the moment."

All right. Maybe she owed him an apology. "OK. So I'm sorry."

"What? That my knee hurts less than my balls? Or that me and the boys are still in the same zip code?"

She turned toward him. His eyes were closed. His legs spread wide.

"That I overreacted."

He grunted. "This is a very enlightening moment for you, considering that you've been overreacting the last few days. Could it be we've actually had a breakthrough with your therapy?"

"That was Katrina Hofsteader on the phone," she said, ignoring his sarcasm.

His gaze shot to hers. "Tiffany's friend from Germany, right?"

"Right. I took a chance she was in the city, left a message. Turns out she's just as worried about Tiffany as I am."

"As *we* are," he corrected.

"Fine. As worried as *we* are."

"And I take it we're meeting her?"

"Your powers of deductive reasoning simply amaze me."

He was quiet for several moments as the cabbie jerked to a stop, laid on his horn, and yelled words in some Middle Eastern language that may have alluded to abusing sheep.

"I don't suppose," McClain said, in a very weary voice, "that you have any ibuprofen on you?"

She rolled her eyes and dug back into her purse. Men. Blacken their eye, split their lip, break their leg, and they'd rather suffer than ask for help. But just touch their pride and joy and they turn into simpering infants.

When she'd worked in the New York field office, Eve had had occasion to deal with socialite types. Park Avenue princesses who were slaves to fashion, plastic surgery, and the vapid men who ran in their circles. She'd expected to meet a grape plucked from the same vine in Katrina Hofsteader, even though Katrina lived in SoHo instead of on the Upper East Side.

She couldn't have been more off target. Katrina may be rich, she may be on a par with a princess based on her lineage, but she was far from a slave to anyone's idea of status quo. Despite Eve's *assumption* that she would barely more than tolerate Katrina for Tiffany's sake, she found herself liking the woman on first meeting. Same went for her significant other, Sven.

"Please come in." Katrina met them at the door herself in bare feet, worn hip-hugger jeans, and a hot pink crop top silk shirt. "I'm so anxious to speak with you about Tiffany."

Eve had seen photos of Katrina in the tabloids. She was an international celebrity for not only her wealth but also her striking beauty. You couldn't stand in line at a supermarket and not see her photograph. Those grainy photos, however, hadn't done her justice.

Katrina was Halle Berry–gorgeous, a stunning mix of her German father's Aryan features and her South African mother's dark, exotic beauty. Her blue-black hair was straight and long in one of those trendy choppy cuts that complemented her oval face and flawless creamy mocha skin tone.

Her longtime love interest, Sven Jorgenson, was a Swissborn Olympic-quality downhill skier slash Nordic god. Sven looked up from a plush white leather sofa when Katrina ushered Eve and McClain into a mammoth sunken living room. He stood when Katrina made introductions.

"I'm sorry," Katrina said, genuine apology on her face when she addressed McClain, "I'm afraid I'm a little unsettled about all this. I didn't catch your name."

"Tyler McClain. I'm an associate of Ms. Garrett's."

Eve raised a brow at that but let it pass.

"Thanks for seeing us." McClain extended his hand to Sven. "We want the same thing you do, to find Tiffany, make sure she's all right."

"Mr. McClain," Sven said, returning his handshake.

Jorgenson wore a white silk dress shirt open over a pair of jeans. He, too, was barefoot, and between all six feet of his statue-perfect physique and McClain, the two of them seemed to fill the cavernous room. Sven's blue eyes flicked with concern to Katrina, who had motioned for everyone to sit down.

"Can I ask you a question, Ms. Garrett?" Katrina curled up in a leather side chair.

"Please. Call me Eve."

"And I'm Mac."

Katrina nodded, smiled. "Then you must call me Kat. Can I ask, what is your relationship to Tiffany?"

On the cab ride to SoHo, Eve and Mac had reached an agreement. Since they'd already decided to work together to find Tiffany for Tiffany's sake, they needed to set some ground rules for their unholy alliance. And until they knew exactly what Tiffany's situation was, they'd agreed to the need to exercise discretion. They had to be careful what they confided to who.

Eve glanced at McClain. He nodded. Which meant he felt, as she did, that Katrina Hofsteader could be trusted. Still, for the sake of expediency, Eve offered only a watered-down version of the truth.

"I've known Tiffany since she was fifteen. And while you and I have never run into each other, Tiffany often mentioned you. She cares a great deal about you. And I care a great deal about her, although I'll be frank with you, Tiffany hasn't spoken to me in several months. She thinks I betrayed her when, in fact, I was looking out for her. It's a long story, but the bottom line is, I care for her very much. And I want to find her. That's why I'm assisting Mr. McClain, who was solicited by Mr. Clayborne to find Tiffany."

"Jeremy Clayborne contacted you personally?"

Mac shook his head. "His representative. Roger Edwards."

Kat tensed immediately.

McClain cut a glance at Eve before addressing Kat. "I take it you know Edwards."

"I know him. Tiffany hated him."

Eve nodded. Tiffany had always made her scorn for Edwards clear.

"She always felt that Edwards tried to fill in for her father. Instead of endearing him to Tiffany, it made her that much more aware of her father's neglect. She wanted Jeremy Clayborne, not Richard Edwards, and Edwards bore the brunt of her anger."

That was the way Eve had always seen it, too.

"Why did Edwards hire you, do you think?" Katrina asked.

"Damage control," McClain said. "Tiffany has been on the move for a few weeks, blowing a lot of coin. Edwards says Clayborne wants her reined in."

"The problem is," Eve added, "we're no longer comfortable with Edwards's take—that she's acting out, intentionally being irresponsible, blowing her trust fund, all to spite her father."

"It's what I would do if I were in her shoes," Kat said
with a concerned scowl. "Her father is a horrible person."

"Agreed, but we're starting to think there's more to it than
Tiffany on the run." McClain paused, then asked point-
blank, "Were you aware that she's heavily into drugs?"

Kat glanced at Sven, worry mixed with denial. "No. I
don't believe that. She went through a phase there where she
experimented a little—we all did—but she would never do
anything hard-core."

When her sharp gaze skated between McClain and Eve
and she saw the truth, her face fell. "Oh God. It's true, isn't
it? Then something *is* wrong. Something's bad wrong.
What's going on?"

Eve shook her head. "We don't know. The only thing we
know for certain is that she's keeping company with a musician and a couple members of his band. Does the name
Lance Reno mean anything to you?"

"No. But I do know that Tiffany makes poor choices
when it comes to men. It's no secret why. She can't win the
love of her father, so she hangs her heart on anyone who will
give her attention."

"When was the last time you had contact with her?"
McClain asked.

"About a month ago." Kat looked toward Sven for confirmation. When he nodded, she continued. "She called. She
sounded so unhappy. I convinced her to meet me in Rome.
Just have a little one-on-one girl time. She didn't show. I've
been worried ever since."

"Has she called you to explain why she didn't make it?"

Tears pooled in Kat's eyes. "She left a message about a
week ago. All she did was cry. I couldn't understand her. She
sounded so . . . I don't know. Lost. When I tried to call her
back, I got a no-service message."

"She's here, you know," Eve said. "In New York."

"Oh my God. Why hasn't she contacted me?" Kat looked
confused and a little hurt.

When McClain glanced at her, Eve nodded. "She might not be able to."

The alarm in Kat's eyes deepened.

Eve felt genuine sympathy for Kat's worry. "We think it could be that she's being controlled or manipulated by this Reno character. He's probably the one who's pushing the drugs on her." She explained about the dwindling bank accounts, the constant moving around.

"Do you have any idea where she might go when she's in the city?" Mac asked, leaning forward—very carefully, Eve noted. "Hotels where she likes to stay? Clubs she might frequent?"

Kat rattled off the names of several hotels.

"Already tried most of those," McClain said, surprising Eve that he'd already checked them out. "She's not registered. Neither is Reno."

"Which," Eve concluded aloud, "suggests they've changed their pattern because they've decided they need to go low-profile. And that translates to the notion that now they're actively hiding, which hadn't been the case before.

"How about nightclubs?" she asked, switching gears.

"Oracle," Kat said decisively. "She loves the place. If not there, there are several others. We made the rounds every time she came to the city."

"If you can give us a list," McClain said, "that's where we'll start then."

"We want to help you look," Sven added with a meaningful nod toward Kat that brought a renewed threat of tears to her eyes. "Besides, you'll need us to get in."

"Thank you." Kat went to Sven, settling on his lap.

Mac glanced at Eve. She shrugged. "Fine. Let's get started."

"Um, there's one little thing," Kat said. "Strict dress codes are enforced in these clubs."

"Dress codes?" they asked in unison.

"You mean like white-tie?" McClain asked with a frown.

"Um . . . not exactly."

The grin that Sven appeared to be fighting made Eve nervous.

"Come on." Kat rose, giving McClain a long once-over. "You're about Sven's size. And Eve, I'm sure I've got something you can wear."

Eve followed Kat from the room—unable to shake the feeling that she was like a lamb being led to the slaughter.

"No fucking way." Mac gave a nervous laugh and shook his head as he glanced from Sven to the bed, where the Swede had tossed several costume items and told him to take his pick.

"You want to get into Oracle? You dress the part."

The studded dog collar made Mac shiver. He hooked a finger under a piece of leather that looked like a masochist's version of an athletic cup. "What in the *hell* is this?"

"A codpiece."

Codpiece. Jesus. Now there was a word he'd never hoped to see in anything but historical literature. And never in a million years had he thought he'd be in the same room with one, let alone use it in a sentence or contemplate wearing it.

"You people are sick."

Sven grinned, despite the gravity of the situation. "It's the going thing."

"Yeah, if you're into sadomasochism."

"Or the pretense of. Although there are plenty of those kinds of nightspots around if it—how do you Americans say it—trips your trigger? With the exception of one area of the club, Oracle is just for fun. To see who can make the most outrageous statement."

Sven laughed again when he saw Mac's expression. "There's an upside," Sven suggested as he shrugged out of his shirt and slipped into a black chain and leather vest.

Mac gave him a look.

"Wait until you see what the women will be wearing."

Mac opened his mouth, considered the possibilities of Eve Garrett dressed as a dominatrix, and eyed the costumes on the bed. Well, fuck. The boys had taken a lot of abuse lately. Looked like they were going to take a little more.

Leather, Mac was soon to learn, did not breathe. Neither did the codpiece. As it turned out, that worked out just fine, because when he walked out of the bedroom looking like a cross between a punk vampire and a bad-dog biker and got a gander at Eve, he didn't think he was going to be taking any breaths any time soon anyway.

All he could do was stare.

"Not one word, McClain," Eve warned.

Not a problem. He couldn't have said anything if he'd been held at gunpoint.

Holy hell. The codpiece was the only thing keeping him from busting out of his pants. And the boys, once again, were suffering mightily.

Wet dreams didn't come any more X-rated than the woman standing before him in spiked ankle boots and black fishnet stockings that stopped midthigh, where lace and black leather garters took over in stark contrast against her ivory skin. The skirt—also leather and all of twelve inches from top to bottom—barely covered the good parts, leaving not only a provocative length of naked thigh but also a generous strip of bare hip and belly circled by a thin silver chain.

Lord help him, if that weren't bad enough, those incredible breasts of hers all but spilled over the top of a leather corset-type thing that was hooked together in front with studded silver buckles.

He contained a gut-clenching urge to drop to his knees and rip the corset open with his teeth.

Black leather and silver-ringed wrist cuffs matched the choker circling her neck. Her blue eyes were heavily rimmed in black. Her lips were painted bloodred. Her hair had been swept up in a sexy, messy *"I just climbed out of a bondage bed"* tangle on top of her head.

In her hand was a whip. At that moment, he'd have sold his soul to be her whipping boy.

"Dominate me, Trixie."

She shot him a droll look.

"Did I say that out loud?"

"Get a good look," she said, between clenched teeth, "then roll your tongue back into your mouth. We've got work to do."

Work. Right.

It was going to be a helluv an interesting night.

14

Eve had drawn lines her entire life, stood by her decisions, and didn't cross them. She wasn't a prude, but she sure as hell wasn't an exhibitionist. And never in a million millenniums had she seen herself playing the lead role in an S and M pay-per-view, with Tyler McClain as her leading man, no less.

Ward and June Cleaver they were not, she thought grumpily as she and McClain followed Kat and Sven out of the backseat of Kat's limo. Eve felt ridiculous. And exposed. Lord, was she exposed. It was amazing that so much leather could cover so little skin and no amount of tugging or shifting could rectify the situation.

Working forward through the line of similarly clad party-goers and those hopeful of admittance, Eve was not surprised to see Kat pull off the dominatrix look with aplomb. Her black leather short shorts and silver ring–studded halter top looked sexy and sophisticated. Her thigh-high black boots hugged her long legs like lotion. Sven, too, looked natural in the part—more so because of the striking contrast of his pale skin and hair to the black chain vest and low-riding leather pants.

And then there was McClain. He'd taken Eve's mind off her own life-threatening situation, that was for sure. It hurt to admit it, but her internal muscles had done a lot of involuntary clenching when he'd stood in the middle of Kat's living room dressed in a black leather vest, boots, and pants and something studded and silver that hugged his package and made her wonder if she had a dark side she hadn't known about.

In the next minute, he'd had her fighting a laugh with a surly scowl.

Dominate me, Trixie.

She shook her head and tried to steady herself with a deep breath—thought better of it when her C cup breasts just about popped out of the A cup bustier—and stuck close to Kat.

"They're with us, John," Kat informed a big, brawny bouncer type who was riding herd on the assembled crowd.

"Ask him if Tiffany's here," McClain said over Eve's shoulder as the bouncer motioned them to enter.

"Haven't seen her," John said stoically, "but I just came on duty, so I might have missed her."

"If she comes later, tell her I'm here and looking for her, OK?" Kat slipped him a hundred.

"Sure thing, Ms. Hofsteader." A wide grin split his face, revealing a gaping space between his front teeth. "You all have a great time now."

While a great time was not on the agenda, Eve couldn't help but be awed by what she saw when they entered the hallowed halls of Oracle, which was billed as one of the most cutting-edge nightclubs in the world. Kat had tried to prepare her for the utter size on the ride over.

"This used to be a church," Kat said above the din of conversation, music, and laughter.

Unbelievable. The entryway was cavernous, the lights alternately dim and vibrant. The sound system was state-of-the-art and filled the echoing chamber with metallic rock like white water boiling over boulders. Modern designs floated in framed rectangles throughout the existing space made up of stone walls and soaring Gothic arches. Hundreds, perhaps thousands, of people roamed the central hall dressed—or *undressed* in some cases—in variations of their leather and chain theme.

"There are five separate areas, all with different elements." Kat pointed to five individual arches above which the names of the elements were carved in stone.

" 'Seduction,' 'Fantasy,' 'Splendor,' 'Escape,' 'Forbidden,' " Eve read aloud.

McClain hung his hands on his hips. "How in the hell are we going to find her in here?"

"We'll split up, as we decided," Eve said decisively. They had talked about it on the limo ride. They all had cell phones and had programmed in one another's numbers. If anyone spotted Tiffany they'd all know within a few minutes and make contact with one another.

"Stay away from Forbidden."

Kat seconded Sven's warning with an adamant nod. "It's reserved for the hard core. Anyone who goes in is considered a player and fair game and up for anything. Bad things can happen in there. Very bad things.

"I'll take Escape," Kat volunteered after a pointed look at Eve and Mac. "Sven, you want Splendor?"

Sven nodded and after a round of "good lucks" and a smacking kiss, he and Kat took off.

"You sure you're up for this?" McClain asked Eve.

"I'm a big girl," she said, and immediately regretted it when his gaze strayed to her plumped-up breasts before crawling slowly back to her face. "You take Fantasy. I'll take Seduction."

"I don't like this," he grumbled as they faced off in the midst of the crowd.

"Noted. Now we're wasting time." She headed for the archway marked: Seduction.

Once Eve passed into Seduction, she entered a realm of ghostly mists and throbbing beats that pulsed all the way to her core. Pure enticement, the room lived up to its billing.

The immediate area was designed with a Moroccan flair and brought images of secret harems and Arabian nights to mind. As her eyes adjusted to the pale light, Eve realized there was a total of three separate rooms that made up Seduction— Intimacy, Night Dreams, and the third, Rhythm, which she had just entered.

Rhythm was a dance floor. Signs crafted of ever-changing colors of pastel neon indicated that Intimacy and Night Dreams were located one level above. Access appeared to be via two suspended Plexiglas staircases that wound sinuously upward, one on either side of the main entryway. Both disappeared in that strange, shimmering mist that permeated the huge room.

She decided to stay where she was and search the dance floor first. The room was cloaked in a shifting blue fog cut only by slow-moving strobes that glinted off silver studs, bare flesh, and dozens of suspended panels of black silk that swayed like sensual energy from the thirty-foot ceilings to the floor. The music was earthy and raw; the eerie light and floating silk panels painted the glut of bodies grinding to the beat with surreal and carnal beauty.

She drifted among the dancers, searching for Tiffany or even Reno or Gorman. At one point, someone grabbed her arm and without a word drew her into a threesome.

"Sorry. Not dancing tonight," she said with an apologetic smile that was summarily ignored.

She ended up moving involuntarily to the music when she was sandwiched between an exotic-looking Asian man wearing a black leather Speedo and a bandolier crisscrossing his chest and a thin blade of a woman in a braided thong and garter belt. Her small breasts were marginally covered in binding leather straps and black star pasties.

With a little careful maneuvering, Eve finally extricated herself. She hadn't gone ten yards, however, when she heard the distinctive sound of a snap clamping shut, followed by a gentle tug on her dog collar.

"I do so love fresh meat," a woman purred with a preda-
tory leer as she reeled in the leash she'd attached to Eve's
collar. "Why haven't I seen you here before, sugar? And
wandering around on your own? It's a little risky, but not to
worry, darling. I'll take *very* good care of you."

Eve forced a smile as the woman, barely wearing a silver-
studded black leather thong, chaps, and lots of chains, looked
her up and down. A two-inch band of leather circled her gi-
gantic breasts as she moved into Eve's space, blatantly brushing her breasts against Eve's arm.

Amazon was the first word that came to mind. *Domi-
nant* was the next and *bi* slipped in a very close third. She
was easily six feet tall; her severely cropped silver hair was
striped with two ink black wings at each temple. She could
have been anywhere from thirty to fifty. Hours with free
weights had defined the musculature of bulging biceps and
well-defined thighs oiled to glistening beneath the filtered
light.

"Actually, I was separated from my party," Eve said, hoping she'd get the message that girl on girl was not a part of
Eve's repertoire.

Silver incisors flashed a little too close for comfort as she
stroked the back of her hand over Eve's cheek. "Pity. Here I
was hoping you might be at loose ends."

When she ran a long, sharp nail painted midnight black
along Eve's jaw, then scraped it slowly down her throat, stopping between her breasts, Eve quelled a shiver of discomfort.

"Of course," the woman continued, slowly pulling her
hand away, "if your party truly missed you, they never would
have let you get this far away. Come with me, dear heart. I
make excellent company."

Very deliberately, Eve reached up and unhooked the
leash. "Thank you. But I really must find my friend. Tiffany
Clayborne? Do you know her?"

Her thwarted seducer made a moue of disappointment as
she tucked her leash into a belt riding low on her bare hips.

"Sorry, darling. I haven't seen her. You truly are exquisite. If you get bored, you can find me in Forbidden."

Eve's skin crawled as she watched the woman, hips sway- ing seductively, saunter away. She spent another half an hour on the dance floor—no one had seen Tiffany—before slowly climbing the winding stairway toward Intimacy. She ended up fielding five more offers of illicit sex before moving on.

In Night Dreams, she stumbled onto a couple having a very private party in a very public place. She was about to give up her search and check in with McClain when her cell phone rang. She ducked into an empty alcove so she could hear.

"I think I've found her." It was Kat.

"Where?" Eve gripped the cell tightly.

"Someone saw her going into Forbidden about half an hour ago. I'm heading there now."

"Call Sven. I'll call McClain. We'll go in together. Do not go in there by yourself, do you hear me? You wait for us."

"Tiffany may not have time to wait."

"Kat—"

"You call Sven," Kat interrupted. "I'm going after her." She disconnected.

"Damn it!" Eve punched in McCain's number as she hur- ried toward the nearest exit.

Her name had gotten them inside the club. Tiffany didn't mean anything to anybody. It was her *last* name, Clayborne, that counted.

She counted. She had to keep telling herself that. She was a real person. She wasn't a dumb slut. She wasn't a coke- head. It was Lance who made her take the drugs.

God, she was so wasted. She wasn't even sure where she was. Oh yeah. Oracle. Forbidden. Not good. Not good at all.

Music blasted from multiple speakers with the subtlety of a freight train; the leaden beat of a bass guitar pulsed through her head like a punctured vein pumping blood. She lay helplessly back on a bed of black silk cushions, brushed absently at the hands groping her breasts. Where was Lance? She was scared. She wanted to leave.

All around her, bodies moved, slid against hers like a knotted clew of snakes, sweaty and oily and smelling of incense and sex. And she wished she were numb instead of just stoned.

She felt a tongue slide across the inside of her thigh. She moaned, curled into a ball on her side, and thought she was going to be sick. Someone pushed her to her back again and held her there. All she could do was stare up at a ceiling filled with murals of depraved sex acts with animals, and blood and unfamiliar faces, hovering above her. She closed her eyes against the shimmer of lights and the disgusting things they were doing to her.

Someone started crying. She opened her eyes, felt the tears on her face, and realized it was her. The tears came in rivers, huge, wracking sobs that shook her body and made her cry harder.

"Stop it!"

Lance's face suddenly loomed above her.

She cried his name. Begged him to get her out of there.

"Shut the fuck up!" he snarled just before she felt the crack of his hand on her cheek. Even the pain was dull, but in the aftermath, her face stung. So did her soul.

Tears blurred her vision, but when she blinked and looked up again, she swore she saw Kat.

"Tiffany! Oh God, sweetie."

The woman dropped to her knees beside Tiffany, shoving the snakes away, gathering her close.

"Get away from her! Get away!"

Tiffany started crying again. It *was* Kat.

"It's OK, sweetie. I've got you now."

She reached out, looked into her friend's beautiful face full of compassion and anger and tears.

"Kat." It was really her. Tiffany clung to the slender arms

that held her. "Don't leave me. Please, please, please. Don't leave me."

"I'm not going to leave you. Sweetie, can you stand? Come on. We've got to get you up. Get you out of this viper pit."

Tiffany tried to focus. Tried to block out the music that pulsed stronger and louder. She struggled to her feet, but her knees buckled. Then Lance was there again and he was shouting at Kat and Kat was shouting at him and telling him to get away. To leave her alone.

"I said back off, bitch. She's with me."

"Not anymore she's not."

"Ask her," Lance demanded. "Ask her who she wants to be with. Tell her, Tiffany. I love you, remember, baby?" His voice dropped to an intimate purr that stroked and soothed and reminded her why she loved him.

But he didn't love her. He couldn't. He couldn't love her and bring her to Forbidden. Hurt her this way.

"I want to go," she managed, pressing her face against Kat's shoulder and clinging. "I want to go with Kat."

"No, no, babe. You want to go with me. Come on. Come with me. I love you, baby."

"She's not going with you. Now get out of my way before I call the cops."

"Fuck the cops," Lance sneered, and from the corner of her eye Tiffany could see Abe walk up beside him. "Help Tiffany say good-bye to her friend, Abe."

Kat's arms tightened around Tiffany as Abe started prying her away. She clung to Kat, but Abe was too strong. Pain shot through Tiffany's shoulder as he wrenched her violently away from Kat and shoved her into Lance's arms.

She sobbed and begged him to let her go.

"Bitch in heat!" Lance shouted above the music. "Bitch in fucking heat! Come and get some!" he yelled, and as he dragged her away, Tiffany was vaguely aware of a swarm of bodies converging on Kat.

"Noooo!" she screamed as Lance picked her up and carried her from the room. Over his shoulder, she watched in horror as leather-clad fetish freaks shoved Kat down on the pillows.

Tears stung Tiffany's eyes, blurred her vision, as they forcefully stretched Kat's arms and legs out and held her down, spread-eagled, as the first of the mob went down on his knees in front of her.

Mac had thought he'd seen it all. But nothing had prepared him for the press of flesh and decadent reality of Forbidden. He'd sprinted for the archway when Eve had called and yeah, he knew he should wait for the rest of them to show before going in, but Kat was in there on her own. So was Tiffany.

He pushed through the heavy wooden door painted with a mural of a satyr with a monster cock feasting on the bloody breast of an angelic naked maiden swooning in trance-induced ecstasy. Inside the dark interior of Forbidden was more of the same. Only a sober eye could discern between the life-size lifelike wall murals of men on women, men on men, women on women, engaging in lewd sex acts and the real thing going on on spotlighted pedestals to a chorus of "oohs" and "ahs" and appreciative applause.

Jesus. Talk about sick. He quickly scanned the room. He didn't spot Tiffany or Kat, but a crowd had gathered on the opposite side of the den. He headed in that direction. A woman's scream had him picking up the pace, then shoving bodies aside as gut instinct told him he needed to get to her. Fast.

He finally worked his way close enough to see Kat on the bottom of the pile.

"Get the hell off of her!" he roared, and grabbed a sick pervert, wearing only bleached yellow hair and a leather thong, by his shoulders and jerked him to his feet.

Pure adrenaline drove Mac as he fought off clutching

hands and sharp, biting nails. He didn't care what he hit—man, woman, or a confused parody of both. Outrage rolled over tact as he threw bodies aside. When he sensed someone behind him, he rounded on her, arm cocked, fist balled . . . and barely managed to draw back before cold-cocking Eve.

Sven tore into the fray right behind her.

"What took you so long?" Mac muttered, and made fast work of a burly biker type who hadn't taken kindly to losing his turn in the rape and pillage line.

Beside him, Sven head-butted the closest sicko stupid enough not to have ducked and run. Eve made quick work of the restraints holding Kat down, and Kat—whom he'd reached in the nick of time—pushed to her feet in a blind rage and jumped on the back of the blonde who had been about to sexually assault her.

With Sven otherwise engaged beating a big bruiser to a bloody pulp, Eve targeted one of the women—an Amazon with some major muscle groups—who had been in on the impending assault and hadn't yet gotten the message that party time was over.

Despite being outsized and outmuscled, the little M&M-loving blonde in ankle boots and bustier had some serious moves—along with a deadly mean streak. Lord above, was she a sight. While a part of Mac wanted to dive in and help her, the sane part realized she'd turn on him if he didn't let her dole out a little justice.

Besides, Eve didn't need his help. She was fast. And she was accurate. And, holy mother of God, she was about to do some permanent damage.

"Easy, Rambo." He caught her around the waist and hauled her off the woman.

"Hey, hey. Easy now. I'm one of the good guys," he protested when Eve kicked and squirmed in his arms, ready to fight to the death if necessary, as the woman took the opportunity to scramble on all fours toward the closest exit door.

"Sorry," Eve muttered when she finally realized it was him.

"Note to self." He set her back on her feet. "Never piss off the blonde."

She shoved a tumble of hair out of her face and adopted a combat stance, ready to take on the next comer.

Fortunately, it was all pretty much over but the heavy breathing. The bulk of the crowd had dispersed, the injured had slinked off to lick one another's wounds, and the four of them were left standing back-to-back in a circle, ready to fend off anyone looking for more action.

"Tiffany," Kat said, rubbing her wrists and catching her breath. "He took her. She was so scared. She wanted to go with me, but he took her."

When Mac asked what he looked like, Kat described Reno and added details on Gorman.

"Which way did they go?"

Kat shook her head. "I don't know. He sicced the pack on me and I couldn't see."

"Are you all right?" Sven squared off protectively in front of her, gently rubbed the circulation back into her wrists.

She nodded, but she looked a little shaky.

"You should not have come in here alone," Sven ground out, his eyes filled with rage and relief and fear.

Kat moved into him. She wrapped her arms around his waist as Sven's arms enfolded her. "Tiffany needed me. And I knew you'd get here."

"Too late to help Tiffany," Mac said, dragging a hand through his hair.

"I slipped her my cell phone."

All eyes turned to Kat.

"Managed to shove it down her skirt at the small of her back. If she sobers up enough before this Reno person finds it, she'll scan the phone book and realize it's mine. Maybe she'll have sense enough to hide it, then use it when she gets a chance."

"You may have missed your calling," Mac said, beyond

pleased that Tiffany had the means to contact Kat. "Good work."

"Better than good." Sven smiled at Kat with unconcealed pride. "Her phone is equipped with GPS."

"GPS?"

"A Global-Positioning System."

"I know what it is, but why in the hell would you have one?"

"Sven and I bought the system to keep track of each other—you never know about road conditions, late hours—and our schedules often find us in different parts of the world. We like to keep track."

"I think I love you," Mac said, and, with a grinning Sven looking on, kissed her full on the lips.

15

THEY CANVASSED THE CLUB BEFORE THEY left. No one they spoke with had seen Tiffany leave. No one remembered seeing anyone matching Reno's or Gorman's description.

"Amazes the hell out of me," Mac sputtered, "given that even among the weird and weirder the three of them were not the kind of characters anyone would soon forget."

"They closed ranks," Eve said beside him in the limo as they left Oracle and headed for Kat's condo.

"We didn't exactly make friends in there." Kat snuggled into Sven's arms in the seat across from them.

She was still a little shaken, but she was holding up. It was Sven who was having trouble keeping it together. "I could kill those bastards for touching you."

"I love it when you go all Terminator on me," Kat said, managing just what she'd wanted—to ease the tension— with her gushy delivery.

Sven heaved a heavy breath. "Just don't pull anything as foolish as that again." He rolled his eyes at Mac. "Look who I'm talking to."

"Tiffany's lucky to have such a loyal friend," Eve said, genuine respect for Kat in her voice.

"Here's to new friends." Kat looked Eve directly in the eye before shifting her gaze to Mac. "Thank you. Thank you both for caring about Tiffany. And for getting to me before it was too late."

If only it hadn't been too late for Tiffany.

Quiet settled over the four of them in the aftermath of the danger they'd been in. Kat leaned back when Sven pulled her into his arms again and kissed her long and deep.

Mac was about two conscious thoughts away from doing the same to Eve as the limo cruised through the New York night. And he might have taken the chance if he hadn't had such fresh, crisp memories of her course in Ball Busting 101 earlier in the evening at Time Squared.

He was horny—an adrenaline kick was always good for a blood rush to the groin—but he wasn't stupid. Still, she could use a little settling. Frankly, so could he. Oracle had been an intense experience, for lack of a better term. So yeah, she could use some settling, but since he couldn't guarantee that if he got his hands on her again he wouldn't take it past the settling stage, he kept them to himself.

In the meantime, though, just looking at his little Conanette had him so hot and bothered he was stretching leather and pulsing against that crotch-hugging codpiece like Jack's damn beanstalk trying to break ground.

Hell. He was only human. And damn, she was a sight. Her hair was a fine mess, her skin still flushed from the fight. Her pale breasts rose and fell above the skimpy black corset, all but popping out of the marginal bra cups. He swore he could see a hint of a dusky pink areola kissing the lip of leather.

Sweat broke out on his brow. OK. So now was not the time, this was not the place, to get bogged down in fantasies of stripping off bits of leather, then using his teeth to unhook her fishnet stockings from the garter belt.

But how much was a man supposed to take? Whatever stuff they'd had burning in the club clung to her wild mass of silver-gold hair just as the scent of sweat and forbidden sex dewed her skin. And he'd seen her sneaking looks at him when she thought he wasn't watching. He'd seen the heat in her eyes. So it was fueled by their brush with danger. That didn't make it any less real. And it didn't make him any less aware.

Adrenaline still hummed through his system like a conductor for a high-voltage power source. If he didn't miss his guess, Eve was fully charged, too. Between them they might not be able to light up the city, but there was more than enough energy to light up his life.

He clenched his jaw. And told himself that if he valued his life, he'd just back away from that little fantasy while the backing was still good.

"You doing OK?" he asked in a whisper so as not to disturb Sven and Kat, who had taken their kisses a little past the tender-mercy stage.

"F . . . fine," she said in an absent, throaty whisper.

From the seat across from them he heard a pleasured groan, couldn't help but notice that one of Kat's long legs was now draped across Sven's lap and the Swede's big hand was gently kneading the back of her thigh and riding higher and higher.

Mac managed a strangled croak just as he felt a small hand land lightly on the top of his thigh. Hot as a firebrand.

He snapped his gaze to Eve's face—only to see her gaze was riveted on the couple across from them. She wasn't even aware that she was touching him.

He was.

Gawd *damn* was he aware.

Just like he was aware that the air in the back of the limo was currently dosed with enough testosterone to fill a pro football locker room on game day. The estrogen level was spiking off the charts, too.

Slender fingers loosely clenched his thigh, then dug in deep, like cat claws, and his leg was her own personal scratching post. And the leather pressure factor became almost unbearable. He looked from her face to her hand and damn near busted a vein when she pressed the heel of her palm into muscle and drove toward bone.

Mother.

When she did it again, then again, setting a rhythm so closely matching the one he'd imagined setting as he pumped into her, he swallowed back a groan and calculated the likelihood of him getting out of his pants before he exploded.

And when he slowly dragged his gaze up, past her amazing breasts, along the length of her slender throat to her perfect profile, he mouthed another silent plea for help. Her attention was rapt on Kat and Sven as she caught her full lower lip between her teeth and drew a breath that was deep and thready and blatantly erotic.

Her grip on his thigh was sensuous and so completely unconscious, there was no way in hell she was aware of what she was doing.

Watching them.

Touching him.

Driving him out of his ever-loving mind.

On a serrated breath he covered her hand with his. Waited, heart pounding, for her to come to her senses and shove it away. When she only gripped his leg tighter, he lost it. He pressed his hand against the back of hers and nudged it higher. And higher. Higher still until, *sweet torture,* her pinkie brushed against his codpiece.

He jerked so hard at the instant and violent pleasure, she jumped, whipped her gaze his way, and blinked like she'd just come out of a trance.

When she realized where her hand was, she snatched it away, turned a luscious shade of hot pink, and averted her gaze to the window.

Mac sat there. Rigid as steel. His cock twitching, his balls tingling, as every drop of blood in his body pooled to his groin and screamed for action.

He felt like doing a little screaming, too.

Thank God the limo pulled to a stop about that time. He ran an unsteady hand across his lower face and tried to regulate his breathing. He almost had a handle on it when the door opened and he was treated to the view of Eve Garrett's premium ass pointed directly his way as she scrambled to get out of the limo.

Covering his face with both hands, he squeezed his eyes shut and committed the sight to memory.

"You coming, Mac?" he heard Sven ask several moments later.

He opened his eyes, realized he was the last man sitting, and with great difficulty managed to exit the car.

"Get me out of these fucking pants," he growled.

Sven grinned and slapped him on the back. "Just as soon as I figure out a way to get out of mine."

Kat poured orange juice into goblets while Sven set platters of food on an elegant glass and chrome dining table positioned near a bank of floor-to-ceiling windows that framed an incredible view of the 4:00 a.m. lights glistening in the city.

"Sit. Eat," Kat offered graciously. "After what we've been through, we need to refuel. And Sven makes the best breakfast on any continent."

Eve sat down opposite McClain and tried to avoid eye contact. Anything to keep her mind off what had happened in the limo. Anything to settle the irrational beat of her heart and the hot, pulsing ache settled low in her belly.

And then there was the voice mail that she'd picked up a few minutes ago. She made it a habit to check her home voice mail when she was out on assignment, but this was the first chance she'd had to do it.

Next time there might not be someone to save you. Or next time it might be someone else's blood on your hands. Will you figure it out in time to stop the bleeding?

She tried not to think about the message now. McClain made it fairly easy. He'd taken his turn in Kat's guest bathroom after Eve had. They'd both showered off the stench of the episode at Forbidden. Like hers, McClain's hair was still wet; like her, he'd changed back into his street clothes. He smelled healthy and clean and male. And she was having a heck of a time not picturing him naked and wet under the shower spray.

All four of them, in fact, had cleaned up before reassembling in the dining room. Judging from the rosy flush painting Kat's cheeks and from Sven's loose-limbed ease and intimate smile, however, the two of them had also taken the time to find a mutually satisfying way to tone down the edgy tension that had followed them out of Oracle.

Lucky them.

Horny her.

Chemistry. Who needed it? Who needed the trouble you had to deal with in the aftermath? And sex with McClain—no matter how hot the prospect—would lead to nothing but trouble.

Sex with McClain. God. It had come to that. She was actually considering going to bed with him. If for no other reason than to dull this edge of painfully acute arousal.

Aftermath, she reminded herself, shoving her fork around on a plate heaped with sausage and eggs and toast. *Remember the aftermath.* But the problem was, the human condition dealt with *aftermath* the same way it dealt with pain. There was a tendency to forget about pain once it passed, just like there was a tendency to forget about dealing with the aftermath when the present was so vital and all-consuming.

And she *was* consumed with McClain. It was a tough pill to swallow, but ever since that kiss in Time Squared and their encounter in the backseat of the limo, she hadn't been able to get her mind off of him. Was alive with thoughts of him.

She should be exhausted. She'd started out yesterday at

6:00 a.m. in Key West, driven back to West Palm, then flown to New York. Since then, she'd experienced a host of fun-filled adventures, and now, at 4:00 a.m.—twenty-two hours later—she was still awake. And she was wired for sound.

It was McClain's fault that she could still taste that kiss. Could still see him decked out in black leather, tearing into the pack of ghouls who'd been about to do any number of despicable things to Kat. She'd been pretty intent on getting to Kat herself, but that hadn't kept Eve from appreciating the spectacle of Tyler McClain in full battle mode. Those creeps hadn't stood a chance. He'd been a machine, running on sleek, pumped muscle and sheer, raw guts.

At that moment, he wouldn't have cared if the odds had been a hundred to one. He'd have taken them all on. And he'd have bested them. His outrage had been primal. He'd been fearless, focused, and nothing short of death would have stopped him. She'd seen the same heroic qualities in her brothers. Admired them for it. Generally, they were her biggest pains in the ass, but always, *always,* they were her heroes.

While she hadn't wanted to recognize those traits in McClain, the episode at Oracle had forced her to. He was cut from the same bolt of cloth as her brothers and her father. What he'd done—going after Kat alone—had smacked of courage and honor. And heroism.

And it royally ticked her off.

She didn't want to see him as anything but what she'd long ago decided he was. Immature. Self-absorbed. Self-serving.

But too many times in the last two days he'd shown her another side. A heroic side that made it difficult to tuck him way high up on that shelf where she stowed the rest of the triple-A's who'd screwed with her life.

That he was a warrior had always been apparent. It was in his DNA. That he was principled hadn't been. Now it was. Now he was about finding Tiffany because she was in trouble. It wasn't about the job or the money for him anymore.

And it had been with a noble rage that he'd saved Kat—not just bloodlust or the love of a fight.

Eve had no doubt that if he knew about the attempts on her life, he'd go into battle mode for her.

Crap. She didn't want that.

And he had a little girl who tugged at his heart, a heart Eve hadn't wanted to believe existed.

Double crap. What if her problems ended up getting Mc-Clain hurt? Then what would happen to his little girl?

"It's not good?"

Startled out of her thoughts, she looked up into Sven's frowning eyes.

"I'm sorry. What?"

"Your omelet? It's not good? You're not eating."

"Oh. Sorry. I guess I'm just preoccupied."

"With Tiffany," Kat put in.

Close enough. "Yeah. With Tiffany." She cut a glance at McClain, saw that he was watching her with both question and heat in his eyes, and felt her cheeks flush pink before getting a grip.

Actually, in between lusting over this new and troubling version of McClain and trying to deal with her reactions toward him, she *had* been thinking about Tiffany. She'd been thinking about her a lot. More so because of the threats to her own life than in spite of them.

She sat back in her chair. "Tell me about your GPS. What kind of range are we talking about?"

"Nationwide," Sven provided as he rocked back in his chair, reached behind him, and grabbed something that looked like a cell phone off the kitchen counter. "This is the tracking unit."

He handed it to Eve, who looked it over, then gave it to McClain to inspect.

"The only problem is, she has to have the cell phone turned on for us to get a fix on her location."

"It was off when I shoved it in her skirt," Kat said. "I didn't think. Didn't have time, really, to turn it on."

"Actually, that may be for the best," McClain said, familiarizing himself with the unit, messing with the settings. "I'm assuming several people have your cell number?"

Kat nodded when he glanced at her.

"Then having it on now would defeat the purpose if Tiffany is to have any advantage. That sucker would start ringing; it'd surprise her and alert Reno that she's got it. With it off and with a little luck, she'll realize what you've given her before Reno does. She can pick her time to call you."

Kat nodded again. "I hadn't thought of that."

"Does she know the phone has GPS capabilities?"

Kat frowned, her beautiful face pinched in thought. "I can't think of any reason why she would. We just got the unit recently and I don't remember telling her about it. Truly, it's been months since I've seen her. When we did talk on the phone, it was only briefly."

"OK," McClain said, drawing the word out thoughtfully. "It might work to our advantage that she's unaware of the GPS as well."

"How so?"

"For starters, it might spook her if she thinks she's being tracked. It's hard telling what frame of mind she'll be in even if she sobers up. And if Reno goes on the move again and Tiffany does manage to call you, all you need to do is keep her on the line long enough to get a fix on her location."

"And notify you," Sven concluded.

"Right. Eve and I can take it from there."

"But she doesn't know you," Kat said, looking at Mac with concern. "And she's angry with you," she said with a sad look at Eve. "She trusts me. I want to be with you when you find her."

"Why don't we just take a wait-and-see approach at this point?" Eve suggested. "We don't even know that she'll call.

Or who she'll call. Kat, are your home phone and Sven's cell programmed into your cell's phone book?"

"They are, yes."

"OK. On the chance she does call, remember to keep her in the dark on the GPS. Mac's probably right. If she finds out she's being tracked, she could go paranoid on us. Especially if she's strung out."

Kat looked sad at the prospect.

"Just let one of us know when you hear from her," Eve said gently. "She may even be able to give you a location. If not, the GPS will nail it for us and we'll move in."

"Provided they don't move again before we get to her," McClain said, voicing exactly what Eve had been thinking.

She nodded. "Yeah. Provided they don't move. Again, we'll adjust as necessary."

"Shouldn't we call the police?"

"We can call them," Eve agreed, responding to Sven's question, "but I don't see them acting."

"Not acting? This Reno creep kidnapped her!" Kat insisted.

"Says us," McClain pointed out. "Look, even if they somehow manage to catch up with Reno and Gorman, I can tell you right now, Tiffany will back up everything Reno says."

"But—"

"He's right," Eve broke in. "Reno will coerce her. He'll threaten her, manipulate her—he's a pro at it. And trust me, she'll deny that she's with him against her will. From everything I know about Tiff, I figure she's in a very bad place emotionally right now. She won't have the strength to stand up to him."

"Then what do we do?"

"*You* do nothing but wait for a call and keep the GPS on for now," McClain said. He looked weary but stern as he leaned back in his chair. "Reno proved tonight that he's capable of violence when he sicced that mob on you. You need to let us take it from here."

Kat exchanged glances with Sven. He nodded. She let out a tired breath. "And what will you do?"

"Until we hear something, we'll keep looking. Chances are slim that Reno will take her out in public again any time soon knowing someone's looking for her, but we'll try just the same. And as far as he knows now, it's just you who's aware she's in the city," he added, nodding at Kat. "They couldn't have made Eve or me, so on the off chance they stick around here, we could get lucky and spot them. Odds are, however, they'll lay low for a day or two, catch up on their sleep. They've got to be as whipped as we are. Regardless, I'm thinking Reno will have them on a plane out of here as soon as he gets a chance to regroup."

And that was the last thing any of them wanted to happen.

16

"WHAT'S RENO'S GAME, ANYWAY?" KAT asked after they'd finished eating and she and Sven were clearing the dishes. "What does he want from Tiffany?"

"Best guess?" McClain shrugged and pushed back from the table. He leaned back in his chair. "He figures he's found the golden goose. As long as he has Tiffany, he's got the means to live high, score big, and have himself one hell of a party. He's milking her for all she's worth."

He glanced toward Eve for confirmation. "What?" he asked, evidently seeing reservation in her eyes.

Eve shook her head. "I don't know. I've got nothing concrete. Just this gut feeling that there's more to all of this than meets the eye."

"Like?" Kat asked, returning to the table with the coffeepot.

Eve waved off her offer of coffee. She was already too wired. A hit of caffeine would send her into orbit. McClain also declined.

"I've never liked it that Clayborne didn't use his own people to find Tiffany," she said, still wrestling with that issue. "He's got a full security team. And his—rather, *Edwards's*—claim that the in-house staff was too close to the situation just doesn't ring true."

"What are you suggesting?" Kat settled on Sven's lap when he held out a hand for her.

Their easy intimacy had Eve looking away—and connecting with McClain's dark gaze again. Her heart did that damn double trip, it was wont to do when he looked at her that way. Like he knew what she was thinking and he was totally on board with the idea.

"I don't know." Eve averted her gaze back to Kat. "I don't know what I'm suggesting. I just know the situation has made me uneasy from the onset."

Kat looked at McClain. "Mac?"

He shrugged and thankfully turned his attention to Kat. "I didn't give it much credence at first, but now I have to agree with Eve. Something's off here. Very possibly, we won't know what it is until we catch up with Tiffany. And that's not going to happen anymore tonight," he added.

He rose, made one of those sinewy male all-over body stretches and sent her heart on a slow dive to her stomach. "I don't know about you all, but I'm whipped. I've got to recharge. Maybe this will look a little less muddy after a few hours of sleep."

"He's right," Eve said, standing, and when she did, she felt herself hit the wall. She was suddenly exhausted. "I've been up for almost twenty-four hours straight."

"You'll stay here," Kat insisted.

Mac shook his head. "I've got a room."

"Me, too," Eve said.

When Kat asked where they were staying, she shook her head. "It will take forever to catch a cab at this hour. I'd send you in the limo, but I don't want to wake Thomas. Please. I insist. You can return to your hotels to change after you've gotten some rest. Tonight, you're staying here. The extra bedroom's yours."

Mac glanced at Eve. "I'll take the couch," he said after a long moment, his gaze locked on her face.

She was too surprised by his offer and too tired to argue. "Thanks," she said instead, with a look that encompassed both McClain and Kat.

"No thanks necessary. It's the least I can do for what you're doing for Tiffany. I'll get you a sheet and some pillows, Mac. Sven will get you some boxers to sleep in."

"Please, God," McClain said, "tell me they aren't leather."

"Silk," Sven said with a grin. "Almost as good."

"Eve, I'll find a gown for you." Kat smiled and she and Sven disappeared down the hall, leaving Eve alone with McClain.

And an unexpected and awkward silence.

"You were something tonight, *Trixie,*" he said, finally walking around the table to stand directly in front of her.

"Yeah, well." She jerked a shoulder, reluctant to be pleased by his compliment, even more reluctant to realize she wanted to smile at his warped sense of humor. "You weren't so bad yourself."

He grinned, crooked and lazy. Amusement and intimacy danced in his eyes. "What have we come to? We're actually being nice to each other. Again."

She lifted a brow. "Must be sleep deprivation. Or something."

"Or something," he agreed, still watching her.

"For the record?" He moved in closer, ran his fingers down the length of her arms, gripped her hands in his. "I'm glad you're on my team."

"Just so you remember I'm the captain."

He tipped his head to the ceiling, exhaled with a heavy dose of Lord-save-me-from-this-woman, then looked back at her. "Wouldn't have it any other way."

Because she was far too aware of his nearness, far too absorbed in the slumberous brown of his eyes, far too tempted to lift her hand, explore the heat and strength of his jaw and the shadowed twenty-four-hour growth of his beard, she averted her gaze to their joined hands.

His hands were large and scarred and dark compared to hers, which were slighter, paler, unmarked. The contrast was an erotic showcase of their differences. Small, large. Pale, dark. Female, male. Very, very male. He ran his thumb over the backs of her knuckles and every nerve in her body stood at attention.

"We need to do something about this, you know?"

His voice was husky, low, and she had no doubt what *this* he was talking about. The sexual tension between them had been building to volcanic levels despite her resistance and her determination to deny it. Her awareness of her own sexuality and of the fact that she liked sex—OK, she *loved* sex—and that it had been a very, very long time since she'd trusted a man enough to engage in a physical relationship was palpable.

Trust. Now there was a word she hadn't anticipated using in a thought involving McClain. And yet, she realized, she did trust him. Go figure.

She swallowed, looked anywhere but at him. Until he curled an index finger under her chin and tipped her head to his.

"Nothing to say about that?"

She saw a devastating combination of hunger and patience in his eyes. And almost—almost—rose to her toes to meet his sensual, mobile mouth with hers. Instead, she managed to slowly shake her head.

"OK," he said, searching her face, all the while sliding his hand from her chin to her jaw, then tunneling his fingers beneath the damp hair at her nape. "Then you just think about it for a while. I'll be thinking, too. About how great it would be between us."

Then he did the damnedest thing. He leaned forward and pressed the gentlest of kisses on her forehead.

Like he was blessing her or something. Or tormenting her when what she was ready for was the taste of his lips, the sleek glide of his tongue in her mouth.

"Just so there's no misunderstanding, though, the next move's yours, cupcake."

And then he shoved his hands deep into his trouser pockets

and walked to the bank of windows looking out over the sleeping city.

She didn't have a chance to analyze the glut of emotions roiling through her blood and setting her fingers tingling. Or decide if she felt more relief or disappointment that he'd backed away.

OK. She felt more disappointment. But really, who could blame him for turning the reins over to her? Last time he'd made a move, she'd put a hurt on him and his precious goods.

His fault for taking her off guard, she thought, mustering a little piety. He'd moved in way before she was ready to admit she wanted him to. And yeah, she'd reacted in the extreme—something she felt guilty about now. Just like she was thinking about another kind of extreme reaction. Like inviting him to join her in Kat Hofsteader's guest bedroom and asking him to remind her with a hands-on demo just how good sex could be when the chemistry sizzled.

Chemistry. There was that word again. As long as she remembered that was all they had going for them, they'd avoid complications. McClain hadn't triggered memories and resurrected dreams of happily ever after. At eighteen, yeah, she could be excused for blubbering around in such nonsense. She was older now. Wiser. Capable of enjoying a hot physical relationship with a hot physical man and not losing her heart in the process.

Kat returned about then with bedding for McClain and an ivory nightgown for Eve and they all said their good nights.

As exhausted as she was, Eve lay awake, however, staring at the ceiling for way too long thinking about what McClain had said.

Next move's yours, cupcake.

Good. Fine. She'd make the next move, damn him. When she was good and ready. *If* she ever was.

Her mind flashed on the memory of a long-ago night in a moonlight-drenched cabana.

"Oh God, am I ready," she muttered, punching the pillow. She rolled over on her stomach, wished for chocolate, and prayed for sleep.

"You did?" Mac sat on Kat Hofsteader's sofa at eleven that same morning, marginally rested from a few hours' sleep and grinning into his cell phone as Ali regaled him with details of a play date with a new friend named Brittany, who had a puppy.

He leaned forward, propped an elbow on his knee, his heart clenching with missing her. "It sounds great, pumpkin."

He could see his baby girl, brushing her straight, silky, fine hair from her eyes because she refused to let anyone pull it back in a ponytail. Her hair was the same color as his, milk chocolate brown. She had his eyes, too. And, praise kismet, a disposition so sweet it was hard to believe she was her mother's daughter.

That wasn't entirely fair. Angie hadn't always been a bitch. Between his job and the dark moods it sometimes gave him, he'd given her plenty of cause to hone the bitch factor to perfection.

Speaking of perfection, he glanced up when he heard movement on the plush ivory carpet and saw Eve enter the living room, heading for the kitchen.

She cut him a glance as he asked Ali what she was going to do today.

"We're going to go to the beach," she answered with excitement. "Me and Mom and Blair."

Blair. Mac wanted to hate the bastard. Not because Angie had cheated on him with the guy. Not even because he'd married Angie. Whatever love she and Mac had shared had died long before their marriage had ended. He wanted to hate Blair because he was there, 24-7, taking Mac's place, watching his baby grow.

Something dark and bleak washed over him and he was

hardly aware of the rest of their conversation until it was time to say good-bye.

"Love you more," he said, to which she replied, "Love you most."

"Love you best." It was a game they played. Part fun. Part pain.

"Love you bestest," she said in that angelic voice that broke his heart to hear, broke his soul not to.

"Bye, baby. You call me anytime. Anytime," he repeated, because it was all he could give her. It was all he could say.

He stared at his cell for a long time after they disconnected. Gave in to the sense of loss and resentment that threatened to suck him in every time he thought of Ali so far away.

He wasn't aware that Eve had walked up beside him until she shoved a mug of coffee under his nose. He looked up, saw the naked compassion in her eyes, and had to steel himself against the urge to draw her to him and bury his face against all that woman softness and just hold on.

She'd let him. At this moment, with her eyes brimming with concern, she'd let him wallow, let him be weak.

And that was the last thing he could afford to be. The last way he wanted her to see him.

He worked up a nasty sneer. "Do I sense the possibility of a pity fuck in the wind?"

Her face went pale in the moment it took her to believe he'd actually said what he'd just said. It took a moment more for her features to harden. And for him to feel like the ass he was.

Fuck.

He propped both elbows on his knees. Dragged his hands over his face. "OK. Can we just pretend I didn't say that?"

She considered him with an unreadable expression, then set the mug on the coffee table in front of him. "You want to talk about it?"

Did he want to talk about a hole in his heart the size of a judge's gavel that gave primary custody to his ex-wife and in effect took his child away from him? "About as much as I'd like my balls in a vise. Again," he added, sucking it up and prying a small smile out of her. "Can we just pretend I didn't *do* that?" He let out a breath that smacked of relief. Because it was. It was important to him that she let him off the hook. They may not be even, but what she'd just offered him was close.

Little Eve Garrett had grown into a generous woman. An amazing woman. Something he'd had a tendency to overlook while he'd been so busy appreciating the package she came wrapped in.

"So, what's on the agenda?" she asked, taking his cue and changing the subject. She filled a mug for herself, then settled into a side chair.

He sent her a silent look of thanks that she hadn't pressed him to talk about Ali. She acknowledged it with an equally silent nod.

"I need to get back to my hotel and check my laptop. Chances are they've made another withdrawal from Tiffany's account. It might give us a fix on their location."

"You're monitoring her account?"

He nodded, expecting a lecture about ethics and the fact that there were laws against that sort of thing. Instead, she let it go. Another point for her.

"I hate to walk out without talking to Kat and Sven, but they might not surface until later this afternoon." He checked his watch. "Hell. We've already slept the morning away."

"I'll leave them a note. They'll call if there's any word from Tiffany." On the move again, she rose, taking a deep sip from her mug. "Special blend," she said with appreciation. "Good."

Yeah. Good. Good coffee. Good woman.

Good God. How was he going to keep his hands off of her until she made a move?

If she made a move.

In light of the fact that she hadn't ripped his head off and shoved it firmly up his ass after that pity-fuck remark, he was cautiously optimistic. But then, he also bought a lottery ticket every week.

17

Eve was still trying to get her pins under her again an hour later as she and McClain walked down the hall toward her hotel room. She didn't think she'd ever seen eyes as bleak as his when he hung up from talking with his daughter. She'd seen much more than pain. Frustrated anger. Helplessness. Defeat.

But most of all, she'd seen bone-deep sorrow.

It had shaken her. Almost as much as his crude suggestion.

Pity fuck.

God. As usual, he'd reacted to his own pain with classic alpha male pride. Don't let 'em see you sweat. Don't let 'em see you bleed—no matter that the anguish he'd felt had been the equivalent of a bloodletting. The man was an emotional cripple. He wasn't capable of an honest evaluation of his feelings.

Or maybe he was just human.

She dug her key card out of her purse, wishing she could be angry with him, but it seemed to be par for the course. Her brothers would react the same way. What was it with the men in her life that would not let them admit to being human? Why was their typical reaction to pain to shut down? She'd seen it happen with Nolan until Jillian came into his life and rescued him. She'd seen it happen with Ethan after his divorce from Darcy. He'd never pulled out of it. No one had shown up to save him.

Well, she wasn't saving McClain. She had enough trouble saving herself.

Suddenly very weary, she inserted the plastic key card in the door and let them both inside her hotel room. She should tell him about the other attacks. But she just couldn't make herself.

"Have a seat," she said instead. "I need to change and do something with my hair. Then we'll move on to your hotel and get to work."

And she needed a little space from McClain. She pulled underwear, jeans, and a short-sleeve red cotton sweater out of the suitcase that lay open on her bed.

"Take your time."

He dropped into a chair. Legs splayed. Eyes closed. Weary.

The look of him plunged her a little deeper into concern.

At least physically he wasn't hurting quite as much as he had been. He was hardly limping at this point, so his leg must be better. The swelling around his eye was pretty much gone, but there were some interesting shades of purple and blue rimming it. His lip appeared to be well into the healing stage, too.

And why was she looking at his lips? she blasted herself as she shut the bathroom door behind her.

Because she wanted him to kiss her again. *That's* why. This wasn't about compassion and rescue. This was about sex.

She leaned back against the door, her entire body trembling.

That kiss in Time Squared had been full of heat and hunger and a sheer animal urgency that had sucked her in before she'd come to her senses and ended it.

Just thinking about it made her face burn hot, her fingers tingle—along with a few other body parts that were going to require another change of underwear if she didn't snap out of it.

What was it about him that riled her up this way? He was just a man. Granted, he was much more than an everyday average Joe. He was bigger, harder, colder. Yeah. He was one tough SOB.

And she'd just seen him at his most vulnerable.

She closed her eyes, groaned, and pounded her head softly against the door.

"You've walked that road before," she reminded herself as she thought about the two of them tangled, bare limb to bare limb, on the bed. "You know exactly what lies at the end of it."

At the core, he was still the same man who had left her. He still owned the triple-A factor.

Yet she kept seeing his face when he'd talked to his little girl. And emotions she didn't want to feel tunneled under her skin and burrowed deep.

That didn't mean they had to be a part of this equation.

She was sexually frustrated, that's all. All that action at Oracle—granted it was on the sick side—was erotic. Erotic, after all, was erotic. And seeing Sven and Kat afterward, all rosy in the bloom of great sex, well, it had all combined to remind Eve that she had a healthy sex drive.

So there, in truth, was the bottom line. She wanted to make love to McClain. They had a physical thing that just wouldn't go away. If she were being honest, the ache had started long before last night and hadn't let up.

Involuntarily she lifted her arm to her nose, sniffed. She imagined she could still smell his scent on her skin where she'd bumped against him getting out of the cab that had delivered them to the hotel. Masculine, evocative, as sensual as silk sheets and a midnight sky. She shivered, tried to shake off the image. Couldn't.

Just like she couldn't shake off the impact of the tractor beam brilliance of his steady brown eyes. Or the dark, dangerous look of the stubble on his jaw he hadn't yet had time to shave. She flashed on the memory of him hauling her against him in Forbidden, her hip pressing against his when he'd captured her close.

She'd never felt so . . . so alive sexually. So supercharged and edgy. So pushed to the limit and in need of release that her entire body hummed with it.

And that's what this was about, right?

"Right?" she challenged her conclusion again aloud, grabbed her brush, and worked it through her hair. It was about release.

It wasn't about that aching vulnerability she'd seen in McClain less than an hour ago. Wasn't about the fact that he appeared to have evolved into more than a hormone on the make. This was about her own sexual frustration.

She was human. She had needs. And the means to satisfy them was just outside the door. Was it really such a big deal to use him to let off a little steam? She glared at her reflection in the mirror—and told herself she saw a wise woman, not a dewy-eyed, starstruck girl mistaking sex for love.

To prove it, she jerked open the bathroom door and marched straight to the bed.

Startled, McClain looked up, suddenly alert. "Forget something?"

Yeah, her better judgment.

She folded up her suitcase, set it on the floor, and threw back the covers.

Behind her, she could hear rustling sounds as McClain straightened up in the chair. "Um . . . what are you doing?"

"What does it look like I'm doing?" She turned toward him, started to work the buttons on her blouse. "I'm making the next move."

This statement was met with dead silence as his gaze followed the action of her fingers, then crawled back to her face. "I . . . umm. Huh?"

Her fingers stilled. And she felt a surge of power at his perplexed and hopeful expression. "Is there a problem?"

"I don't know," he said with the caution of a man about to enter a tiger cage with raw meat and a flyswatter. "Is there?"

"Only if you don't get out of your clothes and come over here."

His brows knit together. He shook his head. "You've got a real romantic streak there, don't you, cupcake?"

Damn him. She wished it wasn't so easy for him to make her smile.

"You want romance or sex?" She shrugged her blouse off her shoulders, undid the zipper on her slacks, swept them down her legs, and kicked them across the room.

When she met his eyes, she managed a steady breath, but an entire herd of wild horses trampled through her stomach as she stood before him in nothing but her sheer panties and bra.

He unfolded from the chair in slow motion, then walked toward her.

"Jesus, you're beautiful."

She steeled herself to keep from melting at the tenderness in his voice, in his eyes. "In case you hadn't noticed, I'm a sure thing here, McClain. You don't have to resort to flattery to get me into bed."

His expression went from soft to hard in a pulse beat. "All right. That's it." He grabbed her shirt from the floor, and tossed it at her.

She was too stunned to do anything but catch it against her breasts.

"I don't know what bug crawled up your ass, but this just isn't working for me."

The blood rushing through her ears was so loud she could barely hear herself think. She was as confused as hell. She knew darn well he wanted the same thing she did.

Desperate times, desperate measures moment.

"Does this work for you?" She threw the blouse at him, reached behind her back, and unhooked her bra.

When she drew the straps down her arms and tossed the cream-colored lace at him, too, his eyes glazed over.

"Yeah." He swallowed, his expression stalled somewhere

between helplessness and self-disgust when he threw her bra and blouse on the floor and reached for her. "It works. But when we get this out of our system, we're gonna talk."

He pushed her to her back on the bed and followed her down, stretching out full-length on top of her. "And for the record, I'm not just some cheap piece you can—"

"McClain," she said, laughing as she reversed their positions. She shoved him onto his back and straddled him. "Would you just shut up and kiss me?"

He fisted his hands in her hair and drew her mouth to his. "Well, if you're gonna get all bitchy about it."

Mac couldn't catch his breath. Couldn't catalog all the flavors and textures and the multiple levels of need Eve conjured as she moved over him. Her mouth devoured his even as she dragged his shirt out of his pants and whipped it over his head.

It was like being caught up in a storm, he thought when she went to work on his belt. All snap and crackle and raw, untamed energy. This was no meek kitten accosting him. This was a wildcat with claws and teeth. She growled in frustration against his mouth as her frantic fingers fumbled between them with the buckle.

"Dammit." She wrenched herself up so she was sitting astride his very happy lap. With an annoyed sweep of her hand, she raked the hair out of her eyes, then attacked the buckle again.

The sight of her consumed him. Her face was flushed with arousal and greed. Her eyes glittered; her lips were already swollen from kissing him. Her hair fell in a wild, silken tangle around her face. Good God Almighty. He'd dreamed about seeing her this way. Her breasts naked and pink and hovering above his mouth. Her hands all over him.

He reached for her, but she batted his hand away.

"Help me." She sank back on her heels in defeat.

Considering the fact that she had him so flaming hot his

fingers didn't want to work, he made surprisingly quick work of the buckle. "You got a bus to catch or something?"

"Or something." She unsnapped and unzipped his pants, then urged his hips up off the mattress so she could drag the pants and his shorts down his thighs. She fished around in his hip pocket for his wallet, then tossed it on his chest while he toed off his shoes and socks and kicked his pants the rest of the way down his legs.

While he fumbled around in his wallet, she shimmied out of her panties, then straddled his lap again, settling over him, her warm, damp heat and constant motion driving him out of his ever-loving mind.

"There'd better be a condom in there."

"I may not have been a Boy Scout," he finally found what he was looking for, ripped a foil packet off a three-pack, then tossed the rest aside, "but I'm always prepared."

She ripped open the packet with her teeth, then did the honors herself.

Mother of God.

If Mac hadn't already been flat on his back, her thorough dressing would have put him there.

He sucked in a harsh breath when she touched him again. Damn near passed out when she got to her knees over him, took him into her busy, busy hands, and guided him home.

Searing pleasure. Consuming heat. He groaned, arched, and, gripping her hips in his hands, eased her onto him until he was buried to the hilt. Then he held on for the ride of his life.

Over and over she took him into her hot, pulsing center. Over and over she moved above him with wild, reckless energy. Over and over she destroyed him with blinding sensation that stalled his breath, scrambled his mind, and drove him to the edge of sanity and back again.

She set the pace. And it was wild. She set the mood. And it was carnal. He swore her name as he rose to meet her, to drive himself deeper, fill her more fully, squeeze out every thready sound she made, milk every drop of pleasure.

She was constant motion, her breasts swaying, her fingers kneading, her slender hips rocking to a rhythm that pleased her, decimated him, and had him digging deep for the strength to hold off.

He swore her name through clenched teeth and dug his fingers into her hips, stilling her long enough to catch his breath, for the haze to lift from his eyes.

"Don't stop," she begged, then lost her breath on a *whoosh* when he reared up and flipped her onto her back beneath him without ever leaving the gloving heat of her body.

Her protest slid into a, "Yes, oh God, yessss," that eddied out on an extended moan when he hooked an arm beneath her knee, pressed it into her chest, and, levering his weight on his good knee, pounded into her.

Hot, wet friction. Shattering need. He lost himself in the maze of it, buried himself in the drugging greed where all he could think of was . . . more. He needed more of everything she gave him and he needed it now. Needed it like he needed to breathe, needed it like he needed water. He fed the need with every shuddering moan that escaped her, feasted on the give-and-take of her body until he couldn't absorb any more.

Release boiled up inside him, thick and heavy and rich. With a fractured groan, he buried his face in her shoulder. And when her inner muscles clenched and she came with a scream that faded to a low, keening whimper, he drove into her like a freight train, then derailed on an explosion that propelled him into pure, mindless oblivion.

When he could breathe again and string more than two thoughts together that made a modicum of sense, Mac hitched himself up on his elbows and studied the face of the woman who had just rocked his world to another dimension.

Judging from the blissful, sated look on her face, the sexy blonde sprawled beneath him and drifting toward sleep was pretty much finished with him.

Too bad. He was a long way from through with her.

"You alive down there?"

Nothing. She was as lax as sand.

He grinned, ducked his head, and drew one of those pearly pink nipples into his mouth. Soft. Responsive. When he sucked her deeper, she sighed and lifted her arms. Her hands, palms up, fingers curled, fell limply on the pillow beside her head.

And despite the warnings wailing like five-alarm-fire bells, he fell a little deeper in lust.

He bussed his nose around her velvety nipple. "Not quite so spunky now, are you, cookie?"

"I thought I was a cupcake," she murmured around a yawn that smacked of exhausted satisfaction.

"What you are," he whispered as he lifted his head from her breast and admired the way her nipple stood at attention, "is a culinary delight." He nibbled at her lower lip. "How will I eat you? Let me count the ways."

"You're no poet, McClain. And I was sort of counting on a nap here."

He ran his tongue along the center of her chest, detoured to the plump curve of her breast, and indulged himself on her other nipple. "Don't mind me. I'll just munch away while you snooze."

"Like *that's* going to happen with you licking and sucking on me that way."

"So," he slid slowly down her body, tasting that tempting flesh just below her sternum, "you're saying you don't *like* my licking?" He trailed his tongue in a slow, wet track around her navel. "Or my sucking?"

"I . . . umm . . ." She squirmed and stretched and caught her breath on a sexy little hitch when he lifted her leg, lightly bit the inside of her thigh. "I don't think that's what I'm saying, exactly, um, no."

"Then what, *exactly,* are you saying?" He slid lower, settled his shoulders between her thighs, and teased her with the warmth of his open mouth against her pubic bone.

"Oh . . . umm . . . what?"

"I may be reading more into this than I should," he whispered, parting her with his fingers, then fanning her clitoris with his breath, "but did you really want to have this discussion now?"

In answer he got a low, throaty moan when he nuzzled deep, stroked his tongue along her pretty pink lips, and feasted.

Eve lay on her back, her arms flung over her head. If her heart beat any harder, it would explode. She was so sensitive between her legs, she was sure she couldn't walk. For sure she wouldn't be riding any bicycles in the immediate future. Although she might be wise to pedal as far and as fast as she could go in any direction, as long as it was away from McClain.

At the moment, though, she couldn't muster enough common sense to even get out of the bed. She just wanted to lie here. Wanton and spent, satisfied and sluggish, and simply drift on the luscious aftermath of one of the most radical series of orgasms she'd ever experienced.

She'd say this for McClain. He was thorough. Of course, he'd been thorough the first time, all those years ago. And now she remembered why she'd been so hot to experience a repeat performance.

The man paid attention. The man gave until her ears rang. The man had an incredible mouth, and the rest of him wasn't too bad, either. Neither were some of his moves.

Beside her, he slept.

She rolled onto her side and watched him.

Even in sleep, his jaw was clenched beneath a growth of beard that was both dark and shadowed. The lashes resting on his cheeks were thick and lush. Movement behind his closed eyelids made it apparent that even at rest, he was on edge.

Yeah, even sleeping, he looked the part of a man who wasn't as easy with his world as he would like everyone to believe.

Danger, Wilhemina Robinson.

Despite her current state of euphoria, she recognized that this was a very dangerous moment.

She was devastated on phenomenal sex. Lying naked with a man who was really little more than a stranger. Mushy headed with an estrogen-induced desire to smooth the furrow in his brow, soothe the boy who was a little bit lost inside the man, fix the man who didn't have a clue that he was broken.

She rolled to her back again and stared at the ceiling. *And what makes you think you could fix him? What makes you think you're in a position to? And what makes you think he's any more in need of fixing than you are?*

And the big question: was she crazy? Hadn't she learned? Hadn't she learned anything from her experience with Troy? Or from Shawn? It was great sex that had started her thinking about fixing them, too. Thinking about forever. And they'd both puked their cheating guts all over her party.

God. Men were all alike. And here she was, thinking mushy thoughts about one who had already let her down once.

Danger. Yeah. Even though she knew the physiological reason for all this tenderness exploding in her breast, there was peril at every turn. She'd read the textbooks. She was a classic victim of the dopamine released in her system by a series of complex neurological and physiological triggers. The short-term effect was what she was currently feeling. Giddiness, warm tingles, the need to touch, to share. In other words, she was dopey.

The long-term effect was even worse. It fostered hope. For love and marriage—which was laughable, since the only man within touching distance was not a man on whom to pin long-term hopes. She'd had plenty of experience with his kind.

And that, Ms. Garrett, is the only factual data to come out of this encounter.

Of course, it didn't help that someone was trying to kill

her. That made for rethinking priorities, fussing with lines that had been drawn, second-guessing even the best of judgments.

She needed to get out of this bed.

"I hope that scowl isn't a direct result of what just happened here."

Just her luck. He woke up before she could make a break for it.

She couldn't look at him. Was fairly certain the tenderness she heard in his voice would also fill his expression and she'd be a goner. She blinked up at the ceiling instead.

"Actually, I was just thinking about getting dressed. We need to get to work."

She started to rise, but his hand on her arm stopped her. She managed to glare at him when he levered up on an elbow and leaned over her.

"What? No, 'Wow! The earth moved'?"

She managed a deep, annoyed breath. "Yeah, sure. OK. The earth moved," she said in a dry monotone. "And now I need to."

"Wait; wait just a second." He pushed her back down on the pillow when she tried to get up again. His dark brows were pinched low over his eyes as he searched her face.

And she told herself she didn't see a little hurt in his eyes.

"Far be it from me to assume, but I thought we had a pretty good time."

"Yeah, it was a real party. You're stud-worthy, McClain. Scale of one to ten, I give you a twelve."

His scowl deepened. "I'll add your glowing endorsement to my résumé. Now what in the hell is wrong with you?"

"Nothing." *Everything.*

"Yeah, I know what *that* means. *Nothing* in that tone means *something*. *Something* is very wrong. And you're not getting out of this bed until you tell me what it is."

She needed to get things back in perspective. For both of them. "Look, we both had an itch that needed scratching. We took care of it and a good time was had by all, OK? If I'd known you'd want to get all touchy-feely afterward I'd have made do with a shower massage."

That finally shocked him into letting her go. It also pissed him off, because he flopped to his back and crossed his arms behind his head. "Fine."

Fine. Just fine, she thought, slipping out of bed and heading for the bathroom. She had to get away from him before she did something really stupid, like throw herself into his arms and beg him to make love to her again.

That would lead to snuggling. Snuggling would lead to talking. Talking would lead to sharing feelings. And right now, her feelings were just too raw to lay out there for examination.

She was too raw. Why? She let out a weighty breath and turned on the shower. Because the earth *had* just moved. And she was scared to death that sex wasn't the only force that had knocked it out of its orbit.

18

SO MUCH FOR TENDER MOMENTS AFTER, MAC
thought as he hunted up his boxers, dragged them on, then
untangled the legs of his pants. Not that he was all that experienced with tender moments, but damn, would it have been
too much to ask for a *little* snuggle time? He hadn't had near
enough of his fill of touching that amazing body of hers.

He jammed his feet into his pants, assuring himself he
was pissed, not hurt. Would he never get a read on this
woman—or his reactions to her? One minute she was throwing shoulders cold enough to put a freeze on global warm-
ing; the next she was wrestling him into bed like a WWF
contender. And the next . . . hell. He didn't know what that
last encounter was all about. Sure as hell wasn't like any pillow talk he'd ever been a party to.

He *did* know they'd damn near set the sheets on fire. And
he knew he'd like to give it another go. Would have, too, if
she hadn't transformed before his eyes from ultimate sex
goddess to ice maiden.

Shower massage.

Ceerist. The woman had a mouth on her.

And he could do without thinking about that mouth at the
moment, he realized as a laser-sharp knife of arousal shot
through his groin. Yeah. She had a mouth on her all right.
And she knew how to use it to reduce a man to begging.

He jerked his shirt over his head, then went sock hunting.

By the time she emerged from the bathroom, all buttoned up and proper in her sweater and jeans, he was dressed, too, and waiting by the door.

She cut him a glance that smacked of nervous anxiety. And that one look was more telling than anything she had or hadn't said since she'd trotted her gorgeous little tush out of bed.

Well, I'll be damned. Little Miss Woman in Charge was feeling a tad bit out of control. In fact, if he didn't miss his guess, she was good and rattled and she didn't quite know how to get back on top of the situation.

He immediately simmered down.

Who'd have guessed that the spitfire who'd taken control in bed would feel so insecure and off balance out of it?

Interesting. There were a couple of ways he could go with this. He could conclude either one, that she really was sorry about their mattress dance and wished it had never happened, or two—which was his pick—that she'd liked it a little too much and wished they could do it again.

Of course, there was always a third possibility. She could be grappling with the same dilemma he was. That maybe what had happened between them wasn't just about phenomenal sex. Maybe there was something more going on—and that was something *he* didn't want to think about.

He'd been speared, filleted, cooked, and devoured by the last woman he'd felt this way about. No way in hell was he going to put himself in that position again.

He watched her quietly as she crossed to the bed, yanked up the spread, then hefted her suitcase back onto the mattress.

"It's a little after three," she said without preamble. "I'm guessing Reno isn't going to be making any moves until evening—if he makes any."

She didn't look at Mac as she sat and eased into a pair of short brown leather boots, very obviously intent on avoiding eye contact.

"Since you've got the means to monitor Tiffany's bank

transactions," she went on as she rose and headed back toward the bathroom, "it would probably be best to do that as soon as possible, just in case there's something telling there.

"Maybe an ATM withdrawal at one of the airports," she added, popping back into the room, securing her hair at her nape with a wide gold clip. "And since we haven't heard from Kat, we can figure she hasn't heard from Tiffany, either."

She lifted a jar from the bedside table, opened it, then worked lotion into her hands. The room suddenly smelled like cucumber and melon.

"And I think you should give Edwards a call. Get a feel for his reaction to an update."

Finally, all put together, she stopped moving long enough to chance a look at him. She wore a contained expression, but he could tell she was maintaining her business face with sheer determination.

"Sounds good," he said quietly.

She considered him with suspicion, then gave him a curt nod. "Well. Then. Guess we'd better get going."

She snagged her purse and met him at the door.

When he just stood there, his hand on the knob, she finally sucked it up and looked at him.

It was sweet, the uncertainty he saw in her eyes, even as she tried to hold on to all that emotional detachment.

She had such an amazing face. Exotic and fresh. Intelligent and vulnerable. And so tense he figured she could benefit from another session between the sheets—or, if she had her druthers, an accommodating bathroom fixture.

Finally, she let out a long breath. Lifted a hand. Let it drop. "Look, for the record, the ah . . . the sex business. It was totally unprofessional. I was way out of line. And I apologize. For . . . for giving you no choice," she added.

She couldn't quite meet his eyes and stared at a button on his shirt instead.

"Yeah, I was going to talk to you about that gun you held to my head."

She gave him a dry look.

"There's always a choice, cupcake," he said softly. "And we made the one that was right for us at the moment. Don't get all twisted up about it."

She managed a tight smile. "I'm not twisted up. I'm just . . . I'm disappointed. In myself. Tiffany—"

"Whoa. We did nothing to jeopardize our search for Tiffany. It's like you said. They're laying low. All we can do is wait for their next move. We could have spent the time sleeping. We went another route.

"Look," he added, gripping her upper arms and forcing her to meet his eyes when she didn't look convinced, "don't beat yourself up about something that was not only inevitable; it was necessary."

She actually grunted. "On Mars, maybe. Not on Venus."

"That BS about what's right for a man and not for a woman is bunk and you know it."

"The only thing I know is that falling into bed with you was a mistake. And if it's going to affect our working together, maybe we should think about going our separate ways."

Oh, no, he wasn't letting her out of his sight. "I thought we agreed that Tiffany had a better chance if we teamed up."

"She does. *If* we can still work together."

"You mean without making any more . . . *mistakes*," he finally concluded, knowing exactly what she meant—and not liking it one bit.

"Right. No more mistakes."

She may have said the words, but he noted a severe lack of conviction. Enough of a lack that he wondered if maybe there wasn't a fourth explanation to consider. She was holding out on him. Something . . . he didn't know. Something was off here. She wasn't telling him something. He'd figure it out. If there was something else going on that he needed to know about, he'd get it out of her sooner or later.

"Tell you what." He opened the door. "I think better on a full stomach. Breakfast was a long time ago." He placed a hand at the small of her back as they walked down the hall toward the elevator. "Let's go grab something to eat."

He could see that she was about to make some protest about not being hungry when her stomach growled.

Caught, she expelled a long breath. "And then?"

"And then we get back to work finding Tiffany."

By the time they'd found a deli, ordered chips and sandwiches, and eased into a booth, she was no longer looking at him like she wanted to smear him on a slide and study him under a microscope.

And she was no longer making noises about mistakes. He even detected a slight relaxing in her shoulders. Which worked really well for him. He liked the other kind of noises she made. The ones that told him what they'd accomplished in her bed was damn near perfect. So perfect, in fact, he had every intention of hearing those particular noises again.

Eve's cell phone rang just as they were about to dig into their sandwiches.

It was Ethan.

"How's it going?" her brother asked.

"It's going." She filled him in on the incident at Oracle and her conclusion that Tiffany was absolutely in trouble and that Reno was the root of it. What Eve couldn't discuss was her growing conclusion that the attacks on her and Tiffany's disappearance were somehow tied together. Neither could she share the subway incident and the subsequent message on her home voice mail with him. She didn't want McClain knowing about that either.

She didn't want him going all protective and macho on her and muddling up his head with worry over her. He needed to concentrate on finding Tiffany. For everyone's sake.

"Did you turn up anything on Edwards?" she asked instead.

"No surprises. Dallas did a thorough search and nothing jumps front and center. Harvard School of Law grad. Top ten percent. Started in the corporate attorney pool for Clayborne right out of the blocks. Worked his way up—caught Clayborne's attention with a major real estate transaction and got bumped up to his personal team ten years ago. Eventually moved to the divine right-hand post and became Clayborne's exclusive public rep about three years ago."

"Any personal data?" she asked, her brows furrowed.

"Upper-middle-class background—small town, Connecticut. Thirty-eight. Never been married. Not linked to anyone—male or female—so if he's got something going on, he's very discreet about it. Seems he's strictly career track."

"To the exclusion of a life? Any hobbies? Golf? Scuba? Kiddie porn, maybe?"

"Married to the man," Ethan said. "If Edwards has ever taken so much as a day off, let alone a vacation, he's played it low-key. No country club membership, no cars in his name—drives a company Chrysler. No boat, plane, not even a skateboard. No outstanding loans that don't match up with his income. And no, no kinky stuff that we could find. So, that's Edwards in a nutshell. As to Jazelle, she's proving to be more interesting."

Eve thought of the cold and polished Jazelle. "How so?"

"What's interesting is that I found out she attended NYU School of Business and started working for the Clayborne machine a couple of years ago."

"And?"

"And that's it."

"This is earth-shattering *why?*"

"This is earth-shattering because that's the sum total of the information I was able to find on her. Period. Nothing before NYU. No family ties. Nothing. She just sort of materialized on campus as a fifth-year senior, then went on to get her master's in business. To say that prior to that point Clayborne's EA's past is murky is like saying the ocean is blue."

"Which tells me you're all over it."

"I've got Bob on it, too."

If anyone could find out information, her old boss at the Secret Service would be the one to ferret it out.

"OK," she said, then after a short hesitation added, "let me know if anything turns up. In the meantime, run these names, too, would you? Margaret Reed, Kat Hofsteader, and Sven Jorgenson."

In the booth across from her, McClain frowned, clearly curious about her reasoning.

"Anything out of the ordinary turns up, call. In the meantime, we're waiting to get a read on Tiffany's next move."

"We?"

Eve cut an uneasy glance at McClain, who was still watching her with interest. "I ran into McClain here. We . . . we're sort of collaborating. For Tiffany's sake."

"Collaborating? With the—let me think—rat-bastard, wasn't it?"

Seems she had mentioned McClain in those terms to her brother at some point. "Um, yeah."

"Interesting," Ethan said. "Frankly, I'm relieved. At least you're not alone out there. Has anything else happened I need to know about?"

"Nope." She was going to go to hell for lying. "I'll let you know if something else breaks."

"Do that. And watch your back, little sister. On all counts."

McClain was still watching her when she disconnected.

"Just being thorough," she said in response to his unasked question. "It's not that I suspect Kat or Sven or even Margaret of anything; it's just . . . who knows. I don't want any surprises blindsiding me." As they'd been doing lately. "You going to call Edwards soon or what?"

McClain slouched back in the booth, looking very male, very brooding, very attractive. She rocked her glass on the tabletop, cut her gaze to it instead of his mouth because it made her remember all the amazing things he'd done to her with his tongue.

Without replying, he punched in Edwards's number. While it rang, she was far too conscious of McClain's dark eyes watching her. Far too alert to the edgy awareness that, despite her determination to discount it, continued to hum in the air between them.

Sleeping with him had been a colossal error in judgment. And now she had to suck it up and deal with the fallout.

"Richard Edwards's office," Jazelle Taylor answered with professional élan after a receptionist had relayed the call.

"Hello, Ms. Taylor. It's McClain."

"Yes, Mr. McClain. We've been expecting a call from you."

"I need to speak with Mr. Edwards, please."

"I'm sorry, but he's in a meeting and instructed that he was not to be interrupted. May I take a message?"

"Actually, no. I need to speak with him directly regarding this matter."

"If it's about Tiffany Clayborne, Mr. Edwards indicated I was to ask you to brief me and I'll pass the information on to him. He's filled me in completely on Ms. Clayborne's, shall we say, situation. And frankly, I'm as concerned about her as Mr. Edwards and Mr. Clayborne. Have you had any luck finding her?"

Mac debated but in the end decided to give Jazelle the report. Clearly Edwards had briefed his EA or Jazelle wouldn't have privilege to even this much information about why Mac was in Edwards's employ.

Before Mac could speak, however, Jazelle said, "The truth of the matter is, Mr. Edwards is becoming a bit impatient. He's been upset that you haven't checked in before now. I'm hoping I can relay some good news to him."

Well. So much for pleasantries. "Actually, I do have something for him. Tiffany's still here in New York."

"Where in New York?" Her voice had sharpened noticeably.

"That's what I'm working on. Ms. Taylor," Mac continued carefully, "I'm starting to think that Tiffany is in trouble."

Silence, then, "I hope this doesn't sound indelicate, but Ms. Clayborne has been in some kind of trouble or other since she reached puberty."

"I'm not talking about mischief trouble. I think she's being held against her will."

Another silence. McClain glanced at Eve to see her face was sober with interest.

"What do you mean, 'against her will'?" Jazelle's tone had changed dramatically—as dramatically as a well-trained EA's could, given she was schooled to suppress all opinions. Still, Mac sensed a shift from barely suppressed cynicism to barely suppressed doubt.

"When Tiffany left Palm Beach, she left with a musician by the name of Lance Reno. Another man, Abe Gorman, is also with them. A third, who I've yet to identify, makes up the final member of the band. In any event, Reno seems to be calling the shots, deciding where they go, what they do. I've also been in contact with Tiffany's friend Kat Hofsteader. Just last night, Kat was involved in an incident where Reno made Tiffany leave with him against her will."

"Ms. Hofsteader actually saw Tiffany? And where was this?"

"At Oracle—it's a club downtown. According to Ms. Hofsteader, the situation was pretty ugly. You may wish to suggest to Mr. Edwards that he consider reporting this to the police. Possibly even the FBI."

"The FBI? Oh, please, Mr. McClain. That's a bit extreme, don't you think?"

Actually, Mac did think it was extreme. He believed what Eve had told Kat about calling the cops. Reno would manipulate Tiffany to the point that she'd deny he was keeping her against her will anyway. But he'd wanted to hear a reaction from the main camp. And he'd just gotten one. Jazelle's professional poise had slipped a rung or two.

He needed to get to Edwards. Mac wanted to hear his take on the prospect of involving law enforcement.

"Actually," Mac added, deciding to play this out a little further, "I think it might be the best option."

"I'll need to speak with Mr. Edwards about this. In the meantime, I strongly suggest that you do not pursue this avenue."

"When can I speak with Edwards?" Mac asked, point-blank.

"I'll make sure he frees up some time to call you within the hour."

"Well, that was interesting," Mac said when Jazelle had disconnected.

"EA with a power complex?" Eve suggested.

"Or something. Lots of alarm on her part when I mentioned the FBI. I have a feeling I'll be hearing from Edwards very soon."

They'd just finished their sandwiches when Mac's cell phone rang.

"Twelve minutes," McClain said smugly after checking his watch. "You owe me a quarter."

Eve's money had been on fifteen minutes at the earliest.

"Do not, under any circumstances, involve the police or the FBI," Edwards stated without preamble when Mac answered.

All righty then. Sounded like they were getting right to the heart of things. "I take it Ms. Taylor filled you in on my report."

"She did and let me make this perfectly clear. You will not contact the authorities."

"You're an attorney, Edwards. You're aware that kidnapping is a federal offense," Mac said reasonably.

"Look, McClain. You're getting way ahead of yourself

here." Edwards's patronizing tone was exceeded only by his anger. "And you're leaping to extreme conclusions."

"Out of concern for Tiffany."

"We all have Tiffany's well-being in mind. But you don't know her like I do. I can assure you that if Tiffany Clayborne wanted to extricate herself from her current situation, she is fully capable of doing so."

"Not if she's being drugged."

"Drugged?" He truly sounded taken aback.

"OK, look," Edwards continued after a moment, his tone a combination of weary patience and absolute authority. "Do not call the police or any other law enforcement agency and suggest this preposterous theory, do you understand? What you are to do is find her, notify me immediately when you do, and I'll take it from there. If you truly are fearful for Tiffany, you'll do your job and find her. And if, at that point, it's determined that she's being held against her will, then and only then will the authorities be notified. To suggest such a scenario at this point, however, will do Tiffany more harm than good. Particularly if drugs are involved. I'd much rather see her in rehab than in prison, don't you agree?"

"But if she *is* being held against her will—"

"Speculation, McClain," Edwards cut in again. "Now listen to me. You are being paid, and handsomely, I might add, to find Tiffany. If one single word of this ridiculous notion of yours leaks to the media or to any law enforcement agency, I assure you, not only your reputation but also the reputation of your business will be dealt such a crippling blow from the Clayborne PR machine that Discovery Unlimited will cease to exist.

"Now find her. No more talk about kidnapping. No more talk about contacting the authorities. And in the future, I expect frequent updates. You will call me daily at a minimum and you will report to Ms. Taylor if I'm not available. Now let's hope for everyone's sake that you call with news of Tiffany's exact location in very short order."

"Jawohl, Herr Kommandant," Mac muttered after Edwards hung up without so much as a fare-thee-well.

"Protest from the peanut gallery?"

"A chorus of boos." He pocketed his phone. "A little Hitler complex there."

"Clayborne taught him well."

"You don't feel any better about Edwards, do you?" Mac asked after a protracted silence.

"Not really, no. I don't know. Maybe I'm just looking for something that's not there."

"Like what?"

"That's what I keep asking myself." She shook her head. "He's just too much of a . . . stereotype," she finally decided. "Career driven. Perfect employee. No life. Just seems there has to be something more going on there than meets the eye. And Kat was right. Tiffany doesn't like him. That bothers me, too."

"You don't like him, either. Maybe he just has one of those obnoxious personalities."

"Maybe," she agreed but felt it was something more. She drained the last of her iced tea. "Logically, there's nothing to pin any of this suspicion to. Even if I don't like his tactics, his motive is sound. All his reasons make sense. Maybe what bothers me most is that the Clayborne public image seems to preempt concern for Tiffany's well-being."

"Then it's a good thing she's got us looking out for her interests."

Eve looked at him with renewed interest. "Yeah. It's a good thing."

"You know," he said after a moment, "I get the impression—have from the beginning—that Edwards is more than just Clayborne's mouthpiece. Like he's making the calls instead of relaying them."

"Interesting. Given Clayborne's lack of parental involvement, maybe it's the route their relationship has taken. You know—maybe Edwards has been more of an authority figure in Tiffany's life than her own father. Maybe Clayborne delegated that role long ago and it's simply status quo."

"Which may account for Tiffany's dislike for Edwards. Like Kat says, Tiffany would rather have her father, but she got Edwards pushed on her instead."

"Maybe," Eve agreed. "In any event, it's Reno, not Edwards, who's the most immediate threat. He's the one we have to target."

"Come on." McClain slid out of the booth and tossed some bills on the tabletop. "Let's go check her bank account activity. See if anything pops up."

19

NOTHING DID. MAC COULDN'T FIND ANY RE-cent withdrawals from Tiffany's accounts when they returned to his hotel room and tapped his laptop. *The happy tribe is definitely lying low. Retooling. Resting. Who knew?* he thought as he switched off the computer.

Rubbing his neck and stretching, he looked up from the desk. Eve was curled up in one of the two chairs in the room, his folder on Tiffany balanced on her lap as she thumbed through pages of printouts.

She must have sensed him watching her, because her head came up. "Nothing?" She notched her chin toward his laptop.

He shook his head. "Either they're bunkered down or they had enough cash left from the last transaction in Key West to get them where they want to go next."

"Wherever that may be. And the big question: to what end?"

She massaged her temples, her face pinched in thought. "You think Reno really is just milking her for money? When he gets tired of the flight pattern and the heat, he'll just disappear?"

"Maybe." Mac rose, walked from the desk to the bed, toed off his shoes, and lay down on his back, his arms crossed behind his head. "Got to be a trip for a starving musician to live the good life."

Eve must have been feeling the strain, too, because she stretched her arms over her head, worked the kinks out of her neck, then let her head fall back on the cushioned chair. She had to be as tired as he was. For close to four days they'd been long on action and short on sleep. The few hours they'd caught at Kat's had helped, but not enough. The hour or so they'd spent playing patty-cake in Eve's hotel bed had depleted a little of the energy their limited sleep had recovered.

"It would be nice to think that maybe the way they hooked up—that it started out innocent enough," she speculated aloud. "Maybe Reno was as taken with Tiffany as she was with him. Maybe he still is. Maybe Kat panicked when she found Tiffany in Forbidden and saw what she wanted to see, heard what she wanted to hear. Maybe Tiffany really is OK."

"And maybe there's a tooth fairy and Santa Claus and maybe you need some sleep, because you don't believe any of that for a minute."

She chuckled. It was a nice sound. Companionable. Like she was relaxed with him for the first time. Ever.

"Well, they were nice thoughts."

Speaking of nice thoughts. He tilted his head, looked at her where she sat across the room. She'd taken the clip from her hair, and the silky blond mass fell softly around her face. She'd also ditched her shoes. In her snug faded jeans, lived-in sweater, and stocking feet, she looked homey and sweet and like someone he could be comfortable with. Maybe after dinner at home with a glass of wine. Snuggled on the sofa with soft music playing while fireflies played tag in the dark outside the window.

He looked away. And wondered what the hell he thought he was doing. Now that he'd had some distance from their intense session in bed, he should be thinking with his *big* head. And the honest truth was, there wasn't any room in his life for squishy ideas about home and hearth. Christ. Even if he had the guts to get involved with a woman again, Eve Garrett wasn't the one. And now sure as the world wasn't the time.

Great sex aside, he had a track record with women that spelled failure with a capital fuckup. And she'd made it clear she regarded any extracurricular activity involving him as a mistake.

He should pay attention. His ex had chewed him up and spit him out, and when he'd landed, he was a different person. Diminished. Jaded. One hundred percent cynical about the institution of marriage and the fairy tale of happily ever after.

Of course, that didn't mean he didn't enjoy women. And Eve, well, his resistance was admittedly a little low when he'd met up with her again. She made him think of his youth, when his life was still ahead of him instead of the reality that he was as worn-out and used up as a bald tire.

Now, this prospect of something more than a one-night stand with her, however, had a hell of a lot of appeal. It implied short-term. That worked. Long-term didn't. The only long-term commitment he could handle was Ali. And she would always and forever remain his priority.

"So you were a cop."

Eve's question—if you could call it that—came out of nowhere. Surprised, he glanced her way.

"Just passing time," she said defensively, in response, no doubt, to the astonished scowl he must have sent her. "Forget I mentioned it."

He should. He should forget everything that had happened between them today. Yeah. Like that was going to happen.

She stretched again, one of those unconsciously sexy lift-the-arms-above-the-head, thrust-the-breasts-against-the-sweater stretches, and *blaam!* Just like that, the little head started calling the shots again.

The picture of her rocking above him, gloriously naked, the berry pink tips of her beautiful breasts stiffened to tight little points, her eyes closed in sensual pleasure, was burned in his mind like a brand. The rush of being inside her, of his hands skating across the silk of her skin, the taste of her when she came, would stay with him until he died.

But if he wasn't mistaken, she hadn't just asked him if he wanted to have another round of brain-frying sex. She'd asked him if he'd been a cop. Slight difference.

Get a grip, McClain.

"Chicago," he said finally, responding to her comment about his police work. "Eight years."

"And that was enough?"

He wasn't prepared for the regret that swamped him. "Not nearly."

She was quiet long enough that he knew she was debating the wisdom of following up on that cryptic remark and the bitterness even he had heard in his voice. He decided to save her the trouble.

"Wrecked the knee," he said like those few words were adequate explanation for a career-altering event. Like he'd reduced what happened to three words when every day he relived the series of surgeries, the months of rehab, and finally the news that he'd never recover enough to go back to the job.

"I'm sorry." The softness in her tone relayed not only sincerity but also empathy. And it was telling. If he didn't miss his guess, she also shared a deep understanding of his regret. So deep, he figured she had some regrets of her own she was dealing with. Possibly some major disappointments.

"So, what's your story?"

She withheld for a moment, until her sense of fair play must have gotten the best of her. "You know my story."

"Up until you were let go. Do you miss it? The Secret Service? Seven years was a long time."

"At the risk of sounding like an echo, not long enough."

"And now you do private security."

She fussed with the crease in her jeans. "Seems we've both had some choices taken away from us."

Intrigued but even more concerned, he rolled onto his side, propped his head on his palm. "You were hurt?"

The laugh she pushed out held little humor. "Only my pride."

He was about to ask what happened, then thought better of it. God. They were dancing around each other like they were wearing tap shoes. Probably with good cause.

If she wanted him to know the details, she'd tell him. It came as a surprise when she did.

"I'd done my six years in the field office and had finally gotten my assignment in D.C. I was part of the protection detail for Vice President Hargrave's daughter. Hadn't been on assignment for six months when they pulled me off and sent me to Palm Beach to provide protection for Tiffany."

"How does that happen? A civilian—a nondignitary—getting Secret Service protection?"

"Presidential order."

"That I know. But why?"

"We're not paid to ask why. We're paid to do."

"And you did. They didn't get her."

"But we lost a good agent and a civilian in the process."

"For that you lost your job?"

"Clayborne was pissed that I let anyone get that close to anything that was his. I don't even think we're talking about parental love here. We're talking about ownership. He owned the chauffeur. He owns Tiffany. And by his account, I screwed up."

"Shame on you for saving her life."

"Yeah. Shame on me."

He thought about it. Shook his head. "That sucks."

"Pretty much, yeah."

A lengthy silence played host to a gamut of emotions that crossed her face. Anger. Disappointment. Stoic acceptance.

"Hey, Garrett," he said, making up his mind to do something to dispel the sad look in her eyes, even if it was wrong.

She looked at him, frowned. "Yeah, *McClain*?"

"Seems to me that if a person is going to burn for doing

things right, she'd just as well indulge in a mistake every once in a while. Sort of balance the scales."

She considered him with a cynical stare. "Is that a back-door approach to try to get me back in bed with you?"

"It is, yeah," he confessed without an ounce of shame, then watched as her beautiful mouth twitched and finally broke into a smile. "So . . . is it working?"

Her eyes held his for the longest moment before dropping to follow the motion of his hand when he patted the mattress in invitation.

"What the hell," she said finally, and, rising, walked to the bed. "Who am I to argue with sound logic?"

Lying on her stomach, naked, her entire body humming with a delicious sexual afterglow while McClain sang in the shower, Eve considered the possibility that she might be a nymphomaniac. Or possibly she was just addicted to sex. At least it seemed that way when it came to falling into bed with him.

She hugged the pillow to her breasts, burrowed deeper into the covers. More likely, she was just stupid—at least where McClain was concerned. She'd never been this much of a wanton. Well, once before. Fourteen years before, to be exact. Any sexual encounters she'd had in between, while pleasant, couldn't hold a candle to the fire McClain had lit and set to a roaring bonfire.

God, he was good.

God, she was easy. One come-hither look from those melted chocolate eyes, one "hey, baby" smile, one vivid memory of the things he was capable of making her feel, one flimsy, fabricated justification for making another a mistake, and she'd folded like an accordion at a hoedown.

"Yee haw." With a satisfied smile she flopped to her back—and threw in a do-si-doe for good measure. McClain had some moves that would take the edges off a square dance all right. And if she didn't stop with these ridiculous down-home country analogies, she was going to break out in freckles and pigtails.

Blame it on the country song he was singing while he showered. And blame her tumble into bed on what it was. Another mistake in judgment, which she had a penchant for making when it came to this particular man.

She forced herself to get up. Tugging the sheet off the bed, she wrapped it around her and walked to the window overlooking the street. Dusk was approaching. Some of the yellow cabs were running with their lights on.

She thought back to what they'd talked about earlier. Specifically, her job. She'd lost her Secret Service position through no fault of her own. She'd proven herself capable— yet four people had died. Now someone wanted her dead. Someone close to her might die. McClain might even be in trouble just by proximity.

Maybe she should tell him what was going on. He deserved to be warned. And yet . . . something kept stopping her.

She didn't want him hurt. She didn't want anyone hurt. So this had nothing to do with their history. A history that thanks to her stupidity was repeating itself all over again.

Would she forever be drawn to the bad boys, like Mc-Clain, who couldn't commit, couldn't be true? She'd never admit it aloud, but secretly, she wanted to meet Mr. Nice, not Mr. Naughty, get married, get a dog, have two-point-three kids, and balance that with a career. What if there were no good guys in her future?

McClain didn't come within a mile of meeting those criteria. Well, he didn't if you didn't count the fact that he was a daddy. A dedicated one. A loving one. Which just mixed her up a little more where he was concerned.

She was watching the flicker of lights and shadows when she heard the door to the bathroom open.

"Hey," he said, walking up behind her. He wrapped his arms around her and tugged her toward him. "You OK?"

She should fight the easy intimacy, but what was the

point? She enjoyed his lovemaking. Enjoyed his body. Regretfully, was even starting to enjoy his company.

She leaned back against his chest. "I'm phenomenal."

"Well," he said, touching his lips to the top of her head, "I guess that should make me smug as hell."

She laughed. "I guess it should."

He gave her an affectionate squeeze, stepped back, and walked to the dresser where he'd stowed his things. "Shower's all yours."

"Thanks."

"Eve."

She turned and felt her breath catch. He was wearing only a towel knotted low around his lean hips. He'd been a beautiful boy. She couldn't help but appreciate what an astonishingly gorgeous man he'd grown into. Broad shoulders, narrow waist, gloriously defined muscle bulked up in all the right places. His wasn't a bodybuilder's form but that of a well-conditioned man in his prime. But for the surgical scars that ruined his knee, he was perfect. He kept in shape. In bed, the man had stamina in spades.

Finally, she managed to drag her gaze to his face. His hair was wet. His expression somber.

"No more beating yourself up about this, all right? We're adults. We're single. We enjoy each other. Not a sin. Not a crime. Not a mistake. Let's not reduce it to one, OK?"

Who'd have thought he'd end up being the adult in this situation?

"OK," she said softly, and headed for the bathroom.

Her cell phone rang just as she stepped out of the shower.

It was Kat. Tiffany had just called her. She was in Las Vegas.

For as wonderfully slow as he moved in bed, McClain was a speedball when it came to business. Eve wasn't even fully dressed and he'd finished packing. Like he said, he traveled light.

She'd decided to travel with a little less baggage, too. McClain was right. Since she couldn't seem to find it in her to fight the chemistry between them, she'd ditched that scratchy hair shirt. It was unavoidable that their search for Tiffany Clayborne bound them together. Who knew how much longer it would take to find her? Tiffany had just called Kat, and the result was leading them to Vegas and, hopefully, another step closer. Until their search ended, though, it was pointless to deny the attraction. And the fact was, fighting it was much more distracting to their investigation than going with the flow.

Or so said a logic Eve somehow managed to twist around to fit into making her feel justified in indulging herself. And that's all it was. A temporary indulgence. As long as she remembered that, when this was over, everyone walked away clean. No harm. No foul.

"Tell me exactly what she said again," McClain said after scooting into the backseat of a cab with her and giving the driver the address of Eve's hotel. It would be the first of several stops. Once they picked up her luggage, they'd head for Kat's for a quick lesson on reading her particular GPS unit—which Kat had agreed to let them commandeer. Then they were off to JFK to catch a red-eye to Vegas that McClain had booked while Eve had dressed.

Eve understood why he wanted her to repeat the content of Kat's phone call. They'd both moved so fast since they'd heard from her that Eve had filled him in on the run.

"Wish there was more to tell. According to Kat, Tiffany didn't sound the best, but she was evidently alert enough to use the cell phone Kat had planted on her. She didn't know where she was, but she was scared and she was crying. Kat got her to look out her hotel window, and when she described what she saw, they both realized she was in Vegas. She had no idea what hotel she was in."

"Was the call long enough for the GPS to get an exact fix?"

"Would have been if the batteries in the tracking unit hadn't died."

"Fuck," he muttered under his breath. "That's one of the bugs with the smaller GPS units," he added with a scowl. "OK. We go with what we've got. We at least know that she's in Vegas. If she calls Kat again, we'll get a fix on her exact location. Provided she doesn't spook."

"And provided she gets another chance to call," Eve added. "Kat said Tiffany hung up so abruptly, she was sure she'd been afraid of getting caught."

"Was she sober?"

Eve shook her head. "Kat didn't think so. But she was scared; of that Kat was certain."

While Eve went up to her room and threw her things together, McClain called Kat back and found out what kind of batteries the GPS unit needed. Then he bought out the hotel gift shop's supply so they wouldn't run into a dead battery problem with the locator once they arrived in Las Vegas—again, providing Tiffany called Kat back. And providing, when they found Tiffany, they could convince her they were the good guys in the mix and she'd trust them enough to let them get her away from Reno.

On the way to SoHo and Kat's, they hashed over what to do about Edwards.

"I think you should give him another update," Eve said.

"Vegas?" Edwards said when Mac phoned and advised him where he was headed.

"Got a lead on an ATM transaction," he lied. He didn't figure Edwards needed to know about the GPS, either. "I'm catching a flight in a couple of hours."

"I want a call as soon as you pin down her exact location. And when you do, I want to hear from you immediately. Do not approach her. Do nothing, do you understand? I'll handle things when I get there, and at that point, your work is done."

"You got it," Mac said, and hung up.

"What?" Eve asked when he sat there deep in thought.

He gave an absent shake of his head. "I'm trusting that guy less and less. He was adamant that I was not to make any move on Tiffany when I found her. I was to wait until he got there.

"Why take the chance on her getting away again?" he speculated aloud. "Why risk it? Or worse, why take a chance on a delay that could potentially lead to Tiffany getting hurt while Edwards had the means in place—mainly *me*—to sew things up? I mean, for all Edwards knows, she'll just run again—or Reno will take her. Then Edwards is back to square one."

"So are you thinking what I'm thinking?"

"If you're thinking that you want a chance to extract Tiffany and make sure she's safe and sound—"

"And hear what she has to say about where she wants to go," Eve added.

"Then yeah, we're on the same page. Edwards plans to drag her home to Daddy. I say we give her another option."

"Kat," Eve said. "She seems to be the only one who gives a fig about what's best for Tiffany."

"Not the only one," McClain said. "You give a fig. You have from the beginning."

Before she could offer up her own conjecture that Tiffany was lucky to have him on her side as well, he dug into his jacket pocket.

"Thought you might have a need for these." He tossed her a sack full of M&M's.

He laughed when she tore into the bag like a tiger on raw meat.

"My God," she said on a sigh, savoring her first taste of chocolate in almost twenty-four hours.

"Figured you were close to withdrawal."

"I owe you, McClain."

"That's kind of the way I see it, too." His grin made it clear that he had a particular form of payment in mind as the cab pulled up in front of Kat's building.

20

TIFFANY WAS STRAIGHT. IT WAS SIX IN THE morning, she was lying on the bed, and she was sober. And she was going to stay that way. No matter how much it hurt. No matter how sick she got. Or how shaky she felt. One hit of weed would take the edge off. One snort of blow would bring oblivion and cut through the pain. But she wasn't going to do it. She needed to stay alert.

With sobriety came truth.

And the truth hurt. But it was time she faced it.

The truth was that Lance didn't love her. He didn't even like her. In fact, she was fairly certain he hated her. It was only her money he loved. The drugs it could buy. The places it got him into.

She heard a noise in the other room of the suite. The sound of voices. Lance and Abe. They were back.

And what she had once welcomed now frightened her.

Scared. She was so scared.

Her heart pounded so hard she was sure it would burst. Tears filled her eyes. She wanted to get up and run, lock herself in the bathroom and hide. But she made herself lie still, dug deep inside to draw on her yoga breathing to calm herself. If Lance came in here, he had to think she was passed out, stoned out of her mind, or he'd force more drugs on her. She was done with drugs. She had to be.

Making him think she was out of it should be an easy sell.

He'd kept her stoned for days. Maybe even weeks. She didn't know. It was all such a blur. Such a murky, horrible blur. Even her contact with Kat.

Kat.

Tears threatened again when Tiffany thought of her friend. Kat cared about her. She may be the only person in the world who did. Eve had once and the fact that she'd deserted her, too, only made it more painful.

But Kat . . . Somehow, Kat had given her a cell phone. Tiffany had no idea how—or when. She'd thought she'd just dreamed about seeing Kat in Oracle, but it had been real. The phone proved it. Somehow, Kat had reached out to her and that little bit of reality had made her think—realize she had a life to go back to, to make of it what she could.

She wanted to get straight. Somehow get her life back. A life she'd lost and had no idea how.

Lance had taken everything away from her. But now she had a phone. And she'd managed to place a call to Kat. She had to be careful. Had to hide the phone so Lance wouldn't find it. Had to disconnect from her call to Kat last night because he'd almost caught her.

She had to . . . had to what?

She lost all train of thought. Panicked. Drew a deep breath. Think. Had to think again about where she was. Vegas. *Yes, Vegas.* And Lance didn't love her.

The bedroom door opened and her heart lurched again. She closed her eyes.

Play dead. Play dead.

"The bitch is still out," Lance said when he walked up beside the bed.

She was lying on her side, her back to him, but she could feel him watching her. Watching. Watching. She willed herself to lie still. To breathe deep.

"I don't know why you don't just do her and get it over with."

Do her?

Abe's statement made her blood run cold.

"I told you. All in good time."

Lance moved away from the bed. She heard him rummage around in a bureau drawer.

"What you keep forgetting, Gorman, is that the minute she's dead, the money tree shrivels up. The longer we keep her around, the longer we play. Besides, it has to look like an overdose or we don't get the payoff."

All the blood drained from her head. Made her dizzy with terror.

"The payoff?" Abe made an angry sound as he walked back to the bedroom door. "You blew the payoff when you didn't ice her two weeks ago when you were supposed to. That money's long gone. We'll be lucky if there isn't a new contract out on us for fucking up the job."

"Stop being so paranoid. No one's going to put a hit on us. Where in the hell did I put that ATM card?" More searching sounds, like he was tossing clothes everywhere. "And we'll get paid, believe me. All I have to do is make noises about ratting to the police and we'll have that money and be long gone before anyone can find us."

"What about Campbell?"

"Billie?" Lance made a snort of disgust.

Tiffany had heard Billie leave earlier. He must still be gone.

"That dumb country fuck hasn't got a clue what's going on. I'm still working on an angle where he can take the fall when Tiffany Rich here does her poor little self in on some bad smack."

"I'm telling you," Abe said again, "it's past time to do it."

"Yeah, yeah. Fine. Found it." She heard the snap of plastic against Lance's palm. "Let's hit the Strip again and tap her account for some more cash."

"When?" Abe insisted. "When are you going to do it?"

"When we get back, all right?" Lance let out an impatient breath. "That soon enough for you, you bloodthirsty bastard?"

"Yeah," Abe said. "Couple hours tops, then we come back and you get it done, or I'm gone and you're on your own."

The door slammed shut behind them.

Tiffany finally let out the breath she'd been holding. Felt her heart lurch again when she heard the unmistakable sound of something being wedged against the door. Lance was barricading her in. So she couldn't get out. Couldn't escape.

So she'd be here when he came back—to kill her.

She shoved her fist in her mouth to keep from sobbing out loud. Lance and Abe may still be out there. She couldn't let them hear her. Couldn't afford to let them know she'd overheard them.

Tears of fear and panic and pain leaked down her cheeks as she eased carefully out of bed and walked as quietly as possible to the door. She placed her ear against it. Nothing.

With everything in her, she wanted to try the door, see if she could force it open and run for her life. But they might still be out there. So she waited. And waited, afraid to make a sound, afraid to give herself away.

Slowly, she sank to her knees, tried to peek through the keyhole. Whatever he'd wedged against the door blocked her view.

Fighting panic, she ached with the urge to light up a joint—just to steady her hands. Just to ease this horrible fear knotted in her stomach.

The cell phone. Yes! Kat had given her a cell phone. She'd call Kat. Kat would help her. She crawled across the carpeted floor, tears streaming down her face, and dug the phone out from between the mattress and the box spring where she'd hidden it.

Then she jumped like a scared rabbit when she heard a door open and close, the sound of footsteps in the other room. Lance. He was back.

She swallowed back a sob. It felt like every muscle in her throat had constricted into a hard, throbbing knot as she waited. Didn't dare make a noise. Didn't dare punch in Kat's number. He might hear. He might come in here.

He might kill her now. Might not wait until later.

Her shaking grew worse. It was so bad she could hardly hold on to the phone. Hating herself, she crawled to the bathroom, shut herself inside. And dug through her makeup case.

She needed a joint. She couldn't help it. She needed to settle herself.

She sobbed openly now, throwing her mascara and blush and lip gloss to the floor, desperate to find a joint. Desperate to feel something other than stark terror.

"Just a little toke. Just a little hit," she promised herself, and finally dumped the entire contents of her case on the floor.

There, finally, was a smoke.

She fumbled with the matches. Cried in horrified frustration when she couldn't steady her hand enough to set the weed on fire.

"Please, please, please."

Finally, it caught. Sweet, sweet relief. She inhaled deep, held the magic in her lungs, exhaled on a long, fractured breath. Again. Again. And again until the panic faded and she could breathe without pain.

She slumped back against the tub. The floor tile felt cool against her butt. Against her bare legs. She stared at the floor. Became fascinated with the tile. Decided to count it. Needed to count it.

One . . . two . . . three.

Her head was all muzzy. She got mixed up and started counting again. It was important, suddenly, that she count every one of those little bastards. Just to prove she could.

She forgot about the phone in her hand. Forgot that she was in deep, deep trouble. And counted.

Over and over again.

Until her head lolled to the side and she drifted into a marijuana-induced stupor.

Something clattered on the tile beside her. She forced her eyes open. She'd dropped the phone. Kat's cell phone.

Kat. She had to . . . had to call Kat.

She reached for the phone, picked it up. And stared. *Where did that come from?* She pressed a button, turned it on. Shushed it when it made a noise.

"Can't let him hear. Can't let him hear."

Can't let Lance hear.

Her eyes grew heavy again. Why couldn't Lance hear? Lance loved her.

Lance wanted to kill her.

She didn't understand. She didn't understand any of this. What she needed was sleep. Lots of sleep.

She curled up on her side, felt the cool floor against her cheek, and counted tiles. "One . . . two . . . three . . ."

Eve and McClain had just stepped off the plane and walked through the Jetway to the arrival gate at the Vegas airport when the GPS tracker went off.

"Something's happening." Bleary from the red-eye flight, Eve dug into her purse, dragged out the unit. "Tiffany must have turned on the phone."

Beside her, McClain dialed Sven's cell phone number. It rang twice before he picked up. "Is Tiffany on the phone with Kat, by any chance?" Mac asked, slinging his carry-on over his shoulder as he and Eve walked toward the rental car desk.

"No," Sven said, sounding half-asleep. "Kat's right here. Still wringing her hands. Tiffany hasn't called. What's happening?"

"We've got a signal on the GPS. I'll hold on a little longer. It only makes sense that she'll be calling."

And yet, five minutes later, at six fifteen, Kat's phone still hadn't rung.

"Look," Mac said to Sven. "Whether she calls or not, we've got a fix on her location. As soon as we ID the address, we'll head there to see what we turn up. We'll keep you posted. In the meantime, let us know if either of you hears from her."

He disconnected while Eve approached the Avis desk. "Excuse me," she said to the clerk. "Can you tell me what's located at this address?" She gave the clerk the street coordinates indicated on the GPS map readout.

"That's the Topanga Bay. Newest casino on the Strip. South Seas theme. It just opened last month."

"Bingo," they said in unison, and waded through the rental car paperwork with barely leashed patience.

"So, do we call Edwards?" McClain asked when they'd finally stowed their luggage in the back of the rented SUV.

Eve glanced at him from behind the wheel as he slipped into the passenger seat. "That's what he's paying us to do."

"Doesn't mean we can't go check things out for ourselves."

"My thoughts exactly."

"Well then, punch it, Martha," he said as he unclipped his cell phone from his vest and dialed Edwards's number. "Let's make tracks."

"That was short and to the point," Eve said after he'd hung up.

"Tell me about it. Edwards couldn't get off the phone fast enough once I'd told him I'd located Tiffany's hotel and given him the name and address. But before he hung up, he reiterated that I was not to approach her."

Eve turned onto Las Vegas Boulevard. "It'll take a few hours for Edwards to fire up the corporate jet and make his way west. Plenty of time for us to accidentally run into Tiffany before he gets here. Say, in her hotel room, where she's probably in bed, where most sane mortals are this time of day."

"Accidents do happen," he agreed with a grin. "Like, oh, I don't know. Maybe I could accidentally finesse her room number from the front desk."

"And we could *accidentally* wander up to her floor, maybe accidentally knock on her door."

"Lots of accidents happening around here. Let's just hope none of them prove fatal—for us or for Tiffany."

It was six thirty in the morning when Billie Campbell let himself into the penthouse suite at Topanga Bay. He breathed a sigh of relief when he found the living room was empty. He'd wandered the Strip all night, just to get his head on straight. Just to think. Now he knew what he had to do.

He'd had it with these guys. He was leaving.

All he'd ever wanted was his music. Lance Reno had looked like his ticket to the top. The man had star talent. And he sang Billie's songs like Billie had always envisioned them sung, with passion and soul and the purest, truest voice he'd ever heard. Three months ago when he'd hooked up with Lance and Abe, Billie had been sure they were on their way. They'd generated interest from a couple independent labels, labels that were making things happen. Mr. Mo Mentum had been on their side—and then Lance had hooked up with Tiffany Clayborne and the music had taken a distant second place to her money.

It was time to face the truth. To give up on Lance breaking the pattern. Hell. Billie felt like some country clod who'd rolled off the turnip truck. It had been three weeks since Tiffany had come on the scene. He'd thought he could wait it out, turn his head and ignore what was happening. Figured Lance would get tired of her and when he did, they'd go back to making music.

But Lance seemed to be as addicted to Tiffany's cash as Tiffany was addicted to the coke Lance scored for her and used to keep her complacent and free with her money and her body. She could have that shit. All of them could. Billie didn't want any part of it.

And yet, he'd be in ass deep if he stuck around any longer. Something was up. He didn't know what. He just knew it made him uneasy and he needed to get away from it.

He stared at the closed bedroom door, brooded over the

way Lance treated Tiffany. Billie didn't much like her, but he didn't like the way Lance abused her, either. Nobody deserved that. He didn't know why she let Lance use her that way. Sometimes he even wondered what had happened in rich little Tiffany Clayborne's life to reduce her self-esteem to the point where she'd allow herself to be abused by Reno.

And then Billie remembered it was none of his business what she did or had done to her.

He settled in to wait for Reno to get back. When he did, he'd tell him he was through. A man didn't just sneak out without a word. A man owned up to his decisions.

He picked up his guitar, strummed a few bars of a new piece he'd been working on. Unable to concentrate, he set the guitar back down. And thought about what Tiffany must have once been. What she'd become. A cokehead.

Well, he wasn't in a position to judge. He didn't much like what he'd become, either. He'd turned a deaf ear and blind eyes to what Reno did to her, justifying it as not his concern. Not his business.

He glanced toward the master bedroom door. Reno had wedged a chair against it. Jesus. She wasn't much more than a prisoner.

Slowly, Billie rose, walked to the door . . . and heard her crying. Nothing new. She was always crying. Either that or stoned out of her head and passed out.

"Please, please."

Her voice was muffled through the door.

"Help me. Please help me."

Something that felt like fear rolled through his gut. What if she was hurt? What if she'd OD'd or something? Did he want that on his conscience?

He glanced over his shoulder toward the front door of the suite. If Lance came back and found him looking in on her, he'd have a royal shit fit.

Still, Billie moved the chair, slowly opened the bedroom door. He stuck his head inside and smelled weed. So what if

Lance would be pissed? Billie was leaving anyway. He'd had enough. Seen enough. It was time to cut his losses and move on.

In the meantime, he'd just make sure Tiffany wasn't dying or something.

She wasn't in the bedroom, but there was a light on in the bathroom and the door was open a crack. Hesitant, he walked over, rapped his knuckles on the door.

"You sick?"

All he got was sobs. Jesus. He was going to have to look inside.

She was stretched out on the floor. A joint was burning itself out on the tile beside her. It disgusted and amazed him that anyone could drop this low.

When she saw him, she pushed herself to a sitting position. And he could see then that there wasn't any blood or vomit. She was just stoned again.

"Help me. Please. Please. Help me."

Help her what? Score some more blow?

He shook his head. *Not my problem,* he told himself, and walked back out of the room.

He sank down on the plush leather sofa, grabbed the remote, and turned on the tube, settling in to wait for Lance.

Five minutes later, Billie shut the TV off. Restless, he picked up his guitar again, worked through the bridge of that tune that kept eluding him.

And he tried not to think about Tiffany Clayborne, crying in the bathroom. He tried not to think about the fact that she was someone's daughter, because that made him think of his own parents and how disappointed they'd be if they knew he was standing back and letting this happen to her.

"Not my problem," he repeated, aloud this time, and snagged a pen to write down a promising lick.

He ignored the soft whimpers coming from the other room, told himself she didn't know what she was saying. Right. Reno wanted to kill her. Paranoid. He let out a deep breath. Came with the territory. The only one who could possibly get killed around here was him if he let her out of that room.

He rose on a deep breath, walked back to the bedroom, and picked up the chair so he could wedge it back under the doorknob.

21

It took longer than they'd thought to finesse Tiffany's room number out of the desk clerk. And it was a team effort that had finally done it. McClain distracted the reservation clerk long enough for Eve to follow her fingers when she punched Tiffany's room number on the phone.

"We make a good team," Mac said as he and Eve rode the elevator to the penthouse level. It was a little past seven.

"I'll cop to teamwork when we find Tiffany and get her out of this mess. Until then, don't count your chickens. We haven't accomplished anything yet."

The elevator doors slid open and Eve stepped out into the hall.

"Wait," McClain said when they reached the door that contained the room number for what they'd determined was Tiffany's suite. "The door's ajar."

Eve immediately tensed. In her experience, open doors didn't always lead to opportunities. More often, they led to trouble.

"Wait right here," McClain said as he eased the door farther open and took a cautious step inside the room.

"I don't suppose you've got a gun on you?" she whispered, disregarding his order and following close on his heels.

"Right. Like I could smuggle a piece through airport security?"

"Just wishful thinking."

Wishful thinking dived deep and stayed submerged when they saw a large pair of feet sticking out at an odd angle behind a sofa.

"Oh God."

McClain swore softly when they rounded the sofa and saw the body. "It's Reno."

Eve's heart pounded like crazy, wild on an adrenaline rush, as McClain knelt by Reno's shoulders. Reno was on his stomach; a pool of blood stained the white carpet around his head.

McClain touched his fingers to Reno's neck.

"Dead," he said, his face grim. He rose, his gaze sweeping the room and stopping on a door that Eve assumed led to a bedroom.

"Stay here," he ordered again as he headed that direction. "And this time listen to me."

This time she did. She studied the body. Best guess was that one bullet, dead center in the back of Reno's head, execution style, had killed him. She made herself touch his face. Still warm. The blood was still seeping.

McClain's face was sober and hard when he emerged from the bedroom.

"Tiffany?" Eve asked, her heart in her throat.

He shook his head. "No sign of her. But Gorman's dead, too. Bought it the same way. And not long ago from the looks of things."

"What's going on?" she asked, at a total loss. "This doesn't make any sense."

"What about this?" His eyes were hard. "Does this make any sense?"

He held out a folded sheet of paper. Blood stained the edges.

She knew. Before she reached out with a trembling hand, she knew.

You're still dead, Eve. Hurry, hurry. Or Tiffany will be dead, too.

"Oh God."

"Come on." McClain grabbed her arm. "You're going to explain this later. Right now we've got to get out of here."

She shook herself out of her shock. "But what about Reno—"

"We can't do anything for them. And as soon as the bodies are found, the desk staff is going to remember the man and woman asking questions about Tiffany. We'll be the first ones they tag for questioning. And the first ones they'll suspect of killing them."

"We can't just leave them here."

"Oh yeah, we can." He hustled her toward the door. "Did you touch anything?"

She thought, then shook her head.

"Then we're out of here. I'll call nine-one-one from a house phone in the casino across the street and tell them about the bodies."

When they reached the elevator, he punched the down arrow, then wiped it clean of any possible prints with his shirttail. He did the same with the floor buttons inside. When they hit the ground floor, he ushered her straight through the casino and out the door. After he'd called 911 from the neighboring casino, they headed directly for their rental SUV.

"The third guy," Eve said once they were on the road. "The other band member. The one we never got a read on. What happened to him?"

"I'm more concerned about what's happening with you."

She let out a deep breath. And told him. About the attack in the rain off Blue Heron that preceded the Club Asylum explosion. About the note on her car in Key West after they were almost run down. About the subway incident and the message on her home voice mail.

"Fuck," he said quietly. "You couldn't have clued me in a little earlier?"

He was angry. She didn't blame him. "I didn't think it was necessary."

"Not necessary?"

"Was telling you going to make any difference in your search for Tiffany? No. Except to distract you. You'd have been worried about me instead."

"Ya *think*? God, woman."

"I don't need you to look out for me. And I wasn't one hundred percent certain Tiffany's disappearance was tied to my attacks until now. It's the first time he's mentioned anyone by name."

"Pull in up there." Disgusted, McClain motioned to a small hotel and casino well off the main section of the Strip. "We'll get a room. Crash for a few hours and regroup. And you will tell me everything."

She wished she knew everything. Something was still missing. There *had* to be something she was missing.

There was.

They both missed noticing the beige four-door that had pulled out two cars behind them and followed them into the hotel parking lot.

MESQUITE, NEVADA–ARIZONA BORDER

Between buying the bus tickets from Vegas to Mesquite and paying for the motel room, Billie was pretty much tapped out. He was also dead beat—and it was only eight thirty in the morning.

He pulled the drapes over the window of the room that overlooked the interstate and Mesquite's miniversion of the Vegas Strip.

Near darkness settled over the room. Which wasn't a bad thing. Number 308 at the Do Drop Inn sure as the world wasn't the penthouse suite at the Topanga Bay, but it was all he could afford. Unlike Reno, who had access to Tiffany's bank account through her ATM card, Billie was down to his last forty bucks.

At least the room was clean and cheap and it had two beds, and that was all that mattered right now. That and the fact that they were at least an hour northeast of Las Vegas. Which meant they were an hour away from Lance Reno. He'd like to have been farther, but he'd hauled Tiffany onto the bus and hauled her back off again here for two reasons. One, they both needed some sleep. Two, this was as far as he thought he'd better take her until she was alert enough to make her own decisions.

He tossed his straw Stetson on the dresser, scratched his head, and yawned. Then he sat down on the bed. And stared at Tiffany.

She was sound asleep on the other bed—had been since she'd dropped there five minutes ago. He didn't know what she'd do when she came around and realized that he'd sprung her out of that locked bedroom and hustled her away from Lance and Abe. She might be ripping mad, no matter that she'd been blubbering that Lance was going to kill her.

Not that Billie believed her. She'd been stoned was all. But still. There'd been something . . . something beyond pathetic about her. He didn't know. And there had been something compelling about her fear. It had finally gotten to him. He'd been about to wedge a chair under the door handle to the bedroom so she wouldn't be able to get out and bring the wrath of Reno down on his head when Billie realized what he was doing.

It wasn't right. Wasn't right at all, what had been done to her. And it had gone on long enough. Right then and there, feeling an urgency that was a little unnerving, he'd made a decision. He'd thrown his stuff in a duffel and tossed her things in a bag. Then he'd coaxed her to her feet, hustled her out of the room, and headed for the bus station.

He didn't know what Lance would do if he found them, and frankly, he didn't care. Hell, it was hard telling what Tiffany would do. For all he knew, she might cry rape. She might cry kidnap.

Fine. Let her. She could holler foul all she wanted. He'd just head on out the door. She could figure out her own way home—or wherever it was she wanted to go.

At least his conscience would be clear. He'd done what his mom and dad would want him to do.

With a weary yawn, he tugged off his beat-up boots, then flopped to his back on the bed. God, he was beat.

He glanced to the bed beside him. She was curled up on her side in a little ball, her knees tucked to her chin, her hands clutched together between them. That permanent tear marking her cheek. Even asleep, she looked lost.

He rolled over on his side away from her. He wasn't going to feel sorry for her. Or responsible. When she woke up, if she wanted to run back to Lance, fine. At least he'd tried.

He knew where he was going. He was going home, and right about now, home sounded pretty darn good. So did sleep.

A few minutes later, he let it take him under.

LAS VEGAS

"Why off Reno and Gorman? All indications are they were working for whoever's behind this. Do you suppose the boys were pulling a double cross?"

Mac considered Eve's speculation about why Reno and Gorman might have been murdered, all the while thinking about strangling her.

Gawd damm it! Someone wanted her dead. And she hadn't thought it was important enough to mention until she'd had—what? *Four* attempts on her life?

He sat with his back propped against the headboard on the motel bed, his legs stretched out in front of him, a paper plate with a half-eaten slice of breakfast pizza lying on the spread beside him. Trying to look casual when inside he was seething with concern and anger.

"Possibly." He tipped a plastic container of orange juice to his mouth. Took a deep pull, then picked up the pizza.

It was around 9:00 a.m. They hadn't slept. Not since New York. The plan was to finally catch a few z's, but there was the little matter of two dead bodies that kept them awake.

Like he could sleep knowing there was a death threat hanging over Eve's head.

He wasn't only frustrated with Eve. They couldn't reach Kat or Sven to tell them about Reno and Gorman so they could warn Tiffany if she called. It was not the kind of news you left on a voice mail. They'd decided to try calling them again later and eat now instead. And hash over reasons for Reno's and Gorman's killings. And reasons why someone wanted her and Tiffany dead.

Mac glanced at her. This business had shaken her. She hadn't said as much. Hell no. Not the bullets-bounce-off-of-her babe. But now that he knew what she was up against, he could see the toll it had taken. Could feel her tension even though she tried to hide it. Knowing she was with him and not out there searching for Tiffany on her own did more than the food to ease his own mind.

Still, he didn't like this turn of events. He didn't like it at all.

"If we'd shown up fifteen, maybe twenty minutes earlier, the LVPD might be bagging four bodies right now instead of two."

She shivered after he stated what they'd both been thinking.

He took another swig of juice, halfway wished it were beer. And suppressed a shiver of his own at the thought of anything happening to her.

"Kidnapping, drugs, and murder," he muttered aloud. "Things are getting dicey."

"Holy crime spree, Batman. What's gonna happen next?"

He sliced her a glance. As angry as he was, he couldn't help but grin. Humor was one way to cut the tension. Action was another. He didn't know what was going to happen next any more than she did, but he knew what *wasn't* going to happen. Eve wasn't going to get hurt. He didn't know when he'd developed this protective streak where she was concerned, but he was going to make damn sure she wasn't hurt.

"Here's what I see happening," he said, pulling his cop face as she polished off her slice of pizza, then chased it with M&M's. "You fly back to West Palm. Get your brothers to go with you to grill Edwards until he's well-done and see what kind of information you can bake out of him. I'll snoop around here, get a read on what the local PD turns up on Reno's and Gorman's murders, and you call me if and when Edwards gives you anything to go on."

He dug back into his pizza, nonchalant as hell, hoping she bought the ploy and he could personally put her on a plane and send her out of harm's way.

The prolonged silence on the far side of the room, however, did not bode well for the plan.

Finally, he chanced a look her way. *Shit.*

She was sitting there, evil-eyed and intent, waiting for him to make eye contact.

"Why don't *you* go back to West Palm?" she suggested with a combative stare. "Instead of grilling Edwards, you can roast him over hot coals. And while we're in cooking mode, you can marinate your thick head in a bucket of brine for oh, say, thirty to forty minutes. That ought to clear out your sinuses and help with your thought process."

He slowly finished chewing. "That transparent, huh?"

"As glass. What is it? You look at me and all you see is blond?" She rose, walked over to the bed. "I'm not stupid. Neither is Edwards. He's not going to roll over just because I ask him to, and you know it.

"Look," she insisted. "I can handle myself. You're not sending me out of the line of fire while you play Mr. Macho and keep the little lady safely on the sidelines."

OK. Truth time. He set the pizza aside. Reached for her hand. "I don't want you hurt."

"Excuse me?"

Oops. Guess *that* was exactly the wrong thing to say. He cleared his throat. Rubbed his thumb over the back of her hand. "OK. That sounded proprietary."

She snorted and mimicked one of his earlier cracks. "Ya *think*?"

"Eve, look—"

"Stow it, McClain. See, this is why I didn't tell you. I don't need you looking out for me, got it? I'm a big girl. I can take care of myself. And you do not make decisions for me. I mean, my God. What do you take me for?"

Now, he hadn't intended to get sidetracked. But he couldn't help it. She was just so vital standing there. Her blue eyes raining sparks, her nostrils flared in defiance, her shoulders thrown back with pride, and that incredible mouth set in an indignant line.

"What I take you for," he said, catching her by surprise when he tugged her down on top of him, "is damn beautiful when you're mad."

As he'd intended, she actually growled as she wedged her palms against his chest and pushed up so she could glare at him.

"You just keep opening your mouth and filling it with your size eleven chauvinist foot, don't you? Want to try for three out of three? You haven't pointed out that I'm the weaker sex yet."

He took it as a good sign that she was smiling—even if it was laced with sarcasm and pity. And Jesus, he needed her pity, he realized as she hovered there above him and a tide of emotion swelled up inside him, sending his heart into overdrive.

Panic had him rolling her to her back on the bed, pinning her with his body. He pushed up to his elbows, caged her head in his hands, and searched her face. He saw surprise, humor, even remnants of shock, and thought, *Damn, I could be in real trouble here.*

All the signs were there. He couldn't bear the thought of anything happening to her. Didn't want to consider the day when they found Tiffany and they went their separate ways and he wouldn't see Eve every day. Hell, he was simply *looking* at her and he felt a groundswell of want and need and—

"McClain?"

He blinked, shook his head in the hopes of clearing it. "Yeah?" The word came out on a rusty croak. As rusty as his ability to deal with all the crazy thoughts tumbling around in his head.

"What is it about this part that always hangs you up? Are you going to kiss me, or what?"

He searched her face, saw everything good and worthy, and at the moment he also saw a healthy level of confusion his sudden silence had caused.

Well, that made two of them who were confused.

About one thing, though, he was crystal clear.

"Yeah," he whispered, and lowered his mouth to hers. "I'm going to kiss you."

And he did. Slow and deep. Long and sweet. Needing her softness. Needing her heat. Craving her hunger that the humming tension of her body, the restless give and the greedy take of her hands, told him was escalating by degrees.

Oh no. He knew what she was about. She wanted fast and hard. She wasn't going to get it. Not this time. This time, he was going to take her slow no matter how easy it would be to let her drag him under in a whirlwind of blinding greed.

Sometimes a man needed slow. He needed it now. Needed to know she was here, safe and secure in his arms. So did she; she just hadn't figured it out yet.

They were exhausted. Their defenses were down and the sexual tension that had chased them from Palm Beach to New York and now to Vegas had nipped at their heels every step of the way.

So he settled her with the deep press of his hips into hers. Set the pace with a languid sweep of his rough hands down the silken length of her body. With a host of lazy, languorous kisses that he scattered along her brow, the delicate rise of her cheekbone, the elegant curve of her jaw.

"Easy, cupcake," he whispered against her mouth. "Let's just take this one easy."

On a thready sigh, she relented. On a protracted moan, she surrendered. Let him undress her. In his own good time.

She let him play with the velvet softness of her breasts, tease her rosy pink nipples to aching peaks, let him explore with unhurried wonder that amazing crease where hip met thigh.

With her fingers gripping the sheets beside her hips, she rose to him, allowed him to savor, sip by thirsty sip, the sleek, wet flesh between her thighs. Let him drink until she couldn't take any more. And when he gently sucked her clitoris, she cried his name and poured like a vessel into his mouth.

He whispered her name over and over as he kissed his way leisurely up the giving warmth of her body, tasting his fill, savoring the scent of her wasted on sex, her breath thready and broken in the aftermath, her heart pounding, pounding, pounding beneath his lips.

Finally, he filled her. Took her on a long, slippery ride that stole them both away from danger and unknown threats and sent them adrift on a haze of sensation. With long, deep glides and a slow, steady ride, he went the same way she had and slid down the path to oblivion.

22

BILLIE CAUGHT THE SACK OF FAST-FOOD burgers and fries between his teeth and inserted the key in the motel room door. He wasn't sure what he would find when he let himself inside. He'd been hoping he'd make it back before Tiffany woke up. Figured it was a pretty good bet that if she woke up in a strange motel all alone, she'd freak. Or run.

He'd feel guilty if she ran. Especially since she didn't have any money. At least he hadn't seen any when he'd tossed her stuff in a carry-on earlier this morning. The only thing Reno had left her of any value was a cell phone that Billie had shut off in case Reno called her and woke her up. Money hadn't been a priority. Maybe it should have been, but he'd just wanted to get out of there.

"Come on," he muttered through the teeth he'd clenched around the bag, and rattled the key around in the lock when the door wouldn't open.

He fiddled with it a little more, was about to give up and go to the office for a new key, when he saw the curtain move. He stepped back, looked, and there was Tiffany, peering out at him.

Now what? She didn't look so sure of herself. Or of him.

The curtain fell back in place. A few seconds later, the door opened as far as the security bolt would allow it.

She stared at him through the crack. And said exactly nothing.

"I brought food," he said, holding up the sack.

She considered him a little while longer. "Where's Lance?"

Billie considered her right back. "Last I knew, he was about fifty miles south of here."

Surprise widened her eyes. Then relief. Then the return of caution. "Abe?"

Billie lifted a shoulder. "Suppose he's with Reno."

She sucked her lower lip between her teeth—and Billie couldn't help but notice how young she looked, despite the layers of makeup and the thick mascara that was smeared all around her eyes.

"Where . . . where are we?"

"Mesquite."

"Texas?" she asked, sounding puzzled.

"Nevada."

Silence, then a soft, "Oh.

"What's your last name?" she asked finally.

"Campbell," he said, and decided to go for broke. "Look. I got you out of Vegas because I didn't like what was happening to you. They don't know where you are or that you're with me. If you want to go back, fine. I'll buy you a bus ticket. But you were making noises about—"

He stopped abruptly when the door closed. Almost immediately, it opened again, wide this time, because she'd unhooked the security bolt.

"You saved my life," she said, and moved back from the doorway so he could step inside.

He entered the room cautiously, still not sure what she might do, even though she looked friendly enough. "Well, you seemed to think it needed saving."

She just kept staring at him . . . like she didn't know what to make of him. Maybe she was scared. Maybe she was still stoned.

"I'm not going to hurt you." He set the sack of food on the dresser. "I just thought, you know, that maybe I'd better get you out of there."

She made a clipped nod, still uncertain. One corner of her mouth tipped up in a short, tight smile. Again, like she was afraid to trust what she was hearing.

"Do you want sex?" she asked flatly.

He blinked. Blinked again. "Hell no!"

She actually looked hurt.

"I mean, jeez. What kind of a question is that to ask out of the blue? I didn't do this because I expected you to, you know, have, um, sex with me." God. If this didn't beat all. He felt blood flood his cheeks with heat.

The smile that tilted her lips this time made her look almost pretty. "You're embarrassed."

"Am not," he sputtered, lifting his hat, then settling it again. "Look, you hungry or not?"

He tore into the sack, grabbed a burger and a box of fries and a Coke for himself, and held the rest out to her. Then he walked to the far side of the room, plunked down in a chair, and gnawed off a big bite of burger.

"Thanks," she said, and took the sack to the bed. Very carefully, she unwrapped the tissue paper from the burger, took a cautious bite.

She made a face. "It has mustard on it."

"So?" he said, feeling cranky all of a sudden.

"I don't like mustard."

"So don't eat it."

She blinked. Eyed the burger, eyed him, then took another bite. "Guess it's not so bad," she said after she'd chewed and swallowed.

Then they sat there and ate in silence. Billie still didn't know what to think of her. Didn't know what she'd do. But it was funny. All of a sudden, he had a hard time not looking at her. Seemed like she was having a hard time not looking at him, too. Weird.

"What were you doing with those guys?" she asked, touching her fingers lightly to the corner of her mouth and brushing away some salt. Her finger caught on one of those stupid lip rings, and she winced but didn't say anything.

"I liked the way Reno sang my songs. Figured we were on our way to a recording contract, maybe."

"What stopped you?"

"You," he said, and he said it mean so she'd understand he thought she was trouble.

She looked at her burger, looked back at him. "I'm sorry."

He showed her his disgusted face because he was just a little too tempted to try to make her feel better by telling her not to worry about it.

She rose suddenly, set the half-eaten burger aside, and headed for the bathroom.

"You aren't going to do something stupid, are you?" he asked, uneasy all of a sudden, like maybe she'd hurt herself now that she appeared to be straight and realized how low she'd sunk with Reno.

"More stupid than what I've been doing, you mean?" She stopped at the bathroom door. Shook her head. "No. I'm not going to do something stupid."

She shut the door behind her. He stared at it for a while, then relaxed when he heard the shower spray hit the bathroom wall.

Now what? he wondered as he finished off his meal. She stayed in the bathroom a long time. Long enough that he picked up his guitar so he'd have something to do with his hands.

He was lost in a song when the bathroom door opened. Steam rolled out of the small room and then she stepped out of the mist like some strange creature who was wary of making an appearance in a brave new world.

Well, for the love of Mike.

She'd wrapped herself up in a towel. And except for that pure white piece of terry cloth, she was as bare as a babe.

Bare feet. Bare face. Without all that makeup, he could actually see it.

Pretty face, he thought again. Even with that single sad tear burned into her cheek. He'd never noticed her eyes before—couldn't see 'em through that thick black gunk she always painted on them. They were green. Soft as meadow grass.

He dragged his thoughts away from such sappy sentiments. This was Tiffany Clayborne. Nothing had changed. Except he got the most concrete feeling that everything had.

The lip rings were gone. Her hair was even a different color. That wild raspberry red was gone. It was still wet, but it looked to be sort of sandy brown.

And standing there, still dripping from the shower, squeaky clean, not hiding behind paint and dye and bling blings, she looked all of twelve years old.

"I . . . um . . . do I have any clothes?"

He must have just sat there because she said, "Billie? Did you bring any clothes for me?"

"Oh, um, yeah. Um . . . in your bag. I just grabbed some stuff I thought you might need."

She smiled at him. Like something he'd said made her . . . he didn't know. Happy?

"Thanks," she said, picked up her leather bag, and set it on the bed.

He stood up, not stupefied, he told himself, and watched her rifle around in it and finally give him a baleful look.

"What? Didn't I get the right stuff?"

"I was just wishing I had some jeans," she said. Then she looked at him. Hard. "What size are you?"

"Me?"

"You got an extra pair? And maybe an extra T-shirt?"

He did. But he wasn't so sure he wanted to see them on her. Still, he trudged to his old canvas duffel and dug out both jeans and T-shirt.

"Thanks."

She disappeared into the bathroom again . . . and came out wearing his clothes.

It made him feel funny seeing her in his stuff. Not funny ha-ha. Funny thinking-about-her-asking-him-if-he-wanted-to-have-sex funny.

"What do you think?" she asked, turning a slow circle with her arms out.

He crossed his arms over his chest, looked at his boot tips. He thought she'd put some bumps in the front of his T-shirt, that's what he thought.

"Where are you going from here?" she asked, looking unsure of herself again suddenly.

"Home," he said without hesitation, because that was the only thing in this whole sordid mess that he was sure of.

"Home? Like, your own home? Alone somewhere?"

"To my folks'."

"Oh." And then, "Where's that?"

He'd never noticed that scuff on the toe of his boot before. Couldn't seem to take his eyes off of it. "Utah."

"Is that far?"

"Hundred miles or so."

He could feel her staring at him. He looked up. She'd slung her weight on one leg, crossed her arms over her middle, uncrossed them. Then she looked at the ceiling and he could see tears form in her eyes.

Well hell. Now what?

"Do you want to come with me?" he heard himself asking just as he realized it was the only thing he could do.

Her face turned all red, and she pinched her lips together, like she was trying not to cry. She lost the fight. A big fat tear rolled down her cheek.

She nodded. Looked at him with so much relief in her eyes that he knew she figured he'd probably just saved her life again.

He figured out something, too, in that moment. Tiffany Clayborne had no place else to go.

LAS VEGAS

Eve woke up thinking, *Wow.*

What had just happened? She glanced at her watch. Strike that. What had happened three and a half hours ago?

Beside her, gorgeous and rumpled and, bless him, naked as the day he was born, McClain slept—with a smile on his face.

Guess that answered the "Was it good for you?" question. It wasn't just exhaustion that had put him in that deep sleep.

And yet the other question remained. What *had* just happened? Three and a half hours ago.

She rose slowly. Headed for the shower, still so relaxed and wrung out, her legs were wobbly.

It was more than great sex. More than anything they'd done before. There'd been tenderness and an underlying urgency he'd taken great measures to hold at bay. And my, oh my, he'd shown a dedication to her pleasure that had elevated her orgasm to heights she'd never reached before. And he'd taken her pretty high in New York.

So, what was it?

Nothing she wanted to think about, she decided with a scowl and a real nervous clutch in her chest as she lathered her hair and let the hot shower spray invigorate her skin. Nothing she could afford to think about.

Chalk it up to heightened senses. Chalk it up to adrenaline—for sure hers had been working overtime since they'd found Reno and Gorman dead. And the note with their bodies.

He was taunting her. Warning her. Either she died or Tiffany did. Who was this guy?

She used the hotel hair dryer, called her hairstyle good, and, wrapped in a towel, walked into the bedroom. Determined not to dwell on the appealing sight of McClain in all his naked glory, she flipped the sheet over his lap, grabbed the remote, and turned on the TV, muting it so she wouldn't wake him. She was reading the news captions, hoping for a report on the murders and popping M&M's, when the GPS went off with a loud bleat.

McClain reared up in bed like he'd been shot.

"What?" Bleary-eyed, he dragged his hands across his face while she ran for the tracking unit.

"Tiffany," she said. "She's turned on her phone."

"Kat said she sounded straight," Eve told Mac as he emerged from a quick cold shower. Less than five minutes had passed since the GPS had gone off and Kat had called Eve's cell, confirming that Tiffany had, in fact, called her.

"Anything else?" he asked with a glance her way. She'd dressed for the heat in a soft yellow tank top and denim shorts. She'd also packed while he'd shaved, then hit the shower. She was faster at getting ready than any other woman he'd ever known. He liked that about her. Liked a lot of things about her. Too many things, in fact.

"Other than the fact that she was doing fine, she was pretty tight-lipped," Eve said, addressing his question.

"I can't believe Kat didn't find out who she was with and where they were headed," Mac sputtered as he ditched the towel, pulled on clean boxers, and snagged a pair of jeans.

"She tried. But for some reason, Tiffany wouldn't tell her. She only said that she was no longer with Reno and that she was going to take some time to think things through. And that a friend was helping her."

Mac tugged a white polo shirt over his head. "She didn't give any indication that she knew Reno was dead?"

"None. Kat said she didn't sound spooked or afraid or even nervous about anything. Just short and to the point before she hung up and evidently turned the phone off. Kat, however, about blew a gasket when I told her about how we'd found the bodies."

Mac let out a deep breath, found a pair of socks, and dropped down on the edge of the bed to tug them on.

"At least we got a location on the GPS. And we know now for certain that she's still alive." It was a huge relief. And a helluva lot more than they'd known—he checked his watch—five hours ago. "Alive and completely unaware that Reno and Gorman are dead and that whoever killed them is most likely after her and you, too."

"I told Kat we'd call her back after we'd discussed what to do next."

He'd given that some thought. "Have Kat call her cell phone and leave a message. Have her tell Tiffany about Reno's and Gorman's murders."

"And what about us? Does she tell her that we're looking for her?"

He rose, looked around for his shoes. "Once she finds out about Reno, she's going to be jumpy as hell. She's not going to trust anyone—especially not you, someone Edwards hired. She might trust me, but she's pretty pissed at me right now."

"Then let's have Kat tell her that *she* hired me once she realized Tiffany was in trouble in New York. We won't mention you."

"That'd work. Have her leave your cell phone number with Tiffany, too. Maybe we'll get lucky and she'll actually turn on Kat's phone, pick up the message, and call."

Eve made a quick call to Kat and relayed the plan.

"Well, that's done. Now we wait," Eve said when she'd hung up. "If Tiffany doesn't call, at the very least, we'll get a read on her location from the tracker."

"Speaking of which," he slipped into his shoes and grabbed the map he'd been studying along with his breakfast pizza, "let's move. The GPS pinpoints her in Mesquite. According to the map, it sits right on the Nevada–Arizona border. We take Interstate Fifteen all the way. With a little luck, we can be there in an hour, hour and a half."

The day was desert hot when they walked out the hotel doors at 1:30 toward their rented SUV. Squinting against the sun's glare, Mac juggled his duffel, the map, and a bottle of water he'd picked up at the casino snack bar.

"Hold it," he said as he managed to fish the keys to the SUV out of his pocket. "Not that I'm getting paranoid or anything . . ."

He got down on all fours and looked under the vehicle. And froze—for all of a nanosecond.

"Run!" he yelled, pushing to his feet.

He grabbed Eve's arm and half-dragged, half-pushed her ahead of him.

"Run, dammit!"

The blast cut off his words right along with his breath. The concussion sent him airborne.

It could have been a second, could have been a lifetime, that he flew through the air. And it was nothing but sheer dumb luck that the blast threw him up and over the hood of a Cadillac. It broke his fall and sent him tumbling to the asphalt beside it.

Pain exploded through his knee just as the secondary blast—probably from the gas tank exploding—rained glass and metal and burning rubber all the hell over the parking lot. It would have killed him for sure had it not been for the Caddy.

He was still shaking his head to clear the ringing in his ears when he realized he couldn't see Eve.

He rose to his feet with a roar, staggered, and made a frantic visual search of the lot. "Eve!"

Nothing.

"Eve!" he yelled again, then felt the air rip from his lungs on a gasp of relief when her head emerged from behind a Japanese import.

Limping, he raced over to her. Gripped her upper arms in his hands and looked her over good.

"I'm OK," she said, one hand clutching her purse close to her chest, the other clasping the side of her head as if she needed to hold it on. "I'm OK. Really," she insisted.

There was blood on her knee, a raspberry the size of an orange on her elbow, and an inch-long scrape on her cheek. He'd bet the farm she was going to turn up with bruises on top of bruises in the morning.

And if his heart hammered any harder, he was going to have a severe case of internal bleeding. He didn't care. Just like he didn't care that his knee hurt like a bitch. Eve was all right. He hugged her hard against him, probably putting a few more bruises on that fragile skin.

His initial panic over, now that he could touch her, his mind finally engaged.

"We've got to get out of here."

She didn't hesitate. She just gripped his hand and took off with him when he hobbled off at a pathetic imitation of a dead run.

23

A HUGE AND HAPPY PARTY CROWD GATHERED in a semicircle around an outdoor stage in a beer garden behind Harrah's on the Strip. Onstage, a Bon Jovi tribute band struck the first chords of "You Give Love a Bad Name."

And the crowd went wild.

Lifting their beers high and rocking with music, Eve and Mac—just another vacationing couple for all practical purposes—partied in the shade on a hot Vegas afternoon. The plan was to blend in like apples in a basket of apples, hiding in plain sight. So far, so good. They were still alive. And they needed a breather.

They'd been on the run for a good hour before they stopped here to retool after ducking in and out of casinos as far down Las Vegas Boulevard as Mandalay Bay. They'd run up escalators, over pedestrian crosswalks, ridden the tram, and cleaned some of the blood off at a Caesars Palace restroom. They'd cut through buffet lines at Bally's and were now at Harrah's. Mac was marginally satisfied they'd lost whoever had been waiting in the parking lot with Mr. Detonator in hand.

Several women stood beside their tables dancing to the beat and swooning over the Jon Bon Jovi look-alike lead singer while a sassy blond bartender jumped up on top of a long horseshoe-shaped bar. With practiced skill and deadly accuracy, she poured red, white, and blue concoctions out of stacked silver containers into twenty or so Tom Collins glasses and never spilled a drop.

Mac was interested in not spilling anything, either. He was particularly interested in not spilling any blood. He was specifically interested in not spilling any more of Eve's.

For that reason, he was barely aware of all the activity around them, except for the need to look like they were a part of it. He resettled the aviator sunglasses he'd lifted from a sixtyish bluehair playing a Lucky 7's machine at the Hard Rock and tugged the UNLV baseball cap he'd also filched lower over his eyes. Beside him, Eve also wore shades and a hot pink ball cap that he'd grabbed for her at the Monte Carlo.

"Your friend is starting to play a little rough." He tipped up his beer, swallowed deep.

"It doesn't feel too much like he's playing. And he doesn't feel much like a friend." They were the first words she'd spoken since she'd assured him she was OK. They'd been making tracks at a dead run ever since.

"Who in the hell is this person?"

"That's what we've got to find out."

She propped her elbows on the table and lowered her head into her hands. "A bomb. God. What if you hadn't checked?"

They'd be dust particles, that's what. Just another million or so irritants for tourists to wipe out of their eyes.

He frowned at her lowered head. "You doin' OK?"

She lifted her head. Gave a big sigh. "Yeah. I'm fine. And I'm ticked. That's going to scar," she sputtered, studying her knee.

Atta girl. She was starting to get pissed.

"We need to find Tiffany before he does. Before we all turn up dead. Just because she got away from Reno before he passed on to the great poppy field in the sky, there's no guarantee she's out of danger."

"You're assuming our phantom bomber hasn't done her in."

"She's alive." Mac sat forward in his chair, palmed his glass of beer between both hands, and rolled it back and forth. "That's part of his game. He wants to make you sweat. He wants a showdown and he's taunting you."

She nodded with reluctance. "The question remains: to what end? Why does he want me dead? Why use Tiffany as a pawn?

"There's something at stake here that we're missing. Money, power, revenge? Love? Hate? Did I miss any possible motives?" Nine times out of ten, murder came down to one of the issues she'd just listed.

She pushed out a weary grunt. "That's the million-dollar question. I don't know. But whoever it is, he's persistent."

Mac lifted his stolen cap, dragged a hand through his hair before resettling it, his mind working overtime.

"OK. So. He's been following you from the beginning. Which means he knows we've been traveling together since New York. Which just prompts more questions. If he's working with Edwards, why hasn't he called me on it?"

"Maybe I've been barking up the wrong tree with Edwards."

That was the logical conclusion and the impossible question.

"Still, it's a little coincidental that the boys were killed shortly after we informed Mr. Comb-over that we'd located all of them in Vegas, don't you think?"

"But he hired *you* to find Tiffany. Why would he add you into the mix? Why wouldn't he just let me fumble around looking for her on my own?"

There was that. "Maybe it was all for show," he speculated. "You know. To satisfy the old man. Make Clayborne think he was looking for Tiffany when, in fact, Edwards was trying to get rid of her—and you, for whatever reason." He leaned back, hooked an arm over the back of his chair. "Try this for size. What if Reno and Gorman worked for Edwards? Maybe he hired them to get Tiffany out of the picture. Maybe the guy after you is just another hired hit man."

"Power?" she speculated, huddling with him over the table. "Is that our motive then? With Tiffany out of the way, does Edwards figure he's in line for something? Something big? Something more than he's already got?"

"What, exactly, does he have? A job as second fiddle to a nutcase."

"An obscenely *rich* nutcase."

"Livin' on a Prayer" ended to a chorus of whistles and cheers. Mac joined the enthusiastic applause.

"OK," Eve said after the band launched into "Let It Rock," which had most of the audience on their feet and rocking all around them. "Let's think here. Who else besides Edwards knew we were in Vegas? Ethan. Kat and Sven."

"You're forgetting someone." He leaned in closer to be heard above the music and the crowd. "Clayborne."

"You're right. It's possible that Clayborne has also known where we've been, the moves we've made."

And the consequences of Clayborne being the powder filling the keg were just too horrible to contemplate. Neither one of them said anything for a while, but they were both wondering if it was possible.

"We'd have to assume he's held a grudge against me for a very long time."

"Maybe you screwed something up for him during that kidnapping attempt."

"Like what?"

"Who knows? Get your friend in the Secret Service to check into it. Or your brothers. Maybe having your job wasn't enough for him."

"They're already on it. But if that's the case, then why didn't Clayborne just have me taken care of sooner? He's got the money, the power, the means. Of course, he's turned completely loony tunes in the last few years."

"Maybe it took that long for things to jell for him."

"But why involve Tiffany? She's his daughter, for Pete's sake. Sure, he's never been much of a father, but still."

Mac shook his head. "You said it yourself. The guy's nuts."

"No," she stated adamantly. "It can't be Clayborne. It's something else. Something I'm missing. Something that does tie Tiffany and me together."

"Well, whatever it is, I hope you figure it out soon."

"I'm sorry you got involved in this."

"Not your fault. It's my fault for not being square with you."

"Look, I was already in this. You had nothing to do with that. And you had no way of knowing these things were going to play into each other."

"And how exactly do they play? And where does all of this leave Tiffany?"

"Dead, I'm afraid, unless we find her. I need to call Ethan again," Eve said abruptly. "Maybe he's turned up something."

"Better do it on the fly," Mac said, draining his beer. "We need to get moving again before we're spotted."

"But I love this song."

He was about to point out that this was probably not the time to indulge her musical ear when he saw her ornery grin.

"Come on, smart mouth. You like it so much, buy the CD. Let's move."

They were riding the tram that connected the casinos from one end of the Strip to the other when she called Ethan. He was dead silent as Eve relayed the details of the bombing. And when she was finished, her brother wasn't satisfied with just the facts. He wanted every little detail. When she'd given them, his voice was flat with concern.

"You sure you're OK?"

"Yes," she insisted. What was it with these men that they couldn't take her at her word? "I'm fine."

"What about McClain?"

She glanced at the sullen man sitting beside her. "What about him?"

"Are you sure you can trust him?"

As if reading her thoughts, McClain turned to her, smiled that tight, reassuring smile that told her everything was going to be OK. *I'm here. You'll be fine.*

Damn chauvinist, she thought with affection.

It was right then that she realized that, yeah, she trusted him. No ifs, ands, or buts.

She told Ethan as much before they disconnected with a final warning for her to be careful and a promise that he'd keep digging and get back to her.

She pocketed her cell phone on a deep breath.

So. She'd just told Ethan that she trusted McClain.

Wasn't that a kick in the pants? Talk about your unexpected revelations. She was suddenly face-to-face with a whopper. Who knew a life/death experience would have a tendency to lay everything out there bare naked and open for inspection?

And as long as she was inspecting, she realized that she felt a little too much of something else for this man, reacted a little too strongly to the way he smiled, the way he moved. But more to the way he looked at her sometimes—like she was the most important thing in the world to him.

A vivid memory dragged her out of fantasyland. She'd seen that look fourteen years ago. And then, she'd never seen him again—until several days ago.

Granted, it had been an amazing several days, but one way or another, she had to face facts. Conquer feelings. Think with her head. Not her heart or her hormones. Nothing had changed. McClain hadn't changed. He was still a charmer, but he was still not a man on whom to pin any hopes.

What she could count on from him was grief. And plenty of it. Well, and good sex. Plenty of that, too.

And trouble. Trouble, quite frankly, wasn't something she needed a lot more of at the moment. Seemed to be plenty of that coming her way from another quarter.

Her cell phone rang again.

It was Bob Gleason.

"I dug out the closed file on Tiffany Clayborne," he said without preamble.

"The protection file?"

"We never pinned down why an attempt was made to abduct the girl."

"Billionaire's daughter. Ransom money. Seemed pretty clear-cut to me."

"On the surface. You were cut out of the loop when you were forced out of service. The two men who tried to nap her? Their names were Petrov Yanev and Stayon Georgiev."

The air just sort of deflated from Eve's lungs. She'd never known their names. Never known the names of the two men whose lives she'd taken.

"That silence tells me you forgot there for a minute that they were the bad guys."

Yeah. It was easy to forget.

"Anyway, they had roots in Bulgaria."

Eve frowned. Thought. "Isn't that where Clayborne was at the time? Supposedly working on some arms deal for his company when in fact he was working undercover for Uncle?"

"So goes the story. But I got to thinking. So I did some more digging on the old man. Lots of loose ends there. Lots of stuff that doesn't add up."

"What are you suggesting?"

"I'm not sure yet. I'll let you know when I tie things up."

"Well, you'd better hurry. Things are getting a little dicey here. But you might be on to something. What's happening with me and Tiffany—it's tied together."

As briefly as possible she led him through the events that

had culminated in Reno's and Gorman's murders and the note at the scene.

"It's like a game or something. Why a game? Why all this strung-out drama?"

"Seems to be the big question, huh? I'll keep digging. Watch yourself."

"Thanks, Bob. I will."

When she hung up, she knew that she was not only going to watch it a little closer, she was also going to think about Bob's idea for a very long time.

"What?" McClain asked beside her.

"We might have our link."

MESQUITE, NEVADA–ARIZONA BORDER

"Up here, take a left at the light," Eve directed as she consulted the GPS unit.

Mac flipped the turn signal on their new rental vehicle. After they'd left the beer garden and taken their tram ride, they'd hailed a cab.

"Where to?" the driver had asked.

"Doesn't matter. Just drive."

The cabbie had taken one look at their cuts and bruises, silently handed them a first-aid kit, and punched it. He hadn't asked any more questions. Guess the ads were right. What happened in Vegas stayed in Vegas.

Eventually, they'd had him wait for them at a pawnshop. McClain was now packing a 9mm Beretta and Eve had made room in her oversize purse for a .38 S & W. They'd each bought extra ammo. The last stop in Vegas had been a car rental agency.

As a precaution, Eve had phoned Ethan again and asked for help acquiring the vehicle. Ethan had charged the rental by phone using Nolan's wife's, Jillian's, card. The news anchor for KGLO TV in West Palm had kept her credit cards in her maiden name, Kincaid, even after she'd married Nolan because that's how she was known professionally in the area. With the rental charged in her name, the transaction couldn't be traced—at least not immediately—to either Eve or Mac. It might buy them a little time from whoever was after them.

They'd left Vegas a little over an hour ago in a white Jeep Cherokee, heading for the coordinates the GPS tracker had provided to Mesquite. No clothes, no laptop. They'd been lucky to escape the bomb blast with their lives and their few personal items. Eve had her purse and cell phone. Mac, his wallet and phone. The GPS had been lost in the bombing.

Now, of course, they each had a gun. Kind of told the tale about the anxiety level. Since increasing Kat's would serve no purpose, they opted not to call her and fill her in on the bombing. And since their luck wasn't exactly holding on the good side, they hadn't been lucky enough for Tiffany to have turned her phone on again before they'd lost the GPS unit. And of course, they had no expectations of actually finding her at the motel pinpointed by the tracker. She was probably long gone by now. But it was a place to start and they actually got a stroke of good luck when they started asking questions at the motel desk.

"Nope. Never seen her." The desk clerk looked to be about twenty. He had a thin, acne-scarred face and spooky gray eyes. His shoulders were scrawny and thin on a tall, spidery frame. His shirt was dingy gray.

"But then, I just came on duty," he continued. "You'd want to talk with Janet. Yo, Janet!" he yelled as a middle-aged woman entered the lobby through a door marked: Employees Only.

Janet had a huge black purse tucked under her arm. An unopened bottle of Diet Coke was tucked in a pocket of the purse, and she held an unlit filtered cigarette in her other hand. Except for the cigarette, she looked like the type who would go home and bake cookies for her grandkids. Since

Mac put her weight at about two-fifty, he figured she'd probably sat down and eaten the bulk of those cookies herself.

"Folks here need to ask you a couple of questions," the
clerk said.

Janet regarded them with suspicion through faded brown
eyes framed with crow's-feet and wire-rimmed bifocals.
"You the police or something?"

"Oh no. Nothing like that," Eve assured her while Mac
stood back and let her handle it woman to woman. "I'm
looking for my sister. We had a little family fight and she
ran. You know how it is."

"Boy, do I. Got two girls of my own. Fight like banshees.
Scream at each other all the time. It's over boys mostly."

Eve smiled with empathy. "Yeah. I know. We think my
sister is with a boy now. Someone who isn't very good for
her. My mom—well, she's sick and all. I want to find my sister and bring her home before . . ." She hesitated, squeezed
out a tear. Got control of herself. "Before it's too late."

Mac laid a supportive hand on her shoulder. He thought it
was a nice touch.

"Oh, sweetie. Don't you cry now. I'm sure you'll find her.
What's she look like?"

Eve gave her Tiffany's description.

"She was here," Janet said, excited that she could help.
"Her and some skinny runt of a cowboy. Checked in about
eight thirty this morning. Left around . . . oh, I'm thinking
three o'clock."

Eve checked her watch. It was almost five o'clock. She
and Mac were two hours behind them. But they had a lead.
Possibly a good one.

Eve took Janet's hand. "I don't suppose you saw what
they were driving? Or if they said where they were going?"

"They weren't driving. But you might try the bus stop.
The boy asked for a schedule. I sent 'em back to the station.
Check Boomer's Texaco down on Sandhill."

"A gas station?"

Janet chuckled. "Honey, round these parts you get a twofer. The bus stop is at Boomer's."

Par for the course, evidently, in a Nevada desert town made up of gas stations, casinos, and, according to the sign, around twelve thousand residents. When they got to Boomer's, Mac filled up with gas while Eve flirted information out of Boomer's boy, Buddy, who just couldn't grin wide enough when she turned a high-octane smile his way.

"A young man—thin—and a young woman buy bus tickets in here earlier today?"

"Mighta," Buddy said, whipping a grease rag out of the hip pocket of his oil-stained blue coveralls. "Chet'd be the one to talk to. He sells the tickets. Come on. We can ask him together."

Mac shook his head. Buddy was smitten. Surprise. So was he.

Grim-faced, ignoring the increasing pain in his knee, he topped off the tank, replaced the gas cap, and washed the windows while Eve worked her magic on the boys.

"OK," Eve said, settling into the passenger seat five minutes later. She handed him a fresh bottle of water and a bag of peanuts. For herself, she'd bought an iced tea and a pound bag of M&M's. "They're headed north."

"Salt Lake?" Mac speculated as he uncapped his water.

"Not quite that far." She buckled up, opened the M&M's. "Parowan, Utah."

"Come again?"

She checked the map. Made a puzzled sound. "Far as I can tell, it's just a little dot a mile or so off I-Fifteen." She calculated the mileage. "Maybe a couple of hours from here tops."

"So, we're off to Parowatsits."

"Parowan," she corrected. "I wonder why they picked there? Suppose maybe this boy lives in that area?"

"I seem to recall the word *cowboy* coming up. So maybe."

They'd seen a lot of pickups and stock trailers on the road from Vegas to Mesquite. This part of the West was a land of cowboys, it seemed.

Cowboys and, unfortunately for Tiffany and for them, a killer.

Things just kept getting better.

24

THE RURAL TOWN, AS IT TURNED OUT, WAS exactly what it looked like on the map. An ink spot. Granted, it was a pretty ink spot that boasted a one-street business district, approximately twenty-five hundred residents, and a really nice little park.

They bought burgers and fries and soda at the Parowan Café, then drove to the park to eat and stretch their aching muscles.

"Do not ask me again how I'm feeling, OK?" Eve advised as she eased gingerly onto a park bench. "We're both battered and bruised. We're both stiff and sore. And don't think I haven't noticed that your knee is bothering you, so don't look at me like I need to be in ICU every time I forget myself and groan."

"OK, tough guy. No more concern."

"If you want to be concerned about something, start worrying about how we're going to find Tiffany and her cowboy before the bad guy finds them—or before he finds us."

Mac set the sack of takeout on the bench between them, dug around inside, then handed her a burger. "All we can do is hope she calls Kat again. And do a little canvassing in town to see if anyone saw them."

So that's what they did after they ate. They stopped in at the local general store, bought a few necessities—like changes of underwear and some jeans and T-shirts—and asked questions.

They came up as empty as a dry well.

"So what do you think about calling Edwards . . . just to feel him out?" Mac asked as they climbed into the SUV yet again after several stop and query missions. He'd received calls on his cell phones from Edwards. He'd ignored them but had picked up his messages. All of them had gone something to the tune of, "Call me immediately with a report or you're fired!"

"On one hand, I'd like to call Edwards and gauge his reaction to the news about Reno and Gorman. On the other, since we have no idea if he or Clayborne is in on this, I don't want to tip him off to the fact that we're still on Tiffany's trail and lead them to her before we can get her to safety."

Mac eased out into traffic and headed for a gas station. "Logically, we should be thinking about contacting the feds or the local law, but I think we should keep them out of it for now, too. If Clayborne is involved, it's hard telling how long his arm reaches. He could have some officials tucked all neat and tidy in his pocket."

"There is that. Money talks. His kind of money shouts. We could actually put Tiffany in more danger."

"Not to mention, we can't call the LVPD without implicating ourselves in Reno's and Gorman's murders."

He dragged a hand through his hair. This was turning into a real cluster fuck. "Let's wait until Ethan gets back to us before we stick our necks out that far."

"In the meantime, want to make a side bet that you can kiss your pay good-bye?"

No shit, Mac thought grimly. And thinking about the money made him think about Ali. Not that he hadn't been thinking about her. She was never far from his mind. And she was probably wondering why her daddy hadn't called her in two days.

He fished his phone out of his pocket and punched in Angie's number.

"Angie," he said when his ex picked up. "It's me. Is Ali there?"

He gritted his teeth and drove, relegated to listening to Angie's sniping denigration of him as a bad father for ignoring his daughter just like he used to ignore her.

"Just put her on the phone, OK?" There was no point arguing or defending. There'd ceased to be any point between them long ago, he thought wearily.

His heart fell when Angie stopped her tirade long enough to tell him that Ali was on a play date.

"When will she be back?"

Apparently it was a sleepover. He let out a defeated breath. "Tell her . . . would you please just tell her I miss her and I'm sorry I haven't called."

He gritted his teeth, waited her out. "I'm on a case, dammit. It's been a little difficult."

That just brought on another tirade, which he cut off. "I'll call her tomorrow. Just tell her that for me, will you? And tell her I love her."

He hung up.

And said absolutely nothing while he tried to get his temper and disappointment in check.

"That's got to be rough," Eve said after a long moment.

Yeah. It was rough. "The worst of it is, Angie's right," he said, admitting the hardest part. "My work does interfere with my time with Ali."

"Yeah, well, I'd really beat myself up over the need to make a living. Most dads are independently wealthy and don't have to pull the forty-hour-week thing, or the eighty-hour-week thing, for that matter. They just stay home with the kiddies and bond by the hour."

He cut her a sideways glance. Leave it to her to overjustify. "Maybe if I'd had a nine-to-five job instead of one that kept me out all hours, things would have been different."

"Are you saying you'd still be married?"

No. That's not what he was saying. He and Angie never should have been married in the first place. "I'm saying I might still have my daughter."

"Or you might not," she said quietly. "It's sad, but sometimes that's just the way things work out. Bad things happen to good people."

OK. This was getting to be too much. "From rat-bastard to good people. Amazing what a little murder and mayhem has done to elevate my less than sterling character."

"And let's not forget the great sex," she added.

Ah. Point for her. She'd just managed to minimize the import of her statements. Couldn't have him start to think she'd begun to like him too much.

And that stung a little more than it should have. Why? Because he liked—genuinely liked—this woman. Maybe even more than liked her. Something about her had gotten to him, dug in deep, and wouldn't let go. Strength coupled with compassion. In-your-face toughness paired with vulnerability. A funky sense of humor that had him grinning as often as growling. And of course—let's not forget the mind-blowing sex.

He couldn't afford to think about what it all meant. He knew there was no future for them. Hell. He wasn't a good bet for the long haul. Besides, she'd made it clear. He was merely a means to an end—help to find Tiffany—and a temporary outlet for her sexual tension. When this was over—if they got out of it alive—they would end their tentative partnership without a long look back.

And he had a sneaking feeling that he was going to regret it for a long, long time.

This was so, so bad, Eve thought, making herself stare straight ahead as they drove west, slowly chasing a sunset that rivaled any she'd seen on Mallory Square at Key West.

She was in a life-or-death situation, aching from head to toe from the beating the bombing had given her, and now she had another ache to deal with. The one in her heart. The one that made her want to reach across the seat, draw that rat-bastard jerk into her arms, and ease the loss he felt, fill the void.

Yeah. This was bad.

She was falling for him.

Again.

Mr. Bad Bet on a Good Day. Mr. Already Lost at Love. And everybody's favorite, Mr. Love 'Em and Leave 'Em.

God. What else could she think of to get things back in perspective?

For one thing, he called her cupcake. That in itself ought to be enough.

He was an emotional cripple. A triple-A.

And he bought her M&M's. No one but her dad had ever bought her M&M's.

And the man made love to her like there was no one he'd rather be with and no place on earth he'd rather be than inside of her.

OK. That did it. Slipped things right back into focus. She was running on adrenaline and lust. Things looked different when seen through glasses tinted with generous amounts of both.

Just because she caught herself enjoying not only the sex but also waking up next to him in the morning . . . just because they thought alike on so many levels and she found herself smiling more often than frowning over something he said or did, or some look he threw her way, didn't mean there was more to it than sex. And adrenaline.

To think otherwise would be insane—she didn't even like the man. And yet . . . she didn't like the idea of not seeing him again when this was over.

Her phone rang, saving her from another rewind of exactly the same limp rationality.

"I came up with nothing on Katrina or Sven," Ethan stated, all business, no hello. "They seem arrow straight."

Which was the same thing Eve had already decided. "Did Bob Gleason call you?"

"Yeah. We're all working on it. Sit tight, sweetie. I'll call as soon as I have something more—on anything. In the meantime, be careful, you hear?"

Yeah. She heard.

"What's up?"

She thought for a moment before turning to McClain. His dark eyes were brooding, lined with fatigue and very clear signs of pain. He needed some rest. And some attention for his knee.

"Pull into that motel up there. You need some ice for that knee. Then you need to soak in a hot tub—then I'll fill you in."

"I'm good to go," he said stoically.

Oh, right. She forgot. Macho mania ran rampant through this man's blood. Which meant she was going to have to grin and bear it if he was going to give himself a chance to re- cover. "OK, then *I* need some ice and a hot bath."

"Well, why didn't you say so?" He pulled up in front of the motel, brows furrowed with concern.

She rolled her eyes and bit back a comment about knights in tarnished armor.

"Sit down," Eve ordered when, stiff-legged, McClain limped over to the bed, then tried to get out of his jeans.

When she could see it was going to be a challenge for him, she bent over and removed his shoes, then tugged the jeans down his legs.

"Oh my God," she gasped. His knee was as big as a bas- ketball. "You need medical attention."

He shook his head, his face gray with pain. "It'll be all right in a little while. Just like it did in the Keys, the swelling will go down, and I'll be good to go."

She was weary of hearing that phrase. He wasn't any- where near *good to go,* but she wasn't about to say as much. "What, exactly, did you do to injure it in the first place?"

"Tore the meniscus and the ACL. Also broke the kneecap."

She winced. "You're thorough, I'll give you that."

"Anything worth doing's worth doing right," he added with a pained grin.

"And they couldn't fix it?"

"They tried. Seven hours of surgery, flat on my back for weeks and on crutches for several more. They threw in a shitload of physical therapy and a knee brace. When they turned me loose it was with a glowing prognosis that I'd never walk without a limp again. Words every man wants to hear."

She couldn't imagine the pain involved then. Or now. A thin film of perspiration had broken out on his forehead.

"Well, I'm the closest thing you've got to a medical expert now, so I'm going to call a few shots. Lay down."

She didn't know if it was a good sign or a bad one that he didn't so much as shoot her a glare of protest. She helped him lift his leg onto the bed, then carefully propped it on a pillow.

"I'm going for ice and aspirin."

"Ibuprofen," he said quietly, and slung his forearm over his eyes. "Helps with the swelling."

"Ibuprofen it is," she said, and went in search of both, praying that he wasn't blowing smoke and his leg would get back to some semblance of normalcy soon.

Normalcy. Now there was a word, one she hadn't made passing acquaintance with since McClain had shown up in her life again.

Mac was almost asleep when Eve returned to the motel room about a half an hour later. She was loaded down with Band-Aids, ointment, ibuprofen, analgesic rub, an elastic wrap, and a plastic ice bucket full of motel ice.

"My very own Florence Nightingale," he said, hitching up on his elbows to watch her.

"Were I you, I'd be thinking more in terms of Nurse Ratched."

"*One Flew Over the Cuckoo's Nest.* I read that book. Saw the movie. Jack Nicholson and Louise Fletcher. She was one demented angel of mercy."

"Speaking of mercy."

He groaned and lay back down.

She grinned at him as she returned from a quick trip to the bathroom with a towel. "I take it you saw what Kathy Bates did to James Caan in that movie, too?"

He lifted the arm he'd used to cover his eyes and peeked out at her. "I'm not going to end up with two broken legs here, am I?"

"Only if you don't do what I say."

He felt the grin crawl up his face. "Are you going to make my day and break out a little leather and a whip?"

"You wish."

"Oh man, do I. I will *never* forget the way you looked that night we went to Oracle."

"How's that?" she asked, ignoring him. She'd poured ice in the towel, then folded it into an ice pack of sorts and, lifting his leg, settled it under his knee on the pillow. "Better?"

Yeah. It was better. When she added another pack to the top of his knee, it actually felt good.

"Missed your calling," he mumbled absently around the three ibuprofen tablets she'd held out to him along with a glass of water.

"Not hardly. This is foreign territory for me. I'm a Band-Aid, McClain. You need a hospital."

He snagged her wrist when she started to move away from the bed. "Thanks," he said simply when her blue eyes, startled by his sudden capture, met his. "Been a long time since anyone took care of me like this."

"Don't worry. Everything has a cost. I'll bill you."

She was actually embarrassed, he realized, to have him see that she was worried about him. "How about we work out some other form of compensation? You've got some bumps and bruises of your own. Maybe I could make you feel better, too."

Her gaze drifted from his face to the tenting action going on beneath the fly of his boxers. She smiled. Shook her head. "I don't recall anything from my Girl Scout first-aid manual that mentioned sex as a treatment."

"Well, there you go. That particular method of treatment is only in the Boy Scout manual. Chapter ten. Page sixty-nine."

Her eyebrows went up at the reference to sixty-nine. "You were never a Boy Scout."

"And you were a Girl Scout?"

"OK. So you got me on that one. Doesn't mean I'm going to take advantage of your invalid status—"

He cut her off by tugging her down onto the bed beside him. "Take advantage," he whispered as he knotted his fingers in the silky thickness of blond hair at the back of her head.

Sexual heat flared in her eyes. He drew her slowly toward his mouth. "If you have an ounce of compassion in you, you'll take advantage."

Turned out, she had more than an ounce. And she liked page sixty-nine of the manual every bit as much as he did.

25

"I'm thinking we've bowed to optimism long enough," Eve said, spreading a map out on the stained tabletop in a corner booth of the Parowan Café the next morning.

After an incredible session of lovemaking, which she absolutely did not want to think about today, they'd slept for a sold eight hours. It was the first real sleep they'd gotten in days.

Maybe it had been the sound of the rain splattering against the motel room windows. It had started sometime during the night and continued this morning at a light but steady rate, packing the dust, streaking the restaurant windows.

"How about we simply start canvassing the area within a hundred or so miles?" she suggested, determined to stick to business. "There aren't that many paved roads in the area. Not that many gravel roads, for that matter."

She watched as McClain finished off his breakfast coffee and leaned back in the bench seat. He looked rested and refreshed. And very, very sexy with his freshly shaven face and some of the pain gone from his eyes.

"Sounds good to me," he said. "We can forget about north. If they were headed north, they wouldn't have gotten off here, agreed?"

"Unless they ran out of money and this was as far as they could get a bus ticket."

"Too early in the day to blow holes in my theories," he said, looking grim. "Don't make me cranky."

Eve couldn't help but grin. Through all of this, the only time she'd seen McClain "cranky" was when he'd been worried the bomb had taken her down. Funny how memories came back with such clarity at the oddest times. But as she sat in that booth two days later, she remembered, for the first time and with vivid detail, the look on his face when he'd finally spotted her. It had been feral. The touch of his hands on her shoulders had been viciously rough. She doubted that he'd even realized how he'd handled her. Adrenaline spikes being what they are, she'd been fairly numb to the full brunt of his touch. Adrenaline must have dulled his pain, too, because he'd barely limped when they'd taken off.

Speaking of his knee, as he'd predicted, it had looked much better this morning. The swelling was down and he seemed to be moving better on it.

"What'd I tell you?" he'd said smugly after he'd iced it down again earlier, then wrapped it with the elastic bandage she'd bought at the local drugstore along with the ibuprofen.

She dragged her mind away from the picture of him, fresh from a shower, unabashedly and beautifully naked as he'd sat on the edge of the bed and let her help him with the bandage. When the waitress stopped by their table with a coffee carafe in hand, Eve shook her head with a "No thanks." Mac did the same and got serious about the map.

"So, which way do we go, O great tracker?"

She angled the map around so they could both see it. "I'm thinking we take One-forty-three southeast until we hit Fourteen, then angle back north on Eighty-nine, stop every time we see a breathing body, and see what we can shake down."

He followed her finger as it pointed out the route, and shrugged. "Better than sitting on our thumbs."

"Who knows? We could get a break."

The look he gave her wasn't exactly optimistic, but since

he hadn't come up with any better ideas, he was going along with hers.

They drove until dark, banking their growing sense of urgency with silence and comments on the scenery as the clouds lifted and sunshine poured over the mountain peaks. The area was beautiful—rich with national parks and rusty rose–colored mountain ranges. But they found no signs of Tiffany. No one they talked to had seen her.

Mac was getting frustrated. So was Eve, but she made great pains not to show it. They booked a room in a mom-and-pop motel somewhere on 89 and called it a day. It was noon, the next day, when they pulled into Ruby's Inn, a huge motel complex nestled just outside Bryce Canyon National Park, that their luck changed.

The decor in Ruby's was right out of a *Western Living* home fashion magazine. Huge roughhewn beams criss-crossed a tall peaked ceiling dotted with skylights and wood planking. Mountain prints and cowboy memorabilia hung from the walls. Spotted cowhides were draped over the backs of bulky mission oak sofas and chairs. And blending in beside a booth advertising Canyon Rim Trail Rides was a wrangler, complete with worn leather chaps, a handlebar mustache, a dusty black wide-brimmed hat, and the requisite bowlegs. He wore a new red kerchief around his neck, spurs on worn boots, and Mac could make out a faded round circle on the left hip pocket of his jeans where he kept his Redman chewing tobacco.

The sign above the booth read: Canyon Rim Trail Rides.

Beneath the sign was a schedule.

The wrangler stepped forward and extended a hand. "Name's Dub. You folks looking for a trail ride? Great way to spend an afternoon, and I've got a couple spots left in the three o'clock group."

Mac shook the wrangler's hand. "No thanks, but we are looking for someone. Maybe you could help."

"Lots of folks come through this stop this time of year. Don't rightly know if I could tell one from another, but I'll give it a try."

He was right about the volume of people. The lobby was brimming with people, some wearing shorts, some in jeans, all of them heading somewhere—whether it was the adjacent restaurant or the gift shop or the pool.

Eve fished Tiffany's photo out of her purse and held it out to the cowboy.

The wrangler frowned, scratched his jaw, and studied the photo. "Well now, I b'lieve I mighta seen someone looked something like her," he said at last, "but this girl had different-colored hair. Brownish, sorta. Not so much makeup. And she didn't have them things stuck in her lip."

Eve, looking disappointed, tucked the picture back in her purse. "Well. Thanks anyway."

"Wait now; wait just a minute. Le'me see that again." He drew the photo closer, squinted at it. "That a diamond tattooed on her cheek?"

Eve glanced sharply at Mac.

"A tear," she corrected.

"Tear, you say?" Dub said absently as he studied the photo again. "Thought it was a diamond. Kids. What'll they think of next?"

Mac was two feet away from Eve and he could feel her energy level buzz up several notches. He was getting a little buzz himself. The chances were slim and slimmer that Tiffany and a girl who looked sort of like Tiffany and had a tear tattoo on her cheek weren't one and the same person.

"Are you saying you saw a girl with this exact same tattoo on her cheek?"

"Well, yeah. Ain't seen nothing like it ever before. Wanted to ask her about it, but didn't seem polite."

"You talked with her?"

"Well, not so much with her, but with Billie. Boy's been gone for a while; it was nice catching up."

Eve shot Mac another quick glance, one that said, *We may have hit the jackpot.*

"Billie?"

"Billie Campbell. She was with him."

"When was this?"

Another frown. Another scratch to the jaw. "Yesterday, round supper time."

"This Billie. He a tall, skinny kid with a guitar and cowboy hat?" Mac asked, working to keep it casual.

"Man, you got him nailed. That boy's a beanpole, and his guitar goes everywhere he goes. His daddy just shakes his head and smiles."

Beside Mac, Eve almost bounced. "Billie's father live around here?"

"Jasper? You bet. Jas owns Canyon Rim Trail Rides—that and some bucking stock he leases out to some local rodeo promoters."

"So, the Campbells are locals."

"Born and bred," Dub said absently as he smiled and tipped his hat to a couple who had stopped and were showing interest in the printed brochures lying on the countertop.

"Where could we find Mr. Campbell, do you think?" Mac asked, sensing they were about to lose their source of information to a business transaction.

"Same place you always find him this time of year." Dub inched toward the interested couple, gave them each a flyer and a smile before turning back to Mac. "Leading a bunch of greenhorns on a trail ride round the rim of the canyon— anyway, that's what the schedule says. Like I said, you folks ought to take that ride if you want to see Bryce up close and personal."

"Does Mr. Campbell have an office?" Eve asked.

Dub chuckled. "Oh, he'd like that—bein' called *Mr.* Campbell. Round here, folks just call him Jas. But yeah, he's got an office, if you could call it that."

He walked them toward the front window, pointed across

the highway. "See that little log building? If he's not back yet, should be a chalkboard saying when he will be. You can wait for him there if you want. Now if you folks will excuse me . . ."

They thanked him and headed at a fast walk toward the front door.

"Can you believe this?" Eve asked as Mac took her elbow and guided her across the highway, which was thick with traffic.

"Your hunch paid off."

"Yeah. Who'd have figured?"

He would. That's who. She had amazing instincts. It was only one of the qualities he'd grown to appreciate about her. She was also cool under fire. Dub had never known she was about two breaths away from wringing out the information the wrangler had taken his sweet time relaying. And she hadn't complained, not once, about her injuries from the bombing—and she'd had plenty. He'd seen every scrape, bruise, and cut when they'd employed a little medicinal sex to take the edge off. He'd kissed every scrape, bruise, and cut . . . and several places in between.

He drew back from the memory while he could still fit in his jeans. There would be time, later, when this was over, to sort things out. To figure out where things were going between them. And they were going somewhere. He was damn sure of that.

Right now, the priority was finding Tiffany and keeping her alive. Since they had to be alive to do it, speed was a priority, too. He'd had that prickly feeling on the back of his neck since they'd left Parowan yesterday. If someone was following them, they were good, because he hadn't been able to make them. In fact, he hadn't been able to pick out a car or a truck or anything that seemed out of place. But his neck still prickled and the ominous knot in his gut kept tightening.

"There they are," Eve said when they rounded the log building.

He followed her gaze toward a wooded area where a string of horses plodded lazily along a worn trail toward the corral beside a lean-to. Buckskins, sorrels, chestnuts, and bays walked in a long, slow line with happy tourists chattering about the exciting ride and in some cases mumbling about their sore butts.

"Mr. Campbell?" Eve asked when what appeared to be the head wrangler had dismounted, said his good-byes to the happy greenhorns, and headed toward the office.

The cowboy stopped with one foot on the office building's steps. He tipped his hat, nodded. "No, sorry. Name's Jed. Jed Barnet."

Barnet was a clone of the cowboy manning the booth in Ruby's—maybe a little younger but still brimming with western hospitality and charm.

"We were told that Mr. Campbell was leading this ride."

Barnet lifted his hat, ran a hand over his hair, then resettled the Stetson. "He was, but we had a last-minute schedule change. Jas called me this morning and asked if I could fill in for a day or two. Guess his boy come home." He smiled. "Billie's been gone for a while, so Jas wanted to spend some time with him. Can I help you folks with something?"

Mac stepped in and extended his hand, introducing himself. "My dad was a buddy of Jasper's. We were passing through the area and I promised him I'd look Jasper up."

The cowboy grinned. "Well, he'll like that just fine. Come on in the office a sec and I'll show you how to get to the home place."

Smiling, if a bit shaky, Tiffany sat across from Billie at a Mission Oak dining room table in a sunny little room that smelled like lemon wax and leather and fried chicken. It wasn't like the dining room table at her father's Palm Beach estate. It wasn't glossy and so massive that you needed telephones to converse with the people at the other end. It didn't have a fresh floral centerpiece that was delivered weekly by a local florist and cost enough to finance a college education. Instead, a green fruit jar sat in the middle of the table, filled with some pretty pink and lavender flowers Billie's mother called summer phlox that she'd picked from her wildflower garden behind the house.

You didn't have to wear designer dining attire, either, or choose from a hundred pieces of silver or a dozen Waterford crystal glasses. There were just plates and water glasses and a knife, a fork, and a spoon. The napkins were paper—with pretty flowers printed on them. There was no butler. There was no maid.

There was just Billie and his mom and dad and her. And a whole lot of warm smiles and easy acceptance.

"Would you like more chicken, Tiffany?"

Tiffany. She loved the way Miriam Campbell said her name. Her father had called her Tiffany, but it was always with an impression of disdain. When Billie's mom said it, it sounded like she loved the name, like she thought it was pretty, like she thought Tiffany was pretty, and like she enjoyed having her at their dinner table.

Miriam Campbell was pretty. Not model or socialite pretty. Tiffany had heard the term *inner beauty.* Now she knew what it was. Miriam had it. Her face was round and tan and her long brown hair was caught at her nape in a no-nonsense ponytail. Tiffany figured her for somewhere in her forties, yet she moved like a much younger woman in her working jeans and soft blue shirt. She wasn't slim, but neither was she fat. She was nicely round and soft and as comfortable with it as she was riding a horse or cooking in her newly remodeled kitchen that was her pride and joy.

"Better eat up," Billie's father said. "Before that boy beats you to it. I swear, if it's not nailed down, he eats it."

Tiffany smiled at Billie. His cheeks turned a mottled red.

"Not that it shows," Miriam said with a motherly smile. "And don't you be teasing him, Jas. Let the boy eat. He's skin and bones."

"It's in the genes," Jasper Campbell said, smiling at Tiffany. "He's built just like his grampa."

Billie was built just like his father, too, Tiffany thought. Jasper Campbell was a big, tall man. His shoulders were broad, on a long, rangy frame. But there was strength in the muscles that molded to that frame. And there was strength in his hands—gentleness, too, though they were covered with calluses and nicks and scars.

Yes, there was gentleness, too. When Billie had brought her to his home and introduced her to his parents as a friend, Mr. Campbell had extended his hand to hers and shaken it, like she was someone special or something. Miriam had hugged her. Just like that. No request to hear her pedigree, no comment about the way she was dressed in Billie's T-shirt and jeans, not a single odd look because her hands were shaking and she looked—she'd caught a glimpse of herself in the hallway mirror—like death warmed over.

They'd just accepted her into their home. Miriam had said, "You look all done in, sweetheart. How about a little something to eat and then let's get you to bed?"

It was the kindest thing anyone had ever done for her— with the exception of Billie getting her away from Lance and bringing her here.

And they didn't seem to mind that she didn't have much to say. They just accepted her.

"The chicken is delicious," she said, and that simple statement was rewarded with a smile from Miriam that was so enfolding, it brought tears to Tiffany's eyes.

"Thank you, dear. Sure you don't want some more?"

"No, thank you. I'm full."

She'd like to have some more. It was the first thing that had sounded or tasted good for days. She'd heaved her guts out on and off for twenty-four hours as her body purged all the poison from her system. She wasn't feeling all that great yet and was afraid the chicken might come right back up along with the mashed potatoes and the sweet corn that

Miriam had grown in her own garden last summer, then frozen.

Yeah. On the way to the Campbell ranch, she'd been dog sick. One hit of weed would have put her out of her misery. But she hadn't smoked a joint. And she wasn't going to. She wasn't going to do any drugs anymore. No matter how much it hurt.

Instead, she was going to OD on all this peace and acceptance Billie had given her. She sat back and listened as the Campbells caught up with Billie on what he'd been doing. Where he'd been. He told them—leaving out the part about Lance and Abe.

So, this was family, Tiffany thought, and smiled when Billie caught her eye as he and his father talked horse lineage, summer wheat, and winter feed. Tomorrow, if she was up to it and it didn't rain, Billie was going to take her horseback riding. She was excited. And surprised by it. She hadn't been excited about anything for longer than she could remember.

The Campbell quarter horses weren't like the horses she'd ridden in competition. They were shorter, stockier, less high-strung. But there were some beauties with soft brown eyes and sweet dispositions. She'd seen them grazing in the pasture along the drive when a foreman from a neighboring ranch who had given her and Billie a ride had dropped them off. She couldn't wait to ride again, even though it made her sad to think of her horses. She wondered about them often. If they were being cared for properly. And felt guilty for not checking in on them for so long.

With determination, she drew herself away from those worrisome thoughts. Billie was going to take her hiking soon, too. The Campbell ranch butted right up against Bryce Canyon National Park. It was rugged and mountainous and all beautiful rust- and cinnamon-colored peaks and valleys full of towering formations Billie called hoodoos.

Billie was sort of beautiful, too, she'd decided. He had

pretty brown eyes, like his mother's. Had her beautiful smile, too, when he let himself give in to it. His mom and dad teasingly called him Pencil Boy, but Tiffany liked the long, lanky look of him.

She thought that maybe he was starting to like her, too. Just the way she was. With Billie she didn't feel the need to hide who she was behind rainbow hair colors and body piercings. Last night, he'd taken her outside to see the sky. It had been full of stars. Had made her eyes full of stars, and when he'd looked at her he'd said so—and blushed. And then he'd told her she was pretty.

"Excuse me," Jas said when the phone rang.

He rose from the dinner table to answer it, and Tiffany thought back to Mesquite. Back to when she'd offered Billie sex as payment for what he'd done for her. At first, when he'd said no, she'd been embarrassed. And then, instead of feeling the familiar panic of rejection, she'd experienced a flooding warmth, a tentative sense of peace, and decided to go with the feeling. To trust Billie Campbell, who didn't want anything from her but for her to be safe. It had made her feel warm all over.

She still felt that way. When Billie looked at her. When Miriam or Jas smiled at her.

Again, the thought came to her. This was a home. And though she knew it couldn't be, she wished she could paint herself permanently into the warmth of this simple, home-spun picture.

She was being selfish by even staying here. She knew that. She didn't know if Lance was looking for her even now. But she did know that he planned to kill her if he found her.

She was surprised to realize that very little pain accompanied that knowledge. Fear, yes. But not pain. She'd thought she loved Lance. Looking around at the Campbells, though, she realized what love really was. It wasn't what she'd felt for Lance. Panic. That's what she'd felt. The panicky need to

feel even the pretense of love in the guise of sex and mud-
died by the drugs she'd let Lance bully her into using.

The shame was almost worse than the worry.

She should leave. She should get as far away from these
nice people as she could. What if someone came after her
here? What if the Campbells got hurt because of her?

The only thing she knew for certain was that someone
wanted her dead. She didn't understand it. Couldn't even
comprehend it. And she didn't know where to go even if she
left here.

Kat? Kat would take care of her. She didn't doubt that for
a minute. But Kat had a life. She didn't need her hanging
around her neck like a ball and chain. Once Tiffany would
have turned to Eve. But Eve had deserted her. It still hurt.

A few more days, she promised herself. She'd just stay
here a few more days. Until she was a little stronger. Until
she could figure out what to do.

Until she could reason out who had hired Lance Reno to
kill her.

"That was odd," Jas Campbell said, returning to the table.
"That was Jed."

"What's up?" Miriam asked. "Trouble with the trail ride
today?"

"No." Jasper rubbed his jaw. "Jed said someone was looking for me today. Said that his father and mine were old
friends and he'd promised to look me up since he was in the
area."

"Really? Who could that be, do you think?"

Jas shook his head. "Beats me. Jed said he got to wondering about it, too . . . figured later that he probably knew most
of my friends and got to feeling uneasy about it. Said he gave
them directions to our place. Figured they ought to be heading
out here about now and thought maybe he'd better warn me."

Tiffany felt her blood run cold. She'd heard that expression. Had never before known what it meant. Now she did.

Her entire body felt like ice. Her lips felt frozen. What if it wasn't a friend of Mr. Campbell? What if it was Lance?

"B . . . Billie?"

Billie looked at her, read the fear in her eyes, and realized what she was thinking.

"We need to tell them now," Billie said quietly.

She swallowed and slowly nodded.

26

It was around four that afternoon when Eve's cell rang. They were on the road to the Campbell ranch, watching the weather and wondering if they'd make the ranch before the rain that was predicted for the area started falling. She checked the number and recognized it as Ethan's.

"Hey, big brother."

"Are you sitting down?"

"Yessss," she said, drawing the word out slowly. Beside her in the passenger seat, McClain gave her a curious look. "I take it I'm going to be glad?"

"Bob came through. He got a lead on Jazelle Taylor."

Jazelle, the EA with no past. "Shoot."

"Let me see if I can summarize. But I've got to back up first. You know that Clayborne isn't only a Donald Trump–type entrepreneur. In addition to his real estate ventures and his computer tech businesses Clayborne was heavily into firearms manufacturing."

"Yes," she said impatiently as the Jeep bounced over a deep rut in the road. "I know all that."

"You also know he was connected politically—that's why you were pulled into civilian protection for Tiffany. OK. This gets a little convoluted, so just hear me out.

"It turns out, Clayborne used to be something of a loose cannon in the thrills department. Thought of himself as a John

Wayne–type patriot when, in fact, he was dealing with illegal international gun exports for years."

"Illegal?"

"Gleason pulled some strings. Got some sealed files unsealed. Anyway, Clayborne was a huge financial campaign contributor to the president and, as a supporter of his administration, was privy to the inner political circle. There was a huge problem—still is for that matter—in illegal arms shipments out of Bulgaria."

"The country's been known for years as a hotbed for illegal arms brokering," she agreed.

"Right. Well, since Clayborne was in the business, the administration asked him how, if he were to illegally manufacture and ship arms to potential buyers, he would go about it, what contacts he would use, et cetera, hoping he could help them break the traffic.

"What happened next was that Clayborne convinced them that he could find the breaches by working undercover, which he did for several years. Still with me?"

"Yeah."

"Those two men you killed during the abduction attempt?"

Eve glanced in the rearview mirror, drew a deep breath. "Yeah—Bob told me they were foreign nationals from Bulgaria."

"Well, these particular men had no overt connections to any particular terrorist organization, but the consensus is that they may have gotten on to Clayborne's covert work for the U.S. government. The attack on Tiffany was a message to Clayborne to back off if he didn't want those around him hurt."

Her fingers tightened on the wheel. "Why didn't I know any of this? Why didn't anyone tell me? It was my case."

"You forget. You were fired."

"I resigned," she reminded him.

"Right. In any event, you were out of the loop. Besides, they couldn't prove that Clayborne was double-dipping. Either way, they figure he must have heeded the supposed 'message,' because it was about that time that he became the reclusive, eccentric, agoraphobic hermit we've grown to love and has holed up in his suite of offices ever since."

"OK. Let me see if I've got this. You're saying Clayborne had been playing both ends against the middle."

"Right. He'd been feeding the U.S. enough info to make them think he was legit and working for the cause while he was actually brokering his own illegal arms deals for both profit and the thrill of the danger with the Bulgarians."

"So the attempt to abduct Tiffany was, in effect, a warning from the Bulgarians who had gotten on to him but who didn't want to lose him as a source of their gun trafficking."

"You got it. But things went wrong. You foiled the abduction attempt. And the two men you killed? Petrov Yanev and Stayon Georgiev? They were the son and son-in-law of the head of the Bulgarian organization, Alexandrov Yanev.

"Eve," he said as her heart fell over itself. "Stayon was married to Alexandrov's daughter, Bianca."

It was like waiting for another shoe to drop. And then it did.

"We have reason to believe that Bianca Georgiev is behind the threats on your life. Probably, she's behind Tiffany's situation, too."

"And do we know where she is?"

"Well, for the past few months, she's been in West Palm. Working as Richard Edwards's EA."

Oh my God. "Jazelle Taylor." She closed her eyes, then dragged her hand through her hair. *Revenge.* "So. We have our motive. She wants me dead because I killed her husband and brother."

"It would seem so."

"But why the theatrics? Why this long-drawn-out drama?"

"Only Bianca has the answer to that one. Are you still there?"

"Yeah. But I'm starting to have a little trouble hearing

you," she said as static drowned him out. "Must be losing the signal."

Ethan's response was choppy. She heard bits and pieces, but what came through loud and clear was, "Stay with McClain. And don't be a goddamn hero."

And then the call dropped.

"I picked up bits and pieces, but you want to fill me in?"

She glanced at McClain. Then back at the road. Then she nutshelled it for him.

"Christ."

"Yeah."

They pondered the impact of Ethan's news in silence as they continued down the rough rural road. Mud gray clouds built and boiled up beyond the mountain range the closer they got to the Campbell ranch. Beside her in the seat, McClain closed his eyes and absently rubbed his bad knee. Trust him to keep the pain to himself.

Trust. There was that word again. She thought back to what she'd told Ethan before they'd left Vegas. And again, without hesitation, realized she trusted McClain to watch her back. More and more it appeared that she was going to need him to.

And more and more it appeared that it was ghosts from her past, not goblins from her present, that were haunting her.

It was closing in on six o'clock when they drove up the lane to the Campbell ranch. Thunder rumbled in the background like a distant volley of mortar fire.

"Right out of *Bonanza*," McClain said, taking in the rolling foothills and rusty mountain peaks in the background. Cattle had clustered together in anticipation of the building storm. Horses grazed placidly in tall grass on either side of the long lane leading to the large two-story ranch house that was flanked by several neat and well-kept outbuildings.

A late-model club cab sat in front of the closed doors of a double garage attached to the white house. The house looked like it might have been built in the eighties to resemble a turn-of-the-century ranch house—either that, or it was a well-preserved older house that had been renovated and added onto.

Flower beds flanked a redbrick sidewalk leading to a porch that ran the length of the front of the house. The porch floor appeared to be newly painted with gray enamel. An old-fashioned swing that could accommodate two, if they sat real close, hung by chains at the south end of the porch. At the other end a pair of antique rockers sat on either side of a small wicker table upon which a Boston fern thrived. On the front door a grapevine wreath with tiny rust-colored birdhouses, metal stars, and a swath of cornhusk ribbon twined through it welcomed visitors.

"Should have named it Peace and Tranquility Ranch," McClain commented as he remembered seeing a huge *Rocking C* formed out of forged steel suspended above the main driveway on their way in.

"Has all the appearances of a peaceful valley, all right," Eve agreed. "Let's hope we're not bringing armageddon down on top of them."

She almost swallowed her words when the front door swung open and a tall, tough-looking cowboy wielding a very big gun glared at them with steel in his eyes and not one ounce of peace or tranquility gracing his granite-hard face.

"Can I help you folks?" he asked, sounding like the only thing he wanted to help them with was finding their way out of Dodge.

"Jasper Campbell?" McClain asked, wary of the twelve-gauge shotgun that Eve knew could be loaded with anything from buckshot to deer slugs, either of which would shoot substantial holes in anything from trees to oh, say, them.

"State your business," the cowboy said. "And don't make the mistake of telling me you're here with a message from your father."

OK. So Jed had called ahead.

"Sorry about that," McClain said. "I needed to find your place and didn't figure the truth was going to get me the information."

"You still haven't told me your business, son."

As in *son of a bitch,* Eve figured, and stepped in to try to diffuse the animosity of the man with the gun.

"Mr. Campbell," she said, and found herself the target of those intense gray eyes. "My name is Eve Garrett. This is Tyler McClain. Mr. McClain and I are private security specialists and we're searching for a young woman who we believe is in the company of your son, Billie."

Campbell said nothing. Since he hadn't lifted the shotgun to his shoulder, though, Eve took it as a good sign that she could continue.

"The young woman's name is Tiffany Clayborne. And I can assure you, we mean her no harm. As a matter of fact, Tiffany is a friend of mine—although she's been a little miffed at me of late."

He still said nothing, neither confirming nor denying Tiffany's presence at the ranch.

"Mr. Campbell," Eve began again, "if Tiffany is here— and we're fairly certain that she is—we understand her reluctance to trust that we're here to help her. Tiffany," she said a little louder, on the off chance the shadow she saw slanting across the floor from behind the open door was her, "it's Eve. Honey, someone's after you. That same someone is also after me. We've got to get you out of here.

"Tiffany," she said again when Campbell's grip on the shotgun became a little less hostile, "call Katrina Hofsteader in New York. We know she slipped you her cell phone at Oracle. That's why we were able to track you this far. She's kept in touch with us, trying to help us find you before whoever is after you does. Please call her. She'll confirm that we have your best interest in mind. Sweetie, we just want to help you."

From behind the door, Eve could hear a woman's voice and then another male voice whispering softly.

"You folks just hold on, right here, OK?" Campbell said when someone behind the door got his attention.

Then he shut the door in their faces.

"Now what?" McClain whispered.

"Now we figure they're having a little come to Jesus meeting. Maybe placing a call to Kat. Let's sit," she suggested. "Present ourselves at our nonhostile best."

When she sat down on the top porch step with her back to the door, he grinned down at her. "Does the term *sitting duck* have any particular meaning to you?"

"He's not going to shoot us. And this will show him we have no reason not to trust him because he has no reason not to trust us."

"Do you ever get tired of being right?" McClain asked after he'd sat down beside her and stretched out his bad leg.

"Actually, I like being right." She couldn't stop herself from smiling at him. Couldn't help but melt a little bit when he smiled back.

"It really is like a movie set, isn't it?" she asked, shifting her attention to the surrounding mountains so she wouldn't have a total meltdown from the ready heat in his eyes. A jagged lightning bolt split the gray above a rugged peak of the range of mountains boxing in the valley where the Campbell ranch lay nestled like fruit in a bowl. Ozone was heavy and thick in the air.

"Let's just hope it doesn't turn into the gunfight at the OK Corral."

The door opened behind them then.

Together, they rose and turned. Campbell, sans shotgun, stood in the open door frame.

"Come on in. Let's see if we can get this business sorted out."

Eve drew a relieved breath. Beside her, she sensed McClain doing the same. On the heels of relief came guarded interest. After all this time, all this way, they were finally going to come face-to-face with the elusive Tiffany Clayborne.

. . .

Mac had expected a coked-out, strung-out wild child. Instead, Tiffany Clayborne appeared before them, a pale but fresh-faced and clear-eyed young woman who looked as innocent as her eighteen years—if you didn't count the hard-won wisdom shadowing her hazel eyes and the panic that sharpened her gaze like a laser.

"Tiffany," he said, extending his hand. "Tyler McClain. And I've got to say, I'm very glad to meet you. At last."

She nodded but was too wary to take his hand. Instead, she sidled a little closer to a boy who could only be Billie Campbell.

"You've led us on quite a chase," Eve said when Tiffany turned an angry glare her way.

"Why do you care?"

"I have always cared, Tiff."

Tiffany met Eve's statement with a stone-cold stare. They weren't going to be mending any fences today.

"OK, look. You talked to Kat, right?"

Tiffany nodded.

"And what did she tell you?"

"She just said I should trust you."

Eve nodded. "And you've had a few too many people let you down in the trust department, haven't you? Including me."

The tension in the foyer became so thick a hacksaw wouldn't have bitten through it.

"Let's go into the living room, shall we?" a pretty forty-something woman said with a welcome diplomacy. "I'm Miriam, by the way. I'm sure you've already figured out that this is my husband, Jas. And this is our son, Billie." She had to reach up to place a motherly hand on his shoulder.

It didn't stay there long, Mac noticed. Miriam Campbell moved quickly to Tiffany's side, placed a bracing arm around her waist. "Come on, honey. I think it's important that we hear what these folks have to say."

With the Campbells rallied around Tiffany like a garrison of troops guarding a peasant princess, Mac sat back and let Eve explain that Edwards, acting on Tiffany's father's behalf, had hired him to find her and that Eve was working with him because she'd been worried about her.

"I'm not going back there," Tiffany stated firmly.

"We're thinking that's a good call," Eve assured her.

While Tiffany's shoulders relaxed some, her combative gaze said she was still suspicious of their motives.

"Until this is all sorted out, we don't think it's a good idea for you to return to Florida."

When she still looked unconvinced, Eve glanced at Mac. He knew what she was wondering. Should she tell Tiffany about Reno and Gorman?

He nodded.

"There's something you need to know," Eve said, holding Tiffany's gaze. "Lance Reno—"

"Was going to kill me," Tiffany interrupted with defiance.

Eve blinked. "That doesn't surprise me, but that's not going to happen now." She waited a beat. "Tiffany . . . Reno is dead."

Tiffany blinked, paled, then found her voice. "How? When?"

Tiffany's shock, Mac noted, was real, but he didn't detect any sorrow on her part. Neither were there hysterics. He was starting to like this girl. She was holding up.

"He was murdered. So was Abe Gorman. We found them in the hotel room where you were staying in Vegas two days ago . . . about seven in the morning."

"Shit," Billie said, sounding shaken. "We must have just gotten out of there in time."

Silent until this point, Jasper Campbell leaned forward in his easy chair. "Why don't you folks just spell out the rest of what you know about what's going on here?"

Mac propped his elbows on spread knees, his hands clasped, and deferred to Eve.

"This all started several nights ago when I got a phone call from someone. They said they were you."

"I didn't call you."

"I've since figured that out. The bottom line, Tiffany, is someone wants me dead. Someone who knew to use you as bait because they knew I'd come after you. Someone who has been taunting me with warnings that if I didn't find you first, they'd kill you as well as me."

"Why? Why would anyone do that?"

"It's a long story," Mac cut in. "And we really don't have time to go into it right now. We're thinking that whoever hired Reno to kidnap you is the same person who's after Eve."

Tiffany glanced from Mac to Eve. "If that's true, why were Lance and Abe murdered?"

Mac looked toward Eve to supply the answer. "It's possible that Reno didn't keep up his end of the bargain. . . . Maybe he was supposed to take care of things a long time ago. Instead, he—"

"Played me for the money he could get out of me," Tiffany finished, and Mac couldn't help but feel sorry for her—until he noticed Billie's hand sneaking over and entwining with hers on the sofa. She seemed to have staunch allies in this young man and his family.

"I'm sorry," Eve said. "And I'm sorry we don't have time to give you more answers, but right now the best thing we can do is get you out of here before they catch up with us. Unfortunately, the Campbells are in danger until we can figure out who's behind this and why."

For the first time Tiffany showed emotion. A single tear leaked out as her mask of indifference cracked with vulnerability and pain.

"Whoever these people are, they're smart and their surveillance is sophisticated. They may be on our trail already."

Jas Campbell cut a glance toward the front window, excused himself, and rose to look outside. "You folks traveling alone?"

Mac looked at Eve, who, like him, had already risen to her feet and was rushing to the window.

A black SUV had pulled into the drive. It eased to a stop, and as if it had been choreographed, all four doors swung open and four people got out.

"Sonofabitch," Mac swore under his breath.

Three of the invaders were dressed in black—complete with black gloves, boots, and hoods over their heads. They were all brandishing AK-47s.

The fourth person, unmistakable at a distance of around thirty yards, was Richard Edwards. He was dressed in a tan suit. He looked a little rumpled. His comb-over lifted as the wind preceding the storm front picked up.

"It's Richard," Tiffany breathed, peering over Mac's shoulder. "What's Richard doing here?"

"We've been suspecting for some time that Edwards is in on this," Mac said, pissed at himself because the extra clip for his Beretta was locked in the glove compartment of the rented Jeep.

"What do we do?" Miriam's voice was barely a whisper but thick with fear.

Eve took control of Miriam and Tiffany. "Get away from the window. Get down behind the sofa."

Reacting immediately, Miriam grabbed Tiffany's arm and pulled her down to her knees with her behind the sofa.

"Billie," Eve continued, her voice steady, calm, and forceful. "Keep low, but go lock the back door and any other door or window they might be able to use for access."

Billie took off at a trot.

With his back against the wall on one side of the window and Jas positioned the same way on the other, Mac chanced another look outside. One of the intruders was moving at a run toward the far side of the house.

"You got local law enforcement around here?"

"Sheriff's office is forty miles away."

"Call 'em."

"I'll do it," Miriam said, and scrambling on all fours, headed for the phone. When she reached the phone cord she dragged it off the foyer table onto the floor. "I can't get a dial tone," she said, sounding shaken.

The third intruder rejoined the others, tucking a knife into his black boot, which explained the dead phone line.

"How about cell phones?"

"We're in a box canyon," Jas said. "Gotta ride to the top of the ridge to get a signal."

Mac cut Eve a glance. He had no doubt that their thoughts ran in tandem. No one was going to be riding to the ridge today. If Edwards and the people in black had their way, no one was going to get out of the house alive.

27

"You people in the house!"

It was Edwards. He'd walked forward from the other three in slow, nervous steps.

Mac moved cautiously to look out the window.

A light rain had started falling, but the wind was far from light. Edwards's comb-over was standing straight up. The lapels of his suit jacket had blown open. His white shirt was plastered against his chest.

"We know that Tiffany is in there," Edwards shouted, tugging his tie down and away from his face, where the wind had blown it.

Eve turned to Tiffany. "Did you call anyone?"

"I thought about it. Even dialed Kat's number, but at the last minute I changed my mind. I didn't want to worry her any more than she was already worried."

Mac glanced at Eve. "They must have found the GPS in the parking lot after the bombing."

Not that they needed it. Seemed the bad guys knew exactly how to find Eve no matter where she went.

"You folks don't need to panic," Edwards continued, his voice breaking. "We just want Tiffany. Everything's going to be fine. We don't want to hurt her. We don't want to hurt anyone, but we need for you to send Tiffany out, and then we'll leave you all alone."

"I was born at night, but it wasn't last night," Mac said under his breath. He didn't buy a word of it.

"I'll go," Tiffany said, standing up. "I'll go with them. That's what they want."

"You'll go nowhere, missy," Jas said with a nod to Miriam, who promptly put her arms around Tiffany and pulled her close.

"I'm putting you in danger."

"We'll sort that out later."

"But you don't even know me," Tiffany said, near tears again. "I can't let you risk your life for me."

"Tell her, McClain," Jas said, and turned back to watch out the window.

Mac's respect for Campbell, which was already high, notched up a couple more rungs on the ladder. He knew the score. The bad guys had three assault rifles. No one was leaving here alive.

"They don't plan to let anyone live even if you go with them," Mac told Tiffany gently.

The girl closed her eyes. Swallowed hard.

"It wouldn't matter," Miriam said. "We wouldn't let you go with them anyway."

Mac had to turn away from the raw wash of emotion twisting Tiffany's face. If they got out of this, it looked like Tiffany may have found, in the Campbells, something her own father had never given her.

"You got any more shotguns to go with that twelve-gauge you use as a greeter?" Mac asked Jas, keeping his voice as calm as possible.

"A twenty- and a sixteen-," Campbell said as he hunched over and made his way out of the living room. "Got some rifles, too. I'll go get 'em."

Billie came hustling back about that time, his eyes wide.

"One of 'em did something at the side of the house."

"They cut the phone wires," Jas said. "Come with me, son. I'll need help with the guns and ammo."

"McClain!" Edwards yelled again. "We know you and Ms. Garrett are in there. You know me. You've worked with me. You know I'm not here to hurt anyone. I just want what's best for Tiffany."

"That would be why you've brought the goons with the heavy artillery, right?" Mac yelled back out the open window.

"No, oh no," Edwards said, hands up in supplication. "They're just here for extra security. We don't want anything happening to Tiffany in transport."

"Nothing's going to happen to her, because she's not going with you. Now why don't you and your playmates hit the road before the cavalry arrives. The sheriff and his deputies ought to be here any minute."

Edwards, looking even more frazzled, turned back to the others. A brief round of conversation followed.

When he turned back, he dragged a shaking hand over his hair. "There's no one coming. We all know it. Look," he stated, and took a couple more steps forward, a hand out as if in a plea. "Don't, please don't, delay any longer. I don't want anyone to get hurt. I want to make this all right."

"For who? You? Tiffany? What about Clayborne?" Mac asked as Jas and Billie came back with two more shotguns and two rifles. A lever-action 30/30 and a bolt-action 30-06.

"Not exactly automatic weapons, but these ought to adjust a few attitudes," Campbell said, keeping the lever-action for himself and handing Mac the automatic.

No, Mac thought, a couple deer rifles and three sporting shotguns weren't any match for three 7.62mm automatic assault rifles that could fire an entire thirty-round clip in one wide, fast sweep.

"You don't understand," Edwards tried again. "The only way we can straighten this all out is to take Tiffany home. Please." He sounded close to panic. "Just do as I ask so no one gets hurt."

"Not going to happen," Mac assured him, and waited to see what the response would be.

One of the figures in black said something to the guy who had cut the wires. He raised his AK-47 to his shoulder.

"Get down!" Mac shouted. "Everybody down!"

A sharp crack split the air.

Then dead silence.

Hunched down beside the window, Mac looked at Jas. The other man's eyes were steady but questioning. No sound of shattering glass. No indication that a bullet had hit the house.

"Send her out," a deep voice said. It was not Edwards. "Or one of you will be the next to die."

Next to die?

"It's him," Eve said. "That's the voice of the guy who attacked me."

Mac chanced a peek out the window.

Edwards lay facedown in the driveway. He wasn't moving. A dark pool of blood stained the tan-hued dirt around his head.

"Jesus," Mac said, and pulled back, facing a living room full of wild-eyed faces. They had no idea what had just happened.

"They shot Edwards." He looked at Eve. She blinked back at him, still steady, still in control. "What the fuck is going on?"

"I guess we'll figure that out soon enough," she said. "Now we need to figure out how we're going to take them out."

"You have a safe place in the house somewhere?" Mac asked.

Jas nodded. "Take Tiffany and Billie to the basement, Miriam. Fruit room. And lock the door. Don't open it for anyone but us. And stay put until we come for you."

"I'm staying here," Billie said, breaking down the double-barreled 16-gauge shotgun and shoving two deer slugs in the twin chambers.

Jas's jaw was clenched, his jaw muscle popping, as he studied his son, whose face was set with determination. The boy was up to it. And Mac wanted Eve out of the line of fire. From the looks of the artillery those three goons were wielding, they'd be in the thick of it soon. The intruders had shot Edwards in cold blood. As far as Mac could tell, he hadn't been armed. They wouldn't hesitate to kill everyone in this house if they had to to get what they wanted.

Eve had drawn the S & W out of her purse and was dropping ammo in the six-shot cylinder when Mac said her name.

"Billie knows the layout up here—inside and out," he said when she looked up. "You don't. You're our best bet to protect Tiffany and Miriam."

She wanted to argue; he could see it in her eyes. But there wasn't time. They both knew it. And she was a pro. She couldn't fault his logic.

She grabbed the 20-gauge. "Can you use this?" she asked Miriam.

"Damn right I can," Miriam said with a clear, steady voice. "You live on a ranch, you learn how to shoot."

"Give me the 12-gauge," Tiffany said, surprising everyone but Eve.

"She used to shoot trap," Eve said when they all looked at Tiffany.

"Works for me," Mac said with an encouraging grin, and tossed Tiffany a box of shells that Jas had dumped on the sofa along with rounds for the other weapons.

"Get the bastards," Eve said with a meaningful look at Mac before they headed for the basement.

"Watch your back," he said as they disappeared down the hall toward the basement.

For the next thirty seconds all he could do was duck and cover as the AKs opened up and strafed the house with a steady and relentless stream of gunfire.

"Go! Go! Go!" Eve shouted, pushing Miriam and Tiffany ahead of her toward the basement steps.

"But Jas! And Billie!" Miriam cried.

"Will be all right. McClain knows what he's doing. And your men look like they can take care of themselves, too," she added, purposefully using the word *men* to help Miriam see Billie in that capacity instead of as her little boy. "They've got their job. We've got ours. Now get us the hell into that fruit room!"

Old house, renovated, Eve decided as her gaze glanced over dark stone and mortar walls as they rushed through two small dank rooms toward the back wall of the basement. Eve shut and locked the doors behind them.

Above them, a low-hanging unfinished ceiling was bolstered up by ancient wooden beams that had turned gray over the years. Dust clung to cobwebs between the two-by-fours spaced every foot and a half or so that braced the floor above. Once the first door closed behind them, they were in near darkness in a small room that smelled of dank and damp and of years of existence with little sunlight.

"Through here," Miriam said, and opened yet another door.

She flipped a light switch, and a bare bulb that couldn't have been more than 40 watts cast both light and shadows across the room, which was approximately ten by ten. A small window near the ceiling was the only source of outside light.

The walls were lined with shelf after shelf containing glass canning jars full of everything from beets, to tomatoes, to beans and Lord knew what else. They provided the only color in an otherwise cave-dreary existence.

The room was cool and deadly quiet now that the shooting had stopped.

"What do you think it means?" Miriam asked, standing in a corner with Tiffany pulled protectively to her side.

"It means they've stopped shooting," Eve said deadpan, then gave them a tight smile. "I don't know," she said. "But I figure it can only be good. It's three to three up there. We have the benefit of shelter and familiarity—at least your guys do."

"But those were awfully big guns those guys had," Tiffany said.

Yeah, Eve thought. *Big guns.* She tossed Miriam a box of slugs for her shotgun.

"Load up. That's an autoloader," she said, glancing at Tiffany.

"You sure you can handle it?" Miriam asked, glancing up from her gun.

In answer, Tiffany pulled back the bolt handle, dropped a shell in the receiver, then expertly depressed the bolt release and dropped four shells into the magazine.

"Guess that answers *that* question," Eve said with an approving grin. "It's gonna be a bad day for the bad guys," she added, her smile encompassing Miriam as well. "OK. Here's the plan. Tiffany, you stand on the left side of the door. If they manage to get to us, when that door flies open, you'll be behind it. The door's made of plywood and it's old and brittle. Just fire like crazy right through it and you'll load 'em up with buckshot and splinters. Ought to do the trick, right?"

"Right," Tiffany said, and moved where Eve directed. "Eve," she said haltingly.

Eve smiled. "It's OK, sweetie. We'll square things with each other when this is over, all right?"

For the first time, Tiffany smiled at her. She nodded and did what she was told.

"Miriam, if they make it down here, they're going to come in blasting dead ahead and to the right because it will be the first thing in their line of sight. I want you to stand next to Tiffany and fire off as many rounds as you can manage as fast as you can manage."

"Why don't I stand on the right of the door?"

God love a brave woman. "Because I don't want you getting hit by friendly fire."

"And where will you be?" Miriam asked.

Eve had spotted a small table loaded down with a box of empty canning jars. She tested the tabletop—it was a good inch and a half of hardwood with a thin metal sheet tacked on the surface. "I'll be behind this bad boy."

She quickly moved the box to the floor, tipped the table on its side, and dragged it a little left of center and to the right of the door and ducked down behind it. When she was satisfied with her positioning and theirs, she set the box of ammo beside her on the floor.

Then she walked to the small window. Rain peppered the glass, washing dirt from the outside window well over the pane. The window provided the only natural light in the room. At least there would be light until sunset. She checked her watch. They had a little over an hour, if she remembered right from the past two nights.

"We need to cover this all but a crack, so they can't see in and only a little light enters the room. Any ideas?"

Miriam raced across the room and dumped the jars out of the cardboard box. They clattered on the stone floor, some of them breaking on impact.

"Gonna need your table," Miriam said, and together they righted it and moved it under the window so they could reach it to cover the dusty and cracked windowpane.

"Perfect," Eve said, and moved the table back into position on its side. "Anyone comes down but our men and we fire, understood?"

Both Tiffany and Miriam gave definitive nods.

"I'm going to turn the light out now."

Tiffany looked terrified.

"It's OK. It won't take long for your pupils to adjust and you'll be able to see—but the bad guys with the big guns won't. We'll have the immediate advantage if they break in, and that's what it's going to take to get the drop on them. OK?" she asked Tiffany.

She nodded, her lips tight.

"Good girl. Here goes. And we need to keep quiet. No matter what happens. Don't talk; don't scream; don't make a sound unless I say it's OK."

Determined nods from both Tiffany and Miriam.

Eve flipped the lights, moved behind her makeshift bunker, and waited for her eyes to adjust.

She'd done everything that could be done to protect them. She hoped they wouldn't need it. And if they did, she hoped like hell it would be enough.

Up above, all was quiet.

Up above, McClain, Jas, and Billie may be dead.

McClain. Dead.

A weakening flood of dread eddied through her.

He wasn't dead. He couldn't be dead. Or critically injured and dying. She refused to let herself think that he might be. Refused to let the hammering of her heart goad her into a fear that she knew would disable, disengage, and ultimately leave the three of them defenseless.

She breathed deep, controlled the adrenaline, and concentrated on what had to be done.

And still she jumped involuntarily when the distant sound of firearms split the silence.

Across the basement room she heard twin gasps.

"It's good," she whispered to calm them. "It's a good sign. Means they still have someone to shoot at. Which means our guys are hanging in there."

At least that's what she hoped it meant.

Truth be told, she was beyond hoping. She was praying like she hadn't prayed in a very long time.

28

THE CLOUDS HAD OPENED UP THE SAME time as the AK-47s. Rain poured like a pulsing showerhead. Fast, furious, and full of force. Only the wind affected its downward path and bent it in sideways sheets that peppered the house along with the bullets.

The initial and unrelenting volley from the AK-47s had ended several minutes ago. All three of the invaders must have emptied an entire thirty rounds. In its wake glass splinters were scattered across the cream-colored carpet of the Campbells' living room. Now wind freely whipped the curtains, but the room was pretty much protected from the rain by the vast front porch.

Mac sneaked a look outside. The rain was so heavy, he could no longer make out Edwards's prone form lying in the drive. Neither could Mac determine if the three black figures intent on blasting everyone in the house to kingdom come were still flanking the black SUV, which he could see—but barely. He didn't know if that meant they'd moved or he simply couldn't see them as darkness approached, to add another element of difficulty.

After the initial round of shots, the gunfire had been sporadic and without warning. He got the feeling, however, that those rounds had been fired from different directions. Some from the left, some from the right of the house.

The next time they opened up, instead of tucking lower,

he took a chance and peeked over the windowsill. He'd been right, he realized, ducking back down. The flash from a single round had lit up like miniexplosions, helping him locate at least two of the shooters.

"They're spreading out," he told Campbell. "How many outside exits from the house?"

Jas was on one knee at the opposite side of the window from Mac. "Front door, side door. Double garage doors and a door into the kitchen from the garage."

"All locked," Billie said from his position on his knees behind the sofa.

"The storm cellar door," Jas said with a hard look at Mac, as if he'd just remembered. Panic flared in his eyes. "It's outside. Lies almost flat against the ground. It's padlocked, but that won't stop a round from one of those weapons they're carrying."

Mac figured he knew, but he asked anyway. "Where does the storm cellar lead?"

Jas's face was grim. "Exactly where you think it leads."

"Directly to where the women are holed up?"

He shook his head. "No. It's on the opposite side of the house. If they were of a mind to search room by room, though, it wouldn't take long to find the women down there."

"Then we just have to make sure they don't get that far."

Another round of gunfire peppered the house. Windows to the left and right of them shattered. Glass flew like splintered ice across the room. Mac felt the sting of a flying shard hit him in the cheek. He ignored it, quickly glancing toward the ceiling when he heard the distinct sound of breaking glass and the thud of boots hitting the floor above them.

"Billie," he barked, heading for the open stairway. "Stay low, but move to the far window. Fire some shots every minute or so, just to let them know we've got a read on them. Jas—"

He turned to see Campbell inching the front door open and belly crawling outside, shoving his rifle ahead of him.

The man was no fool. And Mac couldn't afford to worry about him now. He had an asshole to deal with upstairs.

Speed, Mac knew, was his best ally right now. He had to reach the top of the stairs to the second story before the bad guy did or he'd be a sitting duck on the stair steps.

He hit the steps at a dead run—and fell flat on his face when his knee buckled. He bit back a groan, caught the breath the knifing sensation in his knee had stolen, and made himself crawl, using one foot for leverage, up the stairs.

Above him, he heard a low chuckle.

His head snapped up. He was looking directly into the business end of an AK-47.

The big man holding the gun was smiling through the slit of his black hood as he lifted the assault rifle to his hip and aimed.

He'd be damned if he was going to die on his knees. In a lightning move, he reached up, grabbed a booted foot, and jerked. Everything happened at once then. The staccato sound of the AK going off, the searing pain in his left shoulder, the pounding weight of both man and gun falling on top of him, the bone-jarring tumble to the bottom of the stairs.

Where he lay prone on his back. The wind knocked out of him. Unable to move as a shape in all black rose above him, rifle in hand again, and pointed it dead center at his heart.

He jerked when he heard the shot. Waited for the pain, the darkness, the numbing slide into death.

When none of that happened, he opened his eyes to see the black-clad figure weave, then topple like a tree and land like deadweight on the floor.

"You okay?" Billie asked, coming to stand above him, smoke still drifting from the end of his 16-gauge shotgun.

"Right as rain," Mac managed. "Nice shot."

The boy grinned, wide-eyed and a little shocky.

"Help me up," Mac said, and lifted the arm that wasn't burning. Billie's hand was shaking as he reached for Mac's. But Billie stood firm, put his weight behind his pull and got Mac to his feet.

Ignoring both his knee and his shoulder, Mac bent down and touched the fallen man's carotid artery. He was dead.

Mac whipped off his hood. He'd never seen him before, but he'd bet his life this was the guy who'd terrorized Eve.

The definitive sound of a 30/30 firing several rounds rang through the wind and rain. "Come on," Mac said to Billie. "We need to go help your dad."

Even though it felt like an hour, Eve didn't think any more than a few minutes had passed when she heard the sound of footsteps outside the fruit room door.

She lifted a finger to her lips, indicating Miriam and Tiffany should stay silent, stay calm. It took everything in Eve to maintain her own calm. It didn't figure that anyone should be down here. Not yet. Not unless they'd gotten by the men, and she refused to believe that had happened. Not when she recognized not only the sound of the AK-47s above the storm but also the sound of other ordnance.

"Is there a way into the basement other than through the house?" she whispered.

Miriam's eyes flew wide and she nodded. "Storm cellar door," she whispered back, and, shouldering her shotgun, tucked Tiffany behind her. Tiffany wasn't having any of it. She stood tall beside Miriam, the 12-gauge raised to her shoulder.

Eve nodded in approval—and then the world went Technicolor and surround sound. An explosion rocked the room, blasting her back a full four feet and into the wall of canned vegetables. She was aware of a brilliant flash of fire, of the jars rattling and crashing to the floor, of the door to the room blowing off its hinges and flying into the shelves. Glass fragments and globs of tomatoes and beets and beans rained down all over her as she lay there, stunned and unable to move for several seconds.

When she regained her equilibrium, she pushed herself up to a sitting position, felt glass cut into her palms and her

S & W dig into her hip beneath her on the concrete floor. The cardboard had flown off the window; dusky light cast the room in an eerie glow through the haze of smoke glutting the small room from the blast.

"Stay right where you are, Ms. Garrett. Or I'll put a bullet in you now instead of later."

Eve blinked and tried to focus. And then she recognized the voice of the person threatening her.

"Jazelle," she said even before the black-clad figure reached for the hood and wiped it off. "Or should I say Bianca?"

"So you figured it out."

Eve just looked at her.

"I'm impressed. But not enough to let you live. Unfortunate. And unfortunate for you, Tiffany," Bianca said, motioning with her weapon for Tiffany and Miriam to move from the corner where they were huddled to join Eve by the back wall of the room.

Eve was still on the floor. For the time being, she was going to stay that way and stay close to her handgun. Her head pounded. Her back stung. She ignored the pain. And the wetness of canned fruits and vegetables spilling into her hair and clothes.

"I don't get it," Eve said as Tiffany and Miriam walked shakily to her side. Except for some minor cuts and burns, it appeared they were uninjured. Scared half to death but uninjured. Eve planned to keep them that way. If she could keep Bianca talking until the troops arrived, she might be able to pull it off.

And the troops would arrive. She refused to think of McClain dead.

"I'm feeling generous and we've got a little time to kill until my men finish off yours. So what is it that you don't get, Ms. Garrett?"

Eve winced in pain and scooted back farther against the wall of shelves, nudging her S & W behind her with her hips. "Why did you wait this long to come after me? This is about the death of your husband, right?"

The woman's eyes went hard. "You killed him."

"So you want me dead. I get that part. But why now? Why did you wait so long? Why didn't you come after me back then?"

"Do you have any idea what it's like to lose someone you love? It's paralyzing. You not only killed my husband. You killed my brother. And in the end, you killed my father, too.

"Oh yes," she continued when Eve shook her head. "I had to watch my father grieve; I had to help him through the loss. His grief killed him. He finally succumbed to the pain of all you took away from us."

"I was defending myself," Eve pointed out. "I didn't seek them out to kill them."

"I was with my father when he died last year," Bianca went on, and Eve knew that nothing she said was going to stop this. But she had to stall. She had to.

"He asked only one thing of me. That I avenge his death and my brother's. My husband's. I will keep my promise."

So, Eve thought, the widowed daughter and the father had fed off each other's grief. And now Bianca was determined to extract revenge on the woman who had killed her family.

"I understand," Eve said as calmly as possible. "I understand why you want revenge on me. But why Tiffany? She's the innocent here."

"Ah. But it was Clayborne's duplicity that led to my family's deaths. He needed to suffer as well."

"So Tiffany is merely a pawn?"

"An added bonus," Bianca clarified without an ounce of remorse in her words.

"So, to get to me, you buried your past and managed to get hired by Clayborne. How did Edwards fit into this? And Reno and Gorman?"

Bianca made a sound of disgust. "Reno. The stupid fool got greedy. He was supposed to kill Tiffany immediately and make it look like a drug overdose. But he had too much fun playing with her and her money. So he eluded me, thought he was smarter than me. Well, he'd dead now. And soon, you will be joining him and his ugly friend."

She lifted the gun.

Beside her, Miriam wrapped Tiffany in her arms.

"Tell me something first. You owe me that, at least," Eve said. Anything to keep Bianca's finger off the trigger. "Why this elaborate scheme? Why the taunting? Why didn't you just kill me?"

"Because I wanted you to squirm. I wanted you to know your death was near and feel the helplessness of your inability to do nothing about it."

"OK, fine. You wanted me to suffer first. Job well done. But why kill Tiffany? She'd be much more valuable to you to hold for ransom." Eve was reaching now, but anything, anything, to keep Tiffany alive. "Jeremy Clayborne would pay any sum to get her back alive."

"Clayborne?" Bianca laughed, as if she was delighted with herself. "Jeremy Clayborne is dead."

Behind her, Eve heard Tiffany gasp.

"I had wanted to make him suffer while he agonized over his daughter's disappearance. But he was crazed. I found that out shortly after I came to work for him. He was totally removed from reality, and in truth, he could care less about Tiffany."

"So you killed him."

Bianca's eyes went hard. "He made it easy. One shot, all gone. Has anyone missed him? Of course not, because of the veil of secrecy of his own making. The only one who had contact with him was Richard, and since I control—sorry—controlled Richard, no one was the wiser."

She was gloating, Eve realized. Proud of her manipulation. And she had no conscience whatsoever about murder.

"Richard was a lot of things. But he was loyal to Clayborne.

How did you get him to come over to your way of thinking?"

Bianca smiled again. A cold, evil smile. "Richard's loyalty was attached to his dick. He was easy to seduce."

"Before or after he hired you as EA?"

"Oh, it was all business. At first. And when I had him on his knees, I took care of Clayborne. Poor me. I told Richard that the crazy man tried to rape me."

Bianca smiled again. "I convinced him that no one would believe me. That I'd go to prison forever if I was tried. Begged him to help me, told him I loved him. Of course, he was already in love with me."

"Plain guy like him and all. A beauty like you. He'd do anything for you."

Bianca nodded. "Naturally. He even helped me dispose of the body and go on as if Clayborne was still alive. He had a business head, but Richard was horribly gullible, I'm afraid."

"So Richard didn't know about your plan to kill Tiffany, did he? He really did hire McClain to find her."

"You are truly astute, Ms. Garrett. I commend you. Yes, Richard hired McClain before I could stop him. He actually cared about the girl. My original intent was to slow you down until my people could find Reno and Tiffany and take care of them. But you found her for me."

Bianca considered Eve with regret. "We could use someone with your intelligence in our organization. It's a pity you're going to have to die."

"Yeah. The thing about death—it's so permanent."

"Get up," Bianca said abruptly when the sound of footsteps on the basement steps echoed into the room.

"I don't know if I can," Eve said, moving stiffly into a squatting position, bending forward as if to use her left hand to steady herself.

"Then die where you are like a—"

She never finished her sentence. Eve whipped her S & W

out from under her and unloaded the clip dead center in
Bianca's chest.

Her eyes were wide, glazed over, as she stared through
Eve. The assault rifle fell from her lifeless hand as she
slumped, in slow motion, to the floor.

When the echo of the shots faded, Eve realized she was
still pumping the trigger.

"Don't think she's going to get any deader."

In a haze, Eve looked up, and there he was. McClain. In
all his arrogant glory. His arm was bleeding. His face was
bleeding. And he was holding his weight heavily on his good
leg. He was soaking wet, covered in mud.

And that crooked triple-A smile he sent her made her
heart trip harder than when she'd faced the deadly end of
Bianca Georgiev's AK-47.

Oblivious to the squeals of relief all around her as Jas and
Billie rushed into the fruit room, and only vaguely aware of
a group hug going on in the background, all Eve could see
was McClain.

"What took you so long?"

He limped slowly to her side. "Bitch. Bitch. Bitch."

And then he grabbed her with his good arm and dragged
her hard against him. "You do know that you're covered in at
least three food groups, don't you?"

She did. And she didn't care.

She clung to him, only then realizing how unsteady she
was. She buried her face into the hollow of his shoulder. "I
don't suppose you've got any chocolate on you?"

29

MAC LET HIS HEAD FALL WEARILY AGAINST the headrest as yet one more delay kept him from getting his feet on West Palm Beach asphalt. Heavier than usual air traffic.

He closed his eyes, winced when he shifted his arm, and ignored the throbbing ache in his knee. The days after the episode at the Campbells' had been long and tedious. They'd put him in the hospital, for God's sake—like some weenie. But they hadn't kept him there long. He'd been out the next day, his arm in a sling, his leg in a brace, and back at the Campbells', where the local law enforcement, the Las Vegas PD, the FBI, and even some Company men had set up camp. He and Eve and everyone else involved had been peppered with endless and relentless questions.

Four dead bodies—six counting Reno and Gorman in Vegas—had a tendency to perk up a few bureaucratic ears. And when three of those bodies could be directly linked to international arms dealing, those ears actually twitched. He'd seen it up close and personal.

Kat and Sven had joined them as soon as Eve had called and filled them in. So now Tiffany and the Campbells and the German-born socialite and her Olympic skier were bonding over hot chocolate and long horseback rides.

Mac was pleased for Tiffany. She was a good kid. Who'd have believed it? And now it appeared she had the makings of a family.

Tiffany was going to be OK. It would be a long road to full recovery for her, but with the Campbells' help—and Kat and Sven's—she could get on with her life.

Case in point, she'd already made her first decision as "acting" head of Clayborne International.

Mac had a new job.

He righted his seat back at the request of the flight attendant, who advised him they were about to land.

He'd never flown in such luxury. But it seemed that as the new head of Clayborne International's security, he needed to get used to private jets and top-of the-line resources.

Not to mention more money.

Which equated to only one thing. More Ali.

Right now, however, he had another woman on his mind. An M&M-popping smart mouth who had run like her tail was on fire the minute all the arms of the law were satisfied they were finished with her.

When he'd realized she was gone, he'd had to think about how he felt about that—for all of a second. He'd have been blowing smoke up his own ass if he really thought he was willing to let her walk out of his life.

He was far from finished with the little blonde. And she was about to find out that he wasn't about to let her run too far.

Eve had been expecting him. And when Kimmie, with her tall, leggy, centerfold body and wide brown eyes, walked back to Eve's office door and announced that Tyler Mc-Clain was here to see her, Eve felt her chest muscles clench tight.

Nolan, who, unfortunately, had been walking by, stopped dead in his tracks. "Who?"

"McClain," a voice said from the hall. "Tyler McClain, and I'm staying until she sees me."

Eve glanced up and saw Nolan watching her through narrowed eyes. She recognized that look. He was in full bigbrother mode. If she said the word, Nolan would personally remove McClain from the building without breaking a sweat.

McClain was tough, but with his arm in a sling and his leg in a brace, he was no match for her former Ranger brother.

Oh God. And here came Ethan and Dallas. With scowls just as dark as Nolan's—and that clench-jawed military special ops look they got when they were about to transform into superman mode.

She let out a weighty breath. It was partly her fault that they were reacting this way. She'd been moping around like a surly teenager since she'd returned from Utah. And with good reason, as far as she was concerned.

She was scared. Good and scared. Too many feelings. Too many fears. All of them centering around McClain.

"You gonna hide behind your brothers all day or are you gonna come out and play?" McClain taunted. Damn him.

She didn't figure there would be much play to it. Seeing him was going to be hard. That's why she'd left Utah without so much as a "so long, it's been good to know you." She hadn't wanted to drag things out between them any longer than necessary.

Tiffany was safe and sound. The case was over. Therefore, they were over. A nice and tidy ending for a not so nice and tidy story.

She was tempted to let her brothers handle him—she knew they wouldn't really hurt him because he was injured—but just then he piped up again.

"Look, they can carpet the floor with me if they want. Paper the walls. I don't care. But I'm not leaving until I talk to you."

She hung her head in her hands. Shook it. Then looked up to face the music.

A strange thing had happened. Her brothers had disappeared.

She shot to her feet. "Hey. Where'd you guys go?"

McClain appeared in the doorway. "Guess I scared them off."

"In your dreams, McClain," came a chorus of deep voices from the far end of the hall.

One corner of McClain's mouth tipped up in a crooked grin. "OK. So maybe they decided they wanted to see you sweat a little."

If that was the case, they were going to be happy boys. Her palms were already sweating. And all she was doing was looking at him.

He had stitches and bruises on his face. His left arm was still in a sling over another patently ugly tropical print shirt. She could see the metal shafts of a knee brace beneath his baggy chinos.

And he looked so . . . good that she felt all gooey inside.

Gooey. God. What a girlie thing to feel.

"So," he said, leaning a shoulder against the door frame. "You left Utah in a hurry."

"Yeah, well. They were finished with me. And I'd left some things hanging back here that needed attention."

"What about me? Didn't you figure I needed attention?"

She couldn't quite look at him. She crossed her arms over her breasts. She'd worn a yellow sundress today. Scooped low across her breasts, fitted snug at her waist and hips. Her arms were bare and suddenly she felt cold. And hot. And angry as hell with herself for letting him fluster her this way.

Fluster. Another girlie word, she thought in self-disgust.

"You've been taking care of yourself for years, McClain," she said, rallying a little self-respect. "I didn't figure you needed me around to hold your hand."

"What if I'd just *wanted* you around for that?"

Oh no. She wasn't going to let him lead her down that path.

"I love you, Eve."

Whoa.

Her gaze snapped to his. She stared at him, wild-eyed. Her heart did a little panic dance that reeked of excitement and longing and—hold the phone—wary doubt.

"Where do you come off, coming in here and saying something like that? Just . . . just popping it off out of the blue?"

He limped on into her office. Eased a hip on the corner of her desk and got comfortable. He picked up a round glass paperweight, studied it, set it back down again. "It's what a man says to a woman when he feels about her the way I feel about you. The usual response for the woman is to say, 'I love you, too.' "

She managed to muster an indignant snort. She didn't know why she felt such a pulse-elevating mix of anger and fear and anticipation. She let the anger make the call.

"Look, I don't know what your game is, but I seem to recall hearing those words from you before. I believe it was the night in Eddie Franco's cabana. They didn't mean anything then. Why should I believe they mean anything now?"

He grinned. "Come on. I was eighteen. I was horny. You were hot. I'd have said anything to get in your pants."

"You were a shit," she said, and for some ridiculous reason found herself close to tears.

"I was," he said, his expression suddenly gentle.

She hated it when he looked at her like that. Like he felt sorry for her. Like she needed him to make her feel better.

Well, what would make her feel better would be for him to argue with her, but he wouldn't give her the satisfaction.

"What do you want from me?" she demanded, not caring that she sounded surly and childish. "The case is over. So are we. That's the way it was supposed to work."

"What are you afraid of, Eve? The past? The future? Me?"

All of the above, she realized in a moment of clarity. "Go away. Leave me alone."

"Not going to happen. So. What are you going to do now?"

"Why are you being so difficult?"

He gave her a long, searching look. "Look. I know I hurt you. In the past, I mean."

"You don't know the half of it," she said before she could

stop herself, then tried to cover herself. "But don't give yourself so much credit. You weren't the only one to run out on me."

"Men are idiots," he said. "I know I was. But I've wised up."

She snorted. "Because you think you love me?"

"Because I know I love you. Hell, Eve. I've fought it, too. But it's bigger than me. Bigger than you. Bigger than the both of us."

She rolled her eyes, telling him what she thought of his heavy-handed clichés but longing desperately to believe him.

"It was just supposed to be a sexual thing," she said defensively, but in truth, she had very few defenses left.

"Things don't always work out like they're supposed to."

Unable to sit still any longer, she rose, turned her back on him, and, crossing her arms over her breasts, looked out the window—and saw exactly nothing. She was too aware of him. Of what he'd said. Of how badly she wanted to believe him even though she'd been telling herself for days that walking away from him was the only logical thing to do.

Logic, however, didn't have much play at the moment.

"You think I haven't been dealing with a weighty portion of denial myself? You think I haven't tried to talk myself out of this? Hell. I failed at one marriage. I don't want to fail at another."

She whipped around. "Marriage?"

"Well, yeah. That would be the next step."

"You want to marry me?"

He hitched himself off the desk, walked over in front of her. His dark eyes glittered with emotion and truth and, oh my, love.

"I'm dying to marry you," he whispered, and drew her into his arms. "Now, unless you can come up with a damn good reason to tell me no, you know what I want to hear from you."

She couldn't help it. Hot tears rolled down her cheeks. "I'm scared."

"I know, baby. So am I."

"You? Scared?"

He pressed his forehead to hers. "Damn straight. I'm scared that I won't measure up to the man you need to make you happy. Scared you won't want a washed-up cop with a bum leg."

She lifted her head, kissed his brow. "That doesn't matter. That could never matter to me." Her fingers trembled when she touched them to his cheeks.

"I want to be the best man I can for you. I'm afraid I'll screw that up. Hell, Eve. Look at you. You fulfill every fantasy I've ever had. You're smart and kind and brave and sassy. And you're sexy as all get-out. You're the brass ring, Eve. The one I was always grabbing for. The one I let slip away from me all those years ago. But I'm willing to risk screwing up again. For you. For us.

"Come on," he pleaded. "What's it going to take to cinch this deal?"

What could she say to a speech like that? What could she do but take the plunge and take the chance and wander through life with him—two people scared together?

"M&M's for life might do it," she said, and felt tears of happiness sting in her eyes.

He smiled and it was like the sun came out. "You got it, cupcake. M&M's and me."

She rose up on tiptoe to kiss him. "What a bargain."

Later that night, Eve finally told him about the baby. About the miscarriage. They cried together. And while she had forgiven him completely, it was going to be a while before he forgave himself.

"We'll make another baby," she said, soothing the hair back from his face. "Starting right now."

Much later, Eve gave a lazy all-over stretch and felt her inner muscles clench when she thought about how McClain had made love to her. He'd taken her to bed. He'd turned her on her stomach, drawn her to her knees, and, standing beside the bed, entered her from behind. He'd decimated her with multiple orgasms so strong and intense, she'd felt herself leave her body. Several times.

She smiled. Oh, yeah. The man had some moves.

Right now, he was sleeping; at least she thought he was until she felt a strong, muscled hand cup her breast, gently squeeze, then finesse her nipple into a tight, aching bud with his thumb and finger.

She rolled to her side, toward him, and he immediately replaced his fingers with his mouth as she slung her thigh across his bare hip and let him pleasure them both.

Yeah. He had a way about him. A way of touching her that made her feel very feminine and sexual and ready. A way of convincing her she could trust him with her heart.

"You have the most incredible breasts," he murmured, alternately laving her nipple with his tongue, then sucking as he cupped her breast in his hand, exploring texture and weight and sensitivity.

"And you have the most amazing appetite."

"Not a complaint, right?"

"Um." She loved the feel of his hands on her. Of his mouth loving her. "Not a complaint."

"McClain?" she said on a dreamy breath, and forked her fingers through his hair.

"I'm busy here."

She grinned and kissed the top of his head. "Forever and ever, right?"

He lifted his head, met her eyes with a softness she'd never seen before. "We're taking this to the limit, cupcake. So yeah. Forever and ever."

EPILOGUE

"I DON'T CARE IF YOU *ARE* FAMILY NOW. DO not mess with me, bub. You'll end up raw and bleeding. Case in point," Ethan said, and sent Mac's green ball flying off the course.

It was the annual Garrett family Fourth of July picnic slash croquet tournament and the entire crew was assembled.

"I told you they take their croquet seriously," Eve said as she stood beside Mac and watched his ball sail out of play.

"Bloodthirsty bastard," Mac sputtered, fighting to keep a grin from breaking through his surly scowl.

"Heard that," Ethan said easily as he slung his mallet over his shoulder and popped a cherry Life Saver in his mouth.

"You were supposed to." Mac stomped off after his ball.

Eve was glad to see Ethan enjoying himself. He was just too sober most of the time. Which made her think he was just too sad. It made her wonder if he still carried a torch for Darcy. Eve figured that he did. It had been five years since the divorce. He never mentioned Darcy's name. But then he never said much of anything about his personal life.

But today was not the day to be brooding over her big brother's happiness. Today was a day for celebration.

"Competitive, isn't he?" Dallas commented, coming up to stand beside Eve, his eyes on his new brother-in-law.

"In a word," she said with a grin.

They'd been married a full month now. Once she'd said

yes, McClain had said he wasn't waiting around for her to change her mind. He'd whisked her off to Vegas—his idea of a good laugh, ha-ha—and they'd gotten married at the first chapel they'd run across. She felt she was fortunate an Elvis impersonator hadn't delivered their vows.

He'd made up for the impromptu ceremony with a honeymoon in Italy. It had been the most romantic two weeks of her life. And today was one of the happiest days of her life. She was surrounded by family and friends, all people she loved and cared about. Her parents had turned the Fourth of July celebration into a belated wedding reception of sorts.

Among the many attendees were the Campbells—hey, anyone who stood beside you in a life-or-death situation is as good as family. Kat and Sven were also in attendance, wowing everyone with their celebrity status, striking good looks, and genuine warmth. And then there was Tiffany.

They'd mended their fences. Tiffany was back to looking at Eve like a big sister, and bless them, her brothers had adopted her, too. Eve and Mac made it a point to have her over—they'd moved into Eve's apartment—once a week for a little dinner and conversation. Tiffany was enrolled for the fall semester at the University of Florida, majoring in business so she'd be ready to take her place at Clayborne International in time. In the meantime, Mac, her new head of security, was in the process of running background checks on potential candidates for the CEO position, while the bank had taken over the business on an interim basis until they could install someone capable at the helm.

Eve knew that Tiffany made frequent flights to Utah. And that made her glad.

"He making you happy?"

Eve turned and smiled as Uncle Bud walked up to join her when Nolan and Dallas took their turns on the croquet court laid out on her dad's neatly manicured back lawn. "I'll know who to call if he doesn't," she said, hugging him.

"You got that right."

"I love him, Uncle Bud."

"Yeah. I can see that. I like him," he said after a considering moment, and the passage from outsider to family was
complete.

Her parents had already accepted McClain with open
arms. And her brothers, after eavesdropping on his proposal
in the office, were pretty much convinced he had a few
screws loose, considering he wanted to marry her. "But hey,"
Nolan had said, "it's his funeral."

They liked him. Eve could tell. And though she'd never
admit it, her brothers' approval was one of the most important things in the world to her.

"Look at them," Jillian said, easing into a chair and settling in to watch the show. "Aren't they something? Like
four peas in the same pod. But for the brown eyes, Mac
could be one of their brothers."

Yeah, Eve thought, grinning down at Jillian, whose eyes,
truly, were only for Nolan, *weren't they something?* Four gorgeous testosterone-driven males—and she was linked with
every one of them.

She searched the yard and finally found her father—an
older but no less attractive version of her brothers. Wes Garrett was, as usual, playing barbecue king, smoking up the
neighborhood with the delicious scents of burgers and ribs.
As if aware that she was seeking him out, his head came up.
He grinned and winked at her. She gave him a broad smile
back.

"Take that, you blackguard," she heard Mac say with tri-
umph, and he had another Garrett brother stomping off in
search of his ball.

"Fits right in, that one," Eve's mother said as she joined
Eve and Jillian, who looked cool and sophisticated as always
in snug red capri pants and a loose-fitting tunic top.

Eve's mother, looking more like her sister with her blond
hair short and bouncy, was beaming, as she always did when
she was surrounded by her family.

"And this one fits right in, too," she added, squeezing the hand of five-year-old Ali McClain, who had flown to Florida to join her daddy on this special occasion.

"How's it going, Ali? You having a good time?" Eve asked, looking into eyes so much like Mac's it made her heart hurt with love for both man and child. Tomorrow the three of them were going boat shopping. McClain was as excited as a kid in a candy store over the prospect.

"They won't let me play," Ali said with a pout that only a five-year-old could carry off.

"Well," Eve said, taking her hand. "We can fix that. Come on, sweetheart. You and I are going to show them how the game is played."

"All right," Ali said with a big grin, and marched on out to center court, holding Eve's hand tight in hers.

"Prepare to eat dirt and die, gentlemen," Eve announced. "You've got real competition now."

Mac looked over at the pair of them. She loved how his eyes went soft and warm.

"Oh no, not *real* competition," he said, scooping Ali into his arms and tickling her until she shrieked with laughter. "Don't suppose I could bribe you two hustlers into staying on the sidelines?"

Eve looked at Ali. Ali looked at Eve.

"What you got?" they asked in unison.

With a smug look he pulled two bags of M&M's out of his pocket.

They snatched the candy away like it was gold.

And her husband looked first at Ali and then at Eve like *they* were. Solid gold.

Turn the page for a
thrilling sneak peek at

TO THE BRINK

Book Three in The Bodyguards series

Special Forces motto:

De Oppresso Liber—To Liberate the Oppressed

ZAMBOANGA CITY, PHILIPPINES

PRESENT

"Ethan. Um. Hi. It's . . . Darcy."

Darcy Prescott had known this would be hard. She hadn't spoken to Ethan Garrett in the five years since their divorce. So, yeah, dialing his number had been good and hard; saying his name was painful.

She gripped the receiver with both hands, dug deep for a steadying breath. "Look. I . . . I think I might be in some trouble here."

The admission was as difficult to make as the phone call. Saying the words out loud gave them credence. It did horrible things to the rhythm of her heart which had been getting a helluva workout in the past few hours.

That would show those misinformed souls who wondered in admiration and awe over her seemingly unflappable control. *If they could only see me now.*

"Maybe some bad trouble," she confessed, still reluctant to believe it as she dragged a hand through her hair. "It's . . . it's almost midnight here in Zamboanga. I can't . . . I can't think, you know, how that equates to West Palm Beach time. Maybe one in the afternoon? Two? I'm not sure."

She paused again when she heard a thread of hysteria creep back into her voice. She blinked up at the white ceiling of her hotel room.

"OK, look," she said, if not steadier, at least resolved to

calm herself down. She absently repositioned the base of the phone on the rich mahogany nightstand sitting beside her bed. "I'm at the Garden Orchid Hotel. It's on . . . let me think. Governor Camins Avenue." She rattled off the phone number.

"Can you . . . can you call me, please? As soon as you can, okay?" Darcy slowly closed her eyes, forced them open again. "I'm in Room 333. If . . . if I don't answer when you call, well, try again, okay?

"Look, Ethan. I . . ." She cut herself off as a tear surprised her and trickled down her cheek. She brushed it angrily away with the back of her hand. "Just call. OK? And hurry."

She hung up the phone. For a long moment, she sat motionless, staring at the cradled receiver. And prayed that he would get her message before it was too late.

It probably should have bothered her that her ex was the first person Darcy thought to call the moment she'd realized she had a problem. And it *might* have if she could function on a level separate from the fear. So far that wasn't happening.

This morning, she hadn't been afraid. This morning, she'd had her usual busy day in the Consulate Office at the U.S. Embassy in Manila. But this morning, Amanda Stover had still been alive—and when a co-worker had called Darcy on her cell an hour ago and told her about Amanda's death, a cold chill had swept her from head to foot.

"How?" she'd asked, sinking down in shock onto the hotel bed.

"Hit and run."

It had to be an accident, Darcy had told herself over and over, her heart sinking as she'd scrambled for her briefcase and dug out the envelope Amanda had given her just before she'd left the embassy to catch her flight to Zamboanga.

Darcy stared at the envelope she had promised Amanda she'd open as soon as she had a minute. The envelope she'd ripped open only moments ago.

The minute she'd seen the note tucked inside, Darcy had known. The car that had killed Amanda hadn't done so by accident. Amanda had been murdered. And Darcy suspected that she was now in possession of the reason Amanda had been killed. She was also certain that she would be targeted as the next person to die.

With trembling fingers, she picked up the padded manila envelope she'd resealed as tight as Fort Knox. Then she addressed it and slapped on enough postage to send it to the moon. All the while she fought to gain the upper hand over a damnable rising panic.

Panic wasn't going to help her get out of this alive. Clear thinking was.

On a serrated breath she stood and walked across the room, her sandals sinking into the plush cream-colored carpeting. Slowly, she opened her hotel room door. She looked up and down the empty hall. Reasonably certain it was safe, she slipped outside and headed for the elevator.

"Good evening, Miss Prescott."

Rudy Mar startled her as she hit the ground floor and stepped out of the elevator into a lobby done in soft tropical colors and more mahogany wood so deep reddish-brown it was almost purple. She paused to see the night clerk standing at his post behind the polished registration desk where the older man appeared to be reading the *Manila Bulletin*.

She forced a smile. "Good evening, Rudy Mar."

She always stayed at the Orchid when her duties took her from Manila to Zamboanga. She knew many of the staff on a first-name basis. Had learned that the Zamboangueños people were warm and friendly. As a rule, she enjoyed a little pleasant banter with Rudy Mar whose chocolate-brown eyes and salt-and-pepper hair made him look grandfatherly and kind.

Tonight, however, the rules had changed.

"Going out so late, Miss?" Rudy Mar's wide smile was tempered with concern.

"Actually, I need to mail a letter."

Rudy Mar laid the newspaper on the granite top of the registration desk. Darcy thought of the headlines that would appear on tomorrow's edition: *U.S. Embassy Employee Victim of Hit and Run,* and her blood ran cold.

"Miss?"

Her gaze snapped back to Rudy Mar. His expectant look made her realize she'd completely tuned out something he'd said. "I'm sorry . . . what?"

"I said I'd be happy to take care of that for you. The letter," he clarified with a nod toward the envelope.

Involuntary reflexes had her clutching the envelope in question tighter in her hand. "Oh. Thank you, but I . . . I want to take a walk anyway, get a little air. I'll just drop it at the post office while I'm out."

She smiled in what she hoped was a credible impersonation of a woman who wasn't about to jump out of her skin.

"As you wish, Miss Prescott. Enjoy your walk. But stay on the main streets, all right?"

"Thank you. I will. I'll be back in a few minutes."

As she walked out the hotel door, Darcy understood both Rudy Mar's concern and his puzzlement over her actions. American embassy staff were often targets of terrorists in the Philippines and she was not employing hazardous duty procedure. Normally she followed protocol to the letter—she buried her route to work in the mornings, alternated modes of transportation, and when out of Manila, as she was now, she would normally phone for a car and driver if she needed to go out.

Tonight, there wasn't time. She had to get the envelope out of her possession, in the mail, and get back to her room before Ethan called back. And the bigger problem: She no longer knew who she could trust.

She cut a seemingly meandering path along the main streets, checking often to see if anyone was following her, hoping she'd spot a motorcab or a jeepney and could hitch a ride. One or the other would provide at the least some cover and a little anonymity and make her a little less of a target with a big bull's eye on her back. Tonight, however, both were as scarce as taxies. So she walked. Fast.

It was a typical Philippine evening. Close, hot, tropical. The sidewalks had sucked in the sun's rays during the day and now breathed them back out like heat from a cooling oven. Darcy had dressed for the sweltering night in a white, short-sleeve cotton t-shirt and khaki shorts. Still, her back was damp with perspiration. In her espadrilles, the soles of her feet were damp as well.

She caught a glimpse of herself in a storefront window and realized how tense she appeared. Determined not to draw attention to herself, she made her shoulders relax, deliberately slowed her pace in the face of a warning voice that cautioned her to hurry.

Hurry, hurry!

Struggling to ignore it, she walked on past a towering old cathedral rich with Spanish influence, past a more modern gift shop. The streets were, for the most part, deserted but should anyone see her, they would see an American of average height, a little on the slim side, out for an evening stroll. No one special. Nothing remarkable. Except, maybe, for the auburn hair she'd cut short a year ago when she'd started her permanent change of station with the embassy in Manila.

Tonight more than ever before, she regretted the bureaucratic snafu that had restationed her from Mexico City to Manila. As she'd always done when her rotation was drawing to a close, she'd filled out her dream sheet requesting a PSC in Paris. Paris, Philippines—easy to get the two mixed up, she thought sourly, then sucked in her breath on a gasp when a cat sprang out of an alley and, yowling, ran in front of her.

When her heart dropped back into her chest, she made another quick, visual search around her. Only after she was satisfied that no one was following her did she walk across Corcuera Street toward the post office she'd intentionally bypassed the first time she'd strolled past, playing tourist again, staring at the mayor's office.

Without breaking stride, she walked behind the mayor's office where the post office was located, slid the padded envelope out of her purse, and dropped it in the after-hours mail slot.

Now all she had to do was made it back to her room and wait for Ethan to call and tell her what to do to get out of this fix.

Everything was going to be fine.

And then she noticed the van.

Her heart did that ricochet thing again.

And when the van crept up and kept pace beside her, her heart damn near jumped out of her chest.

But when it pulled up to the curb a few feet ahead of her and the side door slid open, the apprehension churning through her chest shifted to flat-out panic.

Don't stop, don't stop, don't stop. She repeated the command like a mantra.

When the gruff voice belching out from the murky black interior of the van ordered her to do just that, she broke into a dead run.

Something slammed into her from behind. She fell face-first onto the pocked concrete walk. And pain momentarily edged out the panic as the fall knocked the air out of her lungs.

Her breath finally rushed back on a gasp. She tried to scream, but a filthy hand clamped over her mouth. Something jabbed into her ribs, hard.

Oh, God. He had a gun.

"Come with me or die here, Miss Prescott. You decide."

Her attacker stood, pushed her toward the van, then shoved her, hard, into the backseat.

She hit her head on the opposite window and groaned, fighting through the dizzying pain. The van shot off through the Zamboanga streets with a squeal of tires before he'd even slammed the door.

Loss of consciousness was frightening and fast.

Her last coherent thought was of Ethan. His name broke on a sob just before everything faded but the truth: Not even Ethan could save her now.